The Cosy

Charlie Lyndhurst is an award-shortlisted novelist who lives with his boyfriend and cats. He bakes to indulge his dangerously sweet tooth, admires unaffordable classic cars, and drinks pink wine with friends. His favourite sport – of which he's a gold medal winner – is reading a romantic novel in a long hot bath.

Also by Charlie Lyndhurst

The Grooms Wore White
The Lonely Hearts Lido Club
The Cosy Cat Society

CHARLIE
LYNDHURST

THE
COSY CAT
SOCIETY

hera

First published in the United Kingdom in 2023 by

Hera Books
Unit 9 (Canelo), 5th Floor
Cargo Works, 1-2 Hatfields
London SE1 9PG
United Kingdom

A CIP catalogue record for this book is available from the British Library.

Print ISBN 978 1 80436 402 4
Ebook ISBN 978 1 80436 401 7

This book is a work of fiction. Names, characters, businesses, organizations, places and events are either the product of the author's imagination or are used fictitiously. Any resemblance to actual persons, living or dead, events or locales is entirely coincidental.

Cover design by Rose Cooper

Look for more great books at www.herabooks.com

Printed and bound in Great Britain by Clays Ltd, Elcograf S.p.A.

1

MIX
Paper from
responsible sources
FSC® C018072
www.fsc.org

To everyone who works, volunteers or helps our fabulous feline friends around the world, in cat sanctuaries, or in other ways. You're doing such important work. Thank you. Although people say humans rescue cats when we adopt them, I think in many important ways, cats also rescue us.

Chapter 1

Sasha Droxford stared at the message she'd received on one of her mostly dormant social media accounts she'd set up for Fluffy Paws Cat Sanctuary.

> **Lucky L Legs-Crossed:** I think I am your son I'd like to meet you

She read it twice, knowing with absolute certainty she had no children and no partner, so this must be some random person on the internet trying to trick her.

Sasha had been the manager and owner of this cat sanctuary for more than a decade, she thought she'd seen and heard everything, and was, for the avoidance of doubt, very tired and pretty much done with most things. She peered closer at the computer screen, reading the message again: *I think I am your son...*

She sat back in surprise; the chair sprang forwards slightly. Except... What if... The air left her lungs, as if she'd been winded. An icy chill of possibility, of realisation, ran down her spine. *Could it be real? The initial, but what did the Legs-Crossed bit mean?* She'd been told the name had no bearing on... well, anything.

Sasha shook her head, absolutely impossible, the chances were a million to one, worse, in fact. She knew this to be the case because... reasons. Anyway, this was the problem with the internet, setting up an account for Fluffy Paws, one moment you're tweeting, or posting, or whatever it was about stray cats needing their fur-ever home, and then you're sitting at your computer staring at a message from someone crossing their legs. Not to mention one without any full stops.

Sasha wasn't quite sure how she'd ended up here, but life seemed to have given her this furrow to plough, so she must continue. With a sigh, confused and exhausted by social media and computers, she clicked the message away. Gone and out of sight, out of mind.

Unbelievable.

Fluffy Paws Cat Sanctuary was in Wickford, a London commuter town with a love of roundabouts that was, for some, rather too close to the orbit of Basildon, or Bas Vegas, as the locals named it. This was on account of the roundabout announcing in two-metre-high white letters its name as people entered Basildon on both directions of the main arterial road. Sasha had once thought that rather amusing, but now it had become background, like so many things she no longer noticed.

Returning to the spreadsheet showing the income and expenditure of Fluffy Paws Cat Sanctuary, she sighed, long and low. She was no great whizz with figures, but even she could see they were, for want of a more delicate phrase, *absolutely up shit creek without a paddle* this month. With over fifteen thousand pounds of vets' bills still awaiting payment, seven outbuildings containing more than thirty pens full with cats, all needing new homes, a few moggies in the house where Sasha sat now, and not to mention the couple of resident moggies, she didn't know what to do. Never mind the eviction and notice-of-sale letter from their landlord. Three months wasn't very long to find a new premises.

She shook her head and gritted her teeth. Not very long at all.

Paul, one of the volunteers, had mentioned something about social media and how he'd take charge of it. He'd said something about fish cats, or similar. She wasn't sure what he meant, but he'd definitely said she needed to be wary of fish cats, or fishing for cats, when she went on the internet.

Sasha had liked his enthusiasm, and offer of help, even if she didn't fully understand most of that computer side of things.

The last person who'd done the sanctuary's accounts had left suddenly due to a family crisis. Sasha had hoped the woman would return, but nothing doing. *At least Mim's agreed to do them. I'd be lost without the volunteers.*

She left the room, the computer still whirring noisily away. She'd hoped, when she bought it seven years ago, that it would do a bit more than sit there mocking her for not knowing how to use it.

Operating system, programmes, software, folders, files, it was all a bit of a mystery to her.

'You all right?' Anna, one of the newer volunteers, asked.

'Fine.' Sasha paused, trying to think of something to say that wouldn't hint at the truth and make Anna worry about the sanctuary having to close. 'Computers.' She rolled her eyes.

'You're not going to close, are you?' she asked, worry clouding her face. 'I have no idea what I'd do without this place.'

'No fear,' Sasha said firmly and nodded.

Every volunteer said a different variation on that sentiment. They each had their own reasons for volunteering: escape, purpose, loneliness, grief. Sasha ran the full gamut of human emotions. She'd once considered studying to be a therapist, one of those counsellors who sits and leans forwards and asks their clients, *yes, but how does it make you feel*, in an earnest voice.

She tutted. If she charged fifty quid an hour for her time, she wouldn't be in this financial bind. Last month's vet bill was thirty grand. *Unbelievable*.

'Animal therapy,' Anna had proclaimed on her first phone call, asking if she could volunteer. It was clearly to help her through some heavy-duty life stuff, which Sasha didn't want to pry about.

Now, Sasha led Anna from the large Victorian house where she lived. It had bay windows, four bedrooms, a large sitting room and kitchen, referred to as the 'humans' kitchen' since it was where the volunteers ate, and made their hot drinks. Sasha had converted two bedrooms to cat nurseries for the pregnant mother cats to give birth to their kittens in the warm and away from the busyness of the other cat pens. The grounds of the house had outbuildings containing pens for the cats, the largest of these buildings had a desk with paperwork where the volunteers processed admissions and adoptions. Within every outbuilding, there was space for the volunteers to walk about, as well as individual cat pens. Each cat had a folder outside their pen, describing their history, temperament

4

and care they needed that was different from the usual routine.

'What's up then?' Anna asked, following Sasha across the garden, past the wire-framed pens in which they kept the cats.

'Have you done the meds yet?' Sasha wasn't in any sort of mood to be dissecting her emotions. It didn't do to let the others see her feeling below par. She was the illustrious leader; she was the one who helped when everyone else was having an emotional time. Sasha was used to leading out front and pushing down any signs of weakness or worry.

'Half of them. The ginger tomcat in A block scratched me.' Anna held her forearm up, covered in red scratches from wrist to elbow.

'Please tell me you've had your tetanus jab.' Sasha was sure she'd mentioned this at Anna's induction.

'Of course,' Anna said with pride. 'Can't let that sort of thing slip, not considering where I work.' She grinned nervously.

Anna *had* told Sasha where she worked, something to do with doctors, and not far, in the village of Howe Green. Sasha nodded stoutly. 'Of course. Best clean it up though, just in case.' In the largest outbuilding, Anna's arm was washed, and Sasha dabbed antiseptic on the wounds. Then content they'd stopped bleeding and were clean, she said, 'Are you okay to finish off the meds?'

Anna looked worried. 'It's all in the folder, isn't it?'

Sasha nodded. 'Precisely that.'

Sasha didn't want to call them care plans, but it was the one positive she'd taken from her unfortunate dealings with social workers as a sixteen-year-old.

Parent–child visiting centres, adoption packs, days, everything.

A jolt of the memory of that room with the low chairs, toys on the floor, sterilised between clients – also known as children – shot through her. She'd thought all that was left behind her and now this. These messages. *Whoever this Lucky Legs-Crossed person is, he is definitely persistent, I'll give him that. But come on, it couldn't be, could it?*

'You were miles away,' Anna said, shaking her shoulder carefully.

'Just thinking about the folders. If any of them get feisty, let me know and I'll put on the gloves and give you a hand.'

'Should be fine.' Anna stared at Sasha with an excess of confidence given what she'd probably been through, the truth given away in snippets by sharing words and at her regular visits to the sanctuary.

Sasha squeezed her shoulder. 'Thanks.'

'You sure there's nothing on your mind? You know what they say, a problem shared is a problem halved.'

Or just a problem that two people know. 'Nothing.' Sasha looked up. 'It's fine. Once Mim starts doing the accounts, I can stop worrying about them.' Not the actual money itself, but making sure they were accurate at least.

'Wish I could help. Failed GCSE maths. Retook it and still failed. That's me all over.' Anna made an awkward face. 'But I could ask someone at work. One of the doctors or a secretary is bound to be able to help.'

'Don't worry about it. Mim, I've been reliably informed, will take our accounts very firmly in hand and save us.' Exams, watching a child take them, yes, another experience she'd missed, alongside everything else about school since she'd left. *Mind you, the PTA groups sound like more of a pain in the arse than anything else. Perhaps it's for the best that I avoided all that. Avoided, yes, that's better than missed out.*

And then, Anna left, her hair bobbing up and down as she walked away.

It felt like a lifetime ago when Sasha had gone to school, thirty years.

Sasha stepped away from where she'd waved Anna goodbye. Her slower movement towards the cat pens told her there was decidedly more of her now than there had been as a teenager, although she had less to be happy about when younger. Life had been certainly simpler at twenty-six than forty-six.

A small short-haired tabby cat curled herself around Sasha's ankles, meowing loudly. Tiny Tabby was one of the permanent residents of Fluffy Paws, her nervousness around humans meant she'd sat unadopted for almost a year before Sasha and the others had decided to keep her there and spoil her rotten. Her name had started as simply a description, but it had soon stuck: she was a tiny tabby cat, half the size of the male tabbies. It was a better name than Archers Seven – the road where she'd been found in a box next to a bin, and the number signifying she was the seventh cat collected by a national cat charity, before being handed over to the care of Fluffy Paws.

Sasha crouched down, letting out an inelegant groan-sigh she seemed unable to avoid since turning forty. 'Are you hungry?' she said.

Tiny Tabby meowed. She placed two furry dark-striped legs and paws on Sasha's lap, and started making bread with her claws.

She picked Tiny Tabby up, heavier than last time, *must check her diet*, carried her to the cat kitchen, within an outbuilding containing beds, toys and cat accessories for sale. There she opened the fridge and forked some wet food into a clean bowl, adding some of Tiny Tabby's favourite dry crisps.

Tiny Tabby jumped on the work surface, sticking her head in the bowl. Strictly speaking, she wasn't allowed there, but after the life she'd had — born by a rubbish dump, not handled as a kitten and then passed from pillar to post as people couldn't bring her out of her shell — Sasha was disinclined to worry about her paw prints on the grey work surface. She stroked Tiny Tabby's soft fur and the little cat began to purr while eating contentedly. Cats were, for the most part, far nicer than many people.

Her mobile phone rang with the number of a local vet's practice.

At least it wasn't the one she owed money to. *Let's hope they're calling to say they have a veterinary nurse student who wants to volunteer.* It could happen. It was unlikely, but possible.

'Can I help?' she said.

'I've got a cat that's been in an RTA and their owner can't afford the bill, wants to put it to sleep.'

Sasha bit her bottom lip. This was one of the most frequent calls she received from vets. 'Can I speak to the owner?' From experience, sometimes this helped. But not always.

'Why?'

'It's worth a go, isn't it?'

There was a pause, as the vet obviously realised he couldn't say what he was thinking in front of the cat's owner. He handed the phone over.

'Are you gonna take it?' An angry man's voice.

'What's your cat called?'

8

'What's this got to do with anything? Dunno. Pretty. Stupid name, if you ask me. But her indoors said it suited it.'

Sasha closed her eyes. She really did despair for the human race sometimes. When people referred to their pets as 'it' Sasha knew she was fighting a losing battle. 'If I pay the vet's bill, you can't have your cat back.'

'Suits me.' He was very confident.

'What about your partner? Presumably the cat is hers?'

'We can't afford it. But I can afford putting it to sleep.'

As predicted. Sasha unconsciously shook her head in despair. 'Can you put me back to the vet, please?'

The vet said, 'And?'

'Get him to sign the cat over to Fluffy Paws Cat Sanctuary. I want a signed piece of paper explaining in very clear terms, in black and white, that they no longer have ownership of their pet.' She'd been caught out with that before, paying the vet fees then the owner wanting the cat back, until the next big bill came along, no doubt.

'Understood.' A pause, and then the vet said, 'It's looking like three or four thousand pounds.'

Of course it is. Sasha pinched the bridge of her nose as she closed her eyes. 'Will Pretty survive?'

'No guarantees, Mrs Droxford. But based on experience, she's very lucky. Tail and back legs, but her spine's okay.'

'Thanks.' Sasha ended the call.

A volunteer shouted from the far end of the sanctuary's garden: 'I thought I'd be all right, but I think I could do with a hand!'

Sasha stroked Tiny Tabby then strode to help her colleague. Why did she ever think she'd have time for all that computer nonsense when the cats needed looking after? Why couldn't the computer do its own thing and leave her to do *her* own thing, which was caring for the cats?

Chapter 2

Chelmer Village, Essex

Paul Ampfield clicked send and turned his laptop off. He was meant to be off work today, but the client had asked for – no, *demanded* was a better word – a report on the use of their data for marketing purposes.

Just one thing, before I leave for Fluffy Paws, he'd told himself, rising at stupid o'clock this morning and knocking out the report in an hour or so.

It was a far cry from the glamour and pizzazz of his tap-dancing friends. *How did I end up here? How did I end up not dancing with them?*

The house was roomy, far too large for just Paul, but the owners were leaving to travel around the world for a year and the rent was affordable because he had agreed to move in instantly, just as the owners were packing their life into boxes. A three-storey house without a cat wasn't even a house, it was a sad and empty box.

Chelmer Village dated all the way back to approximately 1978, on the edge of the Essex city of Chelmsford, that Paul enjoyed for shopping. He thought any village needing to include the actual word 'village' in its name must have a sense of inferiority. Somehow Paul had found himself living in this home, in this new village, that allowed him to live a very small existence, only talking to the barista at the cafe round the corner, his clients and the women at Fluffy Paws.

Ironic considering he'd travelled most of Europe with George.

Still, it's not forever. Nothing's forever. He'd learned that from George.

Stop that!

He checked his phone, a quick scroll through the socials, noting, to some small degree of shame, he was up to five platforms, and debating joining a sixth. Seeing everyone's posts from around the world – white sandy beaches, azure blue seas, small villages with white-walled houses and blue shutters nestled on hills as people sipped local wine and ate food prepared by hand in family-owned restaurants – made him feel worse rather than better. *So why do I continue to do it?*

What in the name of god am I doing here, in this large house, all alone? A far cry from the Sussex coast.

Why did I pick up my phone? Ah yes, a message notification.

Sasha, who ran the cat sanctuary, had messaged:

> I really need someone to do all the
> computer stuff here. Upload the cats,
> download things, videos and pictures. Can
> you? Please?

She'd seen him photographing the cats and told him very firmly it wasn't allowed.

'They're not performing a play,' he'd replied sardonically.

'What?' She stood with her hands on her hips.

'You can't record shows at the theatre. Everything else is online.' He shook his head. 'Have you been to a concert?'

'Yes.' She pursed her lips.

'When?'

She thought for a moment. 'Not recently.'

'*How* not recently?'

'Before life took over and I didn't have time for that sort of thing.'

'When specifically?'

'I was twenty-two. At the time, it was the biggest UK pop music tour ever.'

'Wow, who was it?' Paul hoped it was someone cool from the Nineties Britpop era, Pulp, Blur, Oasis maybe.

'Steps. Nineteen ninety-nine.'

Paul disguised the disappointment at the total lack of coolness, but didn't want to judge. Paul had been four then. 'I'm guessing you didn't have smartphones?' He knew the answer.

Sasha shook her head.

'Cameras?'

'Not really.' She went on to talk about films and having the pictures developed and sending off for them and them arriving in envelopes. Paul thought she might as well be talking about the time when they set those costume dramas, with the women in bonnets, and the men in tight trousers, with big sideburns. Jane Austen and all that jazz.

'Well, here in the Twenty Twenties, we go to concerts and we take pictures and videos and we post them on the socials. It's all about the social buzz,' he said with care.

'I sort of understand that, but why take pictures of cats and download them to the internet?'

Upload, he thought, but he said nothing. 'Do we have cats that have been here for ages?'

She nodded.

'Do we need to have them rehomed so we can take in new cats?'

Another nod.

'How do you think people know which cats we have?'

'They ring us.'

'And you talk through them and describe them and then suggest they come in to see the cats, right?'

Sasha narrowed her eyes. 'Yes. And?'

'They say they don't want a big cat, or one that meows all the time, or one you can't pick up, cos...'

'They do. Sometimes. And your point is?'

'All of that can be avoided if we post pictures and videos. People can visit the cats they like the look and sound of. You can show the cats' temperaments and personalities with a short video.'

'Can you?'

Raising an eyebrow, he said, 'Well, I don't know if you could, I've seen your pictures. But someone else could.'

'Are you volunteering?'

Paul shrugged, because it seemed like nothing much. 'We could install webcams,' he said, on something of a roll, he felt.

Sasha frowned. 'Isn't that rude?'

Suppressing a grin, Paul said, 'Some people use them for, as you say, rude things. But we wouldn't.'

'What exactly is a webcam?'

'A camera showing something that others can watch if they go online.' He felt it was the simplest way to describe it.

'And the cats would want this, why?' Sasha asked.

'We could install them in the pens, so people can see what the cats are doing. Create a buzz about the sanctuary.'

Sasha shook her head. 'This buzz. Sounds expensive. I think not.'

Knowing when he was beaten, Paul had agreed to focus on the videos of cats, using his phone.

Have a good idea, end up seeing it through. Isn't that what his university mates had said? And before he knew it, he had been chairing the debate society, organising the LGBT soc and much more.

He'd started volunteering at the cat sanctuary to spend more time with cats, because he missed his cat. Another bad George-related decision he regretted.

He'd debated contacting his cat's new owner and asking to visit him, but had read that could cause stress. Besides, he wasn't settling anywhere, and most of the short-term rental places he used didn't allow pets. This one had been very specific.

He was due at the sanctuary shortly and, if he stayed at home, he'd end up being drawn into doing more work for the most demanding client who wasn't paying him nearly enough money.

Three days a week, he should have realised, meant nearly four, which sometimes slipped into five. That had been another reason for the cat sanctuary, some no-phone, no-screen time, when he was unreachable.

Except it felt like his arm had been chopped off without his phone.

Was it unhealthy to stalk both George, his ex, and his cat, Rick, on the socials?

Probably.

He replied to Sasha, obviously in need of his digital nomad skills. Imagining a life without the internet was almost impossible for him, except in the costume dramas with the horse carriages, bonnets and high-collared jackets for the men. The fact that people in their forties, like Sasha, remembered a time before it had existed sort of blew Paul's mind.

He replied to Sasha's message:

> Show me what needs doing later today

No full stop — why did Sasha always bother with them, eh? It always felt so formal and a little bit pass-agg.

Let's see what George is doing at the moment. He opened his ex's favourite social media account and there stood George, smiling, with his arm around a man who looked almost exactly like Paul: slim, pale skin, light brown hair and... yes, he confirmed as he zoomed on the picture, dark brown eyes.

A shiver of recognition and remembering George's behaviour crept down his spine.

George himself had been the biggest mistake of all the George-related errors of judgement. But that smile, the generosity, the charming conversation, always asking more about Paul than he gave to the conversation, soon meant George knew all of Paul's deepest fears, hopes, and carefully began to use them once they were a couple.

'And that's enough of that,' Paul said loudly, and shut off the social media app, locked his phone and put it in his pocket. He stood, walking past his home-made Bradley Cooper wall calendar, a man whose smouldering looks, courtesy — he now knew after some judicious IMDB research — of his Italian mother, had been something of an obsession since stumbling across *Valentine's Day* late one

Saturday night. It was a fabulously cheesy romcom where Bradley was blue-eyed, besuited and adorably handsome for every minute of screen time. And then George had told Paul it was stupid to watch films like that, never mind obsessively watching every film Sir Bradley of Cooper had been in, why should he focus on someone who was straight, unavailable and a Hollywood film star, so why was Paul wasting his time thinking about this actor?

A shiver of George's disdain and control shot down Paul's spine. *At least that's behind me. He's in my past.* On the calendar, he'd scrawled *D* followed by an illegible squiggle, *4pm* in yesterday's box.

He'd received a call yesterday, but let it go to voicemail, hadn't checked that yet. *Who bothers with all that faff anymore? Why don't they just text?*

'Who's D something?' he asked. Speaking in an empty house, without a cat, was a few tiny steps closer to insanity he reckoned than he ought to be comfortable with. Next thing he'd be having a whole conversation with his oven.

Once, he'd done that. And it had been his microwave, if that made things any better. He knew it didn't…

'Shit! D for Dentist.' *Now I owe them fifty quid too for the missed hygienist appointment.* When had he started being so messy? He used to make appointments and stick to them. He still managed that for work, because, well, it paid the bills. But somehow outside of work Paul's standards had slipped. Very far.

As he drove towards the cat sanctuary, he listened to the voicemail left by the dental receptionist: 'I've spoken to the hygienist and dentist you saw last time for your extractions and… well, I think you should reflect on whether you want to cancel your after-care.' Long pause. 'It's very hard to find an NHS dentist, as I'm sure you're aware. At your last appointment you were making good progress with your dental hygiene routine. The hygienist and dentist wanted me to acknowledge this. However, if you don't continue, the dentist said they can't be held responsible for your oral health and it's likely you'll require additional extractions.'

Paul sighed, trying to process it all, returned the call, leaving a voicemail message: 'Sorry, it's Paul Ampfield, I totally forgot our appointment yesterday. I was… work has been… and…' *I'm still not doing any of the stuff you told me to do last time, and I don't want to tell you that again.* 'Can we leave it for a while? I don't have time at the moment.' He bit his bottom lip.

He'd read somewhere that when you think you're too busy to take time for exercise, healthy eating, just to be, to breathe and exist, rather than always doing, that was the time you needed to pause most. He'd also read somewhere about the importance of getting back to 'whatever used to bring you joy'. Which was dance, specifically tap and ballet. They had brought him so much joy, until they hadn't.

George.

He was near the cat sanctuary. *At least I'll be able to talk to someone other than myself very soon.*

There was a silence as Paul turned into the road the sanctuary was on, unsure what to say, before adding to his message, 'A friend suggested I resume dance classes,' he went on, not quite sure why he was saying it. 'And I didn't. Do you know why? Because someone threw away all my equipment. The same someone who shamed me into not going.' Paul coughed, raked his hand through his hair, staring out of the car window, then parking. 'Sorry but my oral health isn't top of my list at the moment. I, mistakenly I now know, believed once the teeth had been removed I could go on my merry way. Which is why I forgot you. It's a me thing, not a you thing. I've got a lot to process and it will, eventually, include my teeth, but at the moment, not so much. So if you could kindly leave me to work stuff out, I'll reschedule soon.' *Ish. God, why can't I just be a messy idiot without people hassling me?* In a very small voice, feeling exhausted and knowing he'd massively overshared and wasn't quite sure why, he said, 'Okay, thanks, all the best, cheers, thanks again, bye,' and ended the call.

He didn't recognise anyone's cars, no small blue Ford belonging to Anna, no sign of Mim's large green BMW. *Let's see if I can pretend I'm holding things together, for at least an afternoon.*

Chapter 3

Moulsham, Essex

Anna Bramley arrived home, to her small new-build terraced house, with a screaming headache, a stress rash over her chest and arms and her breathing shallow and difficult. Her heart pounded as if she was having an attack.

She knew this not to be the case, having spoken to all the GPs at The Grove Practice. They probably humoured her more than the patients as she was a colleague.

After the morning she'd had, she'd have rather been at work. At least audio-typing letters and patient notes, for the six GPs in the practice, was something she could manage. It was contained, quiet, with few difficult variables to manage. And they'd been very good to her in the last six months, letting her take time off to look after her parents.

Earlier that day, walking from room to room of her parents' house in Margaretting, a pretty Essex village, she'd frozen at the wallpaper, at the washing machine she'd bought her mum before she'd lost the ability to use it.

Later, at the supermarket, she'd taken a phone call from the care home explaining she had six months to sell the family home and settle the outstanding bill for her parents' care.

'I can't sell it now,' she'd said, almost beside herself as she stood in the Sainsbury's car park struggling to find a trolley.

'We have estate agents and solicitors we can recommend. They help the whole process go very smoothly,' the care home manager had said.

'It's my home. I grew up there.' She wished she lived there now, in a bucolic village surrounded by green rolling Essex hills.

'Memories. Wonderful things, aren't they?' the care home manager had said with more than a touch of a patronising tone.

'Shame Mum and Dad lost theirs.'

'It's a difficult time for everyone. Which is why we give relatives six months to settle their accounts.'

Relatives, singular for her. An only child had felt such a blessing growing up, her parents' attention showered on her. But now, left all alone to deal with this, Anna wasn't sure how she'd manage. 'I can't deal with this.' Anna had hung up the phone and stormed into Sainsbury's, buying herself clothes and toiletries to cheer herself up. Looking through the dresses, a feeling of power and calm had filled her. For the first time since her mum had asked who she was when she arrived one afternoon, Anna felt a moment's peace and tranquillity.

Now, at home, she knew she was going to be late. *Hate that. So rude. What if the traffic gets worse on the way? Best ring.*

She called the cat sanctuary and spoke to Sasha. 'I'm so sorry, I'm going to be late. I've had a morning of it. On the phone to solicitors and estate agents for hours. Going round and round in circles, jargon I don't understand. And I got a parking ticket in Sainsbury's, didn't know you have to enter your number plate in a machine. Never used to. Then I had a flat tyre. I thought that's okay, because I've got breakdown cover. Except I didn't have it. It had run out, came when I bought the car and I... well, meant to get round to renewing it. But I hadn't. So I had to ask someone to change the tyre in the car park. Lovely lad, pushing the trolleys, he helped me. I gave him twenty pounds. Maybe I don't need breakdown cover now. What are the chances of breaking down twice in one year? Then the bank, they said I couldn't have access to Mum and Dad's account unless I had a letter from them. I said, they're dead. They said I needed an original death certificate and I said I'd sent that to the council and they'd lost it in the post. I went to the doctor who'd certified them and they—'

Sasha said, 'Anna, take a breath. You can tell me everything when you get here.'

'But I'm going to be *late*.'

'Doesn't matter. I'm in the middle of doing four new admissions and we've got six people turning up to adopt their cats. Lots of paperwork. Just what you're brilliant at.'

Anna smiled. She'd introduced new adoption and query paperwork because, before, Sasha had done it on Post-it notes and folders. It didn't cut down on the number of cats, but it made the process much smoother and faster. 'Thanks.'

'Sounds like you've had a right morning of it. Solicitors and estate agents, always, in my experience, only after one thing.'

'Sex?' Anna frowned. She'd given up on all that after a date with a man who'd spoken about nothing but his ex-wife all evening then insisted on paying for exactly what he'd eaten and said he wasn't going halves on the wine since she'd drunk significantly more than him.

'No,' Sasha replied, anxiety in her voice. 'Money. Please do come in. We're all waiting for you.'

'I'll be there' – she checked the time – 'maybe ten minutes, maybe twenty. Depends if there's space to park. Is the car park full? Shall I get a taxi? Mind you, I've lost the card for the local one who doesn't rip you off. Maybe I could—'

'Get here when you get here, drive, the car park's fine.' Anna nodded. 'Sure?'

'You're more use to us here than at home.' Sasha ended the call.

Anna's hands were shaking from the stress of everything. She reached into the kitchen cupboard and tipped two painkillers into her palm, swallowing them with a few gulps of water as if her life depended on it.

Her doctor had prescribed those to help with her migraines and lack of sleep. She was meant to take them at night, but increasingly she found just existing all a bit much without them, so she'd taken to having one at breakfast, and one in the afternoon, just to take the edge off things.

Life.

She grabbed her car keys in the hallway, caught her reflection in the mirror. She couldn't possibly go in these clothes! The cats' claws would play havoc with her lacy blouse and ripped denim jeans.

Now, what should I wear instead? She put her keys in the jeans pocket, scurried upstairs and opened her wardrobe – stuffed with every item of clothing she'd bought since eighteen, carefully arranged by colour. She was lucky to be able to still get into it all.

Anna fondly felt a blue chenille cardigan between thumb and forefinger. *1999, eighteenth birthday present from Mum and Dad, C&A.*

Anna couldn't remember details of when, where and with whom she'd bought every cardigan and dress. The handwritten label was attached to the coat hanger with string.

Too good.

Her fingers walked along the edges of the clothes until she reached a white T-shirt. *2022, New Look, shopping with Mum in Colchester, had coffee and cake afterwards in shopping centre.*

Too close.

She turned away, and fished something out of the dirty washing basket. After a quick sniff, and deciding it wasn't too bad, she changed into a blue blouse and pleated skirt that had seen better days since their purchase in 2002, at Lakeside Shopping Centre, with her friend who she'd somehow lost touch with, along with most of the people she'd been friends with. *Why do people always do that*, she wondered, *say they'll stay in touch then stop returning my calls?*

Chapter 4

'Thanks for coming,' Mim said, waving to the last of her guests as they drove off.

Mim Hursley was a party planner, host par excellence, she made it her personal challenge to throw the best, most interesting, well-catered gatherings in their corner of rural Essex.

Mim's village was one of three which surrounded a reservoir of the same name. Village halls, pubs, thatched cottages, solid Victorian detached houses, village greens, a Norman church and yard overlooking the reservoir, everything you imagine when thinking about a typical English village, and the Hanningfields had them all in abundance.

South Hanningfield was, in Mim's opinion, the best of these three villages, it being nearest to the water and in possession of the most exclusive Farrow & Ball painted gastropub, and almost but not quite feeling as if it belonged in leafy Hertfordshire, or Surrey, rather than slightly overconfident Essex. If Kent were the garden of England, Mim felt some of Essex would surely be the patio.

She returned to the large dining room and folded the tablecloth then decided it needed washing. Placing it in the machine, she noticed the kitchen was full of crockery and cutlery.

'Another successful gathering.' David stacked the dishwasher after carefully rinsing everything in the sink.

I really am so fortunate to have him. She smiled, placed some clothes and tea towels into the machine and switched it on. 'I think I'm going to have a lie down.'

'Paracetamol in the bedside drawer.' He stopped what he was doing, filled a glass with chilled sparkling water from the fridge, handed it to her. 'For the painkillers.'

She smiled weakly, looking about her. Hours ago, the kitchen dining room had been filled with friends, shocked at her wonderful spread of food, amazed at the table decorations and impressed by the ambiance she'd created with quiet background music.

And now it was all over.

'Whose birthday was it again?' David asked.

Mim pressed a palm against her forehead. It wasn't throbbing, not even the merest hint of a headache, but the familiar low that followed such a high had already caught up with her. After being 'on' all day, she'd resigned herself to being 'off' for a while. 'No one. Do you think I'd throw a birthday for a friend here?' She frowned: it sounded very odd.

'You have. Last year. That woman from Sun Burn Holidays.'

Ah yes, her old boss from the Spanish Costa Brava repping days. She lived alone and didn't want much of a fuss, so Mim had offered to throw her a birthday party. After all, you're only sixty once.

'No one's birthday.' She'd not done it again since so many people had commented how odd it felt coming to her house to celebrate someone *else's* birthday. Did she wish she'd gone into professional catering maybe, they had said. Did she want to start a cake–baking business perhaps? Why didn't she sell some of her glass figurines online, since her house was full of them?

David nodded. 'My mistake. Sorry.' He waved her away. 'Go, lie down. Rest. You've been on your feet all day. Would you like a peppermint tea?'

I really am very lucky to have him. Very lucky indeed. Be grateful for what you've got, don't long for what you don't have. Flowers and other decorations always improved plain glassware.

She'd painted a sign for one of the glass figurines with that written: *Be grateful for what you've got, don't long for what you don't have.* Only it hadn't been legible and had looked *very* messy, so she'd dropped it into the sink, smashing into shards of glass. Cutting her fingers as she'd tried to clean it up, until David had heard her crying and taken over.

'Water's okay. Thanks,' she said. 'Do you miss the Sun Burn Holidays days? All the old gang? Costa Brava, sunbathing all day, drinking all night?' She missed it. Very much indeed.

'Great times. Life moves on. Different life stage.' He raised his eyebrows as if he were waiting for her to say something.

'Yes. Of course.' A pause and then: 'Would you like to go back?' She would. Every day. Almost hourly.

'Where would we stay? Everything was put on by Sun Burn. Accommodation, entertainment, transport. No roots there, really.'

'Nearly forty years living and working there. I think we were pretty settled, don't you?' He was unduly irritating her and she could only put it down to slipping into one of her 'off' moods.

'I mean, our own place. Just us. Not grabbing breakfast from the hotel buffet. Living on a fry-up every morning year in, year out.'

He had a point, the thrill of a fried breakfast somewhat lost its appeal if it was the only thing on offer 365 days a year, every year. Except that was the only way one could live: day in, day out; year in, year out. She'd never intended to stay as a holiday rep on the Costa Brava for nearly forty years. But she'd been good at it, had loved the sun and the happy tourists, got settled with a group of British expats who had moved out there. Had felt it would go on forever. Until it hadn't.

'We've been through this,' David said with a great deal of care.

'Have we?' Putting her hands on her hips, she felt a snarky rage building in her chest. It was all part of the her that was 'off' now the guests had left. The her who only saw the negative, the her who dwelled on regrets and missed opportunities.

'We were too old to be reps. People used to laugh at us. Don't you remember?'

She shook her head. That she chose to ignore. 'I feel about a hundred and thirty since coming back to the UK. Out there, the warm sun on my skin, the late dinners, the beach, the mild winters, I felt thirty, forty at most.'

David laughed, shaking his head.

'What?' she asked, very hurt.

'We agreed we'd leave with dignity and come back here.'

'Back here. Back to precisely *what*?' The farewell party had been nicer than the gentle hints at asking her to retire and leave. That way she'd chosen when and how to go, and had thrown – of course – a no-holds-barred, lavish celebration as a sort of full stop at the end of her whole life career in the holiday industry.

'Why do you think they asked us to work on the phones, in the office?'

'That mole on my back. I said I needed to spend less time in the sun.'

David tilted his head to one side. 'I love how you think that's the reason.'

Mim didn't reply.

'Everyone knew we couldn't keep up with the new reps,' he went on, 'bouncing around like a pogo stick, while we greeted guests, leaning against the wall because our legs and feet couldn't cope with standing all day.' He paused, narrowing his eyes. 'A nice sit-down office job, is what we were told. Or we'd be asked to go.'

It wasn't how she remembered it, but anyway. 'Five years of that's better than *this*.' She gestured to the room.

'What's wrong with *this*?' He frowned.

'South Hanningfield? What's *right* with it? Why leave the sun and sea of Spain and come *here*?'

'It's not Spain. But it's gorgeous here. You know why.'

They had a nephew and his family on David's side, who lived in Thorpe Bay, a quiet bit of the coast away from the kiss-me-quick brashness of Southend. David's brother and sister-in-law were in Essex too. Plus, it had been not too hard to find a house in a small village that met all Mim's requirements, and relatively close to London for when they wanted to see a show. The village was nice, as was the house, but it remained unequal to Spain. Mim told him, then tensed her jaw.

'I think,' David said, 'you'd better have a lie down. Leave this to me.'

She felt guilty at snapping and being ungrateful for all she had. Somehow being near to David's family was worse than being surrounded by young holiday reps. Because they were family, through marriage, Mim thought with sadness, and the nearest she had to children. William and Henry, David's brother's children – same age as Diana, Princess of Wales's sons, and deliberately named after them – had been happy to visit them in Spain as teenagers and in their twenties, but now settled with their own families, Mim felt like an awkward auntie, peering into their lives without just cause.

'Your nephews don't want to see us. They have their own lives. I don't want a poor-childless-Aunt Mim pity party,' Mim said, spitting out the 'p's like grape seeds.

'That's not the case at all.'

'I saw his face, as he showed me their beautiful baby girl. He was so proud, and then he saw my sadness at not having children or grandchildren and…' There it was again, the stabbing sadness at what could have been. The ache of the children she'd not had. Combined with the 'off' feeling that crept across her mind, she held her breath, as tears threatened to fall.

David gently took her by the elbow and led her upstairs into their bedroom. He settled her onto the bed, lifting her legs up, removing her shoes. He placed a paracetamol tablet in her hand, held the glass up for her to drink. 'I'll check on you in an hour. Aren't you at that cat sanctuary later?'

She nodded. 'Perhaps I'll cancel. It's not like they're paying me.'

'Hardly the point, is it?' David frowned.

She knew she was beaten; he had a point.

'Besides, I thought you enjoyed it there.'

She nodded. It was her plan, such that it was, having not mentioned it to anyone, that once she'd proved her worth by doing their accounts, she'd pick a select few of the volunteers from Fluffy Paws and invite them to one of her social gatherings. She was growing tired of seeing the same old faces around her dining table. And worse still, none of them seemed to reciprocate, no invitations to others' homes. How inconsiderate. She scrunched her face up at that.

David stroked her cheek. 'Don't do that, if the wind changes, you'll stay like it.' He smiled.

She couldn't help herself and sighed, allowing a small smile to spread across her face.

'That's better,' he said. 'Let's put something in the diary, another garden party maybe? Or a dinner party, like we used to throw in Spain?' He left the room.

Mim stared at the door. Blinked slowly. All the friends from Spain had floated away. The reps were too young, and moved on to other jobs – the expat scene was very transient and people moved back to the UK, or died as they aged. Neither of which had figured in Mim's plans until she'd been forced to move back to the UK.

She knew David wouldn't have *that* conversation. He never did. He'd never been able to face that side of her, of them. But she was very fortunate to have him. To have such a supportive husband who loved to entertain as much as she did.

She rolled onto her side, adjusting the pillow for comfort. Her gaze rested on two glass figurines, a man atop a horse and the other a gentleman sailing a boat. She'd painted them with the same colour hair as David's – *their* – nephews.

They seemed to stare at her, mocking her for attempting to make them like William and Henry, so much that David had suggested she not give them to the men, but keep them for herself. 'Their children may break them,' David had said.

But now, Mim realised how ridiculous it looked to give the grown men a glass figurine decorated to resemble themselves. It wouldn't have worked when they were children either, everyone knows you can't give glass to children as toys. Almost as odd as filling her home with hundreds of them. And decorated glasses. A hobby she'd taken up in retirement, having always adored the look and colour of glass and her mother's china figurines. Glass ones, she'd decided, painted by her own fair hands, were far superior.

Except, she realised with sadness as she lay down, while concentrating on painting and adorning them perfectly, it was one of the only times, since leaving Spain and the busyness of work, when she didn't feel sadness at not being a mother.

Mim rolled over, closed her eyes. She wasn't fifty, not even sixty, she was bloody well seventy. Before she knew it, she'd be eighty, and the thought of her life slipping away from her, having left nothing of note behind, threatened to swallow her whole.

Chapter 5

Bournemouth, Dorset

In the bedroom of his flat, Luke Sherbourne stared at his phone, waiting for a message or notification from the woman, Sasha. Yes, that was her name, he didn't think he'd call her Mum or Mother, not yet anyway. Maybe never.

Nothing.

Jean, his mum, the woman who'd brought him up, walked into his bedroom. She was small and somehow managed to age herself by two decades beyond her fifty-five years, simply from her choice of clothing: pleated brown skirt, pink blouse, leather handbag with a gold clasp. He would never say anything as it was unkind, but it made him wonder what clothes his birth mum, Sasha, would wear.

Looking up, he said with a slight tone of irritation, 'What did I say about knocking?'

'Sorry. I just wondered... has she? Did you send her an email?'

'Message. On the socials.' He shook his head. 'Email, no one uses that now.'

His mum leaned against the wall, picking at the furling wallpaper. 'Do you want me to leave?'

'You've only just got here.' She'd arrived as he was on the third attempt to write the follow-up message to his first, from which he hadn't received a reply. He'd told his mum at every step of the way. She'd been very supportive helping him get in touch with the adoption agency, and she'd found what little paperwork she had about his birth mother.

She'd left him alone to work his way through all of that, how at turning thirty he'd decided he should know who he came from, ought to search for something deeper, more than what his life contained now.

But at the precise moment he was getting the courage to write another message – one more urgent and perhaps desperate even – to his actual birth mum, his real mum of thirty years had burst in. Not having rung the doorbell first, no, she'd let herself in, with the key he'd given her.

'Shall I put the kettle on?' She smiled, that soft and slightly clueless grin he recognised as awkwardness.

'I'm coming now.' Luke stood.

'What if she rings back, won't you miss it?'

He put his arm around her shoulders, led her towards the kitchen. She barely came up to his chest. He used to wonder how a woman so short, very accommodating, with blonde-grey hair and hazel eyes, and his dad, Roger, sixty, bald and forceful, but very short, with dark brown eyes, could produce a boy who by eight was taller than both of them, with jet-black hair, dark features and sky-blue eyes.

'I don't want to get in the way. I'll go.' She looked up at him with kind, slightly tired brown eyes.

He felt as if he did anything wrong she'd break. She always gave that impression, not helped by his dad's over-powering nature. His mum seemed to have spent his whole childhood walking on eggshells. He smiled at her. 'You're not. In the way. Sorry. I'm a bit...' *Worried I'll spoil my whole childhood with you and Dad. That I'll turn up and my birth mother won't want me now, just like she didn't want me thirty years ago.* He sighed.

'I know. Me and your dad just want you to be happy. Your dad didn't want to tell you. Ever. But I insisted.'

That impressed Luke, because his mum hadn't insisted on anything in her life – not as far as he could see anyway. But at nine she'd sat him down and told him baldly that he was adopted. That she had not given birth to him and that her husband, his dad, had nothing to do with his creation either. 'You were given up for adoption by a sixteen-year-old girl, woman, I suppose, and your father and I, well, we'd tried for children but...' She'd looked away then, blushing as if it were the most embarrassing thing in the world. 'Didn't. Couldn't.' She'd hugged him tightly and over his shoulder said, 'And you came along and now you're our son.'

At nine he'd somehow taken it at face value. The people who'd raised him hadn't made him, but the woman who'd given him away was gone, so why waste time thinking about her? As a child it had seemed very simple.

Then it hadn't affected him much, he understood why he didn't look like his parents and that was it. But as he grew, he found himself wanting and needing to know more about who he came from. His people. Wondering why, sometimes, he didn't understand his parents, felt as if he'd fallen to earth and they'd scooped him up and adopted him. Yearned to find out if another human being on the planet would understand him, feel connected to him, explain why he was how he was, through blood.

'Fancy some food?' His mum looked about his bedroom.

'I'm not staying long,' Luke said, 'I've got a practice. Legs Crossed expects me.'

They walked to the kitchen.

'I'll best go,' she said. 'You mustn't be late. Do you need to get your things ready? Do you want a lift?'

'I've got a car. You don't need to do anything except *be* here.'

She looked very put out. Looking about herself in the kitchen. She opened the fridge. 'You're not eating much. How are you expecting to have the energy for all this dancing of yours if you're not eating properly?' She grabbed her handbag from the kitchen table. 'I'll nip out, get you some bits.'

He blocked the door, folding his arms across his chest. 'You don't need to *do* anything. I told you. I'm not going to chuck you out like a bag of recycling. Not Dad either.'

She put her hand over her mouth, blinking quickly, shaking her head. 'I'm sorry. I... your dad said this would happen if we told you. But I think you have a right to know. Even if it means...'

He held her shoulders, staring into her watery brown eyes. 'Do you want to come to my practice? Watch. Like you used to?'

She had taken him to dance lessons after school and at weekends from six years old. She got a part-time job in a supermarket to pay for it, because his dad had said they couldn't afford it.

She took a pink floral hanky from her brown leather handbag with a golden clasp and wiped her face.

But he always wanted to let her be her, and be kind. Because, regardless of how she looked, she loved him and he loved her very much.

And his dad too, although men, Luke had found as he'd grown into one, could be awkward together.

'Sounds nice,' she said, brushing her hair, which was cut into a bob. 'Sure they won't mind?'

'All the members of Legs Crossed love you.' No one ever had a bad word to say about his mum. They often had nothing to say about her, but that was because she was just so accommodating. To everyone. To everything. Although Luke could have moved away from his home town, imagining his mum's disappointed face, although she would never have asked him to stay local, had been too much to bear. Besides, he enjoyed living by the sea, Bournemouth returned itself from the tourists in winter and provided Luke with most things he wanted, including a reasonable gay scene.

His mum had been forever bending her will and wants to suit others around her. He saw her doing it with his father, but that wasn't for now.

'What's this show you're doing, with the group?' she asked.

'Big corporate do. Conference in Birmingham. Chief execs, or HR people. Something public sector. Councils, I think. We're the final session on the second day. It's meant to be the corporate conference equivalent of headlining at Wembley. Apparently.'

'Sounds lovely.' She looked at the clock on the microwave. 'Do we have time for a tea?'

'Course.' He turned the kettle on. 'Do you take sugar? I can't keep up.' Sometimes she was on no sugar, other times sweeteners, and then there had been a phase when she'd been on a teaspoon of honey.

'However it comes, Luke, love. I'm no bother.'

He turned his back to her. If ever there was a phrase that summed up someone, that was it for his mum. And here he was, just about to possibly ruin his relationship with the kindest person he knew. She was so kind she'd risked their relationship for him to meet Sasha. What if Sasha was loads more interesting than his mum? What if he and Sasha got on much better than he did with his mum? Wasn't that the worse option than Sasha not wanting anything to do with him?

'Heard from Ben?' she asked innocently.

His ex.

He finished making their drinks. Handed one to his mum, shook his head. 'No.'

'What happened with you two, I never did understand it?' She blew on her tea then slurped it loudly.

'It… I don't know,' he said simply, leaning against the sink, drinking his tea.

'You must know why? You didn't cheat on him, did you? I thought I'd brought you up better than that. Shame.' She tutted loudly, shaking her head.

'I didn't.'

She raised her eyebrows. 'I always knew he was a bit of a ladies'… I mean man's man. Charm up to his eyeballs, that Ben always had. He's one of them sort who's all nice and chatty to your face and then they rob you blind behind your back.' She tutted again, slurping her tea. 'Nice, is this. What teabags are they?'

Luke had no idea, he just bought whichever ones were cheap and in front of him when he went shopping. 'Tea?'

'I know that, but which make?' She stood, opened a cupboard, found the box of teabags, made a note of the name in a book in her handbag. She sat.

'He didn't do anything either. It just... *Rotto.*'

'Italian?'

He nodded.

'What does it mean?'

'Broken.'

'I always thought you'd end up working abroad, translating for a bank or something,' Jean said wistfully.

'Isn't it a shame I live in real life and not in your imagination?' He winked out of the corner of his eye.

'You know we'd be proud of you whatever you did with your life. This dancing group seems to keep you busy.'

He performed most weeks, it being his only source of income, and kept busy with practice between shows. He could never imagine working in an office and he'd told his parents at eighteen. They had disapproved, his father going on about unstable employment, and the arts always being a bit wishy-washy, but Luke had stuck to his guns. Legs Crossed, his dance troupe, won a TV talent competition a few years ago then sold out a national tour shortly after. They toured the UK and a mixture of corporate events, holiday camp tours, individual appearances in pantomimes, group TV appearances and national events such as the Olympics, Royal Variety Performance and the proms.

'Talking of which, shall we go?' She finished her tea, hanging her handbag over her arm. In many ways she reminded him of the late HM Queen Elizabeth II, except with a worse wardrobe.

He walked past the mirror in the hallway; he had a stubbly face, messy hair and tired eyes. He rubbed the scruff on his chin. His shoulders filled the mirror's width. He wouldn't admit to himself he was handsome, because that felt arrogant, but he'd been told by men and women that he wasn't bad-looking. He had been hit by puberty early and hard, and by fourteen had a square, stubbly jaw, hairy chest and deep voice. Friends used to say he looked like the pictures of men on the covers of his mum's romance books. At the time he'd found it really annoying.

'Ready?' he asked.

His mum had put on her brown raincoat, pulled up the hood. 'What does it mean, again?' she asked. 'What you said, you and Ben?'

'Broken.'

She nodded, looking at the floor. 'Sad.'

He shrugged as they left the flat and made their way towards the dance studio where his group sometimes rehearsed. They rotated the location since members of Legs Crossed were from all over the country, often letting members stay in each other's homes. It had started as a way to avoid expensive London studio prices, and ended up being one way the group's members became so close and synced during their routines.

Upon arrival at the studio, Luke settled his mum with a tea in the corner.

Steve, his manager, frowned. 'What's up?'

'Family stuff.' Luke wasn't about to spill this in front of his colleagues. 'She won't be any trouble.'

Steve nodded, walked away.

The group's leader, a tall man called Romero, who'd been a backing dancer for a well-known pop singer, stood at the front to take the rehearsal. Narrowing his eyes, he asked Luke, without words, if he was okay, nodding at Luke's mum.

Luke smiled. Yes, he was all right. He had to be. He slipped off his baggy T-shirt and jeans, revealing the tight black leotard underneath, showing off his muscular long limbs.

The rehearsal began and Luke disappeared into the dance, the performance; the music was him and he was the music.

It was odd to reflect, as he did sometimes, it had been his natural talent for languages that had unlocked this passion in him, leading him to becoming a dancer. Although not particularly academic, he'd always had an ear for foreign languages at school, managing a top grade at A level Italian. This led him to opera.

Luke had discovered 'opera' meant 'work' in Italian, then disappeared into something of a YouTube voyage of discovery, watching the Three Tenors singing 'La donna è mobile', Pavarotti singing 'Brindisi', the drinking song from *La Traviata* and 'Nessun dorma'. One afternoon at college, at seventeen, as he watched the Italian version of 'Time to Say Goodbye' with tears streaming down his face at the song's beauty, rhythm, and the artful way the dancers moved, he knew, without a shadow of a doubt, he needed to run towards that world and everything it meant.

Now, Romero indicated they were starting the rehearsal.

Luke moved to the front of the group, and taking centre stage, performed his solo dance, while the others knelt on the floor. He twirled, gyrated, moved in time with the music, flipped through a circle in the air, landing gracefully on his feet, like a cat.

His mother clapped excitedly from the corner. Looking about the room, she then stopped clapping, put her hand over her mouth, then mouthed 'sorry' and folded her hands in her lap.

Luke briefly blushed, but saw his colleagues weren't bothered, and they continued dancing until the end of the piece. After a pause, everyone clapped, as was traditional at the end of a practice.

Later, after everyone had dressed and confirmed arrangements for their upcoming conference, on the walk home Luke put his hand around his mum's shoulder. 'It's going to be all right.'

'Wish I had your confidence.' She shrugged, sounding very glum.

Sometimes I wish I didn't have my confidence. 'You know I love you. And Dad.'

She nodded, looking up at him with worry in her eyes. 'It's change. I don't like it.'

Most people don't, he thought. 'It can be good as well as bad.' They were at his home. 'Coming in?'

She shook her head, kissed his cheek, smelling of lavender soap and pear drop sweets. 'Thanks.' She waved, walking towards her car.

It made him feel as if she felt he was doing her a favour by having a relationship with his parents. But they were his mum and dad and he couldn't imagine life without them. It was just that he couldn't go any longer without knowing these last pieces of the jigsaw of who he was. He hoped very hard this change wouldn't damage what he had with his parents.

Inside his home, Luke checked if Sasha had replied to his messages.

Nothing.

So he sent her another, asking if they could meet. Explaining who he was. And he left the rest to the universe to decide.

Chapter 6

Wickford, Essex

Sasha put the phone down, the vet had said she could pick up the cat from the car accident that afternoon. Pretty had been in intensive care, then in plaster, then rehabilitation and a few weeks later could now finally walk and use a litter tray herself. Undoubtedly, she was going to cost them thousands of pounds, but she was going to be all right, and that was the most important thing. Sasha would worry about the vet bill later. They spent tens of thousands of pounds every month on vet treatment for the cats.

The thing to hold on to, after the days of touch and go, when the cat may not have survived the car accident, was Pretty was well and would be rehomed as an indoor cat, or one living far away from busy roads.

They had a strict no-busy-roads policy for adoptions at Fluffy Paws and although there was no guarantee even in small villages, or a cul-de-sac, they wanted to give their rehomed cats the best life possible. And Sasha knew, cats living next to busy roads were much more likely to be injured or worse.

When a man enquiring about rehoming a cat had said it was cruel to keep cats indoors, Sasha had puffed herself up to her full five foot three and said, 'Looking after a cat with a broken pelvis isn't much fun either. Nor is one with a broken back, laboured breathing. I had a cat survive being hit by a car, had surgery to fix him, four grand it cost. I was visiting him at the animal hospital every day, hand-feeding him cos his owner had surrendered him.' She swallowed at the memory. 'Then he died on the operating table.'

'How is that even possible?' the man asked.

'SIRS. Happens to humans too. You can survive a car crash then slip away ten days later.'

'Well, I think they *deserve* to go outside.'

'Well,' Sasha said, putting her hands on her hips, 'you'd be wrong. If a child lived by a busy road, would you let it play outside? No. Well, a cat has about the same intelligence as a small child.'

'It's not the same.'

It wasn't the same, but the principle was. Sasha walked up to him. 'Can you leave, please?'

'I want to get a cat,' he said.

'Well, you're not getting one, or adopting one, as we like to say, from here.' She held her arms out either side of her body and gently shepherded him out of the cat outbuilding, across the drive, past the house, and back to his car.

'You can't do this!' His face was red and his eyes wide.

'And yet, it looks like I just have.' She had turned with satisfaction and returned to the cat pen. *And people wonder why I'm still single. People, they so often disappoint. Unlike cats.*

Now, she returned to the office in the house, sat at the desk and her phone rang. It was a woman with a cat that had just given birth to five kittens. She didn't know how it had happened and could they take them in, please?

Sasha had a pretty good idea *how* it had happened, but she bit her tongue. A knock on the door disturbed

45

her phone call: Paul announced himself. She folded up the landlord's letter giving them notice to vacate. *Worry about that another day.* After telling Paul to wait a mo, she took the woman's details. 'I'll call you back. We're full at the moment. We might have some space in the next few days. I have a man who's helping me with it.' *It*, because she wasn't fully clear how Paul's plan would work, simply being on social media and how it would encourage people to adopt their cats, but he reckoned he'd seen other places do it so she trusted him.

'What am I meant to do in the meantime?' The woman's voice was strained with worry.

'The mum will know what to do. Leave her to get on with it. Make sure Mum has plenty of food and water, and somewhere quiet to look after her kittens.'

'What if anything happens?'

'Usually the mums can sort things out, since their bodies sort of know what to do mostly, but if in doubt ring me. I can talk you through what to do on the phone. Or jump in a car if needed.' She reckoned she would be needed, life being what it was.

'Good, because I can't afford to call a vet.'

If this woman had afforded to have her cat spayed this wouldn't have happened. If the cat had been adopted from a reputable sanctuary it would have definitely been spayed or neutered, that being the main way to reduce numbers of unwanted kittens. 'Understood. Anything else I can help you with?'

'Do you have kitten food I could have?'

Sasha shut her eyes, shook her head and covered the phone's mouthpiece. After letting out her frustrations by muttering, 'For fuck's sake, give me strength!' she uncovered the phone. 'Kittens will feed on their mother's milk very happily until they're weaned at three to four weeks.'

'So I shall need food for then. If I could put in a request for it now, please?'

Sasha's patience was wearing very thin. She took a deep breath, rolled her eyes. 'We'll have space by then, so it won't be your problem. Fluffy Paws will gladly help you out.'

'Good.' The woman hung up. Not a thank you, not a note of appreciation for offering to visit if necessary, nothing.

She told Paul he could enter her office, turning to him with relief washing through her. He was her saviour. 'You're here!' Every time a new volunteer started she always worried they wouldn't gel with the others, but Paul seemed to be getting on well. Plus he had skills no one else had, including Sasha. He'd make a great addition to her merry band of helpers.

He leaned on the door, arms folded. 'Looks like it. What's up?'

Sasha sighed, trying to let all the frustration from the call and the rest of the day leave her body. 'Today has been a rich tapestry of twats and, for an encore, a loud cacophony of the C-word. That woman being the worst offender.'

'That bad, eh?'

Sasha nodded. She'd made this her life's work, had never met a man after her first love, so had no children, she poured all her time, all her money into helping these cats. And some people were just take take take, asking for everything and not wishing to give anything. It wasn't as if the cats had any choice. 'That bad.' She wasn't going to moan to Paul, in case it put him off and he never came back. Some volunteers found it too hard to handle, never returning after their first day when it became abundantly clear it was definitely more than handing kittens to well-to-do homes.

The absolute pinnacle of her day of idiots had been a couple who seemed well-off, if their newish car was anything to go by, arriving with two gorgeous long-haired ginger cats, two brothers.

'Why are you surrendering them?' Sasha had asked, having agreed a while ago to take them today. She'd find somewhere to put them even if it meant having them in her bedroom in the house.

'We changed three-piece suite,' the woman said.

Sasha narrowed her eyes, not following this logic at all. 'Sorry, what does that have to do with the cats?' Sometimes people had a baby and were worried about having a cat, or their financial circumstances changed, or they moved somewhere the landlord didn't allow pets. There were many complex reasons why people surrendered their cats, but this was definitely a new one on Sasha.

'The new one is black,' the man added by way of explanation.

Sasha carefully looked from one to the other, deciding these people may have mental health issues, which she would be very sympathetic to, although the benefits of having pets for depression and anxiety were well documented. Anyway, she took the cat carriers from the man and woman. As she logged the cats into the system, taking age, temperament and any health issues, it became apparent these two well-natured male cats had been given up for the stupidest reason Sasha had ever heard.

'We wondered if we could have two black ones,' the woman asked once the paperwork was completed.

'I see,' Sasha said, having taken the cats into a pen. 'To go with your new sofa, presumably?' she asked, thinking she'd understood what was going on here.

They both nodded.

Wonderful. These two idiots definitely win today's Twat of the Day award. 'If you'd like to leave your details and a description of the sort of cats you'd like, we'll call you when we have a cat for you to view.'

The man wrote his details on a piece of paper, handed it to Sasha.

She read the part about what sort of cat they wanted: *doesn't matter the cat, as long as it's black.* Sasha used all her restraint not to tell these two idiots what she thought. She didn't want the gorgeous cats to return to that household. So she'd grinned, waved them off and returned to her office, ripped up the piece of paper, then lay her head on the desk and had a little cry.

She decided she wouldn't tell Paul.

'Why are people so often such a disappointment, I wonder?' she asked him now.

He looked at her in confusion.

'Rhetorical question. And not you, or any of the others who work here. It's just that I've always preferred animals to most people, but as I get older... Anyway.' She sighed. 'Can you do *all* this?' She pointed at the computer screen.

'What specifically?'

She shrugged. 'I don't know. What do other cat sanctuaries do? Have you checked the Cats Protection League?'

'I can. I've got a pretty good idea. Do you have Instagram, Twitter, Facebook?'

She sat, with less than no idea. 'Probably. Do whatever you need to.' She had got rid of the messages in her Fluffy

Paws social media account from that man who'd messaged a while ago, so Paul wouldn't see them. Very persistent, that Luke person, whoever he was. He'd sent more than one message.

'Where are the log-in details for all the accounts?'

She pushed a piece of paper across the table, folding up the landlord's letter again and putting it in a drawer. She would tell everyone they had to leave, but she wanted to get it fixed in her mind first, needed to put a brave face on things, before opening herself up for questions.

He smiled. 'Remind me not to ask you to look after cybersecurity.'

'Whatever that is.' She shook her head, feeling very harassed and overwhelmed.

'What's up?'

'Five kittens and a cat with two broken legs, that's what.'

'But we're full, aren't we?'

She nodded. 'That's why I need *you* doing this.' She gestured at the computer. 'I want people queuing up to adopt our cats. Clamouring for them. I want us to have a waiting list of people wanting to adopt cats. Not just anyone though, the right people. We've still got to check them out. Anna's forms and all that.' Not just anyone and definitely not the sort of twats she'd seen today.

Chapter 7

Wickford, Essex

Paul made himself comfortable in the computer's driving seat, logging into the accounts. He sensed there was something wrong with Sasha, she seemed jumpy, more than usually stressed. That piece of paper – she'd folded it, then again and then put it in her pocket. Whatever it was she really didn't want anyone to see it. *Shall I ask her? Bit nosy.* A message caught his eye. He glanced at the start of it: *Mum* was mentioned somewhere.

'I don't know how we're going to settle our vet bill,' Sasha said. 'How do other places do it?'

'We could have a fete, like last time.' It had been great fun, it was how he'd first heard of the place and decided to volunteer.

'Something quicker.'

Paul had an idea what other animal shelters did, because he followed some on social media. He'd soon grasp this by the horns and sort it out. 'Are you sure you don't want me to help with the cats?' He'd volunteered to spend time with cats, not sit at a computer, like at home.

'You *are* helping with the cats. If we rehome these, we can take new ones in. Isn't that the point of a cat sanctuary?' Her tone showed irritation.

Shall I mention the message? It's probably spam, just some bot, or someone promising her money if only she deposits cash into a bank account. How do people fall for these scams?

Sasha sat, staring into space.

'Do you want a coffee? Tea, biscuit?' Usually, she was the first to accept such an offer.

'No.' She shook her head.

Paul knew from dealing with awkward clients it was always better to face up to a problem than ignore it. 'If there's something wrong, we can help. Just tell us.'

'You just sort out the computer stuff. Leave the rest to me.'

Closed door. Firmly shut. Right. 'Can I just ask one question?'

'I said, it's nothing. Can't you get that into your head?' she snapped, her eyes wide.

Taken aback slightly, he said, 'That bit of paper you folded up. What is it?'

Sasha sighed, shaking her head. 'I didn't want to worry anyone, since I know how important this place is to you all. I'll deal with it. Must.'

'What is it?' Paul's tone was even but firm.

'Landlord's selling. He's given us a few months to relocate.'

Aha. Paul swallowed, trying to process this. 'Anything I can do to help?'

'I wasn't going to tell you quite yet. But since you've asked me. You could tell the others. It's bad enough having to tell you, never mind the rest of the volunteers. I—' She stopped herself.

'What?' He sensed she felt it was her responsibility to deal with everything to do with Fluffy Paws. But he knew it wasn't.

'We'll find somewhere else. How hard can it be?' She shrugged, shaking her head.

There was a long silence as Paul debated whether or not to ask his next question.

'I'm in regular communications with an estate agent. Promised to find us somewhere nearby.' She smiled, very fixedly, and Paul felt as if she were hiding something.

With a great deal of care, he asked, 'Have you seen this message?' He pointed to the screen. 'There's quite a few from the same person. Going back a few weeks or so.'

Peering closer, she said, 'I thought I'd got rid of them.'

'It comes back when I log in. Unless you meant to delete it.'

'I thought I had.'

'No. Still here.' He pointed to the word *Mum*.

There was a very awkward and long silence.

Paul wished he'd left well alone and ignored the messages. Except he wasn't that sort of person. Finally, he said, without looking at her, 'I didn't know you had any children.'

'I don't,' she replied tightly.

'Right. It's just it says he thinks you're his birth mother. He sounds very polite. I thought it was a scam, but I don't think so. He's not asked for money, has he?'

'And where precisely would I get that?' Very short-tempered.

He had obviously hit a raw nerve. *Definitely a bad idea mentioning this.* He chewed the inside of his cheek in thought. *Too late to abandon the conversation now, might as well continue.* With care he went on. 'If it's a scam they don't know you have no money. They ask, pretending to be someone you know. Or say you need to deposit money in their account to release prize money. It all sounds very far-fetched in the cold light of day but people can get swept along with it.' He looked at her. 'Very easily. Clever, well-educated people can become seized by a firm belief it's true. Easily done.'

Sasha shook her head very stoutly. 'It's *not* that.'

Understood. He swallowed the lump in his throat. 'So it's nothing. Shall I delete it?' He hovered his mouse, about to do as he'd suggested, his hand sweaty.

'Delete it,' she said with absolutely zero patience left.

'Gone. Forever?'

She nodded, staring dumbly at the screen, her face as white as a sheet, as if she'd seen a ghost. 'It's nothing. Time-waster. I've got better things to be doing with my life than chatting to some man who thinks he's my son. Ridiculous.' She walked to the door of the office. 'Delete it.'

Click. Gone. 'I'll get on with this, shall I?'

But she'd gone too.

Chapter 8

Wickford, Essex

After a pleasant drive through the countryside, Anna arrived at the cat sanctuary, carrying three pairs of shoes. The car puttered to a stop, shuddering slightly. *Definitely something wrong there, need to get it looked at. But what if the garage rips me off? What if I haven't got enough money to pay them? What if I need to buy a new car?*

Taking a deep breath, she left the car and walked towards the largest outbuilding while carrying a bag of shoes.

Once inside, Mim greeted her, wearing a long, flowing floral dress, always so impractical yet beautiful.

What if one of the cats scratches it? Or pees on it? This sort of thing always worried Anna.

'The cats don't need shoes,' Mim said with a smile.

'I know.' Anna put them on a table next to the phone. They sat there to complete adoption paperwork. Behind them were pens containing meowing cats. 'I wasn't sure which to keep. I bought all three. But I don't need them all.'

'Why not?' Mim said.

'Wasteful, isn't it?' Her parents had always warned her against profligacy.

Mim shrugged. 'There are worse things you can do than own too many pairs of shoes.'

Unconvinced, Anna went on, 'Or getting rid of stuff when it's perfectly all right.' Which was precisely what her ex-husband had done all those years ago, with their marriage. Married and divorced by her early twenties hadn't been much fun. Without even her best friend's shoulder to cry on. The year she'd turned twenty-two had been an absolute shit.

Cancer can be a merciless bastard too.

The grief had briefly winded Anna at the packed church, the white lilies on her friend's coffin as it was gently lowered into the ground. Her friend's mother throwing clods of earth, leaving a smear of mud on her black skirt and Anna worrying if she'd ever get it clean. Even now, twenty years later, if she allowed herself to dwell too much, what had happened that year felt as close as yesterday and she would easily cry.

Mim sighed. 'Are you all right? Seemed miles away then.'

'Fine. Absolutely.' Anna forced a tight smile.

'You worry too much.'

Anna shrugged, thinking she worried *just the right amount*. It was simply that there was *such a great deal* to worry about in the world. 'I'm going to don the equipment and get on with the litter trays.' It was a dirty job, but someone had to do it and for some reason Anna quite enjoyed it. Changing the litter and paper, making the cats' living space clean and tidy once again. While doing it she got to know each of the cats, sometimes playing with them. It often took most of her morning shift to complete. Nobody seemed to mind, and she worked through in her own little world.

'I have said I'll happily do it and you can show people the cats, but...' Mim waved airily.

Anna shook her head. *Too many worries. Too much that could go wrong.* 'Where's Sasha?' she asked.

'She was with Paul in the house, working in the office with the computer. Haven't seen her since.' Mim inspected each pair of Anna's shoes carefully. 'All of them, I say. Keep them all.'

Worry clouded Anna's expression. 'I don't think I can.'

'Why not? Who's going to stop you?'

Myself. Mum and Dad from beyond the grave. Disapproval of others. I don't want people to think I'm spending my parents' money on wasteful things. Her parents had scrimped and saved to pay off their mortgage years early, it was a bricks-and-mortar embodiment of their dedication to being thrifty. She couldn't simply sell it to the highest bidder! They'd instilled in Anna the value of not discarding things, of saving possessions for best, of ensuring she looked after her belongings. Society may be disposable, but Anna couldn't willy-nilly *just let go* of the items she'd accumulated during her life, since they were her life, the people she'd known, loved, lost.

Anna shook her head, blushing, slipping into a small room where she donned a robust apron and gloves, collected a rubbish bag.

She started at the far end of the outbuilding, unlocking the pen, kneeling to stroke the cat, then emptying its litter tray. While looking after her parents, this had been the only thing to stop her shaking with anxiety. When stroking the cats, and caring for them, she had focused on only that and her heart rate had returned to normal. Animal therapy, a doctor colleague had told her, could help with her anxiety longer-term.

'What's happening with your parents' house?' Mim later asked Anna. She was on the phone at the desk, covering the mouthpiece. Staring at two young cats, she read their care plan folder. Down the phone, she said, 'They're brothers. Must be adopted together. Must.' Mim shook her head, covered the mouthpiece. 'Some people!'

What's happening with your parents' house? Anna repeated the question in her head as she knelt inside a cat pen to stroke a large male tabby cat with a white bib and whiskers. Her shoulders relaxed and the worry about the nursing home's letter, the shoes, and selling her parents' house seemed to fall away. If only she could ask this cat, Tigger, to help her.

At the far end of the outbuilding, Mim finished her phone call, then walked past numerous pens finally stopping next to the one where Anna was working. 'That bad, eh?'

'Don't know what you mean.' Anna finished lining the litter tray with newspaper.

A long-haired tabby emerged from the bed on the ground. Toffee, he was Tigger's brother. Always very shy, second to do everything after Tigger who stood on a shelf, gently pawing Anna's hand.

'He's hungry,' Mim said.

'Shall I give him a little something?'

Mim shook her head. 'Best not. Unless you want Sasha to answer to.'

Tigger's claw rested on the back of Anna's hand. 'He could scratch me, but he doesn't. Clever, isn't he?' Tigger and Toffee had been given to the sanctuary when their human mother had emigrated to Canada knowing the journey would have caused harm, or possibly worse, to the two cats. Her written description and history of the two brothers had made Anna cry when she'd put it in their cat care folder. The woman loved her cats so much that she didn't take them to Canada with her. She'd had them for four years since they were kittens. Tigger was bold and always hungry, keen to do everything first, jumping about and playing with everything, he was a big tabby boy. Toffee, long-haired and another mackerel tabby, was shy, waiting until he felt more confident, but he used to sit on his human mum's shoulders as she walked around the house.

Anna smiled.

'He won't scratch you because he knows it won't get him food. He just wants you to know he wants something.' Mim nodded.

Anna stood, stroking Tigger's ears and cheeks, then left the pen, locking the gate after her as she returned to the outbuilding's corridor. 'Six months. They're giving me six months to repay the bill.'

'Who?' Mim asked.

'Nursing home. It's very generous of them, apparently.'

'That's all right, isn't it?'

In theory it was, but it meant Anna having to make a decision about selling the family home she'd grown up in. 'I don't know what to do.'

'Sell it, surely?'

'I can't just sell it. It's where they lived for seventy years. I grew up there. What if someone changes the kitchen and bathrooms? What if they remove the wallpaper I helped Dad decorate with in the Nineties?' Just the thought of those things had her throat constricting with anxiety. It felt like the actual end of the world.

'I can assure you, whoever buys it will in all likelihood do all of those things. Think of what you could do with the money?'

She hadn't considered that. 'Won't be much left after the fees.' *I think.* She hadn't processed how much she owed, or how much her parents' house was worth. Figures sort of gave her itchy eyes and sent her pulse racing in case she got them wrong. So she avoided them if possible.

'Surely not! Big house like that. How long were they in the care home?'

'Six months.'

The worst six months of Anna's life. That was when she'd started taking the tablets more often during the day. The sleepless nights and the drowsy days. She'd never have managed to hold down her job, so thank goodness for the sabbatical. She'd assumed she'd be paid, but no. Which made the three-pairs-of-shoes decision even stupider.

Mim stroked Anna's shoulder. 'It's hard, but that's over now. They are at rest.'

'Relief. It's a funny emotion.' Anna sounded slightly hysterical to herself. Relief at someone dying felt very wrong. But among the grief, there was an underlying relief and she struggled daily with the guilt of it.

'I always worry before a big party that everything won't be perfect. And when it all comes together – yes, sweet, joyful relief.'

Anna bit her lip. That wasn't quite what she meant. 'Right.'

'You deserve it, the money from the house. You've earned it.'

'Don't say that.' Anna turned away, guilt shooting through her stomach.

'Why not? It's true.'

'It is not. You don't look after people you love for a reward. You do it because you love them. It's like how people do good deeds in life so they are received through the gates of heaven. Like some cosmic slot machine. It's dreadfully selfish. I didn't look after Mum and Dad so I'd get their house. I did it because I love them.' She swallowed. 'Loved them.' Which was why the twinge of relief that it was all over made her guilty, dirty and ungrateful. An itchy wrongness.

'Understood.' Mim nodded solemnly. 'When will you sell it?'

'I don't think I will.' The thought of someone else sleeping in her childhood bedroom, someone else cooking in her mum's kitchen, having a bath in the bathroom her dad had installed with his own two hands in the late Nineties, when Anna was a teenager, all filled her with worry of such unimaginable proportions it outweighed the anxiety about owing the care home money.

'What will you do about the money?'

'I'll take out a loan if I need to.' And she would need to. So that was what she'd do. It was, when she said it out loud, all very simple.

Mim raised an eyebrow and looked away.

Clearly she thinks that isn't a sensible decision. But how can she know how much Mum and Dad's house means to me? Meant to them? Anna shook her head, and turned away, returning to cleaning the cats' pen.

Chapter 9

Mim thought that was beyond madness. Idiocy, in fact. But she dare not tell Anna lest her comments upset her. She'd tried it once before, when they hadn't known each other so well. Anna had arrived in a state of panic. Mim assumed someone had actually died. Anna explained she'd been watching TV when the video recorder had stopped working.

Video recorder, really... had been Mim's first thought, but she'd bit it back. 'Can you buy a replacement?' she asked.

Anna shook her head. 'They don't sell them. I like to watch family films. But now I can't. Dad used to make them when I was a child.'

This made a bit more sense. But not much. 'Can't you get them transferred on to DVD or one of those sticks you put in a computer?' Mim asked with care.

Anna shrugged. 'I don't know.'

'Have you asked?'

She had not.

Mim said with a great deal of kindness, 'I think *maybe* this is a sign for you to move, very carefully, into the twenty twenties, and upgrade.'

'The video's all chewed up. Probably ripped. It's my eighth birthday. Mum made me a cake in the shape of an eight, with a woman on a horse, riding along the eight-shaped path.'

It sounded delightful, and Mim said so, then she tried explaining there were places Anna could take the videos and probably someone could look at the machine itself, see what could be salvaged from the tape.

But Anna became hysterical and shouted: 'You're trying to take over my life. You don't know what it's like. They're my videos. Important to me. I need to keep them. I said I'd look after them for Dad when he gave them to me.'

'Nothing lasts forever,' Mim said with pragmatism. Little did she know how unhelpful Anna would find that fact.

'I know that. I've lost a husband, a best friend and now this.' Anna was beside herself with the loss. It was clearly not about the video, but every other loss poor Anna had experienced.

Eventually, the other volunteers had helped Anna find someone to help with the issue and a few weeks later Anna returned, explaining she had all the videos on her computer and the video recorder had been mounted in a display case.

Mim, knowing better than to ask this time, had wondered quite what possessed a woman to keep a broken video recorder, and video tapes, but she'd kept it to herself.

Now, Mim was itching to point out to Anna that getting a loan to pay off her parents' debt, while keeping their house, *and* her own home, was beyond madness. But she knew it would take Anna a little longer to work through that herself.

'As I say, keep all three,' Mim said.

'What?' Anna asked.

'Shoes. You only live once. And there are no pockets on shrouds.' It was something her mother had often repeated, having nursed her grandparents from her family home in their final years. Mim remembered four elderly grandparents, bed-bound, staying in the back bedroom, meaning she had to sleep in the sitting room on and off for a number of years.

'I know that,' Anna said slowly. 'Having recently seen both parents actually wearing shrouds. But I don't think it's a very kind thing to say to someone.'

Mim had done it again. *Bloody brilliant.* She gritted her teeth. 'Sorry. No offence meant.'

'I'm going to get on. The cats won't clean out their own litter trays, will they?' Anna shook her head and tutted.

'I believe they won't.' Mim smiled.

Anna continued moving through the outbuilding, cleaning the cats' pens, humming to herself quietly, clearly absorbed in her own world.

Mim stayed by the phone, taking details of homing enquiries and requests to take in cats for various reasons. In a brief moment of quiet, she sat back in the chair.

Sasha appeared. 'Okay?'

'Homing enquiries. Why don't people just come in? There's no way I can describe a cat as well as when they meet it.'

'Hopefully, Paul is going to help us on that front.'

'Oh?'

'He's on the computer doing all sorts of stuff.'

'Splendid.'

Paul arrived. 'I've come to see if there's anything I can help with here. Eyes are going blurry from the computer screen.' He smiled awkwardly.

Anna appeared, carrying a large bag of rubbish. 'Just the other buildings to do now.' She appeared relaxed and happy.

Mim was pleased at this. So often Anna appeared in pain with her ongoing anxiety about most things, most recently her shoe conundrum. At least coming here seemed to give her some respite.

'How did your birthday party go?' Anna asked Mim.

'Not a birthday. No special occasion. Very well.' If only she could capture and bottle the feeling when the first guests arrived, as they settled and talked to one another. The lightness in her stomach when someone complimented her cooking, or the theme for one of her bigger soirees. She wished that could continue forever, rather than coming to a sad end as the last guest left.

'How many people?' Anna asked from inside a cat pen, wiping her forehead with the back of her hand, moving a stray hair out of the way.

'Twenty-two.'

'I'm in awe,' Sasha said. 'Just cooking for myself feels too much most nights.'

They laughed.

'I've been looking at the figures, on the computer,' Sasha said. 'And my maths skills aren't great, but I think the technical term is: we're skint.'

'How skint?' Paul asked from behind them.

'Very, but I'm not great at figures.' Sasha looked at Mim.

Mim said, 'I am. So I'll look over them and confirm precisely how little we have.'

'Marvellous,' Sasha said. Turning to Paul, she went on, 'How are you getting on with the internet stuff?'

'I was going to write a plan for what we could do. I've looked at how other animal charities manage their social media. And fundraising too.'

'Splendid!' Sasha waved a hand in the air. 'Whatever you think we should do, as long as it doesn't cost anything. Because we have rather less than fuck all in the money department.'

'Must you swear?' Anna said, shaking her head.

'Sod all?'

Anna shrugged. 'Better. People who have limited vocabulary resort to swearing. It's so common. Mum and Dad used to despise it. Although I know I'm prone to it sometimes. When I'm at a loss for what to do.' She looked at Mim. 'Sorry. Rude of me. It's instinctive, from my parents.'

For a moment, Mim thought about unleashing a torrent of creative, imaginative swearing, because, when she was 'on', she'd been known to hold court, recounting stories to a room of people, held captive by her words. Including many colourful expletives. But because it upset Anna, she held back.

'How much do we owe?' Paul asked.

'This month's vet bill is twenty thousand pounds. They're very good. No rush in repaying it. But we do need to pay it.'

'Can't they give us a discount?' Anna asked.

'That's with a discount. It would be nearly double that otherwise.' Sasha sighed.

They sat in silence for a moment.

'I have some ideas for how to help.' Paul put his hand in the air. 'Although I don't want to be stuck at that ancient computer all day. I came here to spend time with cats, not a computer. I can do that at home.' He looked about him nervously, obviously checking he'd been heard.

'Just until we get ourselves out of this scrape,' Sasha said.

'Which one?' Paul asked.

Sasha's eyes widened, and she nodded almost imperceptibly.

Paul went on. 'Landlord is selling up.'

'And we've been given a few months to vacate. Makes it sound so simple, doesn't it? One word. Vacate.'

'But we won't close?' Anna had left the pen and joined them in the shared space within the outbuilding.

Sasha shook her head. 'Last resort.'

There was a silence as everyone absorbed what she meant: it was an option.

'I suppose we could have *another* fete, for the vet bill,' Mim offered brightly, determined to move the discussion on. The last one had been a great success, raising what they owed the vets. Each month cost, on average, twenty to thirty thousand pounds in vet fees. But she couldn't arrange one every month. Although a part of her would have liked to.

'Can you look into that, please?' Sasha asked. 'And the budget's f—' She looked at Anna. 'Nothing. Can you work with that?'

She'd managed it before. Mim nodded.

The doorbell rang. It was the first of the visitors, hoping to find a cat to adopt. The sanctuary was only open to visitors each afternoon, it gave them time to care for the cats and tidy up their pens without people getting in the way.

'I'll get it.' Paul strode towards the front door.

'I've not finished the other buildings yet.' Anna looked about her frantically. 'They're in a mess. Visitors can't see them like that. What would it look like? Like we don't care about the cats.' She shook her head, pulling at a stray hair in the way Mim recognised signalled she was worried.

Mim put her hand around Anna's shoulder. 'Come on, let's do it together. Six buildings between the two of us, we'll be done in the time it takes for them to tell Paul what sort of cat they're after.'

Anna looked at her with anxiety, blinking quickly, pulling at her hair. 'If you don't mind. In your dress, I mean...' She looked Mim up and down.

'This old thing, I use it as a housecoat.'

They left the main outbuilding, containing the adoption desk and paperwork, and were soon busy tidying and cleaning the pens in the smaller buildings.

A short while later, Anna said, 'When did you buy it?' She held two bags of rubbish.

'What?' The cats' cages were clean with fresh water and they had been checked for any issues to make sure they were okay to receive guests. She put the sign on cage D in a prominent position: *I have been reserved, so no visitors please.*

'The dress.' Anna followed her out to the bins.

'No idea. Why? Do you remember where you've bought every item of clothing?'

Anna shook her head vigorously. 'Course not. What do you think I am?'

Mim waved away the comment. 'Nothing.'

Anna paused, tucked a hair behind her ear, blinked slowly at Mim, almost on the verge of tears. A long swallow as she seemed to gather herself in, compose herself. 'I miss them, but I'm so *relieved* it's over. Not that they're gone, but that it's *over*.' She leaned against the wall, rocking slightly from side to side.

'Your parents?'

Anna nodded.

'The suffering is over. It's natural to feel relief. Guilt is a useless emotion anyway.'

'Is it?' Anna frowned, narrowing her eyes. '*Really* useless?'

Mim nodded. 'Definitely. Anything can be made a little worse or a teeny bit better by adding a *soupçon* of guilt. Human beings are the only animals that feel it. You don't see cats feeling guilty about their behaviour, now, do you?'

'You can't know that.'

'Unless you're hurting someone else, it's a pointless emotion. Move on from it.'

Anna laughed nervously, scuttled off, towards the staff room.

But Mim knew there was a great deal more behind Anna's questions about guilt. She'd have to take it gently, trying to extract the truth from Anna over the weeks.

Chapter 10

Bournemouth, Dorset

Luke returned home from a day's shopping – a few clothes, some trainers and a new phone charger, a cheat lunch of burger and chips, then working off the calories and guilt very hard in the gym.

Reflecting on the rehearsal a few weeks ago, he knew their fifteen-minute performance for the event would be perfect. All twelve members knew their part and they behaved like one animal, of twelve parts, but one united living organism. Luke loved that he got to do this for money.

As he put the key in the door, a hand rested on his shoulder.

'Can me and your mum have a talk?' It was his dad, Roger, short and bald and looking more than his sixty years.

In Luke's mind, his parents were still forty, which was their first *big* birthday he remembered as a child. He was watching them age before his eyes, as he was only a decade from forty himself.

'Where's Mum?' Luke asked.

From the shadows appeared his mum. 'I said you'd be tired. Needed to get ready for the big performance. It's this week, isn't it? But your dad insisted.' She looked to Roger with worry on her face.

The performance was the day after tomorrow. But Luke was prepared and didn't want to talk about anything else now. 'Thanks, Mum. Can we do this another time, Dad?' Luke opened the door.

'Won't take long.' Roger barged ahead, into Luke's home, up the stairs into the flat.

His mum wouldn't hear that he planned to have a protein milkshake for dinner, and instead made everyone beans on toast and a glass of milk – it had been one of his favourite suppers as a teenager. He didn't have the heart to tell her he was doing a low-carb diet so shouldn't eat the toast.

'Sit down if you're eating too,' Luke said between mouthfuls. It was easier to let her make them dinner than dismiss her unkindly.

His parents sat and tucked into the food. It felt almost normal, as it had been when he lived at home, it seemed such a shame to spoil it with *this* discussion.

Luke said, 'I'm going to send a third and final message. She can't ignore me. She's done so for thirty years. Now it's my turn to be heard.' He'd sent two over previous weeks and heard nothing back. Had left it today, too busy shopping, but now he was home, he was bloody well going to message her again.

'You don't know why she gave you up.' Roger cracked his knuckles loudly.

'Do you know if she's read it, this message?' Jean asked.

'Yes.' He finished the food, pushing the plate across the table.

'Sure?'

'I know a read receipt when I see one.' Luke stretched out his legs under the table, folded his arms.

'You should call her,' Roger said, putting his cutlery on the plate neatly.

'I'm not doing that. Phoning someone I've never met.' He scoffed.

'But sending them a message is okay?'

'Course it is.' He was about to mention online dating apps but since splitting up with Ben he'd had more than enough of them. Plus, explaining to his parents the sort of things people messaged total strangers about on certain apps wasn't a conversation he wanted to have any time soon. Ever, in fact.

Jean finished her food, stood, carried the plate to the sink and started washing up.

'I've got a dishwasher, can you sit down, please, Mum?'

'He's calling you Mum now, but what about after he meets this woman?' Roger asked.

'I'm right here. In the room with you. That's almost as bad as talking about yourself in the third person.'

'Don't try and distract us from the real conversation topic.' Roger sniffed loudly.

'Want a hanky?' Jean handed him a blue one from her handbag.

Is there anything she's unprepared for? At least someone's prepared, even if it's not me. In my own home.

Wiping his nose, Roger said, 'Wait for her to reply. Then we can discuss what to do.' Roger stared at Luke with something between worry and anger in his eyes.

'You helped me find her,' Luke said. 'For which I'm grateful. But this now, from this point onwards is my thing. My thing to do how I want to do it.'

'Here's a new idea.' Roger sat upright. 'Why don't you leave the past where it's meant to be left? In the past.'

Luke didn't often respond like this, instead usually preferring quiet reflection, but he was sick and tired of having the same conversation with his dad again and again. He stood up to his full six foot six, leaning forwards, banging a hand on the table. 'Because it's *my* past. That's why I don't want to leave it there. Because it's *who* I am. Because I've always wondered where I came from. Why I look like this. Why I was given up for adoption. That's why.'

Jean folded her hands in her lap, looking at the floor.

Roger folded his arms across his chest, staring at Luke, then looking away.

'Imagine if you had a question you'd wanted answering for your whole life, something that influenced how you relate to others, your relationships with family, friends, everyone. I will always be your son. I love you both very much. But you do drive me mad sometimes. You can't possibly understand what I'm going through. Know I will always love you, always want you in my life. Even if you drive me up the wall. But there's these two pieces of the jigsaw of me that I need to find.' He sat, the heat slightly dissipating from his face.

'Two pieces?' Roger frowned.

'My birth mum and dad.'

'Right.'

'As a child I accepted you weren't my birth parents, didn't think that much of it. But as the thirty-year-old man I am now, I need questions answering for me. Why do I look like this? Why do I love certain things? Dancing, and opera, why can I speak multiple languages, learning them as easily as walking, and why do I feel drawn to seemingly everything that's Italian? Why are those things so important to me? Cos it's not from you two, is it?'

His parents shook their heads, staring at the floor, almost as if they were ashamed.

Luke's heart squeezed with the pain he was causing. 'I don't want you to think I don't love you. I do. But there are parts of me, as I've settled into who I am, maybe it's a big birthday, I don't know. But I need to have answers to these questions and I know you can't give them to me. Even if you wanted to.' He paused, took a breath, wanted to hug his parents. 'I want to answer the question if something's nature or nurture. I've got plenty of love to have two sets of parents in my life.'

'That you have.' Jean said, squeezing his hand as a tear formed in the corner of her eye.

His heart squeezed with sadness at putting them through this. But he didn't see any alternative. 'I promise you I'll always have you in my life. But if you stop me doing this, I can't guarantee what I'll do.' It felt like an ultimatum and he hated saying it, but he needed them to understand the importance of taking this step alone. Of deciding whether to meet his birth mother.

'You're right, we can't answer those questions for you. There's only one person who can.' Jean sighed. She looked at her husband.

He shrugged.

They stood.

'Do you want some warm milk before bed?' Jean held the fridge door open.

It was all too much for him. Such a lot to process, while doing his best not to upset his parents. He wanted them to go before he said something he'd regret. 'Can you both go, please? I need to be alone.' He held his head in his hands, elbows resting on the table.

The chairs scraped across the tiled floor, footsteps towards the door, then the click as it shut.

He'd expected a hug, or another word from his mum, but he had obviously been too angry for her to respond. He hated the thought of scaring his parents, particularly his mum. She was nothing but kind and accepting. But sometimes her offers of help felt suffocating and he needed them to understand he must take this step alone. For better or for worse. With or without their blessing.

The latter wasn't preferable, but if necessary, he would go ahead nevertheless.

Chapter 11

'That's all settled,' the vet said on the phone.

Sasha put her credit card back in her purse. 'Until next month.'

'We'll always be here for you.'

'Thanks.' She ended the call, thinking of the irony that the vets had promised to always be there when the future of Fluffy Paws was uncertain as the landlord's few months' notice marched on quicker than she appreciated. She hoped very hard there would be some give in the deadline.

She left the office, where was Paul when she needed him? He was meant to be in there doing his computer stuff.

'There's someone here,' Anna said, pulling at a stray piece of hair. 'Saying he needs to take photos, for the estate agent, I presume.'

Sasha's strategy of ignoring the letters from the landlords seemed to have limited use. 'I'll meet him. Don't expect you to put up with a bloody estate agent.'

'Everything's all right, isn't it?' Anna's tone was more worried than Sasha felt.

Possibly.

A man in a sharp suit, holding a biro and clipboard, stood by the door. 'From Fareham and Tadley, estate agents. Presumably, the landlord has told you he's selling.'

Sasha ushered him out the front door. 'Of course.' She took a breath. 'Don't suppose you have anything similar on your books we could move to?'

'Not a chance. Anything like this property would be converted into apartments. Lovely Victorian features, and big grounds. Not much call for this sort of set-up, I'm afraid.'

'I think the cats would disagree.' She didn't try to keep the snippiness out of her tone.

He chuckled. 'Mind if I take some pictures and measurements?' He held a biro and aimed it at the building; a red laser shone on the bricks.

'How long do you think it'll take to sell?' In theory, the landlord wanted them out when the sale completed, which could be as little as three months from an offer being accepted, but she was pretty sure there could be some wiggle room there. As long as they were gone by the time the new owner took possession. Vacant possession had been mentioned in the landlord's letters a few times.

The estate agent took a photo of the car park. Shrugging, he said, 'Who can say. Depends on pricing. The market, planning permission. Many factors need to be taken into account. It's a complex business is selling properties.'

'Undoubtedly. But a rule of thumb?'

'Few months, and then at least three to complete the sale. Why? Planning to buy it?'

'Nothing.' *That gives me another five months. An improvement on less than three months. Not too bad. Stand down. Relax. Good job I ignored the landlord's letters.*

'Can I look inside the house?'

'Don't you want to see inside the cat pens?'

He shook his head. 'They'll rip all those outbuildings down before putting it on the market. Makes it easier for prospective buyers to imagine it as a collection of apartments with ample parking.'

There was a noise behind her of shock. She presumed it to be Anna.

Sasha stood still, as if someone had punched her in the guts. Winded. Sick. Sad. All together. It had taken hundreds of hours' work and dozens of volunteers to construct the outbuildings, to design them as cat pens, to include space inside for the volunteers to walk between the pens. This meant she didn't have five months, she'd need to find homes for all the cats much sooner. Very much sooner. Worry bubbled up through her stomach.

She wondered if the landlord could be persuaded otherwise of that and, doing her best to put aside that worry, led the estate agent past the slightly ramshackle outbuildings, a few wood-framed constructions, an old static caravan and a large wooden shed, each containing the cat pens, then they walked into the large Victorian house she'd called her home.

He paused, photographing the large double door and arch. 'Beautiful. Is it just you living here?'

'And sixty cats.'

Stepping into the entrance hall, he said, 'In here, I mean.'

'There are a few nursing queens in here. But usually yes, it's just me in here.'

He frowned. 'I'm not against all of that, but why do you have men like that practising nursing in here?'

Sasha frowned. 'I don't follow.'

'I'm a big fan of Boy George. Erasure, even. Love a bit of Years & Years. But I don't—'

Sasha understood what this nincompoop of a man had misunderstood. Biting her cheek, and with a great deal of care, she went on. 'A female cat is called a queen. Like a male cat is a tom. We let them have their litters in the house as it's warmer. They stay in here until they've weaned them off their milk. Then they go into one of the pens in the other buildings for adoption. Always in pairs, we don't let kittens go alone, unless there's already a cat in the household.'

He stared at her. 'Thank god for that.' He strode into the lounge, looking at the ceiling, coving, windows. 'Lovely period features. Ceiling rose, original coving, sash windows.' He tried to open one. 'Do they work?'

'Of course. But they're closed in case one of the cats escapes.'

He stood at one end of the room, pointing his laser contraption to the opposite wall, writing something on his clipboard. 'You couldn't get me a coffee, could you? Filter, strong, no sugar or milk.'

'No, I couldn't.' Sasha left the room, shaking her head.

A short while later, after checking on the two female cats and their litters, she heard him shouting from the echoey hallway.

'All done.' He looked about, peering up the corner staircase.

'Anything else I can help with?' she asked, wishing very hard he would go away.

'You don't see many properties like this, untouched. This banister is original. Same as the stairs. Under this carpet there will be monogamy. Solid monogamy.'

Sasha debated correcting him, but didn't bother. *Get him out quick.* 'Right.'

'What happened to my coffee?'

'Sorry, but we've run out. It's on the list for when I go shopping. Along with three hundred quid's worth of cat food.'

He raised an eyebrow. 'Rather you than me.'

She wasn't sure why she asked him this, but desperate times and all that. 'If you were me, where would you suggest I look for somewhere to move the cat sanctuary?'

He shrugged, sucking air over his teeth. 'Somewhere land is cheap and no one gives a monkey's about wasting a beautiful property like this on cats.'

'That's very much a matter of opinion.' She ushered him out the house, closing the door behind them. She walked next to him towards the car park.

By his car – a plain BMW, without the estate agent name on the side – he unlocked the door. 'Scotland.'

'Sorry, what?'

'To move this operation. You could pick up a place like this in Scotland, not in the cities, mind, but the middle of nowhere, you'd get it for a song. Or Wales. There are parts of Wales where you could almost buy a whole village for what this place is worth. Essex used to be cheap, but not now.'

'This little operation is saving lives of hundreds of cats every year. Finding them their forever homes, giving so much joy to their adopted humans. The therapy and joy these cats give to their human adoptive parents is proved to help mental health. And you can't put a price on that.'

He sat in his car. 'Unfortunately, that's precisely what I *can* do.' He started the engine. Wound the window down. 'I'll be back with a for sale sign next week.'

'Must you?' *Shall I ask him about pulling down the cat pens so soon?*

'It's pretty usual. Unless you want to speak to the land-lord to agree something else? Pleasure doing business with you.' He drove off, leaving a trail of gravel and smoke.

With a sense of defeat settled deep in her gut, Sasha slowly walked back to the cat pens. *What else can go wrong today?*

Anna appeared from the largest building. A tall man with black hair, a square, stubbly jaw and piercing blue eyes stood next to her.

Sasha would recognise that face anytime. He'd had Sasha's light colouring as a baby, but now he was tanned with azure blue eyes and he looked exactly like his father at that age. Sickness filled her stomach. Cold sweat formed on her forehead. Dizziness filled her head, lightness and an inability to stand upright suddenly overcame her.

The man held his hand out for her to shake. 'Hello, Sasha. I'm Luke, your son.'

Sasha shook his hand. The ground rushed up to meet her and she felt light-headed, overwhelmed, as if she were dreaming. *This isn't happening. I ignored his messages, got rid of them, didn't I? I left him as a baby, with a social worker, signed the papers, knowing he'd never see me again, that's what I agreed to. This day was never supposed to come.*

Then darkness.

Chapter 12

Wickford, Essex

Paul arrived at the sanctuary, he couldn't wait to tell everyone about the last few days. A date from hell and all the shares and likes the cat videos and pictures had received on the socials.

A crowd had gathered. Sasha was on the floor, inside the largest outbuilding containing the rehoming desk and paperwork.

After entering the building, the first thing he noticed, much to his shame, was a tall, dark-haired man with broad shoulders, barely contained in a tight-fitting T-shirt and skinny jeans. He wasn't bodybuilder muscular, but powerful and lithe were two words that went through Paul's mind. The man had a square jaw with enough scruff to look effortlessly rugged. And eyes as blue as a clear summer's day sky.

Whoops.

'What happened?' Paul asked, just managing to marshal his thoughts from imagining the hunky Bradley Cooper lookalike in a pair of Speedos.

Anna was rubbing Sasha's arm. 'Shall we call an ambulance? Is she dead, do you think?'

What on earth is going on?

Mim forged through the throng, knelt and took Sasha's pulse. 'Strong and normal. First-aid trained. Don't panic.' Turning to the man she said, 'Who are you? And what have you done to Sasha?'

'I didn't intend this to happen. I'm sorry,' said the man.

His voice was deep and powerful, well spoken, southern, reminded Paul of a TV presenter he'd spent his early twenties fantasising about. A lot. The echoes of Bradley Cooper remained firm. Focusing on the fact that Sasha had fainted rather than flirting, Paul crouched next to her, slipping his jacket over Sasha's body. Paul looked at the man. 'She should be okay. No thanks to you.'

'Why *are* you here?' Mim asked the man, patience obviously waning.

'I sent her a message. Quite a few of them. But she didn't reply.'

'You could have phoned.' Mim stood, folded her arms across her chest. 'Look at the shock she's in.'

'She doesn't know me.'

'Who rings total strangers?' Paul said, dragging his attention back to the discussion and away from the man who was so prepossessing it was almost as if he'd literally stepped off the cover of one of those thin romance novels his mum used to have delivered monthly when he was a teenager.

'Right!' the man said, smiling briefly. Straight white teeth in a perfect smile.

A grin that would let him get away with murder. Paul chuckled. 'So who are you, again? I feel like I've missed something.'

'Luke.'

From the messages. From the messages he'd deleted on Sasha's instructions, because he thought they were someone starting very slowly to catfish Sasha. 'I thought you were a catfish.'

'What's a catfish?' Mim asked.

'Someone who pretends to be a person they aren't, using a fake social media profile.'

'Why would you do that?'

'Money, notoriety, deception, pretending to live a better life than their own...' Paul could go on but he felt it was enough.

Sasha woke, looking about her, rubbing her eyes, slowly sitting up.

'You're really Sasha's son?'

'I am.' The man nodded.

Paul couldn't believe this. 'From which exotic corner of the world have you sprung?' *With looks like that he must be from southern Europe, an island in the Mediterranean. Sicily, or Corsica, probably.*

Definitely.

Luke nodded. 'Dorset.' He crouched in front of Sasha. 'Sorry, Sasha, I didn't think you'd faint.'

Dorset. Does this guy really think he's Sasha's son? Is he a little bit mad?

'I didn't think you'd turn up.' Sasha stood, with help from Luke.

'What else was I meant to do? You ignored all my messages.' Luke stood with his palms facing upwards.

'Call!' Sasha said with exasperation.

Luke exchanged a look and rolled his eyes at Paul — given they seemed nearly the same age, they were clearly the only two people in complete agreement that calling a total stranger was beyond madness. 'Mind you,' Paul began, 'turning up is *a lot*, and also pretty... unorthodox.'

'Thirty years and I decide to find you, I was impatient. I'm sorry. Didn't mean to make you faint. Turning thirty, it sort of... I needed to know some stuff. Stuff only *you* can tell me.'

'Thirty, how's that even possible?' Sasha frowned.

'Nineteen ninety-three, I was born.'

'Wasn't that about five minutes ago?' Mim asked, then sighed.

'Feels like it,' Sasha said with a shrug. 'I was sixteen. Summer of love.' She stared into the distance.

Paul sensed there was a great deal more behind that. He looked at Luke. 'Funny, you being impatient, cos after waiting all that time, you'd think waiting a little longer until you heard back from Sasha wouldn't make much difference.' Paul put a finger on his chin in an exaggerated pose of thinking. 'You've come from Dorset?'

'Bournemouth,' Luke said.

'Right,' Paul said. *So not Rhodes, Sicily, Sardinia, an exotic island in the Mediterranean?* Paul tried to hide his disappointment and failed. Mostly.

'You seem surprised,' Luke said.

'I assumed...' Paul shook his head. 'Nothing. Sorry. I'm taking over the limelight, this is you and Sasha's thing. Sorry.'

'No, you're all right.' Luke grinned.

Paul's heart beat faster at having that grin directed towards him. Then thought better of it.

There was a brief silence, as everyone seemed to try and process what had happened.

'What now?' Anna asked nervously.

'We leave these two in privacy.' Mim shepherded everyone else out of the wooden building, leaving the cats in their pens behind and moving towards the house and into the humans' kitchen. 'We're British. Tea and biscuits, now, what else?'

There were mumbles of agreement as they filed towards the house and into the kitchen.

'Are we sure this man is actually Sasha's long-lost son?' Mim asked. 'Or is he perhaps something of a con man? Or is it an elaborate joke, maybe?'

'Con her out of what? She doesn't own this place. She has no money, from what I've seen,' Paul said, possibly slightly swayed by his good looks, but not much.

'Funny though.' Anna rotated a digestive biscuit on her saucer.

'Not funny-ha-ha,' Mim said.

'Obviously not. But he traces her and just turns up. After all those years. Early midlife crisis, maybe? Turning thirty: big milestone, I found. Saying goodbye to what won't be, and facing what your life is bound to be. Or so I thought until—' Anna caught herself, stopped suddenly. Looked about her. Smiling brightly, she went on. 'It's like one of those programmes, long-lost family. My mother and father used to watch them. Always made Mother and myself cry.'

'But not pass out though?' Mim asked.

'Suppose not. Funny how life's not like the television, isn't it? It's much neater, more well-organised on the tele-vision than real life, which is so often very dissatisfactory, complex and untidy.'

Paul, noting the conversation had suddenly taken quite a dark turn, said, 'I do have some good news!'

'We could do with that.' Anna looked very glum and worrisome.

'I've raised fifteen thousand pounds towards the vet bill. In the last month or so.'

'How the flip did you do that?'

Mim sat at the table, adjusting her flowing dress. 'It's fortunate I've not progressed too far with the fete. I'll shelve it. I feel you've rather made me and my fete plans somewhat redundant.'

'Come on, it's about the money not who does it,' Anna said.

'True, but I'd have rather it be me who'd done it.' Mim silently dunked a biscuit into her tea with a great deal more aggression than seemed absolutely necessary.

Paul felt embarrassed, being the centre of attention wasn't his thing. He much preferred being behind the scenes, organising things. 'I'm not sure where to start.'

'As near to the end as humanly possible,' Mim said with a wink.

'Social media.'

'You raised fifteen thousand pounds through social media. Isn't that illegal?' Anna asked.

Explaining how he'd done it seemed preferable to guessing about Sasha and the mystery man's relationship. Paul said, 'I've been posting about the cats and the treatment they've needed, how much it's cost. Pictures of them, updates on their progress, where we found them, the sorry state they were in. How they look now, after we've looked after them. When it worked, when it didn't. Some people don't appreciate there's no universal and free healthcare for cats. That if a cat dies, you still have to pay the vet's bill. How we're always here for the cats, even if there's not much hope for them.'

They prided themselves in never euthanising any cats unless it was for health reasons. Some cats had remained in the shelter for many months before being rehomed.

'People sent you money?' Anna asked.

'They did.'

'All from you putting some videos on the internet?'

Paul bobbed his head from side to side. 'There's a bit more to it than that. But you wanted the short version.'

Mim gave him a hug, holding him tightly towards her. She kissed his cheek. 'You're an absolute genius. I said we needed more youngsters like you, didn't I?' She looked around the room and the others nodded.

'I'm twenty-eight, hardly a youngster. I speak to chief executives about data strategies, integrated marketing campaigns.' Paul felt a little affronted, but knew it came from a positive place.

'And we love you for that too. As long as you carry on doing whatever you've done, that problem is sorted.'

Anna held her breath. 'Although there *are* other problems.'

'Are there?' Mim asked casually. 'Other than the landlord's eviction?'

Anna nodded. 'I overheard the estate agent saying he's going to demolish all the outbuildings before putting this place on the market,' Anna said.

'When is it going on the market?' Mim asked.

'He was measuring it today, making notes. So, soonish, I'd say.'

Mim threw her hands in the air. 'Oh well, in that case, why are we even worried today? It's not like they'll turn up to pull them down tomorrow, is it?'

'They could.' Anna's eyes widened. 'I think it's a worry.' She leaned forwards, counting on her fingers. 'A big worry, actually. We thought we had a while plus the time the sale would take to go through. But in actual fact all we've got is a matter of weeks. Unless the landlord is inclined to change his mind.'

'Unless,' Mim said, with a glint in her eyes, 'we have an alternative plan.'

'Such as?' Anna asked.

'That, I do not know at present. But I'm sure we can put our heads together. Or I shall be painting my glass figurines and I'll have a flash of inspiration. Always the way.'

Luke arrived, looking shell-shocked and sad. 'I'm off. I thought I should let you know I was going.'

'How is she?' Mim asked.

'We both have a lot to process. I shouldn't have arrived unannounced, I know that now. I didn't realise she has so much on her plate, with this place.'

'She told you?'

He nodded. 'Like she needs me adding to her woes.'

'Would she like some company?' Mim asked.

'Probably not. She asked me to leave... Said she needed time. To get used to me existing as me now, and not a little boy she...'

Mim brushed her hands together. 'Come along, we must return to work.' She ushered Anna out, leaving Luke and Paul alone.

'I think I've sort of ballsed it up.' Luke's azure-blue eyes widened, with tears almost forming.

'Is she that bad?'

'She cried.' A look of pain crossed Luke's face. 'I made her cry. After you all left, she wouldn't stop crying. I hugged her, but she didn't want me. Pushed me away.' His eyes filled with tears. 'Hurt.' He swallowed. 'Surprised.'

What did you expect, just turning up out of the blue, Paul wanted to ask, but knew it wasn't helpful, so remained silent. 'What else?'

Luke described how he'd sat on the concrete floor of the outbuilding, next to Sasha, and how they had remained silent for a few long moments after she rejected his hug.

–

'I don't know where to start,' Sasha said, staring at him, sitting upright on the concrete floor.

'At the beginning?' Luke asked impatiently. *I want to know everything and now.*

'I was sixteen.'

'Did you love him, my dad?'

Sasha shook her head, awkwardly stood, wiped her eyes with a tissue. 'He looked exactly like you.' She bit her bottom lip, blinked away more tears.

'What was he like?'

Sasha sniffed, shaking her head resolutely. 'I'm not ready, not for that. Not yet. Maybe never.'

'I see,' Luke said, and not really understanding at all. He wanted answers and he wanted them now.

'Do you?' Sasha asked.

After a long pause, as Luke thought nothing had prepared him for this moment, he said: 'No.'

'Why say it?' she asked.

Cos it's what I thought you'd want me to say. 'Sorry.'

'You've said that three times in the last five minutes.' She paused, looking at him evenly. 'Just like him in that regard.'

Him, as in my dad? 'Dad?'

'Biologically.' She looked at his hair, face, jaw, shoulders, hands, torso, legs. Nodded. 'You coming here has totally floored me. And it wasn't as if life was going swimmingly before you arrived.'

'I didn't mean to shock you.'

'Then you should have given me forewarning.'

There was silence as Luke realised what he'd done. How badly he'd judged this.

'He looked like you,' Sasha said, looking him up and down.

'Who?'

'Who do you think, the Italian prime minister?'

'Was he Italian?'

'The Italian prime minister, I should bloody well think so.'

'My dad?'

Sasha shook her head, turned away, sighed low and slowly.

Luke shuffled on his bottom a little closer, put his arm around her shoulder, and she didn't shrug him away as before. He stood, yet giving her space.

She turned to face him, looked up into his eyes, with a look that he thought was affection, mixed with anger maybe. 'Not now. This will take me time.'

Luke saw that rushing to meet her was both pointless and hurtful. He wanted to apologise again, but remembered what Sasha had said about that. He knew he'd either do this Sasha's way or no way, regardless of how impatient he was. He swallowed, composed his thoughts. 'I'm not going anywhere.'

'So we've got plenty of time to get to know each other?' Sasha asked with a twinkle in her eye.

He nodded. 'Afraid so. But I'll try not to make you faint again. No surprises.' He hoped he could keep that promise.

'What will you do with yourself? Haven't you got a job, a life to get back to?'

'I have, but it'll wait.' It was enough to tell her at this stage, he reckoned.

Sasha nodded.

'I was wondering if you could do with some help around this place.' He looked about, a black-and-white long-haired cat meowed loudly from a pen opposite. 'If it's all right with you,' he added carefully.

'I'd be a fool to refuse help. And I am many things, but I'm not a fool.'

He planned to hang around the cat sanctuary, gradually building a relationship with her, by helping, by showing her he wasn't normally this impatient, impetuous, unthinking oaf of a man. That normally, underneath his confidence and bravado, he was sensitive, quiet and reflective. He laughed.

'What?' she asked.

'Me, I'm the fool.'

'Why?'

'Thinking I'd turn up and you'd welcome me with open arms and we'd sit down with a cup of tea as if everything was okay.'

She frowned, stared at him intently. 'You didn't *really* think that, did you?'

He shook his head, but he had believed that. Thought he'd turn up and she'd tell him everything he didn't know about his birth father and Sasha's past. With shame, he said, 'Didn't think any of it through. Idiot.' All he'd considered *very* deeply was meeting her, because that had been the part he'd not been able to let go since his big birthday and a sort of early midlife crisis had settled on his shoulders and in his mind. Luke wanted to hug her, but knew it was too much, too soon.

'You're not an idiot,' Sasha said, 'that fire, get-up-and-go, can be very attractive in a man.' Her eyes shone at, Luke knew, a memory of his birth father.

He was dying to ask more, but knew he shouldn't. 'I'll go. Leave you be. Can I return tomorrow?'

'If I said no, would you take any notice?'

'No.'

She smiled. 'Right answer. But please, with the questions, can you... not? It will come out of me when I'm able to tell you.'

He held his hand out for her to shake.

She held it, pulled him in close, hugging him, patting his back, and shaking her head, a quiet sobbing shaking through his body.

I didn't expect this to happen. I've gone and made her cry. He left her, walking towards the house.

—

Luke finished describing what had happened, sighed. 'I made her cry.'

Paul shrugged. 'But you apologised to her, didn't you?'

Luke nodded. 'I didn't expect this to happen.'

'I know, right. Except *you* knew *you* were coming here.' Paul felt he owed Sasha that. He'd never seen her cry, so she'd been knocked for six.

Luke shrugged. 'You know her better than me.'

'Correct.'

'Feels stupid saying that. When she's my mum.'

'She's the woman who gave birth to you. Presumably, you have a woman who raised you into the man I see before me.' Paul felt very adult all of a sudden. *The man I see before me* – where had that come from?

'True. She was mostly supportive. Dad didn't want me to come. Said the past should be left there.'

'But you told him otherwise?' Paul asked.

'I couldn't leave it unanswered. Not once I wanted to find out. I needed to know.'

'Know what?'

'Why. Who I came from.'

Paul nodded. *Aha, that.* 'What if you leave with those questions still unanswered?'

'You don't think Sasha's going to speak to me? Even if I hang about this place, helping her, you all, the cats?'

Paul shook his head. 'She may not have a reason to open up to you. Or it may be too painful for her to relive it by telling you.'

'Right. She hasn't said I can't help around here, anyway, which is a miracle in itself. My plan is to be here for some time.'

Paul nodded. 'However long it takes for Sasha to come to the place where she can tell you what *you* need to know?'

'Right,' Luke said.

'Yep. Well,' Paul said, 'go gentle on her, will you?' It was a lot to juggle but Paul felt, with help and time, Luke should be able to manage it.

There was a long silence as Luke narrowed his eyes in obvious thought. 'Are you always this perceptive?'

Paul shrugged. 'I wasn't last night.' He wasn't sure where he was going with this, but he was enjoying their conversation, felt comfortable and wanted to share.

'Leading question much?'

'Also, even if you meet your birth mum, you won't necessarily fully *know* who you came from unless you meet your birth dad.' Paul wasn't sure why he felt the need to go straight into a deep and meaningful conversation with Luke, but he had. Perhaps it was something to do with how Luke seemed to command the room as if he were performing in front of an audience. Yes, that.

'Right. Worth a try though?'

Paul raised his eyebrows.

'Wouldn't *you* want to know? Oh, sorry, you said you weren't perceptive. I feel like there's a story there.'

Paul felt self-conscious telling his disastrous date story to this near-stranger. He wished he'd kept his mouth shut and carried on talking about Sasha. 'You don't want to hear it.'

'Oh, I do.' He moistened his lips briefly with his tongue.

I wonder if he's so inclined, whether he'd like to kiss me. 'I fear whatever I say won't live up to the hype.'

'Try me.' Luke raised his eyebrows, folded his arms.

Oh, goodness, if only I could. Flirting, much? Paul bit his bottom lip with uncertainty. 'I went on a date, last night. Not really a date, it was more a pre-meeting with a certain happy ending in mind.' Paul paused, checking if Luke followed him. 'If you follow?'

Luke nodded. 'Got it.'

'I like to meet for a drink before… you know… get to know them a bit first. I can't go straight to the business at the end of the night, without a conversation first.'

'Very gentlemanly of you.' Luke smirked.

Paul blushed very red and very much all over his face. *Why am I telling this very personal story to basically a complete stranger? Do I enjoy watching him listen to it, imagining it was him I'd met and wanted to sleep with at the end of the evening?* 'What are your plans while you're here?'

'As I said, get to know Sasha.' Luke said it very matter-of-factly. 'Slowly.'

'Where are you staying?'

'Hotel. You're not offering me a place to stay, are you?' A flash of his cheeky grin, strong mouth and jawline and a twinkle of his sky-blue eyes, very attractive.

Paul shook his head emphatically. 'Don't be so ridiculous. I've only just met you.' Although he reckoned if they were in a bar, with glass in hand, Luke would have persuaded him to move in by the end of the evening. Probably.

'And yet you were telling me you met someone as a precursor to...'

More comfortable to return to that topic, Paul said, 'Well, we didn't get that far. I went to the gents' toilet and left the bar.'

'Without saying bye?'

'Out the window.'

'Why?'

'He was nothing like his picture. A good fifteen years older. He creeped me out. Stared at me like a hungry cat looks at a mouse. And, he had the worst body odour I've ever encountered. It made the smell of cat piss seem like nice aftershave.'

'He sounds like a real catch.' Luke laughed.

'Hence my escape artist act.' Paul chuckled, letting himself settle into the easiness of their conversation.

'How long have you been single?'

'Few months. Loving it. The independence. I'm a digital nomad. Been travelling around Europe and working.'

Luke smiled. 'Where have you been? What do you do?'

Paul hated talking about his job, so said, 'Data, marketing, digital stuff really. Boring, but it pays the bills.' He shrugged.

'I wish I could do that. But I'm sort of with this group.'

'A band?' Paul liked the sound of that.

'A dance group – we do shows around the country. Sometimes to Europe. We won that TV talent competition a few years ago.'

Paul thought for a moment, trying to remember the talent show and its winner. 'There's ten of you, and it's performance dance art, or something, you were on the Royal Variety Performance last year?'

Luke nodded. 'Twelve of us, but yeah, all that.' His voice was deep and powerful.

Paul wasn't imagining it washing over him like a strong river. Absolutely and definitely not imagining that. *Luke's name in the messages, aha, that makes sense.* 'Legs Acrossed?'

'Legs Crossed.'

Paul was impressed, he'd heard about them performing at the Royal Variety Performance, entertaining the royal family. They'd turned up on breakfast TV a few times too, being interviewed about their journey and tour plans but Paul hadn't paid much attention to the group's individual members. Swallowing, taking in how kind of famous this made Luke, Paul said, 'Sasha said I should get a hobby.'

'You should. She's right. Totally correct. All work and no play makes Jack a dull boy.'

'So they say.' Paul smiled. *How are we talking about this?* 'What would you do?'

'Coming here was meant to be one hobby. But now I'm doing more of what I do at work. On the computer and internet, I mean. I wanted to come here and spend time with the cats. I miss mine.'

'Did yours pass away?' Luke asked carefully.

'Rick, he was called. Don't know if they've kept that name. I had him adopted when we set off for our digital nomad travels.'

'We?'

'Ex.'

There was a slightly awkward silence.

'What sort of hobby?' Luke asked.

'Dancing. But nothing like you do.' A bit of tap and ballet here and there. Practising with no show at the end, but he'd enjoyed it.

'I love dancing in a club, you do too, right?'

'Yeah,' Paul said. 'Same. And I used to do classes. Tap and stuff.' He wasn't sure why he didn't admit to doing ballet, but he just kept it to himself. The comments from George, about doing ballet, still stung. *Yeah, that's why I'm keeping that to myself.*

'Love that for you.'

Paul frowned, thinking that sounded a bit sarcastic. Or was it meant to be genuine? 'I've not done it in ages. Since the travelling.' *Since George, the ex, actually, but anyway.*

'We should find a class and go tapping together.' Luke smiled.

Definitely not sarcastic. Paul's stomach did that little flippy-flip thing it always did when he fancied someone. Oh dear. *Even if he's into men, which he won't be, he's not going to find me attractive. Definitely not.* He swallowed the knot of anxiety in his throat. 'Yeah.' He nodded.

Chapter 13

Chelmsford, Essex

During her lunch break, Anna sat in the bank, waiting to meet the manager. She'd tried online for loans, but they didn't lend 50,000 pounds. She drummed her hands on the desk.

She'd had an absolute shit of a day. The sort of day she wished could be flushed down the lavatory and forgotten. She'd woken worried about the appointment with the bank manager. Then knew she was going to be late for work, rushing about the house frantically, forgetting things, returning and omitting other items, finally arriving at work near to tears, then spending the morning frantic about the meeting at the bank.

And now she was there, and it was, as predicted, as awful as she'd imagined. It hadn't even started and her hands were shaking. She sat on them in an attempt to steady her nerves.

A man in a grey suit joined her in the room, closed the door and sat at the desk. 'Can you explain why you need this loan, please?'

She swallowed the anxiety, having rehearsed this answer all morning, on her journey to work. 'My parents were in a care home and it's to pay the fees.'

'Isn't that linked to the sale of their house?' He frowned.

'I don't want to sell it.'

'Are you going to live there?'

She shook her head, the room felt warm, she pulled at her hair. 'I wasn't planning to. I have my own place. Should I move into their home?' It was very large and empty and so full of memories that she couldn't imagine living there alone. Sadness crept up her spine at that thought.

'You have a mortgage with us. Would you like to convert it to a buy-to-let?'

'Why would I do that?'

'To rent it out, while you move into your late parents' house.' He said it as if it were the most obvious thing in the world.

'I like my place. I don't think I want others living there.' Her place, her things, her home. *No.*

'Are you going to let your parents' home?'

'I could do, I suppose.' Why was he making this so complicated? She just wanted to borrow money to pay off the care home and get on with her life.

'Does your parents' home have a mortgage?'

Anna shook her head. They'd paid it off years ago.

'This loan you're asking for would be unsecured. So, I need to understand what it's for and, because it's unsecured, the interest rate is higher, since it's higher risk for us.'

'Insecured? I'm sure I'll pay it back,' Anna said.

'*Un*secured, means it's not against something. A mortgage has the property secured against it. If you were to default on the loan, the bank repossesses the house. Similar with a car loan. But from what you said in your initial contact, this loan won't be secured against anything.'

'I'll pay it back. I swear. I can.'

'Unless we secured it against your late parents' house?'

Anna didn't like the sound of that, too risky. She shook her head. 'I've got a job.'

He looked at the screen. 'With The Grove Practice?'

'I've been there for twenty years.' It had been something to tide her over after finishing college and she'd never got round to finding another job. They were good to her there, after all.

He interlaced his fingers, resting his hands on the desk. 'I don't think you understand. If we lend you that sum of money, over five years, the interest will be significant and the monthly payments will be considerable. So I'm just trying to ascertain how you will meet those payments, when, I can see from you salary in your current account, your income is...' He chewed his cheek. 'Modest.'

'What am I going to do about the care home fees?' This had been her last hope. She'd spent most of the weekend online trying to find someone who'd lend her this much. 'None of the reputable banks will lend me this. Unless I go to those online lenders and their interest rates are astronomical. I could do that, couldn't I? Or I could get a few more credit cards and put it on them?'

'I strongly advise you against that. Could you let one of your properties, and use the income to repay the home?'

She shook her head. If she were to let one property out, perhaps her parents' home would make more sense, since it was large, and could house quite a few people, a whole family perhaps, since she wasn't sure if she could live there alone. Then she remembered. 'They needed it *all* within six months.' That had been when her parents had died, which was a few months ago.

'I wouldn't be doing my job if I lent you this money. It's a very risky prospect for us, and an unaffordable amount for you. All that sort of thing went out after the two thousand and eight banking crash. We have to do due diligence before a loan can be approved.' He sat back in his chair. 'Sorry.'

The colour drained from Anna's face as she felt cold dread charging through her veins. 'Is there anyone else I can speak to?'

'You can. But I'm afraid they'll tell you the same.' He sat back, obviously signalling the meeting was over, they'd reached the end of the line option-wise. 'Sorry.' He stood and checked the time on the wall clock.

Anna took the hint, stood, gathered her things, tried to gather her thoughts, then left. She walked around Chelmsford city centre for the rest of her lunch hour, in a daze, unable to process what she'd just been told.

Maybe she should move into her parents' home, but what would she do with all their stuff? The thought of sorting through it all on her own had her in a cold sweat, so the thought of leaving it empty was easier. Even if it made no financial sense. She knew she was fortunate to have this so-called problem. But it didn't make it easier to decide what to do, did it? The bank manager didn't seem to appreciate keeping their home; to Anna it made emotional sense.

Or she could sell her place. But her parents had given her the deposit for it so it felt like a part of them and she didn't want to lose that.

She knew she had to sell or let something to get herself out of this mess, but was paralysed by all the options. She wondered which choice her parents would most want her to make. Keep their home, or her own smaller place?

Perhaps I'll sell them both? Up sticks and move far away, but then again that would involve an element of sorting through her and her parents' belongings.

No.

Her circular thoughts continued.

It was too much to think about now, so she decided not to.

She bought some lipstick to cheer herself up, and ate a chocolate bar sitting on a bench overlooking a small park.

When she returned to work, a short drive away, in the small village of Howe Green, the receptionist asked, 'Did you get it sorted, Anna?'

She shook her head, walking past in silence. Very much not sorted. Wished she hadn't told anyone she needed to sort something out today.

Sitting at her desk, she put the headset on and returned to the audio-typing she'd been doing. It was a letter referring a patient to a specialist to have a lump inspected in case it was cancerous. The next letter was a man with back pain who couldn't work and needed an X-ray and orthopaedic referral.

Rebecca Kempshott, the GP who'd started The Grove Practice, and given Anna the job, appeared at Anna's elbow. She was talking, but Anna couldn't hear.

Removing the headset, Anna said, 'Anything wrong?' She couldn't keep the brittleness and anxiety from her tone.

'Just checking you got it sorted.'

Anna bit her bottom lip so hard it felt as if it would bleed. 'Yes, thanks. All done. I'm just in the middle of something, as it goes. I've got a lot to get through.' She turned back to the screen and blinked quickly as her throat tightened. *I will not cry. I will not cry. I will not cry.*

Rebecca put a hand on Anna's shoulder. 'Are you sure? Let's have a little biscuit and a cup of tea and we can talk.'

Anna's mouth remained firmly shut. She couldn't tell the truth because they'd been so good to her, giving her time off towards the end of her parents' lives. 'I'm fine,' she said. She wanted them to see her as organised, efficient, as a senior secretary should be viewed. But her home, her life, were far from that and Anna was ashamed of the mess she'd got herself in and didn't want to ask for help from people who might think she wasn't coping and needed more time off work. Then it would be a quiet conversation with the practice manager about things not working out and then she'd be gone, let loose from The Grove Practice, which had been a consistent and comforting feature in her life, since the divorce, losing her best friend. No, she mustn't tell them the truth. 'I don't want to talk to anyone about it. They're dead and that's it.'

'I know, you said. Come on.' Rebecca nodded and motioned for Anna to stand. 'Just a cup of tea and a biscuit, nothing more.'

Conscious of others watching her, Anna rose, blinked away a tear. 'It's hay fever. Stupid stuff. I've got some tablets in here.' She grabbed her handbag from under the desk, upended it onto the floor, spreading its contents over the carpet. The new lipstick, her purse, tissues, a book she'd been meaning to read for weeks but had never got round to it, her diary, all splayed out.

Rebecca joined her on the floor, kneeling, putting her belongings back into her bag.

Sniffing, she wiped her nose, and Anna met Rebecca's eyes, knowing when she was beaten. 'A biscuit sounds nice, yeah.' A feeling of being defeated at everything flooded through her. *I've tried my best and still haven't succeeded. Ugh.*

Shortly after, they were sitting in Rebecca's disinfectant-scented consultation room, white walls and a blue curtain drawn back around a bed. They both had a cup of tea and biscuits.

'Maybe I should talk to someone about it.' The grief. She'd sort of kept on keeping on while her parents were alive. Because she had no choice. But when they'd gone – died – she'd sort of come unravelled a bit. At the edges. More sleeping tablets, sleepless nights, forgetting appointments, worrying about things more than usual.

'I think it would help,' Rebecca said, resting her hands in front of the computer keyboard on her desk. 'Grief, it's a funny old thing.' She went on, but Anna wasn't listening.

The grief, Anna was happy to talk to someone about that, if it made Rebecca happy, but she wasn't going to discuss the money issue. Not after how stupid the bank manager had made her feel. Like she was some sort of idiot. Surely other people had similar problems. Why was it so hard to keep both homes and pay off the nursing home? Didn't they realise it was the home she had been brought up in? And her place was special. All her own and from her parents' deposit money. They'd been very good to her, so she'd looked after them and now the least she could do was look after their home.

Rebecca had been talking and Anna hadn't heard; finally, Rebecca handed her a business card. 'It's all on there. Call them and say you've been referred as a patient from The Grove Practice. They'll look after you.'

Anna left. She'd been meaning to change her GP practice, so there wasn't a conflict of interest with her employer. But she'd not got round to it. She enjoyed the short drive into the countryside to Howe Green, and apparently the waiting lists were much shorter than the GPs in Chelmsford. And Rebecca and the other Grove Practice doctors, they were so kind and understanding, she didn't think she'd get that elsewhere. Best leave it as it is.

She went home to Moulsham, and tried to borrow money online, managed to secure 20,000 pounds. She'd tell the care home tomorrow she had almost half of it. The repayments weren't too bad, even if it was over ten years. *Who knows where I'll be then, I could have won the lottery!*

She took two sleeping tablets to quiet her mind as it buzzed from thought to idea and back again, not letting her sleep.

Finally, on the verge of nervous exhaustion, she fell into a fitful sleep at four o'clock in the morning.

Wickford, Essex

The next day, Anna finished work at the doctor's surgery at lunchtime, applied her new lipstick and was looking forward to spending time with the Fluffy Paws cats, away from computers and typing and doctors. As she drove away from the village, down country lanes, towards the roundabouts, dual carriageways and rows of houses of Wickford, Anna smiled in anticipation. *Today is going to be a good day*, she thought, briefly checking her reflection in the rear-view mirror.

Sasha greeted her. 'Nice lippy. New?'

Anna blushed. They always gave her such a lift coming here. 'Little treat for myself.'

Closer now, Sasha said, 'You look very tired. Are you okay, you look a bit... ill?'

'Nice to see you too.' Anna checked her reflection in a window. Large dark bags under both eyes. She looked old and knackered and no amount of new lipstick could cover that up. 'Sleepless night.'

'Right.'

'What happened to Luke?' Anna asked. 'He was very handsome. Very dashing. Tall. You're not tall. Was his father tall?'

'From what I remember, yes. Long time ago.' Sasha pursed her lips, looking at the ground.

'Sorry, didn't mean to pry. It must be very raw.'

Sasha nodded, looked away.

'Not having any of my own children, I can't begin to imagine what it must be like for you to have him turn up after all this time. Well, you passed out. As well you might. I think I'd have passed out too. If I had a son. Except I don't.' Anna knew she was getting this all very wrong. She wasn't sure if it was worrying about her own life, or a hangover from the grief, the sleepless night, or the tablets she'd taken that morning to help her through the day, making her feel as if she were wading through cotton wool, here, but not quite here, but she felt very out of tune with what Sasha was undoubtedly going through. She mentally shook herself, tried to put herself in Sasha's shoes. 'Where's he now?'

'He's staying in a hotel. Showing no sign of wanting to leave. Hanging around feels almost worse than if he'd turned up then disappeared. It's harder for me to ignore him if he hangs around being so bloody nice. Makes me look like—' She shook her head, closed her eyes in obvious thought.

'Give it long enough and it'll work out, I reckon.'

Sasha nodded, smiled tightly. 'He's getting on with Paul famously. Someone his own age, I suppose.'

'Course.' Anna nodded. She wasn't sure if Sasha meant the two men were getting on as friends, or as more. She'd held a small candle for Paul since he'd started. A younger man had been one of her fantasies and Paul seemed to tick most of those boxes. Obviously a moot point since he was gay, but she still found him very *visually* appealing. She wondered if he had any nice friends he could introduce her to. She didn't seem to be particularly lucky with men. Since her divorce, she'd never met anyone who came close to how she'd felt on her wedding day. But a nice young friend of Paul's, that could work... Those tablets really were doing the trick today, insulating her from the grief perhaps, making her think of things other than the loss. *Must ensure I don't run out of them.*

'Do you want to hear about our new arrivals and adoptions, or get on with the afternoon kitten cuddle-time socialising?'

'Have all the pens been cleaned?' Anna liked that. She knew where she was, doing that. Playing with the cats was fun, and the kittens were so cute, but they sometimes scratched her clothes and covered them in hair. Last time her yellow cardigan had been ruined and it had been a gift from a friend so Anna didn't want that to happen again.

'Just done. Don't you like the kittens?'

'They're very cute.'

'You look like you could do with playing and cuddling with some kittens. Take your mind off whatever happened yesterday.'

'I'm fine. Nothing happened. I'm okay, but I said I'd see someone about the grief. I mean, it's just in the past now, so I don't know why it's such a big deal. They think it'll help me, at work. So I said I'd do it.' She felt so magnanimous phrasing it like that.

Sasha smiled and nodded.

Does she believe me? I'm not sure I fully believe me…

'Or you could help with the fundraising.' Sasha raised her eyebrows.

That's what I need. 'What are the plans?'

'Mim's in charge, as usual. She'd be able to throw a garden party for the royal family and it would look effortless and totally up to scratch. I do envy her of that.'

Anna envied Mim of the large social circle she seemed to cultivate, which made Anna's work colleagues and her friends from here look very pathetic in comparison. She didn't voice that opinion, knowing no one would be interested in critiquing Saint Mim of South Hanningfield. More and more, Anna found herself having unkind thoughts about others. She didn't say them out loud, but they became intrusive to her thoughts, pointy and spiky and uncomfortable as they drifted through her mind. *Is this the grief, or the tablets, or the stress of it all*, she wondered.

'We raised nearly fifteen thousand in the last few weeks. If Paul carries on like this, we won't need to bother with fetes. Although I think Mim was a touch put out at having to shelve her plans. Perhaps I'll keep a watching brief on that.'

Without thinking, Anna said, 'Maybe *I* should organise a fete, for me, and ask Mim to help.'

'Why?'

'Nothing. It's just…' She shook her head. 'I'm a bit stuck for money, that's all. Not all of it, I got this loan for some. But I'm a little short.'

'The care home fees? I thought you were selling your parents' house.'

Anna's ears became very hot, her face felt flushed. 'I can't sell it. When will people understand? Where would I put all their belongings if I sold it? I can't simply get rid of their possessions. I'd be letting them down so dreadfully.' She shook her head, tutting loudly. Absolutely nobody seemed to understand why she was stuck.

'How much are you short?'

'Thirty.'

'How did you get the rest?'

Anna told her.

Sasha listened in silence. 'Have you got the money?'

'In my bank.'

'When do you start paying it back?'

'End of the month. It's very cheap. That's why I chose them.'

'Can you show me the paperwork?'

Anna brought it up on her phone, handed it to Sasha.

Sasha shook her head, mumbling *no* under her breath. 'Ten years? You're going to pay back sixty grand over ten years, to borrow twenty. Are you mad?'

Anna's pride at having sorted out the problem herself immediately evaporated. 'Don't be nasty.'

'It's them who are being nasty. Taking the *absolute* piss out of you. This sort of thing ought to be illegal. Can you get out of it? Pay it back early?'

Anna shrugged. She'd not looked into that because she knew she'd never be in a position to do so.

'What happens if you pay it all back now?'

Another shrug from Anna as she didn't know what else to do. 'I can't do that. I need to give it to the care home.'

'You bloody well will, if you accept this loan you're saddled with an enormous debt for ten years. And you want to do it again for the rest? I'm sorry, but I'm going to say it: you are absolutely crackers. There's simply got to be another way.'

Anna crouched forwards, closed her eyes; it was all too much, she'd promised herself she wouldn't, but felt it was unavoidable. She cried. At first quiet low sobs, then it built into more of an animal-in-pain sound as she realised her solution had been anything but.

Stupid Anna, does something stupid again. She was the girl at school, not doing very well, being told off, accepting the teacher's advice that she give up on her silly notions about becoming a nurse or a doctor, and settle for something much easier.

Sasha calmed her down, held her in a hug, patted her back, finally said, 'It's all fixable. There's no need to cry. I was going to say nobody died, but unfortunately they did. Sorry for that.'

Anna looked up through teary eyes, smiled briefly. It felt better because at least Sasha acknowledged Anna's grief, didn't tiptoe around it like some people. 'I thought I'd resolved the problem.'

'Ask for help. There's no shame in it.' Sasha held her tightly. 'Apparently.'

Anna let that sink in for a moment. 'How do you feel about Luke?' It was a broad question, without much apparent thought behind it, but Anna knew Sasha had a lot of things to process and she was being kind to Anna, helping her with her financial stupidity. She couldn't imagine how Sasha would feel.

Sasha huffed. 'I don't think Luke is leaving anytime soon. He has the sort of job where he can come and go when he pleases. Or so it seems. He's determined to get to know me. I'm unclear how I feel about that. In fact, I feel a little ambushed, to be honest. In a kind and caring way. He turned up and demanded a relationship with me. By being nice, which makes my ignoring him even worse.' Sasha tutted and shook her head. 'Enough about me.' She turned to Anna. 'What sort of state is your parents' place in now?'

Anna looked up through teary eyes, feeling dreadfully selfish for crying. With great determination she wiped her eyes furiously with the back of her hands. 'Full of their stuff.' Stuffed to the gills, actually. Every room was full of things her parents couldn't bear to part with, clothes they'd not worn in decades, old birthday and Christmas cards, unopened gift packs of toiletries, toys from Anna's childhood…

'And you can't bear to sell it?'

She shook her head. There was too much of it. Too many decisions to make about what to keep, what to discard, and what then to do with it. 'Not at the moment.' *Never. Ever.*

'An empty property is a risk for squatters and damp if you're not using the central heating.'

'Really?'

Sasha nodded. 'Big place like that, no lights on, it's going to stick out like a sore thumb next to the neighbouring houses.'

Damp and squatters didn't sound good. 'Goodness.' The idea came to her, suddenly, like lightning, through her cloudy, medicated mind; she couldn't believe why she hadn't thought of it before. How could she be so stupid, again? 'Luke could stay there. *I* could stay with him. It's better than a hotel. He can make himself more comfortable if he's staying with me. Living there alone in my parents' huge house would be sad, empty, but with someone else, a friend, I think I'd feel differently. I'll work out what to do with my place another time. I've given the care home some money, surely that will tide them over for a while. I can move *all* my stuff into Mum and Dad's place, maybe.' *Save having to sort through it all. Stuff it into the back bedrooms. Maybe. If it all fits.*

'That sounds a bit better than the loan. How would you feel about living with him? You barely know him.'

How well do you *really* know anyone? Maybe it was the medication, perhaps it was Anna herself. But she felt better with this part solution to her problem. Possibly Luke would have some young eligible bachelor friends. 'If *you* think he's all right, that's good enough for me.' With care, she asked, 'Do you think he's okay?'

'He's sensitive and caring. If you put aside that he ambushed me. Apart from that, I think his parents should be proud of him. He owes very little to me, but I don't think he appreciates that.'

That felt good enough for Anna. She nodded resolutely. 'I shall ask if he wants to rent one of the spare rooms in my parents' place and I will move in.' *I'll grab the nettle and shake it very hard indeed.*

'I'm sure he'll be delighted.'

'Sorry,' Anna said, worry returning suddenly.

'What for?' Sasha asked.

'Crying. I didn't mean to.' She thought it terribly common to be so emotionally incontinent. Stiff upper lip was much better. Tablets helped, of course. Helped with brave decisions such as this. Wonderful.

'If you can't cry when you're among friends, when can you?' Sasha asked, squeezing Anna's shoulder.

Anna remained unconvinced. Shaking her head as he admonished herself, she said, 'Twice in one day?'

'I knew you'd had a right day of it as soon as you arrived. Come on, I know exactly what you need.' Sasha led the way to the building where the older kittens were kept, once weaned, with more space than when they were just born, giving them room to play and have human cuddles and socialising time. 'Get yourself in there and play with them. Forget everything else. I'll come in and get you when it's home time.'

'Do you have a jacket I can borrow?'

Sasha removed hers, handed it over. 'Fill your boots.'

Anna perched on a chair, it was cleaner than the floor, and the kittens were soon climbing over her, sitting on her lap, making their way up her legs. It was important to socialise them with humans, otherwise they would be very hard to rehome. For those moments, Anna only thought about the kittens, their large blue and green eyes, white whiskers, and their incessant appetite for adventure, jumping and playing with each other. She held a small white kitten with black splodges. It had been hiding and had taken a while to play with the feathers attached to string.

She stroked the soft fur on its head and it purred. For the first time since waking that morning – with the fear of being late for work, running out of petrol, losing her credit card and not being able to pick the right shoes to wear for work, and the awkward uncomfortable conversation with Rebecca and crying, and spilling her handbag's contents on the floor, then now at the sanctuary, being rude to Sasha, not understanding what she was going through, knowing she herself was doing it all wrong, but not quite being able to know how to fix it – a strange calm descended upon her. Anna's shoulders relaxed and she smiled, maybe tonight she wouldn't need a tablet to fall asleep.

Maybe.

Chapter 14

Mim sat in her large, airy dining room painting a glass horse. It was two inches tall, standing on its back legs, with a man atop. She'd bought it in a car boot sale, always on the lookout for glass ornaments to decorate. It was something of an obsession for her. David never criticised, but after putting up another two shelves, taking the total to well over three or four dozen, she'd immediately filled them with the latest ornaments and painted glasses. She wondered where it would all end.

Anyway.

Turning it carefully in her left hand, as light streamed through the window, she inspected her progress: she'd filled in its saddle with blue paint, the hooves were black and she was debating whether to put colourful stripes on its body. *Does it have to be a real horse, or can it be some sort of magic one? Could I paint wings onto it? Or have it blue or pink maybe?*

David was away with his golfing friends, although the game wouldn't take the whole day, there was a lunch and then a meeting to plan a golf trip abroad. David had said, 'You can come if you want.'

Mim sensed he meant he'd prefer her *not* to join him. They had, after all, spent the last weeks tidying up and

116

living on leftovers from their most recent soirees and David often became a bit antsy, going for long walks alone around the three Hanningfield villages, sometimes doing a circular route around the edge of the reservoir.

So she'd said, 'I have plenty to keep me occupied,' and bid him a fond farewell that morning.

The yawning morning had stretched in front of her as she felt her 'off' personality encroaching. Her shoulders slumped, her outlook on life, the purpose, the point, the reason for doing anything from dressing to eating, all slowly slipped away.

She didn't want to be around others when she felt this way. And yet she felt this way when she was alone. The irony of that hadn't escaped Mim's attention.

The doorbell rang.

Who can that be? Snapped back to reality from her world of blue or pink horses with painted wings, she carefully set the glass horse down, then walked to the door.

Peering through the patterned glass window to the side of the door, she wasn't able to see who it was. *That*, she reflected briefly, *is surely the point of the glass.* Opening the door, she peered through the gap. 'Hello.'

It was Henry, one of their two nephews. 'We were passing. Thought we'd drop in on the off-chance.' He put a hand through blonde hair.

A woman Mim presumed to be his smart wife, Fiona, stood behind their child: a girl, blonde with blue eyes and already the makings of film-star good looks.

Fiona tucked her short black hair back, looked at her husband. 'I said we should ring first.' She shook her head. 'I'm sorry. You're obviously in the middle of something. If we could just use the loo, Tilly's bursting, and so am I, and then we'll be gone.' Fiona mouthed 'sorry' to Mim.

In the middle of something – yes, deep into being 'off' and descending into one of her low moods – *hardly something worth clinging to*. Mim stood to one side. 'Come in.'

They entered.

Mim showed them the downstairs loo.

Fiona entered with the little girl. They wore T-shirts and dark jeans.

Henry hugged Mim. 'We'll go. Sorry. We were passing. Travelling back from Norfolk. Stayed in a yurt for the week.' He grimaced. 'Sounds more fun than it actually is.' He wore dark pink shorts, a white shirt, opened a few buttons, blue deck shoes. He could, Mim reflected, skipper a boat if he had a blue cap.

The loo door opened. Fiona smiled. 'I thought we weren't dwelling on that. I'm Fiona by the way. Pleased to meet you.'

Mim shook her hand, thinking she was very smart and clearly kept Henry on his toes.

Henry said, 'Sorry. Forgot you'd not met.' He introduced them to each other. Folded his arms. 'Fiona's touchy because it was her idea. The yurt. I just went along for the ride.'

Fiona folded her arms, looked at Henry. 'He's along for the ride with the daughter he's jointly responsible for with me. Men, eh?' She rolled her eyes. 'Is David around?'

'Golfing thing,' Mim said.

The little girl said, 'Can I have a drink, Mummy?'

Fiona knelt. 'What do we say?'

'Please.'

Fiona looked to Mim. 'Is it okay? Water. I'm trying to wean her off sugary drinks. Nightmare. Honestly.'

Mim led them to the kitchen. 'Do you want a coffee, tea?'

Henry put his hands in his pockets. 'We'll go. It's very rude of us to arrive unannounced like this.'

Mim put the kettle on. 'During my repping days we always had an open house. Come one, come all. The new reps would descend on our place. It was like having dozens of children in their twenties.' It had been marvellous, twenty years ago, in her fifties, it felt as if she were surrounded by family. Until they moved on, and she never saw them again.

A shard of sadness pierced her heart. Grabbing the teabags from the tin, she then plopped them in the teapot.

'When's Uncle David due back?' Henry asked, sitting on a stool at the island in the middle of the kitchen, rolling up his shirtsleeves.

'Don't sit. We're going,' Fiona said.

'You most certainly are not! How long were you in Norfolk?' Mim asked, holding a cafetière aloft. 'Coffee or tea?'

'Coffee, please,' Fiona said, 'if you don't mind us staying. The yurt didn't have a machine, so I'm in withdrawal. Ten days.'

'Felt like a month,' Henry said with a grin.

'It can't have been that bad.' Mim looked at the little girl playing on a device, sitting on the floor. 'Family time.'

'You can have too much of a good thing.' Henry looked to his daughter, then said, in a whisper, 'Canvas walls means no privacy. For anyone.' He shot his wife a look.

She stood behind him, resting her hands on his shoulders, kissing his neck. 'Next time it's back to a holiday cottage.'

Henry nodded. 'Agreed.'

Mim placed a tray of tea and coffee in the middle of the island, with biscuits. 'Would you return to Norfolk?

I've never been. Pathetic, isn't it? Anywhere in Spain and I can probably tell you a story about my repping days. But the UK, not so much.'

'You must come,' Fiona said, sipping her coffee. 'Actual lifesaver. Thanks so much.'

'And Uncle David. With brick walls and a separate part for you two away from Tilly and us two, I'm sure you'd enjoy it.'

Mim was sure she'd have enjoyed sharing a tent with them, but didn't say so. 'How have you been?'

Henry talked about his job doing something in computers and getting a promotion, which evidently meant lots more work, but also, 'Lots more money,' Fiona said with a grin, stroking his forearm.

They're such a sweet couple. Reminds me of David and me at that age. Except without the child.

Fiona said, 'What's new with you? Settling into Essex?'

She had to do so, for David's reasons of being near family, so it made sense. But living here, away from the coast and sun of Spain's Costa Brava, she wouldn't have chosen herself. It was a reasonable compromise, but wasn't so much of life? 'How far are you from here?'

'Under an hour. Why haven't you been?' Henry asked with a frown.

'I didn't want to impose. I know you've all got very busy lives. You don't want two old fuddy-duddies hanging around. Besides, you've got Hal and Queenie on grandparent duties.'

'If we can catch them.' Fiona ate another biscuit, then folded her arms.

'What do you mean?' Mim asked.

'They're always on bloody holiday. I always thought her name was very apt, but now they're retired, Queenie is behaving like an actual queen.' Fiona rolled her eyes. 'A four-week cruise, then a river boat trip, then a city-hopping holiday around the Nordic countries, then a car holiday, something to do with touring all the ancient counties, or castles, or something.' Fiona put the mug on the tray.

'Have more. Plenty of it,' Mim said.

'Bladder.' She rubbed her stomach. 'Speaking of.' She left for the loo in the hallway.

Henry said, 'Sorry about this. Descending on you en masse.'

'It's lovely.' She put her hand on his forearm, wishing very hard he were her actual son. 'Do it as much as you like. I'm just...' *Sitting around painting my glass sculptures. For no good reason.*

'How are you keeping yourself busy now you're retired?'

'Volunteering.'

'Where?'

'Cat sanctuary.'

'You don't like cats, do you?' he asked in confusion. 'You didn't have them in Spain, did you?'

'No. I don't dislike them. I've just never had the life-style where having one made sense.'

'Now, are you tempted?'

'I'd worry about them breaking things. Jumping up on the sideboard and smashing stuff.'

Fiona appeared in the kitchen. 'She hasn't, has she?' Looking at her daughter she said, 'What has Tilly done? I didn't hear anything.'

Mim explained.

'Dad mentioned something about a gift you'd made for me and William.' Henry leaned his bare forearms on the work surface.

'Don't fish. It's very rude,' Fiona said with narrowed eyes at him.

It was the two statues she'd painted of him and his brother. Mim blushed. She stood. 'Presumably, you've not eaten on your journey?'

'Avoided services because it's all fast food. Said we'd take a picnic but...' Henry began.

'It was left to me,' Fiona continued, 'so it didn't happen. Unless you count a packet of Monster Munch I found in the back of the car we all shared.'

Mim opened the fridge, staring inside. 'I have half a side of salmon, a lasagne or a casserole.'

'We can't,' Fiona said.

'Can't what?' Mim asked, turning to look at her with a smile.

'Turn up, eat all your food and take over your afternoon of solitude. It's entirely unreasonable of us.' She nodded at Henry. 'Come on, let's leave Mim to her afternoon.'

Mim turned, resting her hands on the kitchen island, gripping the cold marble. 'Stay. Please.' She tried to keep the desperation out of her voice, but mostly failed. She was, as expected after the last event, feeling rather flat.

Henry looked to his wife, then to Mim. 'Sure?'

'Absolutely. It'll end up in the freezer otherwise.' She placed the three dishes on the work surface, opened the lids and unwrapped them.

'Why?' Fiona pointed to the large dishes.

'Auntie Miriam is an entertainer, par excellence,' Henry said. 'Mum and Dad used to recount stories of dinner parties in the Seventies, when you were in your twenties. Matchmaking, wife-swapping I shouldn't wonder. Parties where the whole street was invited. What's it called when everyone brings a dish?'

'No one calls me Auntie Miriam, it's Aunt Mim, or Mim is better. The "auntie" makes me feel about a hundred and three.'

Henry nodded and smiled.

'Potluck,' Mim said. 'Although, it can be somewhat risky. Once, when I was younger than you two, I organised one and we ended up with four bowls of potato salad, three rice puddings and two bottles of wine.'

'Honestly, there's nothing I don't love about the sound of that dinner.' Henry rubbed his stomach in emphasis.

Fiona called Tilly.

She arrived, staring at the food. 'I'm hungry,' Tilly said.

'That's the point of these.' Henry gestured to the dishes.

They decided upon lasagne with a salad that Mim whisked up in moments. She'd had three evening gatherings in the past week or so, hence all the leftovers. She told them.

'You don't fancy moving into ours, do you?' Fiona asked. 'Continue cooking and maybe a bit of casual childcare?' She laughed.

Sometimes it was all Mim longed for, when alone with her thoughts, her regrets, the wonderings about what might have been had she and David had a family. 'I could bring something round if you wanted. Nothing special.' She'd get out the cookbooks, really make an effort. Find out what the family liked, make it healthy and modern and maybe ask Tilly if she wanted to help make a dessert of some description.

'I always regretted not visiting you and Uncle David in Spain more often.' Henry laid the table, telling his daughter to sit quietly.

Mim had always wondered why. Perhaps she was too unapproachable. Mysterious. 'Eat.' She put the hot lasagne in the middle of the table, with a serving spoon. 'Help yourselves.'

'Why didn't you? In fact, why didn't we go to Spain before this one?' Fiona nodded at her daughter.

Henry shrugged, a forkful of lasagne in his mouth, chewing in thought. 'We went as teenagers with Mum and Dad, and then when we were old enough, we… didn't.' He raised his eyebrows. 'Teenagers, I suppose. I think I went one summer between university years. Mum and Dad talked about your life like it was so perfect: living in the sun, working with people on holiday. Drinking wine and watching the sun set over the sea as it browned your skin. Whereas we were stuck in Basildon.'

Mim had heard of this place. David had tried to convince her to visit, but she'd resisted. 'So you didn't think we'd want you staying?'

'William and I were quite a handful as teenagers.'

'You're not much different now. Him especially.' Fiona smirked.

'What is he like these days? I've only seen photos recently.' Mim drank some wine, relaxing into the moment, the impromptu gathering she found herself hosting.

'Married, with a new baby. Still exactly the opposite to me,' Henry said. 'Enough about us. I never thought you'd retire. Sounded like the perfect job, working in Spain. And now you're working at a cat sanctuary. What's that like?'

'It's not like working. If I don't want to go, I don't. They're not paying me, there's very little they can actually *make* me do.'

'What do you do?'

'Look after the cats. Talk to people about the cat they'd like to adopt, work out the best one we have for them. Take in cats from all sorts of situations, some I won't describe to avoid upsetting small ears, it's very hard. But worth it.'

'You don't even like cats, do you?' Fiona asked.

'As I said to Henry, I've never had one. But they're rather interesting creatures, I think. They have a degree of self-respect that dogs, from what I've seen, seem to lack.'

'I want a cat,' Fiona said, handing her daughter a tablet computer. 'He wants a dog. But I know who'll end up walking it every day.'

Something for them to work out as a family.

Mim left silence for a moment, watching Tilly swipe and play with the shiny screen. 'I was organising a fete for them. They're in a bit of financial hot water. I had said I'd put my event-planning skills to good use. But, alas I've been somewhat usurped by Paul with his social media fundraising skills. If I weren't such a good person and didn't love him to bits, I'd be as jealous as all hell.' She gritted her teeth, knowing it was for the best but still unable to completely accept not being in charge of planning a fete.

'Better than sticking a thermometer up a cat's bum,' Henry said with a laugh.

Mim frowned. 'I don't know what cat care you've witnessed, but I can assure you, I do not put anything up any cats' bottoms. Certain volunteers are trained veterinary nurses, so they do all the medical interventions. We can give them medication, it's all written down. Each cat has their own folder: where they came from, why they were admitted, how they like to be looked after. If they're violent or shy, whatever. It's all very organised. Anna is a godsend. Sasha would be lost without her. Us all really.'

'Will you get one?' Henry asked.

'A cat? Possibly. Probably. Don't know. They want fosterers when the sanctuary is full. A nice way to dip my toe and see if it's for me. Can give the cat back afterwards, that is rather the point of fostering, apparently.' She and David had considered fostering children when it became apparent they weren't able to have their own. But David hadn't pushed it, and Mim had been too sad at another month when her period arrived and so they'd emigrated to Spain, leaving behind the little house where she hadn't managed to get pregnant over so many years. A fresh start.

The memory normally caused a sharp jab of pain, but now Mim found it had passed, she focused on the family visit.

Later, she said goodbye to them, hugging the little girl, kneeling to look her in the eye: 'Do you like ice cream?'

Tilly nodded.

'Would you like to make it?'

'Why?'

'Because,' she replied winking at Henry and Fiona, 'you can make any flavour you want.'

'Coconut and mint?' Tilly asked.

'Absolutely.'

They hugged her goodbye, Henry said thanks and she must visit them. Fiona thanked her for the food and added how well she got on with Tilly, saying she was a natural great-auntie. Mim smiled at that, watching them drive off in their large, tall four-door car, not quite an estate, not quite an off-roader.

Mim cleaned the kitchen, for once enjoying the silence rather than dreading it. A little. After finishing the washing-up, stacking the dishwasher and wiping the surfaces, Mim sat in silence at the island in the middle of the kitchen, sipping a glass of sparkling water. *Much healthier than caffeine.*

The door clicked with a key. David entered, shouting from the hallway: 'I'm home!'

Mim greeted him, smiling. 'Thanks.' She hugged him, pulling him tightly towards her, inhaling his citrus and woody scent and being thankful for who he was and what he'd done. What they'd done together, over the years.

'What for? I'll go away more often if this is the greeting I get.'

'Henry and Fiona and their little girl visited.'

'Why didn't you tell me? I should have liked to see them. It's been far too long. Before their baby was born. We met Fiona, didn't we?'

Mim shook her head. 'Tilly isn't a baby now. Fiona, I've seen her picture on the computer. But we've never met her. Not that it felt awkward. She's very convivial. Ebullient. Felt like she knew me of old. She was very good at that.' There was silence. 'Busy working. In Spain. These things happen. Can't see everyone, can you? Important thing is that we're here now and... well...'

'So you're glad we moved here?'

Mim pursed her lips, thinking for a moment. She wouldn't go quite as far as saying she was *glad* they'd left the warm, sun-drenched Spanish Costa Brava, for grey and drizzly Essex. But she could at least understand *why*. And the house and village were delightful. 'There was mention of a place called Basildon. I said I had heard of it, but never experienced it first-hand.'

'I said we'd find our groove once we settled here.'

'You did.' She pulled him closer, kissed his lips. 'I didn't believe you, but you were right. As you sometimes are. I do still miss our life in Spain. Don't you?'

'Every day. But we were the oldest employees by a long margin. Who wants to work until they die?'

Mim had never thought of the work as work, it was so intertwined with fun, going to bars, excursions, sampling hotels, sitting by the pool during the day once the tourists were settled in, that she didn't have much need for fun. She preferred work to fun, her whole life. She thought for a moment. 'I've said we'll babysit next time they want to go out without Tilly.'

'Babysit, how old is she?'

Mim indicated their daughter's height. 'At school. Quiet, staring at screens. Didn't speak much, but I'll soon fix that. I want to cook with her. Get covered in flour, sugar and eggs and forget all the screen time.'

'Sounds wonderful.' He led her into the kitchen, where he made them both a drink.

Maybe, Mim thought, *moving back to England, to Essex, wasn't so bad.*

Chapter 15

Wickford, Essex

Luke was spending another night in a cheap hotel in the outskirts of Wickford, sandwiched between a retail park, a petrol station and a recycling centre. He'd stayed in nicer places. But it was near to Fluffy Paws and he'd resigned himself to not leaving until Sasha would open up to him, even if just a little bit. Room service, some scrolling on the socials on his phone, a shower, and then only him and those four walls. After the big corporate performance, his group were developing new dances for their UK tour next year, and he'd told them he needed time away for personal reasons. The troupe would develop a part for him if he returned in time.

Anna had recently offered him a spare room in her parents' house and it was another decision to make and he didn't feel he knew her enough to say yes or no, so he'd thanked her and said he'd think about it.

'She's not rude, Sasha, I mean,' he said to his mum on the phone. 'She's just not kind.' Or so she seemed to him. He was determined not to be rude to Sasha, not to push, but just to be there, to exist in her world, waiting for her to come to a place, emotionally, where she could talk to him about her past. Unless, of course, she actually threw him out of the cat sanctuary, his plan was to turn up every morning, hang out where Sasha was getting on with her life. Make her accept him, get to know him, by a combination of stealth, politeness and helpfulness.

'What did Dad say, leave the past in the past,' his mum said.

'She said she wanted to talk, but not yet.' Luke had hung on to that for the last few weeks in the hotel.

'Well, you did turn up.'

'I tried to contact her beforehand.' Luke sighed. How many times did he have to explain this to people? 'She didn't reply. Multiple times.' Perhaps, he reflected, he could have given her more time. Or tried another few messages, but he'd found it hard enough writing the first one, never mind something to gently jog her memory that he'd sent it. After friendly introductory messages over a few weeks, and still no reply, it had all felt so much simpler to drive there and speak to her in person.

That morning, Luke had arrived at the sanctuary, offered to help. A volunteer let him into the house, where Sasha apparently did things needing a computer. It was an impressively large home, even though she'd given over some of the rooms for the cats.

Sasha was crying in the office, sat at the desk with a computer, covered in paperwork.

'I'm sorry,' Luke said.

She sniffed. 'It's not you. Not everything's about *you*. What is it with people your age, thinking the entire world revolves around them?' She wiped her red eyes with a tissue.

'That's quite a sweeping statement. And,' he went on, leaning against the door frame, 'didn't you, at this age, think *you* had all the answers? Isn't there a time for new ideas to usher out old ones?' Later, he wondered if he'd gone in a bit strong with this, but at the time he'd been so frustrated at her knee-jerk response he couldn't bite his tongue.

Sasha shook her head, waving away his words. 'I'm not doing this. Not now. Could you go, please?'

'Okay. But I'm not leaving. I'm going to stay until you acknowledge who I am.' He said it firmly, but quietly. He was aware that his deep voice could be intimidating, but he wanted to be clear he wasn't going anywhere soon. He would simply wait until she was ready to speak to him. Properly, about everything that had happened.

'I gave birth to you. I know precisely who you are.' She bit her bottom lip, staring at him, with deep sadness in her eyes.

Guilt flooded his veins. A cold prickliness in his hands. Perhaps that had been a step too far. Regret washed through him. Going in too far, too quickly. 'Sorry. Didn't mean to upset you.'

'I was upset far before you turned up. Today, yesterday, or when you first rocked up here. I've got plenty of stuff to sort out regardless of you.'

'Shall I go?' Luke asked, feeling very dejected and deflated.

'You can't help, so you might as well.'

If I knew what was wrong, maybe I could. He chewed the inside of his cheek in frustration. 'Try me.'

She stood, walking forwards. 'I didn't want to say this, but will you please just piss off and leave me alone?'

Luke walked backwards out of the room, shocked how he must have pushed her to anger.

She slammed the door in his face.

Right. That's a pretty clear message. Luke left the house, strode towards the largest outbuilding containing a good number of cat pens.

In a cage, the nervous woman, Anna, who had offered him a place to stay, was stroking a large black cat, called Slinky, sitting on her lap. 'Hello,' she said with care, looking up at him with a sadness in her eyes. 'Someone didn't handle this beautiful girl as a kitten, so she didn't trust humans.'

Luke nodded a hello. 'Oh. Why?' he asked, knocked by this unexpected comment.

'They thought she had an infection, so she was kept in a small room with her mum and sister until we took them. I try to sit with her every time I'm here. Just now she lets me stroke her.'

'Impressive,' Luke said, briefly calmer, glad he'd left Sasha to deal with whatever she had on her plate, away from him.

'You're still here?'

'Evidently.' Luke gave a fake grin, nodding farewell to Anna, walking past. Best not to be sarcastic, they could easily ask him to leave the premises.

Paul was in a pen at the far end, using his phone for something.

'Mind if I join you?' Luke walked to the far end of the building.

'Still here then?' Paul asked.

Luke sighed. *Is everyone from the school of the bloody obvious today?* 'Are you like *The Midwich Cuckoos* in here?'

Paul shrugged. 'Dunno, are we, whatever that is?'

Luke was too frustrated to explain. 'When one says something, they all say it. Cuckoos, they lay their eggs in other birds' nests.' It felt enough explanation at the time.

Later he'd realised he was taking his annoyance out on Paul, who was completely innocent and undeserving of his rudeness.

'So does that mean *you're* the cuckoo, or *we* are?' Paul asked with confusion. 'What's the hotel like?'

'Have you stayed in a hotel before?' Luke was feeling pretty done with this day and it had only just begun.

Paul nodded.

'It was remarkably like that,' Luke spat, anger getting the better of him. He was allowing himself to take it out on Paul because he was a man. Which made Luke feel even stupider. *God, why do I do this sort of thing?*

Paul put his phone down, stroked the long-haired grey cat. 'Are you going to disturb me all morning, or do you think you can make yourself useful in some way? I'm not about to manhandle you off the premises, and we don't have security, so unless I call the police you're probably going to stay here.'

Instinctively, he wanted to leave in a huff, but he decided he'd ignore that and try to understand why Sasha wasn't able to talk to him yet. The thought of Paul manhandling him wasn't the worst thing imaginable either. Besides, short of the police arriving, he would remain here all day. Carefully, Luke said, calming his anger, 'I was hoping you'd be free for a talk. But don't worry.' He brushed his hands together, took a deep breath. 'Anyway, what are you doing?'

'I was,' Paul began, 'taking a short video of this one, and talking about him.' Paul nodded at the grey cat.

'Why?' Unwanted frustration in his voice. *Must do better.*

'You know they say a picture paints a thousand words?'

Luke nodded, kneeling on the ground outside the cage, looking at Paul and the cat through the wire, doing his best not to snap again. 'I have heard them say that, yes.'

'Well, turns out a video and me talking to the cat is better than a five-hundred-word description and a few pictures. People go mad. Love them. We've had a threefold increase in homing enquiries since using the socials and videos.'

'Right. How many are you doing today?' It sounded interesting.

'Sasha said the youngest two litters of kittens are old enough for rehoming now. She wants us to be over-whelmed with suitable adopters.'

'Kittens. How many?' Luke couldn't believe his luck. Perhaps today wasn't going to be so bad.

'Eleven.'

'Can I help?' The anger and frustration slipped away, replaced with a focus on something positive, a tiny bubble of optimism, perhaps?

'If you're well behaved, then yes.' Paul smiled.

Happiness bubbled at Paul's smile. Luke hung his head in shame. 'Sorry.'

'Let me finish this big boy, Oliver,' Paul said, 'and then we'll go to the nursery block.' Paul explained the grey cat was over ten years old, and had been adopted from Fluffy Paws before, but had been found roaming the streets in a very sorry state: matted fur, ulcers from fighting, thin and malnourished. They checked the microchip and contacted the owner, who said he didn't have room for the cat, now he had a new kitten.

Processing this, Luke said, 'He got a new kitten and discarded the old cat?'

Paul nodded. 'Like an unwanted pair of shoes.'

'Why?'

'Old cats can be expensive. Vet bills, special food, plus they sort of *do* less than younger cats. They're kind of less cat, if that makes sense.' Paul kissed the large male cat's head, stroking it. He purred loudly. 'I'm going to make the best video and nobody's going to be able to resist him. Cos he's a lovely old boy, right?'

Luke nodded, feeling a small sense of calm and a hint of happiness bubbling through his chest. He slumped on the floor, leaning his back against the wire of the cat pen. *If I'm not going to leave, just hang around near Sasha's orbit, I reckon doing it with Paul is better than sulking alone.*

Later, when Paul had finished, he left the pen, locking the door behind him. 'Better? Calmer?'

With contrition, Luke said, 'Sorry. I know it's not your fault. It's just…'

'I was there when you happened to be angry?' Paul raised his eyebrows.

Luke nodded. *About summed it up.* 'And now here you are, helping me. I don't know why I took it out on you.' He knew why, but he didn't tell Paul.

Paul led them to the house and into the room Sasha used as a kitten nursery, where the queens brought up their litters until they were weaned.

There was a litter of black-and-white kittens, long white whiskers and azure-blue eyes dominating their faces that had Luke's heart beating faster and he was unable to stop saying, 'Aaah, aren't they sweet?'

Paul let them into the pen, closing the first door before opening the second leading into the space containing the cats. 'Concentrate. This is work.'

Luke nodded solemnly.

Paul played with each kitten in turn, talking about them, talking to them, describing how their mum had arrived at the sanctuary, none of them had been named, just sexed. Luke filmed with his phone. Each video was about two minutes long, meaning it could be shared on all the socials.

Paul said, 'Got them?'

'Six videos, six kittens. Do you want to see them?'

Paul sat next to Luke and watched the videos in turn. Each kitten behaved slightly differently, some were boisterous, others shyer, a few became a little too enthusiastic with teeth and claws as they played, and one lay on its back, letting Paul stroke its stomach and purring with its eyes shut.

Paul settled himself on the floor. 'So you can make yourself useful, that's good.' A pause, and then: 'What did Sasha say?'

Luke told him.

'She's got a lot going on at the moment.'

'What else?'

Paul shrugged. 'She doesn't talk about it. Keeps it to herself. She's in charge, so I think she believes she has to steer the ship calmly and not let us know about any problems.' Paul huffed. 'I think it's very unhelpful. Toxic positivity, apparently. I had a client who talked about it. Very dangerous, it can be.'

'What should I do?' Luke understood more, that perhaps it wasn't *all* about him.

'I'm not running this place, I just come here a few days a week and post on the socials the rest of the time. But time's usually good.'

'I hear it's a good healer.' Luke smiled.

'Apparently so. You should talk to Anna again, she's got a big empty house, doesn't know what to do with it. It would save you staying in a hotel. Unless you think you're leaving soon?'

Luke shrugged. He should take her up on that offer. 'No rush. The group says they can manage without me for a while.'

'Nice work if you can get it.'

'Says the digital nomad who's working his way around Europe.'

'Theoretically.'

'What does that mean?' Luke frowned.

'Six months in each European country where we could get a digital nomad visa, was what we planned, and all I've managed so far is three months in Croatia, Spain and Portugal. And then back here.'

'Doesn't sound like a fail to me.'

'Nine months to give up everything we, *I* had here. Hindsight's a wonderful thing, right?'

'What happened?' Luke asked gently.

Paul stood. 'George, is what happened. And I'm not getting into all of that now. I wish I'd noticed it sooner.'

'What?' Luke stood.

They left the pen and moved to the next one, letting themselves through the first door, shutting it, before opening the second leading to the cats.

'Do you want to play while I film?' Paul asked. 'Unless you don't want to be on the socials.'

'I'm all over them, I mean, isn't everyone?' Luke shrugged, then sat on the floor, allowing the kittens to climb up his legs and body.

'Ready?' Paul asked.

Luke nodded, played with one kitten, as it chased a tiny ball about. Luke talked to the light grey ball of fluff with the largest bluest eyes he'd ever seen. Long white whiskers made the kitten look so adorable. He played with three more. 'I want one.'

Paul stopped filming. 'Everyone does. Except they're only kittens for six months, they're cats for fifteen to twenty years. That's the bit some people forget.' He put his phone in his pocket. 'George seemed like the perfect boyfriend. On paper anyway. It's funny what you find out about someone when you're travelling together.'

Luke raised his eyebrows, sensing this was as much as he'd get out of him for now. Holding a tiny calico kitten, he nodded to check Paul was ready to resume filming.

Paul nodded, started videoing.

Luke stroked the kitten, describing it, and repeated this until all of the second litter had been filmed. With a sense of satisfaction, Luke left Paul behind the chicken wire with the cats in their pen.

Later, Luke spoke to Anna. She was wiping the cat kitchen work surfaces. 'I've been thinking about your offer of a place to stay.' A few days had passed and although she was quiet and said little about herself he could see she was kind and broken and seemed lonely and in need of help, but was, for some reason, unwilling to ask except disguised by offering him a place to stay. He thought he'd say yes and see how it went, it had to be better than a budget hotel room. 'Is it still open?'

'It is.' She nodded, tucking a stray hair behind her ear, glancing about the room nervously. 'I think it's better for me to live with *someone* rather than alone. And I'd rather a someone I know, than a someone I don't.' She stared at him, smiled. 'Plus, having you around I'm sure may come in handy for fixing little jobs around the house. It's in need of repair, Mum and Dad's house. I couldn't decide what to do, with the house, so I'm doing nothing. Except letting it out. To you!' She grinned.

'Very sensible,' Luke said. 'No big decisions so soon after losing someone.'

Her face brightened. 'Is that right?'

'Read it in a book, so it's got to be, right?'

She told him about the house, said she was thinking about selling *her* place, but not quite sure. She seemed very indecisive and at sea, but he reckoned it was grief, or medication. She explained she would eventually need to make a decision about whether to sell it, but in the meantime her offer stood, he could live there, keep the heating on, it would stop it becoming damp.

'Shall I pay for each night?' Luke asked.

'Whatever you think.'

'If you're happy with that?' Luke wanted to do this right, after making such a dog's dinner of his arrival. Anna was a friend of Sasha's so he didn't want to do anything that would upset her, and therefore Sasha.

'Better having the house occupied than empty. You're doing me a favour really.'

'And you me.' Luke shook her hand, wondering if she'd mention paperwork, contracts, all that stuff. 'Can you give me your bank details so I can transfer the money? Unless you want something formal, written down?'

Anna shook her head. 'I trust you. I trust Sasha.' She suggested a nightly rate that sounded very reasonable.

Luke agreed, making a note of it and her bank details.

Anna looked at him from the corner of her eyes, staring at the floor, only briefly making eye contact. 'Wish I could do that.'

'What?'

'Turn up. Out of the blue. Drop everything and just go.' There was a sadness to her tone, a sense of missing things from her life.

'Why can't you?'

'They've been very good to me, at work. I can't up and leave again.' She shook her head nervously.

'You can. If you want. You can do anything.'

'Don't be silly.' She blushed, looked away.

'There are always choices in life. You've just got to take them.'

'What if my choice is to have everything stay the same, forever?' She folded her arms on her lap.

He'd never considered anyone would want that. Except perhaps his mum. Maybe it was a more popular fantasy than he imagined. *Interesting.* 'Impossible.'

She got a faraway look in her eyes, stared out of the window. 'Yes, it is.' She swallowed. 'Sad.'

'Or does it mean life's always developing, changing, new?' That was how Luke thought of it. Like a dance around the room, when he'd done ballroom dancing, moving about the floor, twirling, stepping side to side, adjusting to your partner's movements. Otherwise life would be like someone standing as still as a statue. Luke didn't like the sound of that.

She shook her head. 'Sad.' She turned away, and stood over the sink, fastidiously washing each cat bowl in hot soapy water, carefully stacking them on the draining rack, then drying them, each with a clean tea towel.

He thought he'd leave it there, feeling sure Anna would come to him when she was ready to ask for help, and he would absolutely be there to do whatever she needed. He thanked her and left.

Chapter 16

A few days later, Sasha noticed Luke seemed to have disappeared. She'd certainly not seen him since their last discussion. Well, she had told him to piss off. Perhaps that had been a bit much, she reflected, but she had just put the phone down on the landlord who'd refused not to pull down the outbuildings as soon as possible, explaining they were putting off prospective buyers and they needed to go now. He'd asked the estate agent to return for more photos as soon as the demolition was done. Leaving Sasha up shit creek without a paddle.

She knew Luke was only trying to help, but it had been so overwhelming, such a lot to take on, she was far from ready to open up about why she'd had him adopted all those years ago.

Sometimes she caught his name from the volunteers, but she had not seen him. Ironic since she'd wanted him to leave, and now he'd done precisely that, she missed him, wanted to know where he'd gone.

Anna was in a pen, sitting with a plump female tabby cat, waiting for the animal to sit on her lap. The cat was nervous and wasn't showing well – when people came to view her, she stayed in her bed, only two eyes visible from beneath a blanket at the back of the pen.

Sasha had asked Anna to take a break from cleaning the cats' litter trays and washing their bowls, and spend the morning with Duchess, this female tabby, trying to gain her trust, since she'd done so well with Slinky.

'How's Duchess?' Sasha asked.

'She's let me stroke her face. Then disappeared into her bed. I've been sitting here doing nothing since.'

'Have you talked to her?'

Anna shook her head, worry clouding her expression. 'What should I say? I've never had a cat, I don't know what to talk to them about.'

'You should adopt one of your own.'

Anna shook her head. 'Shall I introduce myself to her?'

'Could do. Talk in a low voice, make it clear you're no threat. Let her sniff your hand before you touch her. Sit a bit closer. Tempt her onto you with some treats.' Sasha reached into her pocket, placed a handful into a hatch.

Anna retrieved a few. 'All of them?'

'That's it.'

'I didn't talk to Slinky, just sat with her. Is that wrong?' Anna asked with worry.

'Whatever makes them trust you. You did a great job with Slinky.' Sasha was proud of how Anna was settling in and clearly becoming more relaxed.

Anna nodded slowly. 'Are you going to talk to Luke?' she asked, as she spread out some cat treats on her lap, tapping herself to attract Duchess.

'He's staying at your place?' Sasha knew this, but she wanted to check.

'A few days. Taking it one day at a time. He said he could go any time, but...' She looked away.

'What?'

'He won't, not before he's spoken to you. Properly.'

'How do you know?'

'Nothing he's said to me. I just get a feeling. He seemed pretty settled when I checked on him at the house.'

'What's he been doing, just waiting?'

'Working with Paul. Helping out here.'

Sasha reckoned she should have told Luke to leave, rather than ignoring him. It would have prevented this mess. 'Why haven't I seen him?'

'He's avoiding you.'

'Deliberately?' Sasha frowned.

Anna nodded. 'I think so. You clearly didn't want to talk to him. So he's not tried to talk to you. Very sensible, I reckon.'

At least that showed some degree of emotional intelligence, even if the turning-up-unannounced part left a lot to be desired. 'Where is he now?'

'Probably playing with his phone with Paul. They're getting on *very* well.' Anna had a glint in her eye. 'It's very sweet.'

Sasha frowned. 'You don't think? Do you?' She wasn't sure how she felt about that. Not that she had anything against it as such, but she'd not fully appreciated it could happen, them being both so inclined, so to speak.

Anna shrugged. 'Anything's possible.'

Apparently so. 'Let her eat from your hand. Stroke her. Talk to her. If you do that every day this week, she'll soon come round. Time, is all it takes.' Sasha left Anna doing as instructed. She searched all the outbuildings for Luke and finally found him playing with Smokey, the large male cat who lived in the sanctuary.

'Why doesn't anyone want him?' Luke asked. 'He's adorable.'

'Smokey is very old. He's diabetic and needs medication and injections. He used to need his bladder massaging to have a wee. He's not a lap cat either. If you knew what he'd come from, you'd understand why.'

'Dare I ask?'

'Probably best not.'

There was a silence as they stared at Smokey.

'I've gotta go.' Luke knelt to stroke Smokey's head, then turned to leave.

He was clearly very hurt. With contrition and regret at her first reaction, Sasha said, 'I came to say sorry. I shouldn't have told you to... you know. I sort of lash out when I'm hurt or confused, or it's too much. I'd just had some bad news. About this place.'

Luke nodded, smiled. 'Right.'

That was something. He accepted her apology. It was the same smile of his birth father, all those years ago. She couldn't continue keeping him away. He was part of her, she part of him. She spoke very carefully, not wanting to be so rude again. 'It's not *you*. It's who *you* remind me of. Which isn't your fault. I know this.'

Luke turned. 'My birth father?'

Sasha blinked, looked at the ground, nodded. 'And, I would have appreciated some notice of your arrival. It's not like I have the luxury of spare time.'

'Sorry.' He toed the ground. 'Mum and Dad said I should call. Well, sort of.'

'They're not wrong. I like them already.' Sasha coughed. 'How are they about everything?'

'Supportive. Now.'

'Now?'

'Mum didn't want me to contact you. It's cos she thinks I'll like you more than her.'

'Well, my behaviour has certainly prevented that.' Possibly, she'd done him a favour in that regard. Sasha smiled awkwardly. Although telling him to piss off was definitely not her finest moment. At least she'd apologised. 'What do they do, your parents?'

'Mum used to work in a post office, then a shop. Dad works for a local law-firm business as a paralegal.'

'Where do they live?'

'Bournemouth. South coast. Sandy beaches. I had a great childhood there.'

'I'm so glad.' That was nice. She had made the right decision, even if he'd turned up thirty years later to question her on why.

'Is that why you gave me up for adoption?'

Just like that. She wasn't prepared for this, quite so soon. 'How do you mean?'

'Because you thought I'd have a better life with someone other than you.'

It had been a whole range of reasons, some she could no longer properly recall since she wasn't the scared sixteen-year-old she had been then; she was forty-six and different in almost every way. She nodded. 'I could barely look after myself, never mind a little baby.'

'Right.'

'I was at school. Retook my GCSE year, did all right, except maths, did A levels. Meant to go to university but didn't.' It had been one of her biggest regrets. She felt guilty for not keeping Luke since she needed to continue her education and, at the most important stage, she hadn't bothered.

'What would you have studied? I did performing arts. After a term of sociology.' Luke grimaced. 'What on earth was I thinking?'

'People make mistakes.' A pause as Sasha remembered who she'd planned to be as a teenager, contrasting it with who she actually was now, thirty years later. Disappointment lodged itself in her gut. 'Veterinary medicine.' She swallowed. 'I was planning to be a veterinary nurse.'

'Why didn't you?' Luke asked.

Because I'd had a baby at sixteen and my emotions and hormones were all over the shop. Because I carried a heavy guilt about doing it, making every decision afterwards so important to get right, that I was unable to make any. Bracing herself, for further questions about this, Sasha said, 'Because I failed my A levels. Turns out maths and sciences aren't my friends.'

Luke nodded. 'I'm not great with them either. Scraped through my GCSEs.'

'I thought if I had private tutoring and retook them I'd be good. Mum said I'd be better, but not good.' It had hurt at the time, someone telling her she had no natural ability for what she wanted to do, but eventually she'd recognised when she was beaten and needed another plan.

'The shade!' Luke said.

Sasha frowned. 'What?'

'Your mum saying that. It's... I don't think mine would do that.'

'It was the kindest thing. Not the nicest, but the kindest.'

Luke thought for a moment. 'Suppose.' He raked his hand through his hair. Carefully, he asked, 'Can you tell me about my birth father?'

'Please?'

'Sorry, please will you tell me who he was?'

Sasha knew this was coming. So she'd mentally prepared herself. It was wonderful since she'd relive what had been a perfect fortnight's holiday with her parents. But it had also led to the hardest decision she'd ever made, that still stung now. 'It was my last holiday with my parents. After that I was too grown up to go with them. Southern Italy, Sorrento. The town was busy, lots of bars and restaurants along the seafront, full of hotels, bursting with tourists.'

'Is he Italian, my dad?'

'Your *dad* is a paralegal in Bournemouth. He's the man who made you who you are.'

Luke swallowed. 'Right. But he's not why I look like this? You are. And him.'

'Luca was as tall and broad-shouldered as you, black hair, green-blue eyes and a presence I couldn't ignore.'

'Luca? Is that why I'm called Luke?'

That was why she'd named their son Luke. She hadn't expected him to retain the name she'd given him, the social worker had said it rarely happened. Not that it mattered, since she knew she'd never see her son again. Except... She told him.

He nodded in silence.

She huffed to herself. 'Sometimes I wish I had ignored him.'

'Well, I don't!'

'No. He was in his late twenties. Maybe early thirties.' She hadn't exactly asked to see his passport.

Luke scrunched up his face. 'Is that a *bit* problematic?' He waved his arms about in emphasis.

His father used to do that, when he talked enthusiastically about his country, his home town. Sasha swallowed the lump of memory that had formed in her throat. 'The age of consent in Italy is fourteen and sixteen in the UK, so, no, it isn't, as you say, problematic.' He was becoming

147

a bit tiresome. Did he want her to share her story or not? Was he going to interrupt her with annoying questions at every opportunity? She paused, swallowed in thought.

'How did you meet?'

'I walked to the shops to buy a postcard and was browsing the tourist shops, fridge magnets, bottle openers, mugs, hats, T-shirts, those sorts of shops.'

Luke nodded.

'Luca asked if he could help me. I said I was fine choosing my own postcards thank you very much. When I bought them I asked if they sold stamps and he showed me the nearest shop selling them.'

'It was his shop?'

'Evidently. Probably. The next day I was back with Mum and Dad, and we were lost. I went into the shop, asking for directions and Luca helped.'

'Nice.'

'I thought so, yes. The following night, Mum and Dad had gone to bed early, Mum had a headache – she was exhausted after the day of sightseeing, and Dad didn't want to leave her alone.'

'Nice.'

Sasha frowned. 'Is that all you're going to say as I recount this?' *Very private and painful story…*

'Sorry. It's just, I…'

'You what?' She couldn't keep the irritation out of her voice. A tiny bit snappy even.

'I wondered if you came from a broken home. Hence…'

Hence… Sasha sighed, gathering all her patience to continue. 'No, Mum and Dad are still very much alive *and* together,' she said with emphasis and shot him a look. 'Can I go on?'

'Sorry. You left your parents sleeping…'

There was an awkward silence as Sasha debated walking away. Carefully, she went on. 'I wanted to explore a bit, without them. I knew this would be my last family holiday. My school friends were already starting to go away in groups without their parents. I didn't want to sit in a bar alone because I was too shy and Mum always said it sent a certain signal to men.'

'And you didn't want to give off that signal?'

Sasha shook her head. 'I didn't.'

'And yet…'

Sasha nodded. 'Life can be funny like that.'

Luke scratched his high patrician forehead, another thing he'd inherited from his birth father. 'Right.'

'I saw a family who I recognised from our hotel, sitting at a table overlooking the sea. I walked past very slowly and one called to me, saying they'd seen me by the pool earlier that week.'

'That's kind of them.'

'I thought so. I joined them, didn't feel hard since I'd already spoken to them at the hotel. Didn't know their names. They'd eaten but I joined them for a drink. They let me have some of their wine. I said I couldn't, because I wasn't eighteen and they said it was okay because I was eating and hadn't bought it.'

'Not sure that's how it works, but anyway.'

Sasha folded her arms, unable to disguise her irritation. 'Do *you* want to take over?'

'Nope.' Luke held his lips tightly together. 'Sorry.'

Another awkward silence, before Sasha resumed her story: 'One minute it was early evening, next it's late and they're going back to the hotel. I said I wanted some water.

They waited outside while I went into the bar for water and when I left, they had gone.'

'I thought they were waiting for you.'

'So did I.'

'Where were they?'

'Later I found out they'd rushed back because one of their friends at the hotel had food poisoning. They'd planned for one to stay back and wait for me, but they all got in a taxi.' Pre-empting his next question, she said, 'I didn't have their numbers. And, it was nineteen ninety-two, so...' *No mobile phones.*

'Right.'

'Luca was at the bar with friends, he recognised me, asked if I was all right. I told him my friends had left.'

Luke leaned forwards. 'Did he seduce you in the bar?'

Sasha shook her head. 'Sorry to disappoint you, but no.'

'What was he like?'

'Tall and strong, but also very gentle. He took charge, but was also quiet and reflective. Listened to me. Didn't dominate, unless it was better if he did.' He'd been, Sasha admitted, pretty bloody perfect. No man had ever lived up to her albeit brief experience of Luke's father.

'He sounds faultless.'

'He was. Although aren't all holiday romances?' She was under no illusions much of the perfection of Luke's birth father was down to their brief relationship and avoidance of the everyday dullness that can sometimes take over a relationship – or so she'd heard from friends anyway.

Luke shrugged. 'Right. My fortnight with friends on a Greek island confirms this.'

'Tell.'

Luke blushed. 'Met in a club on the first night. Went back to his. Stayed there for four or five nights. He came back to my hotel for the next three. I didn't see my friends at all. As in, not at all. Then back to his place, making house and feeling so permanent and perfect. Until it wasn't.'

'Flight home and then nothing?'

Luke nodded, with pain in his eyes. 'Nothing. He didn't answer my calls, texted back a few times but then nothing. Totally ghosted.'

'Ghosted?' Sasha asked.

'Disappeared, no contact, without a goodbye, or even a sod off. Nothing.'

'Nothing.' She let that settle for a moment, enjoying how he'd shared part of himself as she shared part of herself. It felt, for that brief moment, as if they'd been mother and son all his life. A sharp jab of nostalgia for the relationship they could have had, shot through her. 'If I could do it all again, I don't know if I'd make the same mistakes.'

'Giving me up for adoption, sleeping with my dad, which mistake?'

'I was told I couldn't have any contact with your adoptive parents, or you. Once that process was complete, I would never see you again. Unless you sought me out. It's for the protection of both parties, so they say. Didn't feel like it at the time.' She'd signed a form confirming she would not attempt contact with Luke, or his adoptive parents. On that day a piece of her heart closed, she couldn't think about it, so she hadn't. This was one reason why she kept herself to herself, wanted to remain self-reliant. All she knew back then was his adoptive parents' names, no address, no internet to research, so she'd soon left the whole sorry episode in the past. And there it had remained until…

'What would you do differently?'

'If I knew I was going to fail my A levels and not go to veterinary college, I think I'd have kept you.' She imagined being a mother at sixteen, her parents' reaction, the shame they'd felt, how clueless she'd been then. 'Feels like such a waste.'

'What does?'

'All of it. None of it. Me. You. Us. Him, your dad. If I'd stayed in Italy, maybe we could have been a family. If I'd not had you, perhaps I'd be a vet now.' She looked at him, her handsome, tall, confident son, who she'd missed watching grow up from a baby, being a child and teen-ager, into the man who sat next to her now. She closed her eyes as regret, anger at her mistakes, bad decisions, overtook her. She squeezed her eyes, willing herself not to cry. Determined not to make a terrible show of herself. Despite her best efforts, she sobbed. That closed-off part of her heart had, after all those years, opened slightly, for Luke, as it should have done had she kept him.

Luke held her close, tightly to his large body, squeezing her arm.

He didn't say anything, probably didn't know what to say, how do you comfort your long-lost birth mother when she finally realises she made a mistake giving you away thirty years ago? There's hardly a greeting card for that.

Finally, she composed herself, wiped her eyes, sat upright, took a deep breath. 'That's more than enough of that for today.'

'I was waiting.'

'For what, the story of meeting your dad?'

'Yes, but no, not that. To see who I came from. To understand why I'm me.'

'Rubbish. You're you, because your parents raised you that way.' She thought he probably got his persistence from his birth father, but didn't tell him.

'I don't think it's that simple.'

There was a silence. Sasha decided she wasn't ready to tell him the rest of how she met his father, how he'd seduced her, made love to her, so said, 'How's Anna's place?'

'Big. Full of crap. And I mean, full. Of. Crap. Piled up in every room. Stacks of newspapers and magazines, boxes of clothes. Three broken TVs in my room. Christmas cards going back to the Sixties.'

'How do you know?' Sasha thought Anna had issues, but hadn't appreciated it was this bad.

'Each envelope has a diary with it. One for every year.'

This really did sound like something Anna would need help fixing. 'Better than staying in a hotel?'

'By miles.'

'When do you need to get back to your life?'

'Whenever. I'd like to continue helping here if you'll let me.'

More of that persistence again. She liked it. 'Looks like you've been doing that without my blessing.'

He smiled, that was the charming grin that his birth father had, that had no doubt allowed Luke to get most of what he wanted, precisely when he wanted it. 'I couldn't sit around waiting for you.'

'No. He was always doing stuff, up and at 'em.'

'My dad?'

'The man who made you with me.'

Luke nodded, smiled. 'Do you have a photo?'

It was his father's smile, she remembered it so perfectly. The look he'd given her when she was lost and a bit drunk. The way he'd driven her back to the hotel and dropped her off, like a perfect gentleman, that was why the next night she'd wanted to see him again, secretly hoping he wouldn't be so gentlemanly.

Guilt, regret, nostalgia mixed and Sasha knew she couldn't tell Luke more. 'No. We didn't photograph everything back then, like we seem to now. I hope that's enough. For now. I can't go through it all again. Not yet. It's too…' She choked with tears as her heart closed to protect herself. Besides, she had bigger things to worry about, such as what to do with sixty cats once the pens were pulled down.

He squeezed her shoulder, nodded. 'Thanks.'

Chapter 17

Paul and Luke had gone to a tap-dancing class in the outskirts of Chelmsford. Luke had seemed quiet and Paul wasn't sure whether to pry.

Discovering that Luke not only liked dancing, but was also a professional dancer, had been a wonderful surprise and Paul was determined to make the most of their friendship, no matter how short-lived. Paul was, after all, only staying in the UK for a while, due to return to a digital nomad life around Europe very soon.

They had changed into T-shirts and tracksuit bottoms and stood in the corner of the village hall, opposite a mirrored wall.

Luke held on to the barre fixed to the wall.

'Have you done ballet?' Paul asked.

'Yes.'

'Would you do it now?' Paul used to enjoy dance classes until George made him stop.

'Maybe. Why?'

'I miss it.' Paul missed all of it. The ballet part he'd particularly enjoyed until George had told him he shouldn't.

'I thought you were into this. Hence why you asked me to join you.'

'I am into it. It's just I've not gone dancing in a while.'

'Travel?'

'Partly, yes.' *And partly, no. Partly George.*

The instructor arrived, called the room to order and began the class. 'This is new, so follow me.'

Music played, a jaunty pop song with a fast beat. Paul didn't recognise it at first, then at the chorus he knew it was 'Foundations' by Kate Nash from a few years ago. He smiled at the memory of dancing to it a while ago, the last time he'd made time to come somewhere like this.

Their conversation ended and Paul kicked himself for giving up something that made him this happy. George really had a lot to answer for. Or was Paul equally to blame for allowing himself to be controlled like that? *No more of that.*

The instructor first tapped his toes, then heels, then clapped along with the music. 'You copy me now.' He turned to one side, and demonstrated the first step, clapped, tapped his heels then toes, then turned to the other side and repeated it. He built into a high-tempo sequence, ending in two jumps into the air. He stopped the music. 'Are we ready?'

Paul reckoned he'd memorised most of it. He followed the instructor's lead and was soon jumping in the air, twirling, clapping and tapping with his heels, toes and the front of his shoes.

He looked to one side and Luke was, of course, effortlessly smiling and dancing along with the music, as befitted a professional. Normally, Paul focused on his own reflection in the mirror, but this time he couldn't take his eyes off Luke.

Mesmerising.

Luke moved with such grace and art, it almost made Paul stop dancing. But seeing Luke's smile, as he seemed to look at Paul doing his best at dancing, spurred Paul on and he soon relaxed into the moment, still drinking Luke in with his eyes, the sensual way he moved, the confidence with which he held himself, all had Paul imagining them moving together, in other ways than dancing...

The next song was 'Anything Goes' from the musical of the same name. Paul knew this well as they'd danced to it a number of times.

Paul joyously flung himself into the song, twirled, danced on the spot, ran forwards, backwards, really throwing himself into the dance. When the music stopped he could hardly breathe, sweat poured down his brow.

Luke handed him a bottle of water.

'Thanks,' Paul said, regaining his breath then drinking some. 'Okay?'

Luke nodded, smiled, leaning against the wall for a moment. It was as if he owned the wall, the hall in fact, the confidence he oozed was mesmerising. *Alluring, even. Where did that come from?*

'Aren't you dancing the next one?' Paul asked, deciding he needed to shake that thought away immediately.

'Maybe, but I'm really enjoying watching you. You're *very* good.'

Paul blushed, waved away the compliment. *He's probably just saying it.*

There followed 'Dancing Queen' by ABBA, to which they gave a bouncier dance, moving from one side to the other, hips swaying, and jumping up and down with a great deal of arm waving in the air. Paul's favourite part was dancing the actions of the lyrics, like peering under their palms to show 'searching', jumping high in the air for 'high' and claps in time with the beats, and the chorus was accompanied by hands twirling around like rolling a barrel in front of their own chest.

Paul had felt a touch self-conscious dancing to this the first time, a few weeks ago, not least because it was *very gay* and he knew George would have tutted, shaken his head and walked away in disgust. But Paul no longer needed to worry what George thought, so now he danced and tapped along with reckless, wild, fabulously gay abandon.

Taking a breath, Paul leaned against the wall, sipping the water for a moment.

Luke was dancing to the ABBA song, joyfully, unashamedly, beautifully, with a wide grin and twinkling eyes.

Paul couldn't take his eyes off him, allowing his imagination to run wild, consider how splendid Luke would look without clothes, his muscular limbs, his taut stomach, with what Paul reckoned had something of a six-pack, the little trail of dark hair from his navel going down into his trousers that he'd caught a glimpse of when Luke's T-shirt rode up as he lifted his arms in the air.

Paul shook away that fantasy as the music stopped. He was here to dance not ogle Luke, although it was almost as much fun.

The instructor thanked everyone, wishing them a good evening. 'And now, we clap and then we go home!'

Sweating, full of happy hormones buzzing around his bloodstream, and tired, Paul joined the rest of the class in clapping and thanking the instructor, who shortly left.

'Fun?' Paul asked Luke.

Luke huffed, wiped sweat from his brow. 'I've missed this as I've not been rehearsing for a show.'

'I've missed it too,' Paul said.

'You said. Surely there are places like this around Europe.'

'Probably.'

'Probably?' Luke frowned. 'How hard is it to look for them, a quick google, surely?'

'If I could.' Paul didn't want to discuss this.

'Why couldn't you? Is this some sort of quiz? Sorry, I'm tired. And a bit thick too. What are you saying?' Luke seemed exasperated.

He's going to make me say it and I don't want to. Because of the shame. 'I didn't search for them during the travels because I didn't do this when I was at home either.' *Not for a long time.*

'But if you like it, why wouldn't you?'

'Do you *always* do everything you like?'

'Pretty much. Don't you?'

Paul slowly shook his head. 'I used to. I can now. It's just me.'

Recognition crossed Luke's face. 'Is this because someone disapproved of you dancing?'

Tightly, Paul nodded, the memory of that conversation with George flooding back to him. The shame, the fear, at the time, and the guilt for allowing himself to be ground down like that. 'George liked things how George liked things.' *For everyone. Including me.* Paul felt weak, useless, powerless, ashamed of telling someone else. And yet he needed to, because they'd just shared this wonderful dance class together and had bonded over a shared passion, one Paul was rediscovering now he could.

'I'm sorry,' Luke said, holding his arms aloft, indicating they should hug.

Paul let all inhibitions dissolve; the kindness Luke was showing him felt so marked in comparison to how George had treated him that Paul almost, but not quite, cried. He surrendered himself to the hug, to Luke's strong arms holding him, patting his back, to his chin resting on Paul's shoulder as they held tightly.

Luke said, in his wonderfully deep voice: 'It's easy to ignore what's in front of your eyes, if things change very subtly. There's a saying about how someone will die in a bath of hot water as it slowly heats from a flame below, until too late, they're gone. Your ex's behaviour was that flame.'

God, he's so perfect, isn't he? Paul reluctantly let go of the hug. He could have remained in Luke's arms all night. *All. Night. Long.* 'Thanks for coming tonight.'

'Thanks for inviting me.' Luke slung his bag over a shoulder. 'Can you give me a lift back, please?'

Perhaps now I've been all messy in front of him, he'll open up to me in the car. There was something about sitting next to people, rather than opposite them, that Paul found helped people talk when they'd not managed before. 'Of course.'

'Appreciated,' Luke said, striding towards the car park.

On the silent drive, Paul said, 'What was he like, your biological father?'

Luke looked out of the window. 'We don't say that. Makes him sound like washing powder.'

'What do we say?'

'Birth parents.'

'Understood.' This was going to be much harder than anticipated. Usually, Luke was confident and chatty. Something must have happened to change that.

They drove in silence through the countryside, until they arrived at Luke's place in the small village of Margaretting, to Anna's parents' house. It was a large and impressive, if slightly dilapidated, Victorian home, with peeling paint and cracked tiles, the garden in serious need of attention with weeds and brambles overgrown where lawn and flower beds should have been.

Paul turned the engine off. 'You're clearly not going to tell me what's wrong. So I'm going to ask you.'

'If you want,' Luke said with tiredness.

'You're actually going to make me ask, aren't you?' Incredulity and frustration frosted his tone.

Luke shrugged. 'Makes no odds to me. Ask, don't ask.' He shrugged.

'Are you *always* this hard work?' Paul knew the answer was no, because usually Luke was a pleasure to be around. 'What did Sasha say?'

'It's more what she didn't say.'

'Such as?'

'She told me how she met my birth dad, and then she stopped. Clammed up.'

'Sounds like a good start. Come back to it. It's *a lot* for her. Like I said, she's got other stuff going on.'

Luke turned to face Paul, his brow was furrowed and seemed to be in serious contemplation. 'I've really hurt her. Coming here. She said she's glad to see me, but when she talks about back then, it's really painful for her.'

'What did you expect?'

Luke shrugged. 'I'd just turn up and she'd tell me about my past, her past, herself.'

'Maybe that's the problem. You're prepared. But she's not. Still. She's not ready to relive that time.'

'It sounds like she was a totally different person then. I...' He shook his head.

'Thirty years ago, she *was* totally different. Who'd have thought it?' Paul's tone aimed for humour.

'Mum and Dad have always been the same. I thought Sasha would be the same.'

This was going to be harder than Paul expected. *At least Luke's talking, that's something.* 'Have *you* been the same all your life?'

He shook his head. 'I've always felt unsure who I was. When Mum and Dad told me I was adopted that made sense as a little boy. But as I grew up I realised I didn't have the answers. When I turned thirty, for some reason it changed how I viewed my life. Midlife existential crisis.' Luke shrugged.

'And now?'

'I still don't have all the answers I was hoping for from Sasha.'

'Is it reasonable to expect the woman who gave birth to you, and who you've not seen since, to give all this to you? And all at once?'

Luke shook his head quickly. 'I really haven't thought this through, have I?'

'Are you usually a think-things-through sort of person?' It amused Paul that despite a few weeks of hanging out together at the cat sanctuary he didn't really know who Luke was.

'Not once I've made up my mind. Then I'm on it. Like a dog with a bone, Mum says. Until I'm on to the next thing.'

'You're not going to leave Sasha like this, are you?' It worried Paul that Luke would sweep in, disrupt Sasha's life then leave just as abruptly. He also didn't want to think about Luke leaving, but for his own reasons. And the dance class had confirmed those.

'Like what?'

'Dredging up all her pain from the past.'

'That. Right. Yeah. I mean, no.' After a pause, Luke said, 'Don't know.'

'Why not?'

'I can't stay here because every time she sees me it's painful for her. I can't go home because my dad told me not to go in the first place, and I've made a mess of everything. They'll...'

'Tell you they told you so?'

'No,' Luke said.

'What then?'

Luke shook his head, put it in his hands. 'If there was something to think through, this was it, right?'

Right. You think? 'Maybe. Although I don't have a great deal of experience of retracing long-lost parents. Nearest I've come to that was telling my parents they could always get hold of me wherever I travelled as long as I had Wi-Fi.'

Luke chuckled. 'How did they take to you leaving for travel?'

'Well. I didn't do it before university, so it sort of made sense to do it when I did. Plus, I was working, not just holidaying for a year, like those endless students on their gap yars!'

'Yar! I went to uni with a few of those.'

'Didn't we all?' After a pause, Paul asked, 'What now?'

'I could go back and work. There's rehearsals for our new show. We're improvising it and practising. It's like totally immersive. And I really miss dancing every day. As tonight has shown.' Luke rubbed his hand across his stubbly jaw.

Paul totally didn't think about what it felt like. *Nope. Not considering that at all.* 'For what it's worth, running away from your problems doesn't sound particularly healthy. You've met Sasha, you might as well give her time to finish telling her story to you. Or it's a bit hit-and-run, don't you think?'

'What about working off my problems? Throwing myself into another show, rehearsals, forgetting I ever started this.'

'I don't think even *you're* convinced about that,' Paul said. He felt Luke had a duty to see this through with Sasha, and for his parents' sakes. He'd started this, created the mess, so he needed to work through it until it was less messy and some sort of new normal for him and his family.

'Do you have to be anywhere tonight?' Luke said quietly, staring into the footwell.

'Is that you asking me to come in?' Excitement and anticipation scuttled up Paul's spine.

'If you want.'

'Well, if you're going to put it like that, how could I resist?' Paul chuckled. Luke's unenthusiastic offer somehow made Paul keener. He must remember that if he wanted to use casual allure to attract a man.

'Is that a yes?' Luke asked.

'It's an okay, if I must, I must, you've really twisted my arm.'

'Good.' Luke nodded.

They were soon in the kitchen and Luke had poured them wine. 'It's cheap.'

'Can I have a coffee?'

'At this time of night?'

'I'm driving. And don't you have decaf?'

'Like having alcohol-free lager. Pointless. Besides, coffee isn't proper unless it's black and strong enough to jolt you into the day.'

Paul put the wine glass on the table, sat at the far end, folded his arms. *I'm not drinking this and I'm not letting him charm me into wherever this is heading either.*

'Water?' Luke stood by the sink. Handing him the drink and sitting at the nearest corner, he said, 'They're an interesting lot, the volunteers at the sanctuary, right?'

Paul's brain had clicked back to Luke handing him water in the dance class and he really wanted to kiss Luke. Very hard. He shook away that thought. 'Interesting, how?' A nice change of subject from his ex, from Luke's birth mother, and now this. They really were covering all the bases tonight.

'Nothing. Just people, and how they relate to one another, and observing them this past week I've noticed stuff.'

'Stuff? Go on.' Paul was enjoying how Luke was finally opening up. Even if it wasn't about his own problems.

'Everyone's there for their own reasons, but they don't say why. Unless it sort of comes out when chatting. When they're unguarded.'

'Why am I there?' Paul asked, thinking, *This ought to be good. See if Luke has sussed me out.*

'You miss your cat, Rick,' Luke said, leaning back in his chair, balancing on the rear two legs.

Just like the cool boys at school. 'Correct. And?'

'That's it. You've not said much more. Travelling, dancing, that's you.'

And a controlling ex-boyfriend. 'Right,' Paul said, grateful he'd not mentioned George to the other volunteers, and only Luke, just now. He kept that vague when asked at the sanctuary. Not that many of them asked.

'Being single is easier,' Luke said.

'True.' After a pause, Paul went on, 'Or is it just a different sort of difficult? Compromise, waiting, sharing space.'

'If I was with my ex, I wouldn't have come here.'

If I was with my ex, I wouldn't have been allowed to the dance class. Paul swallowed as that thought trickled through his mind, imagining the battles he'd have had about it. The arguments they'd had. 'Why not?' *This ought to be interesting.*

'He liked to do stuff together. Got a bit antsy if we didn't. Not that he ever wanted to. I used to... but in the end it wasn't worth it.'

'Sounds delightful.' Paul couldn't think of anything worse. Except maybe an ex who forbade him from doing stuff. Like dancing, because it was too... much... gay... flamboyant.

'It was. Until it wasn't. So why do you volunteer there?' Luke narrowed his eyes at Paul.

'We were going to travel Europe for a few years. Digital nomad visas. We couldn't take the cat with us. So I had him adopted.'

'Whose cat was he?'

'I had him before I got with George.'

'So *he* made you give up *your* cat, and then you split up while travelling?'

'Pretty much.' God, it sounded dreadful when described in that way.

'Sounds delightful.' Luke smirked at repeating Paul's phrase.

'Nine months. Three countries. It wasn't bad. But it wasn't... that good either...' What they'd planned, hadn't been as enjoyable as he'd hoped. Sadness settled in his gut. He missed being part of a couple, not necessarily with

George himself, but the stability it seemed to give him. The status it seemed to afford them in their friendship circle. Paul and George, George and Paul.

'What was the final straw?' Luke asked.

Paul shook his head, unprepared to go there, quite so soon. 'Not now. Let's talk about you.'

'Not now.'

'What shall we do?'

Luke held Paul's hands as they rested on the table, stroked them, leaned forwards and pressed the lightest of kisses on Paul's lips.

Yes, well, this is a good idea. Paul closed his eyes, the firm lips pressing on his own, the scent of hair product and a freshly mown grass odour filled his senses. As desire uncoiled within his stomach, lust pooled in his lap, he pulled back. 'Sorry. I'm not. We're not. Not that. Not now. Not ever, in fact.'

Luke looked surprised. 'Never?'

'I'm giving it all a rest.' Even if one part of his anatomy very much wanted not to do so.

'What?'

'Dating.' *Be clear. Be strong. Be you.*

'I didn't think that's what *this* was going to be. I thought...' Luke waggled his eyebrows suggestively.

Not that Paul didn't think he'd enjoy himself, but after the last few times when he'd met men for a coffee and gone back to his place, or theirs, he'd been left feeling empty, like after eating fast food. As if he'd got what he wanted, but it ultimately turned out *not* to be what he needed.

'Don't you like sex?' Luke asked.

'Who doesn't?' Paul shrugged.

'Some people don't. But not you.'

'Not me.' Paul didn't want to say the line about spoiling their friendship because they hardly had one to spoil. It felt stupid saying he needed to guard his heart. Although that was closer to the truth. Nearer to what he allowed himself to say: 'I sort of do this thing where I fixate on someone, and ignore all their faults. It's why I stayed with George for so long.'

'He can't have been all bad?'

He really was. 'He was organised – controlling, had high standards – controlling, liked to lead – controlling, can you see a pattern?'

'Didn't you see it?'

'Didn't want to. Until I couldn't ignore what was in front of my face. I found a lump, down below. Saw a doctor, waited, went to hospital, waited more. During the whole thing, he didn't talk about it.'

'But it's your health, so that's a good thing, right?'

Paul shook his head. 'Not when I was talking about the next appointment, waiting for the test results, researching what an ultrasound entailed.'

'You're okay now?'

'Both bollocks, all present and correct.'

'Good.'

Not that you'll be seeing them any time soon. Paul narrowed his eyes, he would need to watch himself with Luke, who was obviously used to charming men into bed with as much effort as removing a yoghurt pot lid.

Not me. Not today. Not ever.

'Sorry,' Luke said, with contrition in his eyes. 'Earlier. Lizard brain reaction. I have a lot of feelings I need to have sex about. Shouldn't have. Bad idea. Instinct, but wrong. Sorry. Picked up a vibe from you, but it's obviously not the vibe I thought.'

I'm not going to fall for this guy and ignore all his faults. I will not do that. If I don't sleep with him, all will be well. Paul swallowed, looking away from Luke's azure-blue eyes. 'Totally understandable. So you're not leaving, but you can't stay, what's your plan?'

'Do you think Sasha wants me to stay?' Luke asked slowly.

'If she *really* wanted you to leave, you'd know.' Paul had seen her usher people off the premises if they had questionable motives for adopting a cat. So an unwanted son, he felt sure, she'd have sent away had she not, underneath, wanted to build a connection.

'I need to think about it. I don't want Sasha to see me as her problems and mistakes from thirty years ago, walking on two legs. I want...' Luke frowned.

'What *do* you want, when you boil it all down, what do you really want?' Paul asked, sensing Luke didn't know.

'She's told me why she put me up for adoption, and how she met my birth dad, but I'd like to know who my father was. Who *I* really am.'

'You're really you. Regardless of who he was, or wasn't.'

'I want to understand why I am me, this way.' A lost look flickered across Luke's face.

As far as Paul could see, Luke was sometimes messy and shambolic, but always, delightfully charming. 'I think you're great, whatever the reason.' Paul looked downwards. 'How about finding out who Sasha is first, and then you can move on to him, in time?' *If at all.*

Luke shrugged.

Paul stood, he'd had enough of this for one night. 'I'll leave that thought with you. See you tomorrow.'

A look of worry crossed Luke's face. 'Are you going?'

'Looks that way.' *If he asks me, I'll stay, but if he can't even make himself appear vulnerable and a bit helpless, then I'm not rescuing him.*

'It's a very big house. Ridiculously large. Four bedrooms. I'm in the front one. There's bedding for more. Load of sheets and pillowcases.' He raised his eyebrows.

'Interesting.'

'I'll behave myself.' Luke looked at the floor. 'Promise.'

Not that *all* of Paul wanted Luke to behave himself, if he relaxed into the lust he felt, but he said nothing. 'Right.'

'The back bedroom's very nice. It has three old computers piled up in the corner. You, as a digital nomad, will feel very at home. I believe.'

Is he going to actually ask me? 'I believe you might just be right.'

'Is that a yes?'

'I've not heard a question yet.' Paul was enjoying making Luke squirm slightly. *Make him become vulnerable and ask for help, when he clearly never usually needs it.*

Luke sighed loudly, stubbed the floor with his foot. 'Do you have plans tonight?'

'No.' Paul bit his bottom lip, stopping himself asking what he wanted Luke to ask.

'I shouldn't have lunged at you earlier. Sorry.'

'You said,' Paul replied, thinking he hadn't minded Luke's lunge at all. In fact, he'd quite enjoyed it. Was secretly hoping Luke would lunge again now. 'Well, if that's all, I'm going home.' He walked towards the door, opened it and stood on the drive, pausing before he stepped over to his car.

Having followed him, standing by the car, very quietly, Luke said, 'I wondered if you could, if it's okay, but it would be nice for you to...'

Paul turned, leaning against the car.

'You're enjoying this, aren't you?' Luke said with some frustration.

'What I fail to understand is how the same person who turned up in search of Sasha, is unable to ask *me* a simple question.'

Luke shrugged. 'I don't feel the same about *her* as *you*.'

This ought to be interesting. Paul grinned, mischief twinkling in his eyes. 'I see.' He walked towards Luke standing close to him. *He really is very handsome, in an obvious sort of main-character-in-a-movie sort of way. Ugh, cos that's like the worst sort of handsome. Not.*

In a very small voice, Luke finally said, 'Stay the night, would you?' He looked at the ground, his arms folded.

'I'd be delighted.' Paul walked through the door, Luke walking backwards, until pressed against a wall, they stood hungrily kissing. Paul was left in no doubt how Luke felt after that, how much he wanted Paul. The desire in Luke's eyes, the hardness in his trousers, left nothing to Paul's imagination.

And so, putting aside the worry that Luke would surely be careless with his heart and hurt him, Paul leaned into the moment, the joy of what was happening. Paul told himself he wouldn't let Luke play with his heart, and instead he'd let Luke play with the rest of his body, and decided he could do much worse than spending more time with Luke, especially if it involved a bed, and a distinct lack of clothing.

Chapter 18

The next morning, Anna arrived at her late parents' home, parked on the large drive, knocked on the door loudly, rang the bell, then entered using her key. *No answer, don't know why I'm knocking on my front door.* 'Anyone here?'

Two pairs of shoes in a heap by the door. She was sure Luke hadn't packed to stay. Unless he'd gone home first. Or bought some new shoes.

Crouching to inspect them, she decided neither pair was new.

Walking up the wide staircase, she called Luke's name. A shower was on, his bedroom door open, the bed unmade, clothes on the floor. Peering inside, there were two pairs of men's underpants on the floor. Two pairs of trousers, two T-shirts.

Interesting... although Luke isn't the tidiest of people, they're probably all his, as he's making himself at home.

Deciding she'd intruded enough, she crept downstairs, and sat at the kitchen table with a cup of coffee. She texted Luke: *I am in the kitchen. Wanted to check how you are.*

The shower stopped. Two sets of feet clomped across the landing, the bedroom door shut.

'SHIT!' Luke shouted from the bedroom.

Anna waited for a reply to her text.

None came.

She rotated the mug so the handle was lined up with the closest edge of the table. She pulled her hair a little as worry bubbled up within her.

Loud footsteps came down the stairs. Luke, looking flushed and embarrassed, stood with wet hair at the door. 'Didn't hear you.' He nodded upstairs. 'In the shower.'

'Alone?' She tried to sound as innocent as possible. Why was she the one feeling embarrassed? It was, after all, her house.

'Not quite.' He looked at the floor.

'Look, I'm not fussed. It's your life. Just don't make a habit of it. And I don't want any parties.'

'No danger of that.' He sighed, folded his arms across his chest. 'I think I'll go home soon. Leave Sasha to get used to the idea of me being in her life, rather than forcing it.'

Anna nodded. 'Very sensible. She's got a lot on her plate.'

'Everyone says. Do you know what else?'

Anna shrugged. 'Apart from the sanctuary being sold, no. She keeps her cards close to her chest. A closed book, is that woman.'

'Why are you here? Sorry, it's just I'm about to see Sasha.'

'I'm moving in,' Anna said proudly. It seemed the simplest solution.

'Here?'

'Well, unless you know any other properties I have.' She smiled, enjoying the red of his cheeks from whatever he'd been doing with whomever it had been in the shower earlier. It was so enviable how some people seemed to slide through life, without a single worry, playing it all by ear and everything turning out perfectly.

'What about your place?'

Anna shook her head. It was full of her belongings, and she was going to let it, but she needed to empty it, or find a storage facility. Next week. She'd do that then. 'I'm renting it out.' *I think.*

'Could I stay there?'

'It's not quite ready. A few finishing touches though. Besides, I thought you weren't staying here long.'

'No. You're right.'

'I just need to get something from the car. But do get on with your day. I can lock up afterwards.' She left, banging the door tightly shut.

Shortly, she returned to the house with a tape measure and a digital camera her father had bought her a few years ago. She wasn't sure how the camera connected to a computer, but she probably had the wires somewhere at home. In that drawer full of computer bits and pieces she'd kept, just in case. *Yeah, it'll definitely be in there.*

She opened the door.

Paul stood in the kitchen. Luke sat at the table, his head in his hands.

Anna walked into the room.

They turned to her, horror on their faces.

'I thought you'd gone,' Luke said with guilt written all over his face.

'I didn't say so. I need to measure up and take photos.'

'Why?'

'Sasha wants me to foster some cats in the spare rooms. Fluffy Paws is at capacity and she can't bear to think about stray cats who need our help waiting.'

'Have you owned cats before?'

Anna shook her head. 'Too much mess.'

'And you think this will be different, because?' Luke asked.

'I've been socialising this female cat and I think I was quite good at it. I'd like to do the same with another one. It's the only time I don't worry, or feel sad. So I think I'm going to sort of run towards that, rather than away. If that makes sense.'

'Sasha's idea?' Luke asked.

'Indeed.' Turning to Paul, she said, 'This could be really awkward, so I'm just going to ask it.' She knew the answer already. 'Why are you here?'

Paul blushed deep red. He pointed upstairs. 'Shower, bed, wine.' He shrugged.

'In that order?'

'Reverse, actually.' He made a yikes face. 'We were in the shower when you first came in. The water stays hot for ages, doesn't it? Very impressive. Is it a combi boiler or hot water tank? I ask because we must have been in there for a good twenty minutes—'

'Enough,' Anna said, putting her hand up to stop him while slightly grinning. 'I don't need you to draw me a diagram. Well, this is an interesting turn up for the books, isn't it? What do you think Sasha will think?'

'Like it's any of her business,' Paul said, rinsing his mug in the sink.

'You don't think she'll want to know her son and one of her staff are…' Anna pointed, waving her hand about a bit in an effort to gesticulate what was going on here.

'Do you want a lift in?' Paul asked Luke.

'Do you think maybe I ought to leave it for today? Back off a bit?' Luke made a pained expression.

Anna looked from one man to the other. 'She'll want to see you both. As soon as she knows. I suggest you follow me in.' Keeping secrets could tie one up in knots, and Anna didn't want to remember she had to keep this from Sasha. She'd tell Mim, ask *her* what was best.

'I thought,' Luke began, 'you were measuring up.'

'This takes precedence.' Anna put her clipboard under her arm. 'Best get it out in the open. If Sasha asks me I'd prefer not to lie to her face.' She'd done enough of that already.

Shortly after, they left the house and, in her car before they set off, Anna remembered what her morning was going to consist of, until she'd been dragged into this drama. She beeped her horn, shaking her head vigorously, admonishing herself for forgetting, for being swept up with the men's drama. *This is what happens when you don't stick to a rigid plan.*

'What?' Paul stood by her car door.

'I'm going to a storage place. For my home. Put everything in. I've got to sign up to it today, because I've got a discount code. Runs out tomorrow.' This would buy her time to sort through her parents' belongings and with the discount it was money well spent. She hoped.

'Go there first and we'll meet you at Fluffy Paws.'

'I've got an interview.'

'Haven't you got a job?'

'It's not really an interview, more like a chat. To see if I want it.'

'What?'

'Nothing much.'

'When?'

Anna checked the time. 'In an hour. I must go. Tell Sasha I'm sorry but I can't come today.'

'Good luck with the job interview.' Paul waved her off.

Anna left for the storage facility. The loan repayments had started, she really needed this job. The storage locker was more expensive than she'd anticipated. Maybe she should get rid of some of her belongings. Or put them all in her parents' house. Save a bit of money.

But where would she start, working out what to keep and what to do with the stuff she didn't want? As she turned that over in her mind, she arrived at her destination, an out-of-town industrial park of new car garages, small businesses, and parked next to an enormous grey corrugated metal building.

Later, after a tour of the facility, and after the employee, a pushy man in a yellow polo shirt and trousers, had explained how it worked, he stood next to the space she could rent for nearly her budget. It was the size of two large bedrooms at her parents' place. 'Do you want it or not?' he asked.

'Do I need to say now?' Already the anxiety built from the bottom of her stomach, tightening, sickening, up through her chest as if someone were pressing down on it.

'If you want the discount, yes. This deal is only for today. If you want it, you need to sign up today.'

Now. Since she had no time to return here today. 'Right.' She swallowed, her throat dry. Logically, she should say no, sort through her parents' and her own belongings, declutter and therefore need less space. But the thought of having to decide what to keep and discard of her late parents' lives was too much for her now. The cost of the storage locker was worth buying herself time.

Half an hour later, she left, feeling flustered and confused, having signed up to three months. She'd have everything sorted by then, wouldn't she?

Later that afternoon, the supermarket interview went well. 'I'm happy to do weekends.' Because she didn't work then for the doctor's surgery.

'References?' the woman interviewing her asked.

'I've got one from my neighbour. They've known me for years. It's a shame I'm leaving, but I'll keep the place. Still see them, I expect.' Another problem with letting her place.

'We'll need a professional reference.'

'What?' *What if The Grove Practice gives me a bad reference? What if they're pretending to think I'm good and really looking for any excuse to get rid of me?*

'Your previous employer. You said you're leaving them, wanting to cut your hours, fancied a bit of a change?'

She nodded, smiled. That was what she'd said. Minutes ago. And on her application form. 'Yes, I'll ask them.' *And work out how to explain I want a second job, when I only work there part-time.* Anna wanted a job that was easier, less stress, less responsibility than asking for more hours at The Grove Practice. They had suggested she apply for a full-time practice manager role, but the job description stressed her out, and writing the application would have taken hours, hours she didn't have, so she'd declined. *No, I need to keep these two jobs separate. In case they won't give me a reference. In case they say I'm not coping with my work at The Grove Practice with the rest of my life, including the supermarket job. Besides, it's none of their business anyway what I do in my spare time.* Admitting she needed a second source of income fell into the broad category of 'failing', which

Anna wanted to keep away from The Grove Practice and their impression she was organised and efficient at work.

She left, shaking the woman's hand, holding a letter with a conditional job offer.

A missed call from a number she recognised. Checking the message, she walked to her car, feeling exhausted from a busy day, and yet strangely dissatisfied. The storage locker man had probably taken advantage of her good nature, she wasn't sure she *really* needed that space, but it seemed too good to ignore the special offer. And how was she going to get a reference without any of her colleagues wondering why she wanted a second job?

She'd seen all of the doctors' signatures hundreds of times. She could write a reference, print it on the surgery's headed notepaper, sign it with an illegible scribble and the supermarket wouldn't know. They weren't going to call the doctor's surgery to check, were they?

The voicemail was Mim: 'Hi, Anna, it's Mim here, just checking you're all right. I wondered if you were okay. We missed your organisational strengths at work today. Anyway, give me a buzz, it would be lovely to hear how you're getting on.'

Anna deleted the message. Felt Mim had been somewhat fishing, a touch intrusive maybe. Just because Anna hadn't turned up at Fluffy Paws today, didn't mean she owed anyone an explanation. She was absolutely fine, didn't need anyone's help. Had everything absolutely under complete control. She could handle two jobs, and renting out her little house, and transferring her parents' life into the new storage locker, and volunteering at Fluffy Paws, perfectly well on her own. Far better than being dependent on others for help.

Chapter 19

Moulsham, Essex

Mim hadn't seen Anna at the sanctuary for a week or so. Anna had called to apologise for the first two instances, then just hadn't turned up. Mim had left a few messages, but hadn't heard anything. She had a bad feeling as she sat in her car one evening outside Anna's small home.

It felt a teensy bit stalkerish, Mim admitted to herself, as she stared at Anna's house, nestled in a curved road of a housing estate of newish homes on the edge of Chelmsford. The house had no lights, and Mim wondered where Anna's car was. But Mim knew her motives were good and she'd watched a documentary with all sorts of stories about people isolating themselves from friends and doing the worst thing, when they couldn't see any other way out. A permanent solution to a temporary problem. Less likely, as Anna wasn't in the demographic with the highest risk profile for taking their own life, but it was something that niggled in the back of Mim's mind.

Sasha had said to leave Anna alone, but in fairness, Sasha had her own issues to deal with.

It was very late and Anna was still not there. Hadn't she said something about moving into her parents' house? Sasha had said Anna was getting it ready to foster some of the cats they had no room to house at Fluffy Paws.

There had been some such drama about the long-lost son, Luke, and Paul. Anna texted something about Luke and Paul sleeping together and Anna had said she didn't want to keep it a secret, so what did Mim think she should do? But Mim had better things to worry about than keeping that a secret. She'd resolved to not lying if asked, but otherwise keeping this to herself. The gist of it she'd grasped was Luke and Paul had become acquainted *in the biblical sense* of knowing someone and now Paul was behaving as if nothing had happened, while Luke was moping about like a wet weekend.

'What on *earth* is the matter with you?' Mim had asked him that morning. 'And, while we're at it, how's Anna? I've not seen hide nor hair of her except a scant text.'

Luke had shaken his head, rubbed his large hand over his stubbly chin. 'Anna's never home. She's seems all right. Nothing's wrong with me.'

Mim sighed, and wondered why most men took such a lot of hard work to open up about their emotions. 'Then why,' she went on, 'do you look terribly miserable and why haven't you said a single word to Paul in the last week?'

'We fell out.'

'Over what, precisely?' *This ought to be good*, she thought, since she knew they'd slept together.

'A misunderstanding.'

'Involving?' *Goodness, this is like trying to get blood from a stone.*

'We'd had such a great night at Paul's dancing class. Back to his place, few drinks and...' Luke looked away, blushing.

'If you're embarrassed to tell me, because I'm an old fogey, let me assure you, I've heard it all before. Almost four decades of working with holiday reps in Spain and there's nothing, and I do mean nothing, that will shock me.'

'He danced so well. Like, almost professional-well. It showed me another side of him I hadn't appreciated. I was a bit sad about Sasha and how much I'd ballsed it up. We'd had a great evening, dancing, got all hot and sweaty, had a drink round at Anna's place to sort of cool down and...'

'Got all hot and sweaty again? Cool down, you did not, I'm presuming?' Mim said. She didn't need to tell him she'd heard as much from Anna.

Luke nodded, staring at the concrete ground of the cat pen.

'And presumably one of you was more into it than the other?' she guessed airily, not wanting to *quite* get into the ins and outs of their ins and outs, but feeling it needed establishing in terms of why Luke was so down in the mouth.

Luke shook his head. 'The night was awesome. Like' – he looked out of the corner of his eye – 'really good. Both of us were really into it. But the morning after, he went very cold.'

'How so?'

'I, wrongly I now know, assumed he'd want to at least have another date, start seeing each other. We'd had such a connection at the dance class. But apparently, as far as Paul was concerned, not.'

'Not?'

'Not,' Luke said. 'I said I'd fancied him almost from when we first met. He blushed at that. Then I stupidly said, must have been post-sex hormones making me dumb, that I thought we worked together and did he want to go out for dinner that night. That I—' Luke stopped himself, shut his eyes, shook his head. 'God, why am I such a monumental twat?'

'Love, lust, and everything in between is my guess.' Mim asked carefully, 'You asked him out for dinner, and then what?'

'I didn't exactly ask him to move in with me, but I might as well have done. God. I'm an idiot?'

'Wearing your heart on your sleeve can be a very attractive quality.' *At the right time*, she thought.

'I said I really liked him, more than just fancied him, like really *really* liked him. Might as well have said the other L word. And he went quiet.'

'Quiet, how so?'

'Slipped out of bed, dressed in the bathroom and didn't want breakfast together, then left.'

'Aha.' *That really is quite the fight-or-flight reaction.* 'And since?'

'Since, I've had my heart crushed, feel like a monumental idiot and don't know what to do.'

Mim coughed. It had all felt so much simpler when she was their age. Or perhaps she was lucky since David had never been the sort of man to play games. If he said he'd call the next day after a date, he called. If he said they'd see each other on Thursday, they indeed did so. But all this bed-hopping and pretending one didn't have feelings for someone you'd just slept with. Mim couldn't get her head around it. Not wanting to judge Paul and Luke for whatever casual arrangement they'd had, since they were both consenting adults, Mim simply said, 'If you give it time, these things sometimes work themselves out.'

'You think?'

'Seen it hundreds of times before, when I was repping in Spain. Holiday romances, trysts between colleagues. If it's worthwhile it'll come to something. If something is for you, it won't pass by you, is I believe the saying. If not...' She let that hang there since the alternative, especially from Luke's perspective, was somewhat less palatable than what she'd said.

He looked very lost, which for someone of his appearance struck Mim as odd. She'd wrongly assumed men of such stature and prepossessing appearance would be spoilt for romantic attachments.

She patted his shoulder. Better than saying more on that subject. It struck her Luke would possibly have done better focusing on his relationship with Sasha than this, whatever *this* was, with Paul. But she bit her tongue. 'You're very charismatic.'

'I didn't think I'd feel this hurt. Snubbed. Used.'

'Give it time.' After a pause, she said, 'Want to play with some kittens?'

'That sounds good.' His face lit up with a smile.

A smile Mim felt, no doubt, had broken a fair few hearts, and would break more in future. Just like in Spain, she felt energised, youthful by spending time with people younger than herself. As with the young people from Fluffy Paws. And that time she'd video called with Henry and his family had been a welcome disturbance from her solitary thoughts. Tilly was joyful, unfiltered, innocent, and Mim loved her almost instantly. Far from being painful spending time with them, as it had been at an age when she could have had children, now, as the grandmother figure, it was a salve to her soul. Keeping her youthful, enthusiastic for life in all its complexity and mess.

She had led Luke to the correct pen, let him in, and left him socialising a litter of ginger kittens that had been found in a cardboard box in a forest by a dog walker. They'd all been weaned then left there. If they hadn't been found, god alone knew what would have happened.

Now, Mim decided in her car, as it was dark, late and she felt cold, Anna wasn't coming home. Perhaps she'd moved into the big house. Mim's hand was on the ignition key, poised to drive off.

Anna's car pulled up, stopped outside the house. The headlights were switched off.

Mim waited for Anna to get out, but nothing. Deciding she'd had enough of waiting for Anna this evening, Mim knocked on the window of Anna's car.

Anna was crouched forwards, leaning on the steering wheel. She jumped, turned towards the window. 'You made me jump. What are you doing here?'

Mim opened the door. 'I was worried. Where have you been this late?' She knew Anna seldom went out, particularly at night, preferring instead to stay in, watch TV and clean her home.

'Work.' Anna stood, slammed the car door shut. She wore a beige polo shirt pinned with a name badge. Underneath was a supermarket's name.

'Don't you work in a hospital?' Mim narrowed her eyes in confusion. *Something's not right here.*

'Doctor's surgery.'

'And this?' Mim pointed at Anna's name badge.

Anna's bottom lip stuck out, her eyes filled with tears. No sound came from her mouth. She stood, shaking, as Mim led her indoors, quickly made her a hot, sweet cup of tea in the small kitchen.

'I couldn't afford the loan,' Anna said.

'Loan? But you own an enormous house, don't you?' This, Anna's mess, Mim feared would have very possibly grown arms and legs, threatening to entangle the poor woman.

'The care home wanted their money.' Anna leaned in front of the oven, sipping her tea.

'Right.' Mim feared this would be worse than she'd at first thought.

In the tiny kitchen, Anna told her, slowly, about the loan, the second job, that she'd faked her references from the doctor's surgery and about the storage locker she didn't need but had signed up for a three-month contract she didn't seem able to cancel. After a sniff and a shaken head, Anna said, 'I've been working ten to four at the surgery, Monday to Friday, having a Mars bar, then five to midnight most evenings at the supermarket.'

'No time for Fluffy Paws, I presume?' Hence why she'd not seen Anna there. As suspected, this was a mess that Anna had got into that reached every part of her life. Clearly, Anna was very unwell. Her mental health was making her take bad decisions, jeopardise aspects of her life.

Anna shook her head. 'I needed a job where I could do lots of hours, more than I could have ever worked at The Grove Practice, but less mentally taxing than working there.'

She wished she'd shared her opinion when Anna had mentioned the loan, but that ship had sailed and Mim needed to deal with the problem in front of her friend, so she asked with care, 'Show me the paperwork for the loan, please?'

Anna returned, led them to the small sitting room, laying it out on the coffee table. It was worse than she'd imagined, double-figure interest rates, ten years to pay it back.

Mim sat next to her on the small sofa. 'Didn't you know how much it would cost each month?' Mim asked, in near incredulity.

'I needed to give the care home some of the money owed, to tide them over, so I still went ahead with this loan.'

Oh god, honestly what a mess! She really is very poorly. 'Why didn't you tell someone?'

'I can't say anything at work, because they were so good to me when Mum and Dad were dying. I couldn't ask them for more. Not after how they'd helped me. I wanted to show them I could cope.'

'Can you?' Mim asked, knowing the answer.

Anna shook her head, sadness crossed her expression, a sense of feeling very lost, like a small child who'd done something very wrong, but had no idea how to fix it. 'I couldn't ask them for references. I don't like to bother them. Wanted to keep the two parts of my life separate. In case they didn't give me a reference. I don't think they want me there. Only putting up with me since I've been there so long. Any excuse to get rid of me, I reckon. Besides, it's funny, me working part-time there and getting more hours at the second job.'

'Couldn't you have asked for more work at the practice?' Mim asked carefully.

'I didn't want them to know I was struggling. With money. Failing. They might think I'm ungrateful. I'm not. They think I'm well off. They know about the house, and some of them suggested I sell it. But I can't. I didn't want to get into all that with them. In case…' Anna pursed her lips, a look of serious worry crossing her face.

'In case what?' Mim asked.

'Mental health. I've seen what doctors can do. I didn't want any of that. I'm fine.'

Mim could see Anna was very far from being fine. Her heart broke for this poor woman. It was so sad, Anna's delusions, paranoia and lack of rational thought. Yet she couldn't see how irrational she was being. This was very bad.

Anna brightened, forcing on a slightly brittle-looking smile. 'I'll be fine. It'll all sort itself out in the end, won't it?'

Mim shook her head gravely. 'I'm afraid with things like this, based on experience, it very much will not.'

'What should I do?' Anna looked very small and child-like, sitting cross-legged on the chair, tears staining her cheeks, hunched forwards, as if she'd had the weight of the world on her shoulders. 'I want my mum.'

Happy to be a second-best alternative, Mim pulled her into a hug, sitting at the kitchen table, rocking back and forth, stroking her head. 'It'll be okay. Trust me.' She said it with as much confidence as she could muster, but even she wasn't sure quite how to disentangle the mess Anna had got herself into.

Later, after more tea and small talk, and a little bit of TV together, which seemed to calm Anna, Mim hugged her goodbye, left her calmer and promised her she'd sort it all out. She took the paperwork and returned home to South Hanningfield.

David walked down the stairs, bleary eyed, in his pyjamas, worried. 'Where on earth have you been?'

Mim bustled past, placing the paperwork on their dining room table. 'Sorry to wake you. A friend in need.'

'Who?' David said, looking confused, following her.

'Anna. From the cat sanctuary.'

'Why do you *always* have to get involved?'

'Because,' Mim said, with a great deal of feeling, 'it's *who* I am. It's *what* I do.' Was it because they had no children, or was it just her wanting to help others? She'd never know. A bit of both, probably. 'And I'd hope that by now you'd know this about me, and be supportive.' She heard the terseness in her tone and didn't regret it.

Pulling her into a hug, he kissed her hair, said, 'Let the dog see the rabbit.' He made them coffee.

They worked until well into the small hours, checking the figures, trying to make them balance, thinking up options for Anna, until finally they went to bed.

Mim was grateful for David's support and ideas for what had felt, at some points, in Anna's home, earlier that night, like a problem without a possible solution.

Chapter 20

Luke had arrived at the cat sanctuary early, he'd fallen into some sort of routine. Sasha didn't want him to leave, or at least she'd not told him so. They'd fallen into something of a friendly relationship, both steering clear of the conversation about his birth father. But as he worked alongside Sasha more, he began to see parts of himself in her: his desire to help others, the importance of family and friendships.

He knocked on the house's front door, waiting for Sasha to answer.

'I hope you're ready for a busy day,' she said with a smile, letting him in.

'Why?' He stood in the airy, tiled hallway.

She walked to the large, well-lit area he knew everyone called the humans' kitchen. 'Three collections this morning, and we have twice as many adoptions to process this afternoon.'

'That's good, isn't it?'

She shrugged, handing him a coffee. 'You'll need this.'

They drove to the first call, parking outside the house. A woman had seen a long-haired black cat in her back garden and had been feeding it for a while. She showed

190

them the shed where she had fed the cat last night and kept it in, on Sasha's request.

The cat was in a very poor state: matted fur, almost just skin and bone. It lay in the bed in the shed, sniffing the air.

Without very much fuss, they coaxed it into a cat carrier.

'How long have you been feeding it?' Sasha asked the woman.

'Since we moved in. Few months ago. Apparently, the people who lived here before had been doing it for years.'

Sasha sighed, closing her eyes. 'Thanks.'

They left, Luke carrying the cat in the small metal cage. He placed it in the back of the van. 'What's wrong?'

Sasha shook her head. 'Months, if not years, the previous owner of that house had been feeding this poor cat. It's as plain to anyone who can see this cat isn't well. It needs more than feeding.' She used a colourful feather-covered fake bird toy to get the cat's attention, moving it outside the cage. Shaking her head, she said, 'He's blind. How can someone not realise that?' She sighed. 'We'll call him Jessie.'

Luke made a note, then started the ex-post office van, with Fluffy Paws painted on its pinky-red bodywork. 'Is it always this difficult? It's a good job you all do. Carry on going when it's hard like this.'

'We have to. Because who else will care for these poor cats? Anyone who thinks it's all fluffy kittens will be sorely disappointed very swiftly.'

They sat in silence as he drove, following the satnav to the next address, which was a vet's practice.

Luke parked the van. 'Shall I wait in here with the cat?' he asked cautiously.

'If you'd like. This one won't take long. Take a breather.' She shut the van door.

Luke turned, the black cat was meowing quietly. Probably hungry. A bit of his heart broke for the poor creature. He wanted to help, but he didn't know if he could handle the pain and sadness.

Before he had time to consider that any further, Sasha returned with a long-haired mainly white cat with black markings. He meowed loudly. She settled him in the back, next to the black cat. 'Are you okay, or would you like me to drop you off? This work is difficult and sad, I know.'

Luke turned to face the back of the van. 'Why's she here?'

'He,' Sasha said, with not an inconsiderable sigh, 'was surrendered by his owner.'

'Too ill?'

'Too poor.' Sasha bit her bottom lip. 'I could say more, but I won't. It's not for us to judge why people surrender their cats. All I know is this beautiful boy shouldn't be PTS.'

'PTS?'

Sasha tapped the dashboard. 'Let's get going, please.' She leaned forwards, put the next address in the satnav app on her phone that sat in a holder, stuck to the windscreen.

Luke set off.

'His owner was an elderly man. Pensioner. Didn't look like he had a lot of money. That cat had a blocked bladder. The owner asked the vet to put him to sleep. PTS.'

Luke swallowed. 'Right.' A pause as he thought. 'And the vet didn't?'

'Called me. I've paid the vet's bill, the elderly man has signed over the cat to our care.' She shook her head. 'He was very apologetic. Said he wished he could afford it, but he can't.'

'How much?'

'Fifteen hundred pounds. Catheterisation, X-rays, medication, it all adds up.'

'So he's all right now, the cat?' Luke asked, really wanting the answer to be yes.

'He'll be on special food for the rest of his life. Just in case. All because a stupid human did this to him.'

'His owner?' Luke asked with horror.

'He lived in a block of flats, used to come and go through the front door, the old man lived on the ground floor near the entrance. Someone kicked the cat as they entered the flats.'

Luke couldn't understand why anyone would hurt someone else's loved pet. Sometimes he despaired for people, the human race. He told Sasha.

'I agree. But not all people are like that. Some are very kind and caring.'

Luke nodded slowly. 'Same reason why I don't follow much of the news,' he said, after a while driving in silence. 'It's like a showcase of the worst of human beings.'

'Me neither, I've much better things to be doing than watching the news. Too depressing.'

'This cat, the black-and-white one, he'll be okay now the vet's done what needs doing?'

'He should live a long and happy life. Eating special food, but apart from that, totally normal.'

That someone would destroy a cat, for financial reasons, Luke found hard to believe. But he knew his parents, although not rich, hadn't been poor. He supposed people with limited budgets would have to prioritise animals or themselves or their children. And it was easy to see why some decisions were made.

Luke drove and they were soon out of Essex and into east London, next to a twenty-storey block of flats. There were three concrete tower blocks in a line, off a busy A-road, each grey, with tatty-looking green and blue cladding beneath the windows.

A tall woman in a white blouse and blue skirt emerged from a car and met them at the flat's entrance. 'Fluffy Paws?'

'People tend to call me Sasha.' She held her photo ID for the woman to see.

'Linda Sherfield. Who's he?' She nodded at Luke.

'One of my volunteers.'

Pride swelled in Luke's chest. It was certainly better than being asked to leave, or ignored. He was, despite Sasha's best efforts, trying to build a relationship with her.

'I don't think you should come in,' the woman said to Luke. 'I'm a social worker. The little girls'... The dad can be a bit...' Worry crossed her face. 'I think he's encouraging the girls to play with the kittens too roughly. He should be okay with two women. I worry that if he sees a man he may...' She smiled awkwardly. 'Punch first and ask questions later.' She grimaced.

'Shouldn't you have the police here?' Luke asked, taking in the risk of the situation.

'If you're happy to wait a month of Sundays, then yes. But otherwise it's down to us two.'

Sasha held a wicker basket with a caged door at one end. 'And this.' She turned to Luke. 'Wait here.'

All his protectiveness, his desire to help, his masculine pride, surged through him, coursing through his veins as he tensed his muscles, unconsciously puffing himself up to his full height, setting his shoulders back, holding his head high. 'Are you going to be all right?' He looked from Sasha to the social worker and back.

'No guarantees, I'm afraid.' Sasha looked to Linda.

'I know the family. I've been working with them for months. I've got the mum's trust. The little girls' too. Not the dad, but I understand what agitates him. And a man like you…' She looked Luke up and down. 'Let's just say *you're* not going to defuse the situation.'

'Okay?' Sasha asked him.

'It's got to be, hasn't it?' It felt like a very unsatisfactory decision, but he understood why.

Linda nodded. 'First call will be the police; second call will be you. Promise.'

It hardly inspired him with confidence. Worry tasted bitter in his mouth. Impotence at not being able to do anything settled in his gut.

Linda buzzed the flat, said who she was and why they were here. They slipped through the main entrance.

Luke couldn't sit. He could barely stand. His birth mum and a social worker were inside that building and probably in danger and if he entered he'd definitely agitate the situation, so instead he had to remain outside, completely useless.

He wondered if his birth father had liked animals, had any pets.

Sometime later, the main door slammed and Linda and Sasha stood outside. Linda held her clipboard under her arm and Sasha held the cat carrier with one hand.

'What happened?' Luke asked with anxiety bubbling in his stomach.

'*She* was magnificent.' Sasha nodded at Linda.

Linda smiled. 'You weren't too bad yourself. Is there any paperwork I need to complete?'

'You've got enough of that with the two children. We've got it from here.'

Linda waved, returning to her car then driving off.

Safely in the van, the third cat carrier in the rear, with three kittens meowing loudly in a more high-pitched cry than the two adult cats, Luke said, 'Can we eat something?'

'I think we deserve it. Once we're back at the ranch.' She grinned.

Her ability to smile and make light of such a grim situation was very impressive and enviable. He hoped some of that would rub off on him.

'I always wanted a ranch. Like in *Dallas*. I used to watch it as a child in the Eighties. It was meant for adults, but I was allowed to watch it if Dad was working late.'

Luke started the van and set off. 'A ranch of cats?' He was enjoying her sharing some of her childhood. Giving him a glimpse into who she was.

'Horses. I used to dream of having my own. But Dad didn't let me. Well, I doubt we could have afforded it even if I was allowed.' She paused. 'I used to help look after the horses at a nearby stable, and there was a very handsome older man who worked there, mucking them out. As soon as Dad found out he stopped me going.'

'Older?'

'He was twenty-ish. I was fifteen.'

Luke grimaced. 'Possibly for the best.'

'Who knows what would have happened otherwise? Well, I can think of one end result. You wouldn't be here.'

He didn't like the sound of that. 'Did you used to ride the horses?'

'Sometimes. Not too often. I just liked being with them. Helping look after them. It felt like good, honest, worthwhile work, you know?'

As someone who'd not had much to do with animals, but liked them, he could understand the sentiment. He nodded. 'Yeah.'

'Thanks to Dad, I stopped going to the stables, shortly after I turned sixteen and we went on the holiday when I met your dad.'

Luke had heard the first part of how they'd met, but she'd held back how he had seduced her, how a sixteen-year-old had ended up pregnant. 'What was he like?'

'Just like you. You've got all that from him not me. Short, plump, pale genes from me.' She laughed.

They arrived at Fluffy Paws, Luke turned the engine off. 'Was he an animal lover?'

'I think so. There were cats hanging around his restaurant. He fed them. I don't know for sure.' She looked out of the window. 'There's a lot I don't know about him. I suppose that's what happens when you only see someone for a few days.'

Luke waited for her to open the door, start collecting the meowing cats and take them to the main building for admission.

She did not. 'It was, in some ways, the perfect relationship,' Sasha said wistfully. 'None of the boring everyday drudge, just the interesting, romantic, fun part.' A pause, and then, 'He recognised me in the bar, then helped me back to the hotel after I was left alone, when the others had disappeared. He asked if I wanted him to show me the real Sorrento, away from the touristy bits.'

Luke grinned, it was the sort of chat-up line he'd had used on him while holidaying. He'd fallen for it hook, line and sinker. Gladly.

'I said I'd have to ask my parents,' Sasha went on. 'I didn't. I told them I'd met a girl my age and we were going out for the day. Mum and Dad were *very* trusting.'

Luke sensed some latent guilt behind that.

'Too trusting, as it goes. But hindsight's a wonderful thing, isn't it? We had a wonderful day, your birth father and me, he held doors for me, took me to the best cafes, restaurants. We visited a church where his sister had married. He introduced me to his family, who ran the restaurant. They didn't speak English and I didn't speak Italian, but somehow, we understood one another.' Her voice cracked slightly, stopping her from talking.

'Don't go on. If it's too painful.' Luke put a hand on her shoulder.

Sasha sat up. 'It's fine. I'm fine.' She coughed, and then: 'It was in the evening, at the end of that perfect day, when he said, "I would like to see you tomorrow." And I wanted to see him again but knew my parents would get suspicious. I told him. I yawned and he said, "I must take you back to your hotel." I didn't want to return. Not until I'd kissed him.'

'So you kissed him?' Luke asked with care.

'I wanted and did much more than that. I didn't always look like this. I was younger than you. Hormones fizzing through my veins. Lust rising as the temperature rose and I fell in love with Italy and an Italian man who was perfect. For that holiday anyway.'

This came as a surprise to Luke. He'd expected to hear how Sasha had been seduced. But when she described it, he realised that Sasha had seduced his birth father as much as he'd seduced her, and it was just that his father had let Sasha take it at her own pace.

'I asked him for a coffee,' Sasha went on, 'I yawned and when he placed it on the table, I pulled him closer, and kissed him. He didn't stop, and I forgot who I was, where I was, I only wanted one thing.'

'And he gave it to you?'

'We gave it to each other,' she said with feeling and eyes shining at the memory. 'I stayed the night, told my parents a terrible lie about how my friend had become very drunk and we'd had to stay in her room that night in case she was sick. I did the walk of shame the next morning, back from his place. I felt as if I looked different. Now I was a woman. I blushed as I lied to my parents.'

It sounded very romantic to Luke. Even if it involved lying, but what teenager hadn't lied to their parents at one point? He told her. 'Did you see him again?'

'The last night. Our schedules didn't line up. Plus I didn't want to arouse suspicion. Mum and Dad didn't ask about this friend with the hangover who they'd never seen. Perhaps they knew.' Sasha shrugged. 'Our last night I asked to go to his restaurant, as a family, and he was so pleased to see me he treated us like royalty. After he'd been charming and attentive to Mum and Dad, I said I wanted to go for a walk alone on the final night.' Sasha smiled. 'He said he'd make sure I returned back to the hotel safely. I went for a walk with your father. But we didn't do much walking.' Her eyes lit up at the memory.

Luke chuckled. He stupidly forgot that people his parents' age had been horny teenagers too, just like him. 'Nice.'

'We exchanged addresses, no emails back then. I wrote him a letter but he didn't reply. Then a few months later, I found out I was pregnant. Didn't know what was happening at first. Forgot when I was due and another month passed. Gaining weight, feeling a bit sick in the morning. I thought it was continuing to grow into a woman. It was. Didn't know I was expecting. Until it was too...' She opened the van's door.

'Late?' Luke said under his breath, wanting to ask if she'd known, would she have had an abortion. But he knew that was both pointless and unnecessarily cruel.

Sasha opened the van's rear doors, avoiding his gaze. 'Can you give me a hand with these cats, please?'

They carried the cages containing the cats into the sanctuary. There was much activity and commotion as people commented on the poor state of Jessie. They confirmed he was blind, but with care and treatment he would make someone a wonderful indoor cat and be very grateful to live out his days like that, rather than crouching under a hedge in someone's back garden.

The black-and-white cat who'd had the blocked bladder was called Domino, and they said they'd wait to name the kittens until they knew more about their personalities.

Chapter 21

Wickford, Essex

That afternoon, Sasha had been in the seating area in the largest outhouse containing a large proportion of the cat pens, processing half a dozen adoptions as people collected their cats, taking them to their forever homes. There was an adoption agreement, explaining the individuals agreed to pay for further care and treatment for the cat, as they were responsible.

Sasha knew people would get out of it if they could, but it made it at least feel more official than simply handing over the cats with a wave and a goodbye.

It had been a busy but fruitful afternoon. Sasha couldn't keep her news to herself any longer. She gestured for Luke to join her, feeling they'd bonded after that morning in the van.

'What?' he asked.

'I'm not good with bad news.'

'And I'm much better?' He raised his eyebrows. 'What is it?'

'It's not good.'

'Is it easier if you tell me and then I tell everyone? Presumably, it's to do with this place.'

She told him about the landlord wanting to demolish the cat pens. 'He wanted to do it much earlier, but I persuaded him to wait. Apparently, they're putting off buyers. He's going to pull them down in the next few weeks. I've begged him for some more time, but he said he's given me plenty of that already. He's arranging for someone to do it now. Very soon.'

'What are we going to do?' Luke asked.

'No idea. Which is kind of why I'm telling everyone. I've run out of options.' She'd run out of options a month or so ago, but didn't say.

'If you need help, just ask,' he said.

It seemed very simple, but usually Sasha tried everything to manage on her own before asking for help as the last resort. She looked at the floor. 'It makes me feel as if I've failed.' She couldn't keep the sadness out of her voice.

Luke shook his head, squeezed her shoulder. 'That's not how it works. Not with friends. Or family. Trust me.'

She'd never considered it that way before. The failure that had lodged in her guts seemed to shift slightly.

'Do you want me to tell everyone, or you?' Luke asked with kindness.

The failure seemed to shrink, the shame at needing to ask for help was still there, but much smaller. She knew she should do it, but still couldn't shake the niggling doubt that it made her look incompetent, incapable. 'I'm the big cheese here and I should be able to deal with it. With anything, right?'

'Except when you can't. Because you're not Wonder Woman. Even if you try to be.'

She nodded slowly. He'd totally summed her up. 'I *like* being Wonder Woman.' It made her feel valued, in charge, knowledgeable. If she couldn't study to be a veterinary nurse, she needed this at least as her castle, her kingdom, where she knew everything and sorted out all problems.

'I bet even *she* asks for help every now and then.'

Sasha couldn't remember if this was true, it had been a long time since watching the TV show as a child, but she understood Luke's sentiment. 'If you tell everyone, I'll take questions.' The latter felt less splashy and more practical, which suited Sasha just fine.

'I'm happy to help, but it might be better coming from you,' he said carefully.

Knowing she was beaten and he was, slightly irritatingly, right, as she realised he often was about this sort of thing, she nodded. 'Fine.'

Luke gathered everyone around, announced Sasha had something to tell everyone.

Once she had silence, Sasha said, 'As you all know, the landlord is selling. And you know he's going to pull down the outbuildings. I begged him to wait, but he's doing it in the next few weeks. No extension to that. Said he's losing out to buyers cos they're there. I've tried looking for alternative accommodation, but it's basically impossible. Nowhere near is suitable. Any possible places won't allow animals or they're earmarked for redevelopment as residential property.'

'Because,' Mim said, 'apparently, the only thing we need in this country is homes. No infrastructure, no community facilities. Just overpriced tiny housing units.'

'Indeed. I found somewhere suitable.' Sasha shot Mim a look.

'Great,' Luke said.

'In Yorkshire. A large barn we could convert into cat accommodation. A farmhouse where I could live. Except I don't want to.' Her roots were in Essex, she knew everyone. She'd made it her home for most of her adult life and starting again, as well as setting up Fluffy Paws afresh, felt too much. She knew she was unequal to it.

'We'll hold a sit-in,' Mim said with enthusiasm. 'Just like a CND protest. I'll round up all my CND friends and the landlord won't know what to do.'

'What about a campaign on the socials?' Paul asked.

'What about it?' Sasha asked.

'If I can raise twenty grand in a few weeks we must be able to do something.'

Mim raised her hand. 'If I may, I've been ruminating about this for some time. Looking through your finances it occurred to me, it's very apparent what your biggest costs are, after vets.'

'Right,' Sasha said. 'And?'

'The rent on this place.'

'I don't follow,' Sasha said.

Mim nodded. 'I do have one option.' She paused, in obvious thought. 'A *virtual* cat sanctuary.'

Anna frowned. 'How would that work?'

'A network of volunteers who take cats into their homes.'

'No building?'

'Wouldn't require one.' Mim shook her head.

'I see,' Anna said with undisguised disappointment.

'Temporarily, until we find somewhere permanent.'

'Unless,' Anna went on.

'What?' Sasha asked.

'Even I acknowledge I don't need two houses. I've decided I can't sell Mum and Dad's so I shall sell mine.'

'Good for you,' Mim said, patting Anna's back. 'But I think we have a somewhat more pressing issue to deal with.'

Sasha smiled at Mim, glad she'd persuaded Anna to return. 'I don't think the landlord will *actually* evict us. And it'll take months for a sale to go through, so we could retain some of the cats in the house. But it's nowhere near big enough for them all, once the pens are demolished.' However, she realised with a slow, plodding sadness, it would not resolve itself of its own accord. The landlord was selling, and they didn't have the funds to purchase the sanctuary off him. He was also definitely pulling down the outbuildings as soon as possible.

'I'll sell my little house and I wondered,' Anna said, 'how would it be if I gave you the money?'

'It would be very generous. But totally unnecessary. It's your money. To do with as you wish. And oughtn't you repay your loan first?'

'Of course. And if I want to give the rest to you, then what should I do?' Anna asked quietly.

'Where will you live?'

'My parents' home. Besides, I've got two jobs. I have plenty of money.'

'I think,' Mim said, 'that's a matter of opinion.'

Anna looked from person to person, with worry clouding her face. 'It's my money. This place is very dear to me. I look forward to my time here. It's my oasis of calm. We save the cats, but I also think they save us too. In their own ways.'

There were nods and murmurs of agreement.

'This is me paying for my animal therapy. Repaying the cats for helping me,' Anna went on, 'I know what you're thinking. You think I'm not well enough to make a decision like this. Well, you're wrong. I'm absolutely fine. Very well in fact. It's being here that's made me so well.'

There was silence.

Anna went on, 'I'm not happy my parents are no longer with us. Of course not. However, they're no longer suffering, slipping away from me, day by day. I want to do something positive, that's bigger than me, with the money from selling my small home. My parents would approve.'

'It's very generous of you, but it's absolutely unnecessary. We'll find another way,' Sasha said with a confidence she didn't feel. 'I shan't hear another word about it. This is my problem and it's for me to solve.'

Anna shook her head, walked away, slipping into a large cage, where she sat on the ground, stroking a chunky long-haired ginger cat. She looked serene and happy, Sasha reflected. Certainly different from how she'd appeared on her first day at Fluffy Paws, worried about everything, and exhausted.

But even if Anna felt the cats *had* saved her, Sasha knew she couldn't accept that sum of money, not from a woman who was still clearly very mentally fragile and risked making poor decisions. She was always grateful for the volunteers' help, but this went way above and beyond.

No, as Sasha had said, this was her problem and she would solve it herself.

Mim's virtual cat sanctuary idea sounded interesting, if temporary, but Sasha had no idea how it would work, on a practical, day-to-day basis. Perhaps she could ask Mim to explain it to her in more detail. It certainly felt better than worrying about it all herself.

Chapter 22

'I suppose you know what happened with me and Luke?' Paul asked, not looking away from the computer screen in the office in Sasha's place.

'Of course,' Mim replied, calmly. 'I saw you two weren't talking.'

It was quite a while after the night he'd shared with Luke. He and Mim were dealing with the last set of homing enquiries, having briefly closed for new admissions. Some of the pens had been demolished and the cats were in Sasha's house, slightly more crowded than was ideal, but as Paul had said to Sasha, their whole situation was far from ideal.

Paul said, 'I didn't mean for it to happen. I was thoroughly resigned to being single. Preferring it, in fact. And then...'

'Luke arrived?' Mim said.

And all our clothes seemed to magically fall off. 'I absolutely didn't see him coming. That night, after the dance class... Quite,' Paul said, not wanting to get into the whys and wherefores, the albeit pleasurable ins and outs, because he didn't fully understand them himself. He'd resigned to not settle down again, not after how disastrously it had gone with George, and then, well, then Luke had arrived, being handsome, and charming and almost bloody well perfect. And then they'd slept together and Paul had fixated on Luke, knowing it was unhealthy, and so had denied it vehemently and ignored Luke, despite his best efforts at charming Paul.

'He asked me to stay the night. But not after a lot of pushing. God, that man's persistent, and charming. And I was fully intending on sleeping in the spare room. But then—'

'Then?' Mim asked.

'He kissed me. And while he was kissing me, he undressed himself, so he was standing there, naked, very much enjoying our kisses. I was still fully dressed.' It had felt odd for a brief moment, then Paul found it very erotic. Very sexy. Almost as if Luke wanted Paul to have all the power. 'I think he knew what he was doing.'

'I'm sure he did.'

'I have never wanted anything more in my whole life than what I wanted at that moment, in that bedroom with Luke.' And god, had he wanted it. Paul had been so entranced by Luke's body he hadn't been able to take his eyes off him.

His muscular arms and legs Paul had seen during the dance class, but the rest of his body... magnificently masculine were the only words Paul had to describe it. Paul was wholly unprepared to see Luke so naked and so close that night. Luke's torso had black hair covering his stomach and pectoral muscles, they were so hard, Paul remembered.

Luke had stood smiling, watching Paul looking at him, still fully dressed. 'Do you want me to undress you?' Luke had said.

Paul couldn't speak, his throat was so tight, his underwear tighter as lust strained to escape, he nodded.

Standing close, facing Paul, Luke undressed him slowly. Between each garment he carefully laid on the bed, Luke kissed him, his lips hard, his mouth open and the memories of them dancing scuttled across Paul's mind.

Finally, when Paul thought he was about to burst with lust, pure animal desire, Luke pressed his chest against Paul's and the chest hair sent electrical desire through Paul's stomach, down, to his groin. Their hips were close as the hardness of their desire jostled, pushed against each other.

Paul blushed at the memory. Luke had laid Paul down and after reaching for a silver packet in his wallet, protected them, and then so thoroughly and passionately showed Paul how he felt, how completely he'd wanted to take and possess Paul, that now, talking to Mim, Paul wondered if he might *possibly* have made the wrong decision.

'He charmed you into bed and you chucked him out next morning?' Mim asked, having listened to him sharing what had happened that night.

Paul shook his head. 'We were at Luke's place, where he's still living with Anna. The morning after we were very adult about the whole thing, amiable.' *Until I wasn't.* He clung on to why though and said, 'He *would have* dumped me. People like him always do. So it saves me the heartache to nip it in the bud, after that night.' *That perfect, passionate, sexy night.*

'Because you don't want to be with him, or you don't want a boyfriend?'

'Both. Either. Yes.' Paul knew his logic wasn't perfect, but he knew Luke would hurt him if they became more

209

romantically involved, so he wanted to stave off the relationship stage, and keep things as two people who happened to have slept together once. *Or was it twice, if he counted the morning after? Before their super-awkward conversation when Paul had frozen and left.*

Twice, no more than three times, definitely.

Mim raised her eyebrows, then turned back to the computer screen.

They continued working their way through the spreadsheet, each row containing a potential adopter's details.

'I'm just about to go travelling again.' Paul wasn't convinced, even though he was saying it. He'd been telling everyone at Fluffy Paws he was due to leave for Europe at any moment, and yet, months later, he remained resolutely in Essex.

'So it's a moot point,' Mim replied. 'Shall we do the home visits Sasha asked us about?'

Paul was sick of sitting in front of a computer, too much like his job. 'Anything to get away from here.'

'Avoiding Luke?' Mim asked.

Paul shook his head. 'A computer. Sitting at a desk.'

Mim nodded, but didn't seem convinced.

They took the little faded red van and drove to the first house.

Mim was driving, and seemed to take charge of the conversation too, which Paul didn't hate. 'I used to see it all the time at the holiday company. It was practically compulsory, bed-hopping. Comes with the territory of the job to some extent.'

'Not with this job it doesn't.' Paul felt glum. Stupid. 'It's something I'd have probably done at eighteen. It's a bit less charming now I'm twenty-eight.'

'Age shouldn't be a barrier to anything, really.'

'Including making a tit of myself?' This, Paul knew, was the worst part of it. Being resolute in his commitment to being single, and yet absolutely falling at the first Italian-romance-hero-shaped hurdle. Onto him, in fact. It was all so cliché, wasn't it? And there was Paul, sure *he* was more sophisticated than that. Evidently not.

'Aren't they the best times? When the most interesting things happen, perhaps?' Mim asked.

The first house visit was a third-floor flat with a small balcony. A man and woman lived there with two young children and a dog. Although their home wasn't tiny, it was far too hectic for nearly all of their cats, almost all of whom had some sort of trauma in their pasts.

Mim completed the form on a clipboard. 'I'm sorry, but we're going to have to say no.'

'Why?' the woman asked.

'You can only have a house cat and there's precious little space for it to escape and be alone. Children, although well meaning, so often mistake cats for toys. We hear some terrible things.'

Luke had told them about the kittens they'd rescued from the tower block, where the children had been playing with them very roughly after their dad had been boxing with them. 'It's sad but true,' Luke had said. When Paul heard Luke recounting the story, he'd wanted to hug the cats, and then Luke. Very hard.

It had been one of the few times they had spoken since *that night*.

I'd best switch off from that right now.

'I'll buy a kitten from the pet shop then.' The woman stood with her hands on her hips.

'That's your choice.' Mim put her clipboard under her arm, staring at the woman. 'But they won't spay or neuter them, or have their vaccinations up to date. And they'll charge you to *buy* the poor creature.'

'We believe,' began Paul, 'you shouldn't buy a pet, like an object. You should take on the responsibility of having it as part of your family for maybe twenty years. Which is why we're unable to say your situation is suitable.'

'But my son wants a kitten.' The woman huffed loudly.

'Sorry if you think I'm patronising you, but they're only kittens for a matter of months. They grow up to be large adult cats. Capable of having kittens of their own from one year old. If your son wants a kitten, can I suggest you buy him a cuddly toy?' Mim raised her eyebrows at Paul, indicating they should go before things got ugly.

Paul thanked them. 'If your living situation changes, you can always apply again.'

They left, just catching the woman shouting something about interfering old busybodies.

Paul wasn't sure he could cope with this. He'd hoped volunteering would take his mind off Luke, but instead it was making it worse. At times like this, he just wanted to cry and for his boyfriend – even though he didn't have one – to hug him.

They sat in the van.

'Ready for the next one?' Mim asked brightly.

'Do you think Anna will let us help clear out her house?' It felt as good a conversation as any to have at the moment.

'Anna, I think, needs a bit of a firm hand to steer her in the right direction.'

'I could do with that.' It was why he'd agreed to work with Mim today.

'Do you want me to tell you to run after Luke, because he's devastatingly handsome and you're destined to have babies together? Because I can tell you that if you want. But it doesn't mean I believe it.'

'What *do* you believe?' Paul asked with uncertainty.

'I believe it's not always possible to be absolutely certain about matters of the heart. I also believe that if you don't throw yourself into something you think is right, you'll never know what could have been. And,' she said, with a final flourish, 'I believe there's a lot to be said for kindness. I had dozens of boyfriends before David, but he was, and still is, the kindest person I know. Which is different from being nice. He's not brilliant when it comes to certain topics of conversation, but we shan't go there today.'

'Oh?' Paul asked, hoping she'd say more.

Mim pursed her lips. 'Do you want children?'

Paul hadn't really considered it before. 'George, my ex, didn't want them. So, I sort of agreed. And in those two sentences I've just summed up what was so very wrong with my last relationship.' Paul sighed. 'Shall we get to the next place?'

Mim turned up the radio and they drove in silence.

Paul pointed at the address they'd put in the satnav. 'Who knows what we'll find?'

It was a bungalow with a neat garden and two newish, shiny prestige cars on the drive.

'Do you want to do this one?' Mim handed him the clipboard.

He'd hoped to be along for the ride, and not take charge, at least not so soon. 'Can I?'

'You've watched dozens. There's only so long you can get away with saying you're the new boy. Luke's been doing rescues with Sasha, he's not far off doing an adoption and he'll soon be doing home visits too.'

It felt a bit like throwing down the gauntlet to Paul, but he didn't say so. 'Is he too perfect to really be perfect?'

'Entirely possible,' Mim said casually, waving her hand about.

'How will I know?' Paul needed to know this, to have certainty if he was making the right decision or not.

'You won't, until you've given it, whatever it is, some time.'

They waited by the door after Paul had rung the bell. 'I might do,' he said to Mim.

'What now?'

'Want children.' *With Luke? On my own? Who knows?*

'I do,' Mim said quietly with a tinge of sadness to it. 'Did.'

Paul sensed there was a lot more to it than Mim was going to share, now at least.

A smiley man in a football shirt and shorts opened the door. He was what Paul described as beefy, rugby-player build. Very nice, in fact.

A lithe woman appeared behind him. 'You the cat people?' She introduced herself as Kathryn.

Paul nodded. 'We are.'

Their home was clean, large and set back from a quiet road.

'Eighteen, he was,' Kathryn said, after a long story about their cat and why they loved him so much.

Her husband, Wayne, kissed her hand. He looked as if he was about to cry. Wiping his eyes with the heels of his hands, he said, 'You don't appreciate how they get under your skin, do you? Furry little buggers. Not until they're gone.' He coughed, composed himself. 'How many cats do you have?'

'One. But now none.' Paul coughed, feeling rather inadequate.

'I'm planning to foster them. I can't have my *own* permanently for... complicated reasons.' Mim waved about.

That was news to Paul. Perhaps it was Mim's plan to foster cats, she'd definitely not told him. 'I went travelling, it wasn't fair to put my cat in a cattery. There was no end date to the travelling.' He shrugged apologetically. Nine months it had ended up being until he and George had parted ways. It was odd how accommodating Paul had been to George's... peculiarities, he now saw.

A while later, Paul handed the couple a yellow piece of paper. 'This confirms you're authorised to adopt a cat or kitten from Fluffy Paws. When you visit, just bring it with you and it'll expedite the process.'

'Good news,' Kathryn said to her husband.

Wayne nodded. 'Made up, we are. Feels like passing a test or something.' He showed them to the door.

'It is a test,' Mim said on the doorstep.

'And you passed it with flying colours,' Paul added with a smile.

The couple stood at their door, waving them goodbye.

'There,' Mim said once they'd set off, 'you did very well. I knew you would. You've just to have confidence. Why are you so hard on yourself?'

Paul scrunched his nose up. 'George was quite... particular about things. If he was a judge on one of those celebrity dancing shows, he'd never give above a seven.' *Or a five for me.* In the end, it had become very hard being with someone that critical.

'Difficult.' Mim patted Paul's back.

Paul nodded, and drove in silence for a short while. Finally he said, 'I think I'd prefer to be the cool uncle, do all the fun stuff, then hand them back at the end of the day.'

'Children?'

He nodded. 'Not that I've considered it *very* deeply. I always thought, growing up, that being gay meant I didn't have to do all the stuff that some straight people sometimes sort of fall into, take for granted, without making a conscious decision.'

'Such as?'

'Marriage, children, buying a house. Settling down.' Those two words were something he'd unconsciously railed against his whole adult life, he now realised.

'How many serious relationships have you had?' Mim asked gently.

'One.'

'George?'

Paul nodded.

'Can I suggest,' Mim said, 'if I may, that perhaps you're not basing much of that on a large enough sample size to be really robust with your hypothesis?'

'What now?'

'Basing how you feel about settling down, on one boyfriend, with whom it seems you're better off having not settled down, may be a tad narrow-minded.'

Paul reflected on this for a moment. He knew George had been untypical in many ways. Numerous ways, which he'd only realised having separated from George. 'The one thing he gave me is a taste for travel. Adventure. I intend to hold on to that at least.'

'Admirable.' Mim nodded, staring ahead at the road.

They were approaching Fluffy Paws.

'I definitely wanted children,' Mim said. 'But it didn't happen. David is wonderful at most things, but alas, with discussing that side of things he… was not.'

'That must be very hard for you.' Paul parked the van, then touched her shoulder in a sign of solidarity. They'd had quite a day of it, a lot of water had passed under the bridge of their friendship since setting out that morning. Paul hadn't expected to become close friends with someone as different from himself as Mim, but here they were.

'David's… *our* nephew and his wife have a child. Same with our other nephew, apparently, although I've not seen him or his family since we've moved back to the UK. Anyway. What I'm saying is it's as if I have grandchildren. I'm sure there are others my age without that.'

Paul considered this for a moment. 'Some would say you have the best of both worlds. The joy of grandchildren without the stress and sacrifice of having children yourself.'

'I wouldn't have minded the sacrifice.' Mim looked out of the window. 'It was rather stressful not having children too. Became something of an obsession.' She shook herself as if trying to discard that painful memory.

They sat in silence.

Sasha walked up the drive to greet them. 'Good day?'

'One yes, and one no,' Mim said, getting out of the van.

'I'd rather that than rehome and have to take the poor cats back after a fortnight because they're not doing much.'

Paul walked with them towards the house and into the humans' kitchen.

As they discussed a woman who'd adopted a mother-and-daughter pair of cats who'd been found in a cardboard box by a busy road – Meryl and Grace, named after the actress and her daughter – and who, after a week, had returned them, demanding a refund on her adoption fee, because they 'hadn't done much' and were 'still under the bed most of the day', Paul wondered how he'd know if he and Luke were well-suited, or were only as such in bed. For, that night, had been one of the best he'd enjoyed in his life. He blushed slightly at the memory. He might only have one relationship to speak of, but he had much more experience in the fun-for-the-night department and, without hesitation, his night with Luke had been uninhibited, enjoyable, tender and sexy.

Perhaps that meant something, after all…

'What do you think?' Sasha asked him.

He'd not followed the last conversation as he'd been musing on his and Luke's whatever it had been. 'Sorry. I was miles away,' he said apologetically.

'I was saying, do you think we need something on the website about no refunds for the adoption fees? That when you adopt a cat from Fluffy Paws, you're not buying a cat, you're committing to take it into your life, and care for it until its final day? Our adoption fees are to cover some of our costs, vaccinations, desexing the cats, etcetera?'

'Very sensible,' Paul said. 'I'll put something on the website.' But already his mind had wandered back to Luke and the night they'd shared.

Chapter 23

Anna sat outside her boss's office at The Grove Practice. She'd been summoned that morning, to discuss references in relation to a request from a supermarket.

She'd driven the short distance to the small village, the same journey she'd done automatically for twenty years. Howe Green was a village of six hundred people, two main roads, and a few facilities including a church, primary school serving other neighbouring villages, and the surgery where Anna worked. The GP surgery had been built there as part of an agreement with the local council to encourage more people to live in villages rather than the creeping suburbs of Chelmsford. She parked round the back of the yellow brick building with a sloping roof.

A little squiggle on a letter using headed paper, it was hardly bank fraud, was it? She'd been a loyal employee for twenty-odd years, with a blemish-free record, and this had simply been her using her role to reduce admin for one of the doctors.

Rebecca poked her head out of the door. 'Ready, Anna?'

She stood, entered and sat at the desk.

Rebecca took a seat behind the desk, holding a piece of paper. 'I know you've had a lot to contend with. But we take the probity of our employees very seriously.' Handing Anna a letter, she said, 'Can you explain what this is, please?'

It was the reference letter Anna had typed and squiggled Rebecca's signature on, then sent to the supermarket. Anna put it on the desk, swallowed. 'I'm very sorry. I was desperate.'

'I appreciate that, but why didn't you ask to increase your hours if you were short of money? Better still, why didn't you say you were having money problems? We could have helped. You own two properties, almost outright, it makes no sense for you to have financial difficulties.'

If I explain it carefully, this whole thing will surely go away. 'I needed money while I decided what to do with the two houses. Temporarily. I didn't want you to think I wasn't coping financially as you'd think I wasn't coping with the job. After turning down the full-time manager job I thought it would seem odd, my asking for more hours. Arouse suspicion I wasn't okay.' Anna coughed. 'I love working here. But I wanted something less stressful, with less responsibility, to earn the money.'

Rebecca nodded, wrote on the paper.

'I can't sell Mum and Dad's house. I tried. But I can't imagine anyone else owning it. Living in it, with me, okay. I'm going to let out two of the spare bedrooms, use one for fostering cats.' Anna bit her bottom lip. Maybe not the latter. Perhaps she was doing enough for the cat sanctuary giving them the money from selling her small house. Which Sasha still insisted she didn't want. Well, Anna was just going to do it and give them the money.

'I just need you to explain what you did in relation to this letter, please?' Rebecca asked calmly.

'I didn't think I could ask for more help. Not after how you'd been so good for the last six months before Mum and Dad—' She broke off, the grief lodging itself in her throat.

'Are you seeing someone to talk about this? I gave you the number of someone, do you remember?'

Anna had taken the card, put it in her diary and then she wasn't sure what had happened. 'I'm sorry. I won't do it again.'

'This is very serious. You are entrusted with our finances, this brings into question your trustworthiness to oversee that on behalf of the practice.'

Anna shook her head. 'I've never even taken a paper-clip or notebook home. Twenty years, nothing.' Her face heated, her ears felt as if they were burning. 'I thought it was easier than bothering you for a reference. Didn't want to tell you as you'd think something was wrong.'

'You never gave us a chance to help you. But something was wrong, though, wasn't it?' Rebecca asked.

Anna nodded. 'I wanted a *different* job. Didn't want to ask to increase my hours here, fancied a bit of a change.'

Rebecca rested her elbows on the table. 'You just said you couldn't ask us after we'd been so good to you. Now you've said you wanted a different job. So can you please clarify, what drove you to forge my signature and fake a letter on my behalf?'

'I do it all the time, with you and the other doctors' signatures.'

'PP–ing a signature on a letter someone else has dictated and you've typed up, is very different from what we have here.' Rebecca tilted her head slightly. 'You must understand that, Anna, surely.'

With a feeling of being defeated, she could fight and squirm away from the truth no longer. She said, 'I am so sorry. I kept everything secret from you because I worried what you'd think if I wasn't coping and I hoped I'd have worked out what to do, with the houses, soon and then I was going to give up the supermarket job.' It had felt logical in her muddled mind at the time, but saying it now, it was clear how wrong she'd been. 'I'll never do it again. I promise. One thing in twenty years, that must be worth something, surely?'

Rebecca nodded slowly. 'It certainly is. A blemish-free record definitely counts in your favour. But this, I'm afraid, is a significant problem for us. It calls into question your honest and trustworthy nature for how you carry out the rest of your work here.' She coughed. 'Can you give me your ID badge, please?'

Ceremoniously, Anna looped the lanyard over her head, handing the photo-ID badge to Rebecca. 'What will you do? Fire me?'

'You're suspended, while we carry out an investigation.'

'Suspended? I might as well go now.'

Rebecca shook her head. 'I have been assured by the HR service provider that suspension is a neutral act and doesn't reflect any outcome from an investigation. It is normal procedure. Twenty years ago, we would have approached things differently, but we are where we are, and the HR business partner has advised us. So, with their advice we will go.'

The shame and regret threatened to engulf Anna. She was sick to her stomach. Had never wished she could rewind and do something again more than now. She shook her head, as tears fell on her cheeks. 'I'm so sorry. So so sorry.'

Rebecca stood, helping Anna to her feet, led her by the arm out of the door, through reception, where patients waited and the receptionist stared at her as she walked past, and into the car park. 'You mustn't return here. We'll write to you. You'll need to be interviewed by the HR person, who's investigating.'

'Is this it?' Anna said in a very small, very contrite voice.

'For now, yes.' Rebecca turned and walked back to the building.

Anna had no idea where to go. Couldn't really process what had just happened. Was this serious? Could it mean she'd be sacked? Surely not, for a little squiggle on a letter. Hadn't Rebecca said something about fraud, surely that wasn't right?

The supermarket had fired her when they found out she'd forged the references. She'd been called into an office, asked if she was still working for the doctor's surgery, and who had written the letter. They had spoken to Rebecca, who obviously knew nothing about Anna's letter. They'd asked her to return her uniform and leave immediately. It had felt as if she were sorting out her problems, that things were falling into place.

And now it was all unravelling, rather like herself, the way Anna felt now.

How could she be so stupid? Why hadn't she just asked Rebecca for a reference? Or seen if she could have increased her hours, rather than getting the supermarket job? So many stupid decisions stacked next to each other, all in a line, seemingly taunting Anna. And how was she going to repay the loan, having lost one job and been suspended from the other?

She drove, not paying attention to where she was going, and somehow ended up in Wickford, at Fluffy Paws.

After parking, she sat in silence, trying to absorb what had just happened. Unable to, she walked into the main outbuilding.

Paul greeted her. 'You're not due until tomorrow.'

'Nice to see you,' Mim said, patting her on the back. 'We're just going for a break. Luke's out with Sasha in the van.'

'Bodes well,' Paul said with a smile. 'I thought he'd be much more hit-and-run.'

'A man with staying power, something to bear in mind,' Mim said with a wink, walking towards the house.

Anna followed them in silence. She was trying to work out how to recount her morning. How to explain why she'd been so stupid. So many times. All in such quick succession.

'All right?' Mim asked, pulling her in for a hug as they walked.

Anna nodded. If she started to tell the truth it would all come tumbling out, en route to the big house, and she'd soon be standing in the car park in floods of tears. She, at least, wanted to be sitting when she dissolved into a heap of crying.

Shortly, while they made drinks, Mim and Paul talked about the cats, their mornings, and how they expected a busy afternoon of visitors, hopefully reserving many of the cats, so they had room for the next intake. Anna remained silent, holding her mug of coffee as if her life depended upon it.

'Aren't you usually at work?' Paul asked.

That was it. That did it for Anna. She shook her head, sniffed loudly. 'I've been suspended.'

Mim scoffed. 'You're joking!'

Anna closed her mouth tightly, furiously shaking her head. 'Investigation.'

'What for? Surely it'll all blow over?'

'I faked a reference for another job.' Best get it out in one sentence. Then take questions that would inevitably arise.

'Sorry. Start from the beginning, would you? The supermarket has fired you?' Mim asked.

She told them. The loan, the supermarket job, the made-up reference, the squiggle of Rebecca's signature.

'So they've fired you?' Paul asked.

'The supermarket has. Offer was null and void. Fraudulent references. Done and done.'

'Very much,' Mim said, 'it seems you have been.' Quieter now, Mim went on. 'And by your own doing, it very much sounds.'

Anna nodded. Mim had summed it up correctly. Shame flooded her and she wished the ground would swallow her whole.

'But you've not been fired from your main job?' Paul asked.

'Neutral act,' she said. 'Suspension.' Anna shut her eyes. 'But I did it. Open and closed, surely?' She stared at Mim and Paul, hoping for some sympathy, some words of wisdom that it would all be all right in the end.

Mim sat back, folded her arms across her chest. 'I did jury service once. Twice actually. Before Spain and recently now we're here. It's never open and shut, is what I'd say. Mitigations, context, all sorts. Have you asked to do a statement?'

'Will I have to sit in court, in front of a jury?' It had never occurred to Anna. The thought set terror shooting through her veins. She could barely speak to one person, the thought of imagining doing so in front of an audience stopped her frozen.

'This isn't that. No judge, no jury. But the principles are similar, evidence, beyond reasonable doubt, all that jazz.'

Relief washed through Anna, she sat back in the chair. 'What am I going to do?'

'Wait,' Paul said. 'Although, it's not beyond reasonable doubt.'

'What isn't?' Anna asked.

'This sort of thing, employment law. It's on the balance of probability. The threshold of truth is lower than in crown court, as Mim described.'

Anna's mind was buzzing with thoughts, worries, terms, regrets, if she'd only just asked Rebecca to sign the letter, would things have ended differently? 'So that's better?'

Mim shook her head. 'Worse.'

Paul added, 'I did a four-month contract for a solicitors' firm, sort of picked it up through osmosis. I'm not an expert, but I do know that's true.'

Anna felt as if the world was closing around her, tighter and tighter until she couldn't breathe. 'I think I'm going to be sick!' She ran to the loo, slammed the door and her prediction came true. Shortly, after rinsing the acrid taste from her mouth with water, splashing her face to cool herself, her forehead felt red hot, she returned to her friends.

'Better?' Mim asked.

Anna nodded, with surprise, she did feel slightly less worried, having talked it through, and emptied her stomach.

'We wondered,' Mim went on, 'if you'd like something to keep you occupied while you wait for the investigation? Because my advice is to continue, to march on. Don't sit around waiting, like you're at an airport departure gate awaiting a plane that may not arrive for weeks. Months even. This could drag on for a very long time.' Mim caught Paul's eye.

He nodded. 'Months.'

Anna liked that analogy, she was one of those people who arrived at the airport four hours before the flight left. Once she knew something was to be awaited, she went into her own special waiting mode. Nothing else could continue, until the end point, the thing she was waiting for, had happened. It was a terrific fear of missing the flight, or whatever she was queuing for.

'Yes,' Anna said with anticipation, anxiety and a tiny smidgen of hope. 'I'd like something to keep me busy.'

'We can help you sort through your belongings, so you can live in your parents' house and enjoy the space. Imagine all those extra rooms to use. All that extra space into which you can grow.'

She couldn't let them see her wardrobe, with her labels of where, when and with whom she'd bought each item of clothing, or the collection of old media she'd been unable to dispose of from her parents.

Her father had, it seemed, taped most of the televisual output from the mid-Eighties to the late Nineties and catalogued and labelled it in one of the spare bedrooms. There was a recently fixed video recorder to view them.

'I think,' she said quietly, 'I'd like that, but I should like to sort it myself before you arrive, if that's okay.'

'When?' Paul asked.

'Next week, maybe?'

'When?'

'Can I let you know?' Anna didn't want to come across as ungrateful, but she didn't feel ready to let them loose on the contents of her little house. Luke staying at her parents' home was one thing, he kept to his bedroom, and she'd locked the others, the rooms containing the old video tapes, one with multiple old computers stacked in the corner, although she thought Luke and Paul may have seen that one...

Paul and Mim exchanged a look; there were raised eyebrows.

Mim said, 'I think, rather, if we're to help you, we need to help you with all of it. We believe you'll need help with the part you've said you'll do alone.'

Feeling very defensive and not just a little irritated, Anna said, 'I know what I need help with. Thank you very much. And I'd ask that you respect that, please.' *There, that ought to tell them.*

'Luke told me there's a lot to sort through at your parents' place,' Paul said.

Aha, I knew Luke saw the contents of that bedroom. Anna narrowed her eyes, her shoulders tensing as she prepared to defend herself.

'Do you definitely want to sell your old place and move into your parents' home?' Mim asked.

'It's the only solution.' She'd gone over it many times but nothing else seemed to work. 'If I get lodgers, it'll help me if I'm not working. After...' She waved about indicating the investigation but not wanting to return to it.

'Presumably, you won't give the money from your little house to Fluffy Paws?' Mim asked.

'Do I have to say now?' It was certainly her intention, but given that morning's events, she wasn't sure which way was up and down, never mind a decision like that. There were fewer cats in the remaining pens, many were inside Sasha's house, in makeshift pens all around the home.

'Course not.'

'It'll take me a long time. You two don't want to spend your free time going through my stuff, do you?' She looked at Mim and Paul.

They nodded and smiled. Paul said, 'We really do. Sooner the better, actually.'

Moulsham, Essex

The next day, after much persuasion, Anna let them into her small home and they began in the kitchen, sorting through crockery and cutlery so she only had enough for eight places – not that she ever hosted dinner parties for eight, but Mim had said that was a nice even number. Anna knew she needed help but had never understood why she held on to things.

Feeling pleased, with the two small boxes now destined for charity shops, they moved on to the drawing room. That proved easier than Anna had anticipated, she was surprisingly able to let go of piles of newspapers and magazines her father had given to her, when he'd run out of space, and she'd kept with the intention of making clippings, but hadn't quite got around to.

Later that morning, as they tackled Anna's spare bedroom, Paul said, 'I got in touch with a library and they're interested in some of the magazines as cultural artefacts of the time.'

'What time?' Mim asked, scrunching up her face in obvious disgust.

'The Eighties and Nineties,' Paul said.

Was that how old the magazines were? Anna hadn't looked at them in ages. Decades, probably.

'Cultural artefacts?' Mim shook her head.

'I was born in nineteen ninety-five, so like the Eighties are very much a long time ago, and the Nineties, I don't remember a great deal since I was five in two thousand, and I'm not alone in that.' Paul shrugged.

Anna was pleased at this. *So it had proved useful to keep Dad's magazines so long. Marvellous.*

'I can see what you're thinking,' Mim said, wiping her brow. 'This is not carte blanche to keep every magazine you buy now. Please tell me that's not crossed your mind.'

Anna blushed. How come Mim was so perceptive, she wondered. 'Have we earned lunch yet?'

'I should think so.' Mim opened a wardrobe full of children's games: jigsaws, puzzles, Lego, Playmobil, plastic yellow ducks and small boats. 'Dare I ask?'

'My toys as a child. Mum and Dad had run out of space. So, I took them.'

'Would you like children?' Paul asked.

Mim shot him a look that said: *End this now.* 'Lunch?'

'If I'd met someone, who stayed with me, I would have liked children. But it must be such a worry. As babies, if they're ill, or fall over, and then when they're older it never ends. They're driving and doing all sorts of things and who knows what might happen to them?' Just saying it made her anxious as worry trickled down her spine, making her stomach rigid with terror. 'Probably best I'm divorced, I suppose.' The divorce had left her heartbroken and broke and her parents had helped her buy the small house they were in now. A fresh start, away from a man who'd cheated on her multiple times over their short marriage. It still stung, thinking how he'd lied to her face repeatedly.

Mim shut the wardrobe. 'I'm stopping. Kitchen.' She led them out, down to the kitchen.

Anna opened her fridge. It contained two ready meals for one, skimmed milk and sparkling water. 'I sort of got out of the habit, when Mum and Dad weren't well.'

'Out of the habit?' Mim asked, staring into the fridge in obvious disbelief.

'Eating,' Anna added. The fizzy water was because it felt like champagne but didn't get her drunk and after she didn't descend into a morass of loneliness. Plus, the sleeping tablets she'd been prescribed were not to be mixed with alcohol, so that made her feel slightly virtuous. In an odd sort of way she wouldn't share with others.

'How,' Mim replied in disbelief, 'does one get out of the habit of eating? Isn't it something one needs to do three times or at least twice a day?'

Not if you're rushing around, watching your parents die before your eyes. Anna managed a shrug. 'There's a macaroni cheese and a stew, that'll do you two. I'll microwave one of these and have a cup of tea.' She reached into the cupboard and retrieved an unopened box of mince pies she'd bought and never eaten at Christmas.

Mim shook her head. 'I don't want to come across all mumsy, but I do not think this is healthy. Nor is it acceptable, not while I'm on your watch. Paul? What do you say?'

Paul took the box off Anna. 'I'll order an indoor picnic from that organic deli round the corner. We've a lot to get through.'

Anna sat, and allowed them to continue to take over her life somewhat more than she had at first anticipated. She found herself beginning to lean into it, to perhaps enjoy it a little. 'When do you think we'll reach my wardrobe?' she said with uncertainty, thinking of her labelling system and worrying how she would ever be able to explain it to them.

'Tomorrow?' Mim asked Paul.

He shrugged.

'Okay,' Anna said, and not meaning it. Tomorrow was definitely too soon. She'd rather sit around worrying about the investigation than have them interrogating her, one item of her wardrobe at a time.

That afternoon they finished downstairs, the bags for charity shops to one side of the hallway and the ones for other destinations along the other. The rubbish was left by her wheelie bin and Anna knew she'd have a little check through once Paul and Mim left.

That evening, Mim said, 'Nine tomorrow morning, okay?'

'I wondered if we could not.' Anna held on to the door frame too tightly. 'Tomorrow at least. I received an email about the investigation.' Anna bit her tongue at the lie. 'I'd like to prepare for that. Shall we say... I tell you what, I'll let you know next time we're at the sanctuary together?'

Mim, with undisguised disappointment on her face, nodded, pulling Anna in for a hug. '*Adios*.'

Paul rolled his eyes at her. 'In your own time.'

She shut the door, leaning against it, closing her eyes, wondering if she'd made a big mistake, letting them in so soon, allowing them to be so ruthless with her belongings. She opened a black plastic sack in the hallway. *Nice stuff in there. I'll just rescue this plastic box, and those shoes, I'll wear them more than I managed before...*

Chapter 24

Wickford, Essex

Mim was standing in the hallway at Fluffy Paws, on the phone to the landlord. Sasha was helping a very young cat give birth to her first litter of kittens. Mim had said the phone call was for Sasha, but Sasha had replied, 'Tell him to piss off. Tell him I'm doing my best and we'll be gone when we can. But until then, he can whistle for it.' And she'd disappeared looking very flustered.

Mim had scuttled back to the phone and was in the middle of a conversation about their absolute latest date when they would need to vacate the property.

'Vacant possession is one of the conditions of sale. If you remain after the sale has completed, you will be trespassing,' the landlord said.

'I'm sure Sasha wouldn't want that.' Mim kept the bit about telling him to piss off and whistling for it to herself. One attracted more flies with honey than shit, or so the old expression went. 'We're exploring all avenues,' Mim said stoutly.

'Good. You've had plenty of notice. I'm not being unreasonable.'

'What would it take for you to call it all off?' Mim asked, holding her breath for the answer. It was worth asking.

He named a price. 'In cash.'

'I see.' Mim swallowed, feeling very much unequal to that, even with all her best event-planning skills absolutely at full tilt. 'At what point during the sale will we need to be out?'

'Originally, I wanted you out when it went for sale. Obviously, that didn't happen. When the sale is agreed. Technically. But I am *not* an unreasonable man.'

He'd said that at least three times during this phone call and Mim reckoned he was protesting too much, else why bother making such a song and dance of it? 'Of course,' she said soothingly.

'However, I realise that isn't possible. And it's much more complex than a residential sale. You have the residential aspect, plus the animals. I've held off demolishing the last few pens as long as possible. Don't need to show that part of the grounds for the pictures. I am trying to be reasonable, but they will all need to go eventually. I believe there are two left.'

'They house twenty cats. Give or take.'

'Indeed. So if we were to say four weeks from sale agreed.'

That gave them another few weeks' grace from their previous estimation. Better than nothing. 'Thank you.'

'Can I ask you to relay that to Sasha Droxford, please?'

'Consider it done.' She ended the call then found Sasha to tell her the relatively good news.

Sasha listened. 'It's hardly great news, is it?' She looked stressed and exhausted with a tinge of sadness thrown in for good measure.

'How are the kittens, and mum?' Mim wanted to move on to other conversations.

'Three girls, two boys and a very tired mum, feeding them as we speak.' She smiled.

This was the part of the sanctuary that Sasha had told the volunteers she loved. Not worrying about the landlord and fundraising and unhelpful members of the public.

'I wondered if we could use the next few weeks to move to the virtual sanctuary model I suggested.' Mim had read about it online, when researching fostering cats, to determine what it was likely to involve. A cat sanctuary in Yorkshire had moved to a virtual model, saving huge overheads while they found a new location, and still rehoming as many cats as before. She told Sasha.

'How many volunteers do they have?' Sasha asked.

'Dozens. We'd need to recruit. Check them. Visit their homes. The arrangement with our vet would remain. The website, everything, stays the same. But the visiting takes place at volunteers' homes. There are some insurance issues I need to research more to fully understand, but it would give us some breathing space to find another location.'

'What if people weren't happy having strangers in their homes viewing cats?'

'Ensure there's a senior volunteer there for all viewings. We'd need volunteers to look after, others who could ferry the cats about, some to supervise. A system to coordinate who had which cats, when they needed moving about, etcetera. That's obviously your role. A spreadsheet, probably. Anna would be a whizz at that, I don't doubt.'

'How is she, after your house clearance?'

Mim didn't want to get into all that now. It had been difficult and Anna had never allowed them back to complete the job. Which worried Mim. 'A start. More to

do,' she said. 'Paul seemed to prefer that to coming here...
since they fell out.'

'After falling *in* bed.'

Mim nodded. Sasha had asked what was wrong with
the two men and keeping to her plan, Mim hadn't lied.
Sasha wasn't too bothered, although them falling out
wasn't ideal.

'They'll come round, I expect,' Sasha said. 'Luke's very
forgiving.'

'How are you and he getting along?' From what Mim
could see, they'd spent more time with each other than
anyone else lately.

'A start, more to do,' Sasha replied with a smile. 'Can
you work out the details of this virtual thingy, and come
back to me soonish? Number of homes needed, number
of volunteers, different roles, the whole shebang. How
long you think it'll tide us over. It's not something I've
ever considered. Sounds like you might just have saved us.
For now.'

'More sustainable than another massive fete. Not that
I don't think we should have one too.'

'A sorry-we're-closing-give-us-money fete?' Sasha
grimaced.

'Something like that.'

Sasha stood still as worry clouded her face. She shook
her head. 'I don't think so. Feels a bit desperate. The fete
of last resort.' She paused, then said, 'Want to see the new
kittens?'

'Wondered when you'd ask.'

Sasha led them upstairs to the two bedrooms she'd
converted into nursery pens. A white cat lay on her side,
with five kittens suckling her milk. Two were white, two
white and ginger, and one ginger.

They stood in silence, listening to the contended purrs of the kittens and tiny suckling noises until, one by one, they detached themselves and lay in a heap next to their mum.

'Can't tempt you to take in a pregnant queen?' Sasha asked.

'I will definitely sign up to foster cats in our home if we go virtual. David will love it.' He'd wanted pets while they'd worked in Spain, but Mim had said they never knew how long they'd stay there. Almost forty years, and they could have had more than a few pets. It was shocking how one moment she'd been in her twenties, resigned not to having children, leaving the UK to be a holiday rep, just for that summer, and now she was seventy with all that behind her and back in the UK. It was almost as if none of it had happened. But it had, she reminded herself, when at home alone, looking through the piles of photo albums she'd filled with her parties, friends, new teams, leaving parties, birthdays, everything, over a lifetime.

'Go home, you've been here all day,' Sasha said now.

'I don't mind. You must all come round to dinner. Everyone.'

'If you think Luke and Paul can be in the same room together?' Sasha raised her eyebrows.

'Paul was very hurt by his ex. There's a lot of baggage. Although given time…'

'Luke says Paul definitely doesn't want anything more than what they had. Although Luke says he doesn't want anything from me except meeting me, talking about his father. And that's patently untrue too. So…'

'There may be hope.' Mim waved goodbye, left the house and walked to her car in thought. What was it with men, not talking to each other? If it were two women she felt sure they'd have talked and discussed this until the cows had indeed come home. Whether they'd then decide to be together was another matter entirely, but at least they would have had the chat.

South Hanningfield, Essex

A few days later, Mim was awaiting the arrival of Henry and his daughter Tilly. She had, mercifully, been far too busy with the virtual cat sanctuary idea and her shifts there to even contemplate feeling a little 'off', which she welcomed. She had tried to encourage Luke and Paul to be in the same room together, but had failed.

'If he wants to be single,' Luke had said, in the humans' kitchen, 'who am I to disagree?' He'd shrugged and sat with a very defeated look about him.

'If I may?' Mim said, joining him on the sofa, to have Tigger sitting between them, purring and demanding attention. 'Isn't that how *you* felt about relationships, until you met him?'

Luke sighed and nodded, looking very glumly into his mug of tea.

'Why did your last relationship end?'

Luke shook his head. 'It wasn't good. I see that now. I shouldn't have let it get so bad. I fell out of love with him. Very slowly, one day at a time. But one morning in bed together I realised it was like living with a sibling, or a friend.' He turned away, pursing his lips and looking out the window. 'I *was* enjoying being single, a lot, until Paul. But if he wants to stick to his guns about not wanting a relationship, who am I to change that?'

Mim had left it there, stroked Tigger and Toffee in preparation for taking them to her home to foster. She felt sure separately she'd coax Paul out of his shell and, carefully, obtain the truth from him about why his last relationship had hurt him so much. And why he'd felt perfectly able to throw caution to all of that and fall, in some small way at least, for Luke. It would no doubt help her sort out the two men and ensure they saw how well-suited they were.

She'd wanted to tell Paul about how assiduously David had pursued her when they'd met, charming and showering her with gifts, until finally, she'd acquiesced and agreed to go for a drink with him. Content she had Luke's side of the story, she'd speak to Paul.

Now, the doorbell rang.

Mim sprang up, surveying the house, she'd packed away the wine glasses she'd been painting with flowers, didn't want to spoil the surprise, they were for Henry and Fiona's Christmas present.

Henry smiled, standing on the doorstep, Tilly standing in front of him, gazing up into Mim's eyes.

Her heart beat faster. She had a whole day of activities planned for them. She didn't want to appear too keen, aimed to give the impression of being effortlessly in control and just so happening to know what she was doing vis-à-vis entertaining and caring for an enthusiastic seven-year-old.

'All her stuff is in here.' Henry held a pink backpack aloft, handing it to Mim.

She peered inside: paper, colouring crayons, books, a change of clothes and a few toys. 'Will you come in for a coffee?' Mim asked carefully, she wanted to make sure what she had planned met his approval, without actually asking him outright.

He nodded back at his car. 'We've got to get on, actually. Fi has us booked into a spa. His and hers spa day, then we're going to the cinema. There's an action film out, it's a sequel to one of my favourite Eighties ones and… well, Fi reckons the reviews are good, so she's giving it a go.' His eyes shone.

'Do you want me to keep Tilly overnight?'

He frowned. 'Hadn't considered that. We didn't have any plans for this evening. But I'm sure a bottle of wine and *Pretty Woman* or *Dirty Dancing* and an early night wouldn't be too bad.' He grinned cheekily.

Mim instantly saw why Fi had fallen for him. He really was very similar to David at that age. Charming, unassuming, friendly and not quite Hollywood–film–star dashing good looks, but definitely BAFTA-actor handsome. Mim ushered Tilly into the hallway, holding the door for Henry.

He pulled his phone from his pocket, nodded and walked away from the house to call his wife.

'What would you like to do?' Mim asked Tilly.

The little girl shrugged. 'Do you have a cat? Mummy says we can't have one. But my friend Sean, he has lots. He had one, and she had babies and we weren't allowed one of the babies.'

'Cat babies are called kittens. I don't have one, but I might,' Mim replied with a smile.

Henry joined them. 'One of what?'

'Sorted?' Mim asked.

'If you could have her tonight, that would be great. She has spare clothes. Otherwise just throw them in the machine. Use the old T-shirt for sleepwear. We'll collect her first thing tomorrow.' He knelt down, pulling his daughter in for a hug. 'You're going to be good for Aunt Mim, are you?'

Tilly nodded. 'We're getting a cat.'

He looked at Mim.

She shook her head. 'I thought we'd go to the sanctuary. I'm going to foster a cat. I thought she'd like to come along for that.'

'What does it entail?'

'Unsure. But I'm sure they'll lead me through by the hand. Basically, I take a cat or two, care for them here, but they're not mine. Any vets' bills, the sanctuary covers them.'

'We're not having cats. Fi isn't keen.' Henry grimaced, then smiled.

'Do you like drawing?' Mim asked the little girl.

She nodded.

'Painting?' Mim asked.

'You could show her your glass painting. I'm sure she'd be fascinated,' Henry offered helpfully. He kissed them bye, then left.

The door shut, it was now Mim and Tilly, David being away on a golfing trip until tomorrow morning, and she couldn't have felt happier.

They discussed the activities for the day and agreed first to do some colouring and drawing, and Mim would show her how to paint on glass, then they'd go to Fluffy Paws to collect the cat.

'What sort of cat is it?' Tilly asked.

'One that needs my help,' Mim said with a smile.

The little girl nodded.

Later, after hand painting and reading and a short spell digging in the garden in search of snails, they arrived at the cat sanctuary and Sasha greeted them in the car park. 'You're here! The cavalry arrives!'

Mim introduced Tilly and Sasha to each other.

Sasha led them to the main building, with cat pens. They arrived at a cage containing a small grey cat. She meowed loudly, strutting around as if she owned the place.

'Stray. Been on the streets of Harlow for who knows how long. She'll eat everything. Has had who knows how many litters, but no more. From eating god knows what, she has a stomach condition. Something to keep an eye on. We'll pay if she needs any treatment.'

'What's her name?' Tilly asked. She was enchanted, staring at the cat.

'Sparkle.'

'I'll take her,' Mim said resolutely, sure she'd get along with the two male sibling cats she was fostering.

'She just needs lots of love. Keep her inside, obviously. Get her ready for rehoming. Someone is bound to happily take her on with the small health conditions.'

'Does she have belongings I need to take?' Mim said, feeling slightly overwhelmed with the responsibility, but then upon reflection reckoning if she could be entrusted with her great-niece, she'd be okay looking after a cat.

Sasha gestured to the inside of the pen. A blue cuddly elephant toy, some feathers on the end of string, attached to a stick, and a blue blanket. 'Take it all, it'll smell of her. Leave her carry case in the room with her, so she can seek refuge if required. Give her a room of her own, and leave her to settle.'

'What do I need in the room?' Mim asked, wishing she had a notebook and pencil.

'Litter tray, water and food bowls, bed – use the carry case as a bed. Toys.'

Mim nodded. 'Now, do you want us to take Sparkle?'

'Now, or if you can stay. If Tilly wants to see how we look after the cats?'

Tilly jumped up and down and said, 'Can we stay? Stay, I wanna stay!'

'I think,' Mim replied, 'you have your answer.'

They watched kittens being fed by their mother, looked at some of the older cats who had been awaiting homing for a long time 'People always want kittens,' Sasha said, 'but they're a handful. Old cats are much easier to look after.'

'Do they go outside?' Tilly asked.

'Some of them. But not here. You won't let Sparkle outside, not until she's in her forever home.'

'Can I have one?'

Mim shook her head. 'I don't think Mummy would be very happy. Let's see what Daddy says tomorrow.'

They had lunch in the humans' kitchen, then Mim completed the rehoming paperwork for Oscar, a ten-year-old tabby, who'd been at Fluffy Paws for three months. His new human parents had lost their cat to old age and cancer, and had fallen for Oscar, a slightly unkempt tabby with a strong personality and inability to share with other cats, shortly after, but waited another few months until reserving him for adoption.

'It was too soon, before,' his human mum said, stroking Oscar through a hole in the top of the cat carrier.

'Felt like an empty house,' his human dad said, signing the paperwork.

Mim saw them to the car park. 'I hope you spoil him rotten!'

'We will!' The woman got into the car and the man placed Oscar in his carrier in the back seat, slipped into the driver's seat, then drove off.

'One down, only nineteen left in the pens,' Mim said, walking back to the house, knowing she needed to forge on with the virtual cat sanctuary plan because the land-lord's patience was wearing thin.

That evening, they had settled Sparkle into the smallest spare bedroom and given her food. Tilly and Mim sat on the bed, while Sparkle ate a whole bowl of wet food, without pausing. She finished, meowed loudly, walked towards Mim and Tilly.

Mim sat on the floor – better to be at their level, Sasha had said – and held her hand out.

Sparkle sniffed it, then licked the back of Mim's hand with her rough tongue.

'Does it tickle?' Tilly asked.

'Not really.' But it felt odd. Strangely calming and exciting at the same time. As if Sparkle knew Mim was responsible for looking after her and she wanted to thank Mim.

Perhaps.

Whatever Sparkle meant by licking Mim's hand, the way Tilly had listened when Mim read a book at bedtime, kissed Tilly good night, and fallen asleep, Mim knew she hadn't missed out on spending time with children. It had taken Mim until this life stage, before she could feel satisfaction, serenity and acceptance at her role as fun auntie and second grandma. Now she appreciated the life she had, rather than grieving the life she'd missed.

Chapter 25

Margaretting, Essex

Luke was at his temporary home, in his bedroom in Anna's parents' house, speaking on the phone to Steve, the manager of his dance group. Luke perched at the bottom of the bed, the belongings he'd acquired since moving in a few months ago – clothes, toiletries, a few books – splayed over the floor. He'd tidy it up later. He needed to make a decision about whether to join their next tour and rehearsal schedule, or if he was going to sit this one out.

Steve had listened to Luke describing what had happened. 'I know it's important for you to do this, but you've been there a while,' Steve added. A sigh and then: 'I thought you'd meet her, swap numbers and be back on the road with us. Any chance you're coming back soon?'

'She's my birth mother, not a blind date.'

'Of course. Look, no pressure to return. It's just I need to know when we're developing the next routine, booking future events. Okay?'

Luke let that sink in. Nodded, although Steve couldn't see him.

'Stay,' Steve went on, 'if you want, just let us know. We're holding your spot for this tour, but we're starting rehearsals soon. Either you're in for this new tour, or you're not.'

After a short pause as Luke considered the options, confidently, he said, 'Not for this tour, please.'

'Do you want to take time to consider it?'

He'd had quite a few weeks here to do that. 'She's got a lot going on and I'm helping her. She wants me to stay.'

Sasha had broken down to him about the landlord having the pens demolished, each pen being smashed felt like a piece of her heart breaking and she didn't want to lean on the other volunteers, since they all had their own problems. Luke's heart had broken for her.

'Right,' Steve said with disappointment.

'I've spent years with the group and now it's time for me to come first for a while.'

'What do your parents say about this?'

'They're supportive,' he said, biting his bottom lip. In truth, his mum had stopped calling weekly for an update, but he could feel her worry from the daily messages. His dad had totally disengaged and didn't speak to Luke directly, only via his mum.

'Impressive,' Steve said, 'not sure I would be, in the same position.'

'Dad, less so. Perhaps he's sulking a little. Mum's okay though. Seems to think I'm going to cast them aside once I've installed myself into Sasha's life.'

'I wonder how she could have reached that conclusion?' Steve said, with sarcasm lacing his tone.

Luke decided not to rise to the bait. 'Do I have to sign something?'

'Releasing you, temporarily, from the group and this tour, etcetera. Yes. I'll send it later.' There was a silence, then: 'Good luck?'

'You don't sound convinced.' Luke tried to keep irritation out of his voice, but probably failed.

'I've never seen someone pausing a very successful career like yours, for something like this. It's brave.'

'I'm guessing the people who raised you are your birth parents? There are no unknowns in your past?'

'If there were, I don't think I'd go digging it up. Leave the past—'

'In the past, yeah, I've heard that.' Many times, from a few people. But it was easy to say when you didn't have much to discover in your past.

'I am me, because I am me. I'm not fussed about genealogy, descendants, long-lost relatives, all that jazz. I've got enough to be dealing with in the here and now, without going digging in the past for people I've never met.'

Easy to say when you're not adopted, he thought. 'And that is where we differ.' Luke could have said so much more, but he bit his tongue. 'I'll sign the thing when it comes through.' He ended the call, wondering how he'd been managed by Steve for so long, yet knew so little about him. And how, he continued to muse, could someone who made his money from working with creative people have such little curiosity about his own past, what was, what might have been, and what wasn't?

There had been some activity in the house's other rooms, with Paul and Mim helping Anna sort her belongings, or her parents' belongings. Luke hadn't wanted to get in the way, so he'd spent most of his time at Fluffy Paws, mainly helping Sasha. He had helped her move the cats from the pens into the house before they were pulled down. He told people on the phone they weren't open for new admissions, were trying to decant their cats as best they could.

He'd soon realised helping her with what she found most important gave him access to more of the *real* Sasha, the woman who'd fallen in love with his father and then given him up.

He wanted to ask her if caring for the cats was compensating for not caring for children, for leaving him to be looked after by Jean and Roger. Unsurprisingly, he'd not worked out how best to ask this, or how to do it delicately. So he hadn't.

There was noise downstairs in the kitchen, he needed some breakfast before going to the sanctuary, so he left his bedroom, walking down the wide stairs, standing in the large hallway – it really was a beautiful house.

Anna stood by the kitchen table, staring at four cake stands, shaking her head.

'All right?' Luke asked as he walked into the kitchen.

'They've been so good to me. We've almost done my place. Just my wardrobe left.' She blinked, looked away, then back to Luke.

'What's this?' he asked.

'I need to get rid of some of their stuff. So I can rent out the spare rooms, or use them for cats. Or both. I'm not sure. But whatever, I need to sort through and declutter.' Anna sat at the table. 'But I *like* clutter. I enjoy living in it. I think I love it, in fact. Makes me feel safe and secure. If I get rid of it, I feel as if I'm letting Mum and Dad down.' She shook her head, blinking quickly. 'Sorry, you don't need this, when you're making your breakfast. Don't mind me. Pretend I'm invisible.' She moved the cake stands about on the table, switching their positions again shortly.

Luke reckoned Anna had spent quite a bit of her life with people behaving as if she were invisible. And that was probably much of the problem about why she couldn't let go of belongings. He made coffee. 'Want some?' he asked, his back facing her.

'If it's no bother. I should be going. But I don't have anywhere else to be. It's going on for a very long time. Have you had anything like that, at work?'

'What are you talking about?'

'I thought you'd know. Mim or Paul would have told you?'

Luke shook his head, leaning on the work surface waiting for the coffee to brew.

Anna told him about the forged letter, the investigation. 'They've interviewed me. Well, they asked me a few questions on the phone, didn't even want me to come in. Said I could. Happily would. But no.'

Luke gave her a mug of coffee.

The four cake stands were in a different order, running in a line from left to right. Anna stood in the middle.

'It'll all blow over,' Luke said. 'It's not like you killed anyone, is it?'

'No,' Anna said, blowing on her coffee, taking a sip, then carefully putting it on the table, adjusting the handle so it was aligned with the table edge.

'Nice cake stands,' he said, hoping it would spark a conversation about what she was actually doing.

'They're *all* nice, aren't they?'

He nodded, gently said, 'What I thought too.'

'That's the difficulty, you see. I thought I'd make a start here, before the others come too. Except I can't.'

'Can't what?'

'Start. Decide. Pick. Choose.' Anna looked very worried.

'Sorry, I don't understand. You can't pick which cake stand to...' He thought he knew what she meant, but didn't want to charge in without being in full possession of the facts and reflecting about how he might help her.

'To keep, to use, to give to charity, to see if it's worth anything to sell online.' Anxiety deepened on her face. She shook her head. 'Because it's too hard, I don't. I put it all back and leave it for another day.'

'Is that what you parents did too?' He knew the answer, but he wanted to help her see it wasn't all her fault.

'Upstairs,' she pointed to the ceiling, 'there's a box of papers and letters from my grandparents' christenings. And the gowns they wore. Ballet shoes my mum used to wear as a teenager. She liked baking, did it for charity events, so she used these, I expect.' Anna pointed at the four cake stands. 'I don't want to let them down,' she said, as if she had the worries of the whole world on her narrow shoulders.

'Who would you let down?'

'Mum, Dad, Grandpa, Grandma, Nan, Grandad...'

Aha. Now it made sense. This is going to be harder than expected. 'I see.'

Anna put the cake stands back in the cupboard. 'I'll worry about it another day.'

Which Luke would have thought healthier, if she couldn't reach a decision now, alone, except he felt sure she would continue worrying about it until she returned. 'I'm off to the sanctuary shortly. Are you working there today?' It felt better than continuing the cake stand conversation. He didn't feel remotely qualified to carry on with that.

'I'm meant to be going, but I've such a lot to get through here. Or I could do my wardrobe first. At my house.'

'Does it need moving, your wardrobe? I reckon me and Paul could help.'

Anna shook her head. 'The clothes, not the wardrobe itself.' She stood. 'I'll leave you to it.' She left, without saying goodbye, thanking Luke for the coffee, just silently slipping out, the door clicking faintly and then she was gone.

A light pink lipstick stain remained on her mug and Luke wondered what he should, could do to help her. If not himself, then who?

Shortly, Luke arrived at Fluffy Paws and didn't recognise Anna's car. He soon established she wasn't there.

Paul returned in the van with five cats in carriers.

Luke walked out to greet him. 'Need a hand?' He thought they weren't meant to be taking in any more cats.

Paul looked slightly put out, but honestly, it had been weeks since their night together and they were both adults – if Paul couldn't sleep with someone and then get along as friends, what hope was there for him?

'Everyone else is busy, or not here,' Luke said.

Paul opened the back of the van, five cat carriers, filled with cats all meowing in various tones, and a faint smell of cat wee. 'I told Sasha I shouldn't go on my own, but she was trying to sort something with the landlord, so I went alone.'

'Should have called me, I'd have gone with you.' Luke retrieved a carrier, waiting for Paul.

Paul held a cat carrier with both hands. 'Would you?'

'Definitely.' Luke led them towards the outbuilding, resisting saying anything more for fear of it developing into an argument.

They collected the other cats from the van, then with all carriers on the floor inside, Paul checked for empty pens, nope. The two remaining ones were full. With some clever cat Tetris, he just about found room to accommodate them in the house in some makeshift cages someone had made from parts of the outbuildings. Some cages were divided into smaller spaces with walls, if the cats wouldn't get along together.

Paul sat at the desk in the main outhouse, completing paperwork for the new cats. 'Who'd have thought there'd be so much work that wasn't looking after cats?'

'Varied though,' Luke tried.

'I'll miss this place,' Paul said without emotion.

'I thought you enjoyed it.'

'I have a new job that pays much better, and I'm having the following few months off to travel.'

Sounded amazing. Luke said nothing. So this told him all he needed to know about how Paul felt about him. It would forever remain one night of passion and nothing more. Just like the night he'd been conceived.

Mim arrived, looked from one man to the other. 'Am I interrupting?'

'Don't be ridiculous,' Luke said. 'Why?'

'I've had a call from someone. Their neighbour has died and the house is full of cats. The neighbours don't want them. No family, I asked.'

'Or at least, no family that cares,' Paul added, shaking his head.

Imagine what that's like, was on the tip of Luke's tongue, but he bit it back.

'Two-man job?' Paul asked.

'At least. There's six cats. One big house.' Mim shrugged. 'I'd go, but I'm trying to put the finishing touches to my proposal for Sasha. I've a whole list of volunteers lined up, some have taken cats already, if they had space. It's going to save us. Or at least buy us some time.'

Luke frowned. 'I thought you'd rehomed a lot of cats very quickly?'

'Virtual cat sanctuary,' Mim said proudly. 'They're under our care, but not our roof. Since we shan't have this roof much longer.'

'Sounds like the answer to a cryptic crossword clue,' Paul said.

'It's going to be the temporary answer to our cryptic cat conundrum.' Mim smiled.

'I'll go. You stay here with your cryptic whatever.' Paul nodded at Luke.

So we're going, together, in the van. Right. Luke reminded himself he'd given up his place in the dance group, temporarily anyway, for this. So he might as well make the most of it.

Paul drove; Luke put the address in the satnav, another tiny village just out of the orbit of Basildon's new-town vibe. It was a large three-storey house, bay windows, red bricks, enormous ramshackle garden.

From a neighbouring house, a woman left her front garden to greet them. 'You're here. I'm so glad.' She nodded back at the house. 'They're emptying it. Dread to think what'll happen to the cats otherwise.'

Luke knocked the front door. It was ajar, so he pushed it open, shouting into the tiled hallway: 'Hello, we're here for the cats!'

The acrid smell of cat piss hit his nostrils; he covered his nose with a sleeve.

A long-haired Burmese cat lay on the bottom step, washing its nether regions. A black cat sat on top of the hallway radiator. The kitchen table had two cats – a tortoiseshell, and a black one with white bib and paws. There were empty cat food tins on the floor. Four over-flowing litter trays were arranged by each kitchen wall.

'Can I help you?' a voice came from behind them.

Luke turned to face her. 'Fluffy Paws, we were told the cats needed to be rescued.'

'Who told you?' She was a woman in her late sixties, wearing an apron over jeans and a baggy blouse, with grey hair tied back in a bun atop her head, who with a pinched expression stared at them.

'The lady next door. Said the woman who lived here has passed on and—'

'That bloody nosy cow.' She shook her head. 'It's none of her bloody business. I said I'd deal with them. Bloody cats. I never understood why she had so many. Seen one bloody cat, seen 'em all, is what I always said.'

Luke introduced himself, holding a hand out.

'Eunice. Busy, tired, stressed and fed-up Eunice. When will you get rid of them?' she asked. 'And, can you take away all their shit with you as well? Might as well have the food too. I'm not going to need it. Do you have any ideas for how to get rid of that terrible smell?'

'Whose house is this?'

'Mine now. But it was my sister's. Shared it with the cats, and never anyone else. Said she was happy, but I can't see it myself. Not the state she's left this place in.'

'You don't want to keep the cats, since they were your sister's?'

'I do not. Why should I want to do that?'

Luke felt it was a bit sentimental, but having just rediscovered his mother, felt able to voice it: 'Part of your sister. They were important to her so...'

'Not to me they're not. If it was up to me I'd chuck them out into the street and leave them to fend for themselves.'

'How many does she have?' Paul asked.

Luke felt grateful for his company. He was very much out of his depth.

'Four, six, don't know. Just get them gone by the time I'm finished today, otherwise I'm chucking them out into the street.' She turned. 'Don't think about nicking anything. Cos there's nothing worth taking. Except the house.' She left the room.

Luke had no idea what to say. He couldn't believe people could be so callous. 'What should we do?'

'Get all the cats, get all their equipment that's worth saving, and get out of here.' Paul stroked one of the cats on the table. 'These look to be easy to catch. Otherwise I've got a few trapping cages in the van.'

'Why?'

'Better safe than sorry,' Paul said. 'Can you get some carriers from the van? I'll work out how many we're catching.'

Shortly, Luke returned from the van with four carry cases. He had seen some metal cages packed flat on the sides of the van and presumed these were the trapping ones. He hoped, very hard, they wouldn't need to use them today.

'Eight,' Paul said as they met in the hallway.

'Eight?' Luke swallowed. 'We don't have enough carriers.'

'They'll have to go two to a carrier. They're all bonded as they're from the same household. They might not be best friends, but they'll get along.'

'Like us,' Luke said, without thinking.

'No thanks to you,' Paul replied with narrowed eyes.

'You're leaving.' Luke couldn't believe it.

'You're not staying either.'

'Hardly the same thing,' Luke replied. 'I'm not from here. I don't really live here.'

'You're in Anna's parents' place.'

'Temporarily. Staying there.'

Two cats shot across the room, meowing and hissing.

Paul shook his head. 'Can we *not* do this now? Cats come first, right?'

'Right.' *When then?* Luke wanted to ask.

But Paul was in the kitchen gently coaxing the sleeping cats on the table and work surfaces into carriers.

Working together, they put six cats in three carriers. Mostly, they allowed themselves to be picked up and placed inside. Two required a bit of cat food in the carrier. One was younger and followed a ball containing a bell into the wicker basket carrier.

'Two more,' Paul said, having deposited the others in the van.

'Are you done?' Eunice stood on the stairs, scowling with her hands on her hips.

'Two left,' Luke said.

'You'll never get them two. Pair of little bastards, they are. Scratched me to buggery.' She held a hand aloft, red welts on her forearm.

'When did that happen?' Luke asked innocently, catching Paul from the corner of his eye, as he shook his head.

'Clearing out a wardrobe, they were in the bottom, on top of some coats. Real fur, so worth something. Covered in cat fur though, but it sort of blended together. I've got a friend who sells antiques and he took everything that's worth something. I picked up the cat, but it scratched me, didn't like being held. Bloody little bastard. Threw the stupid thing away. Never came near me again.' She raised her eyebrows, clearly believing she was an astute animal handler.

Luke, in his relatively limited experience, knew it to be untrue.

'I wish you well.' She walked down the stairs into the kitchen. 'They all gone from here?'

Paul shouted, 'Yes.'

'Aren't you taking the shit away too?'

'Once we have the last two.'

She mumbled something, then slammed the fridge shut with a bang.

Luke mouthed, 'Are we?' to Paul.

Paul shook his head, nodding towards the last room, where the two remaining cats had been trapped.

Carefully opening the door, it reminded Luke of something he'd read in a book for school: a dressing table, bed, piles of clothes, everything covered in cobwebs. There had been a wedding cake in the book he'd read, but here there stood an urn on the dressing table, with a black-and-white photo of a man and woman on their wedding day.

'Wonder when he died?' Luke asked.

Paul inspected the urn, found a card and a pamphlet. 'Ten years ago. This order of service asks for no flowers, and donations to another local cat sanctuary. He must have been into cats.'

There were trophies along the edges of the dressing table. Luke read the engraving: 'Best Burmese, in show, nineteen ninety-seven.'

'They used to show cats.'

'People do that?'

'Like Crufts, but for cats. Of course.'

Paul, who was clearly much more experienced at this than Luke, used the cage trap and, in that small room, gave the cats no choice but to walk into it. There was quite a bit of time when the cats were running around, there was a great deal of them grabbing cats with thick leather gloves that came up to Paul's elbows, and he briefly picked up one cat and placed it in the cage, before Luke shut the cage door.

Soon, they had both cats in the cages. Paul wiped the sweat from his forehead with the leather glove. 'Let's go,' he said with a sigh.

Luke carried the metal cages containing the two cats, who were meowing with the occasional hiss. 'What about the litter trays, bowls, all their other stuff?'

'Get it if you wish, but we have the cats, which is why we came here.' Paul took the cages, left for the van.

Luke, more through duty than desire, collected tins of cat food and bowls, carrying armfuls to the car. 'I left the litter trays.'

Paul nodded. 'Wise.' He started the engine.

Luke climbed in, the items on his lap.

They drove off.

'When will you go travelling?' Luke asked, relieved they'd got on well saving the cats from whatever terrible fate awaited them.

'Few months. This contract is two months. But it pays more than usual. So I'm rewarding myself with a few months' travelling.'

Luke thought for a moment. 'Very sensible. Did I tell you I'm taking some time off from the group?'

'I'd heard.'

'I've been in the group since uni. Never had more than a week or so off at a time. I love it. Don't get me wrong, it's just...' Luke struggled for the words.

'You fancy a change?'

'That's it.' Luke nodded.

'It's easy to find yourself in a rut. Between seventeen and twenty-one, I took my A levels, went to uni, and got a proper job. Well, it was one of the clients I'd worked at during the summer holidays. Moved from home, to uni and my own place. But twenty-one to now, well, before I went travelling, I got a place with George, and nothing else changed.'

'I was with my ex, from just twenty-two until recently, same time. Basically.'

Paul nodded.

'Have you always wanted to travel?' Luke asked.

'George did, but once I got going I loved it too. Haven't you travelled?' Paul asked.

'With the group. But it's not the same. Or at least I think it isn't. I don't know.'

'Where have you been with the group?'

Luke thought for a moment. 'Portugal, Spain, France, Sweden, Norway, Iceland was cancelled, Lithuania, Estonia.'

'Impressive.'

Luke shook his head. 'Not really. I didn't see any of those places. It's hotel, a bar or two, then the venue where we perform, then back to the airport. Most of the time I didn't know where I was. Hotels, airports, and most bars are the same. I never got to see the real cities.' He left that hanging wistfully in the air between them.

'I intend to see much more than hotels and airports during these few months.'

'Where are you going?'

Paul shrugged. 'No idea. I need to plan a route. Some sights.'

Luke nodded, raising his eyebrows. 'Nice.'

They had arrived at the cat sanctuary. Paul switched the engine off. The cats were meowing loudly from the back of the vehicle. They were making the slight crying noise cats did when hungry or a little distressed. It wasn't unpleasant.

Paul left the van, opened the back and carried one carrier into the largest outbuilding, leaving them on the ground next to the desk where they processed the paper-work.

Luke followed with the wicker box of two cats.

'Do you want me to ask if you'd like to travel with me?' Paul asked, leaning on the open van door.

Luke hadn't expected that. 'Don't know. It sounds appealing, that's all.'

'Not that it was you, but I went travelling with a boyfriend, and… well, I don't want to do that again.'

George had obviously done many things Paul wasn't going to share, but Luke needed to bear that in mind in whatever he asked next.

They finished carrying the cats to the admissions desk in the largest outbuilding, and Sasha greeted them. 'Eight?'

Paul nodded.

'The woman said six.'

'I wouldn't trust her with anything she said. Least of all about the cats.'

'Bad?'

'She was going to throw them on to the street. It's sad that her sister died and that's how she treats the house.'

Sasha shrugged. 'People, eh?' She sat at the desk. 'Shall I do these admissions, or do either of you fancy doing it? Who knows where we'll fit them. In the house, I expect. I'd like to speak to Mim about her marvellous new idea.'

'Go,' Luke said with as much authority as he felt appropriate.

She stood, gesturing to the chair for one of the men to take her place. 'You two seem to be getting on well enough.'

They shrugged.

'Only I thought...' She looked from one man to the other. 'Doesn't matter.' She walked through the building, past the meowing cats in their pens, some sleeping, others playing, towards the exit, shouting, 'I'll bring tea for the workers shortly.' She disappeared.

'Do you want to do one?' Paul asked.

'I've not done one before,' Luke said with slight embarrassment.

'How do you think *I* learned?'

Reluctantly, Luke sat at the desk. He hoped Paul would be a good teacher.

Paul talked him through the process, showing him what to put on each part of the form, dictating the description of where they'd been rescued. 'Temperament?' Paul asked.

'She didn't scratch me. These two went in the carrier easily,' Luke said.

'Put that.' Paul tapped the form with a finger. 'We'll do videos later, this is so they're in the system.'

Luke nodded, wrote in the form.

A while later they had finished the new cats' paperwork and Paul had left to confirm where to accommodate them. They put all eight cats into one of the larger bedrooms of Sasha's house, since they all came from the same home.

Paul said it was best to keep them all together. 'If they can be rehomed together, that's best. Unlikely, but best.'

Luke smiled with the satisfaction of a job well done. The cats had been saved from a dangerous situation and now they were safe. 'I don't want to tread on your toes, with your travel plans. I'm just interested.'

Paul raised his eyebrows. 'I think you're awkwardly trying to ask if you can come with me.'

Luke shook his head slowly.

Paul led them to the kitchen in the house. 'I can be friends, an adult about this, if *you* can.'

Luke barely caught what he'd said. 'What?'

Paul leaned against the door frame, evidently trying to look as unbothered and relaxed as possible. 'You heard.'

Luke reckoned he was managing it very well. Paul also looked very attractive, with those come-to-bed eyes that had been Luke's undoing that night and the morning after, the way Paul had remained in control, until he hadn't. It was so sexy. *He's so sexy.* Luke swallowed the lump in his throat. 'Is that a yes?'

'It's a twin-beds-if-not-separate-rooms yes.' Paul looked Luke up and down briefly. 'If we want to do separate things while we're travelling, hook up with other men, spend days apart, only meet for dinner, that's also fine. I don't want to feel as if I'm coming on someone else's holiday. Understood?' Paul closed his eyes slowly.

'Understood.' Luke reckoned there was a great deal more behind that statement than Paul would share at the moment. That George ex of his must have really scarred Paul, relationship-wise.

Paul walked through the hallway, towards the front door.

Luke, against his best efforts, couldn't help but notice Paul's wide shoulders, narrow hips and tight buttocks. He was, after all, a very accomplished non-professional dancer. *Moved very well, elegantly. On the dance floor and in bed. I wonder if we'll go tapping together soon…*

Chapter 26

Sasha was in the drawing room of the house at Fluffy Paws, with Mim and Anna. They were agreeing what remained to implement the virtual cat sanctuary idea. Between Anna's offer of money and Mim's incisive brain with figures, Sasha knew she was lucky to have these people, friends, in her life. *Not every person lets you down,* she told herself.

The landlord had accepted an offer for the property. The final two pens had been pulled down and there remained far fewer cats at Fluffy Paws than seemed right. Sasha had asked what had happened to them and Mim had said not to worry, all was under control and the cats were safe.

'We haven't talked about my money,' Anna said with some fortitude that Sasha hadn't seen before. 'I've accepted an offer on my little house, the sale's going through very quickly.'

'I don't feel comfortable accepting such a large gift.'

'I don't need the money. I'll have my parents' house. Lodgers, maybe cats too.'

She paused. 'I beg to differ. Hadn't you ought to repay the loan you took out?'

'Of course. But what's left, I mean.'

'Perhaps,' Sasha said delicately, 'we can move on to that shortly. It's part of the virtual cat sanctuary discussion. Are you saying you're ready to accept cats to foster? It's just I wasn't aware that you were okay with the... disturbance and... mess they would make.'

Anna sat back in the chair, folded her arms. 'Why does everyone think I'm some basket case? I've survived burying both parents, a divorce, lost one job, probably going to lose another. I'm still here. What makes you think I can't handle a few cats in my enormous house?'

'You won't be able to keep your home as scrupulously clean as you'd like,' Sasha said, very carefully.

'I know that!' Anna shouted, then burst into floods of tears.

This was the regular pattern, had been since her work travails. Anna had disappeared for a few weeks again, not turning up to Fluffy Paws but instead sending long, rambling, slightly incoherent messages, she was ill and they didn't need her anyway. Fluffy Paws would be better off without her. Sasha had always replied to the contrary, telling Anna to rest and get better soon, then a while later she'd receive another from Anna, still unwell, didn't think she'd be back for a bit longer.

Sasha maintained Anna wasn't in the right place to offer such a generous benefaction, being both nearly unemployed and, probably, even to Sasha's untrained eye, suffering from poor mental health.

Mim rubbed Anna's shoulder. 'There's no rush. I've been slowly decanting cats to the network of volunteers over the last few weeks. Can we look at your place to see if it's suitable?'

Sasha frowned. 'You've done what?'

Mim repeated herself. 'Call it a pilot of the idea. There was only so far I could go writing it down, so I sort of started to do it. A cat here and there, a volunteer's house visit every now and again.'

'Without asking me?' Sasha asked, open-mouthed.

'Would you have said yes?'

'I wouldn't.'

'Which is why I didn't ask. The cats are all safe. Safer than cramming them in your house here. Do you trust me?'

The anger left her and Sasha knew when she was beaten, she couldn't control and worry and do everything. She nodded. 'Thanks.'

Mim smiled. 'Eventually, after we're out of here, have moved on from the virtual cat sanctuary, once we've found permanent *new* premises, we should have a ball. In aid of the sanctuary, a celebration of all the hard work.'

Sasha liked that idea, nodded at Mim. 'All in good time.'

'Of course,' Mim said.

Anna looked from one woman to the other. 'You've come to my place. And Paul. Emptied most of it out. I want to help too.'

'We did that to your small house. Most of the contents of your parents' place remains in situ.'

'What do I have to do to convince you I can foster cats?' Anna sounded exasperated.

'As with all volunteers, as is described within Mim's very comprehensive proposal, we would need to inspect where you intend to look after the cats. Check your history with pets.'

'Which is precisely what I've done with the new volunteers' homes, where many of the cats have already gone.'

'Can we do that for me, please?' Anna sounded down-trodden.

Sasha took pity on her. 'We may not even need your money, not that I'm saying we'd accept it. But when we get this virtual sanctuary up and running, we'll save a considerable amount and won't need a building.'

'For now,' Mim put in.

Anna seemed happy with that, folding her arms.

'We'll include you on the list of homes to rehome the cats,' Sasha said to Anna. 'Won't we?' she asked Mim.

Mim nodded. 'Indeed.'

'Thanks,' Anna said.

Turning to Mim, Sasha added, 'Can I include you with that, taking on some cats to home as part of your wonderful scheme?'

'Of course,' Mim replied with a smile that seemed to say there was more she wasn't telling Sasha.

Later, they gathered the volunteers in the house's drawing room. Sasha explained the concept of the virtual sanctuary, including the names of the senior volunteers.

There was a lot of nodding, implying many of the volunteers knew more than Sasha thought.

'It's only a temporary solution,' Sasha said. 'Eventually we'll need to find new premises. It's not my idea, I'd have been lost without Mim's help, but I recognise a good idea when I see one. If you can take cats, assuming you're not already doing so, since Mim has sort of jumped the gun with this, please leave your name and how many cats, with Mim. If you know people who are well-proven cat carers, please ask them to get in touch to build our network of homes? I'm putting Mim, Paul and Anna in charge of the virtual pens.' She looked to Mim. 'Is that what we're calling them?'

'Each home will need to show cats,' Mim said. 'They'll need to take visitors, people who are looking to adopt cats. We'll direct them to the most appropriate cats, but you'll need to manage the showings. So anyone who doesn't own their own home, or who's in a leasehold property, may not be able to do this. To ensure the safety of volunteers, every showing will be chaperoned by one of the senior volunteers Sasha has just named.'

And so she left Mim in charge of the virtual cat sanctuary project, who effortlessly steered them through all problems, kept calm and was generally absolutely unflappable and indispensable. It took longer than anticipated, but Sasha was grateful for Mim's unofficial head start, and Sasha kept the landlord appraised of their progress, assuring him they would indeed have vacated the property before the sale completed. It wasn't quite what he had wanted, empty at the point of sale, but he realised he had little choice, so accepted it when Sasha explained her plans.

A few weeks after the announcement, in time for the landlord's deadline, Sasha carried the last cat from its pen into the boot of a volunteer's car. 'Thanks, much appreciated,' she added, waving them off.

It had taken a very concerted effort on social media, led by Paul, contacting people who'd expressed an interest in volunteering, but had never followed up, as well as the clients who'd adopted cats, but they now had a network of thirty homes into which all cats had been placed. There were half a dozen senior volunteers who chaperoned house visits to show the cats and it was all coordinated by a splendid spreadsheet of Anna's making, with a social media group for the volunteers to communicate. Anna really was a marvel sometimes.

It was surprising to Sasha how amenable most people were, especially once they had publicly shared the sanctuary was being sold and they had no real alternative. One option had been passing the cats to nearby cat sanctuaries, but they were all at capacity with long waiting lists.

With a sense of sadness and despite her believing it would never happen — as this signalled an end to this chapter in her life — for the final time, Sasha locked the house front door then posted the key through the letter box.

She was moving out.

Mim, Anna and Paul had gently led her by the hand through this, asking for her decisions, keeping her informed, and she would have been absolutely lost without them. Her belongings were packed into a removal van. Among all the virtual cat sanctuary activity, she had *almost* forgotten about herself. Except the volunteers hadn't let her.

Sasha had no income, she couldn't get another job, so the decision had been made for her.

'You'll live with me,' Anna had said. 'Means you can keep an eye on *my* cat fostering skills.'

Secretly, Sasha had thought that rather a good idea, but to Anna she'd said, 'That's very kind of you. I wouldn't dream of doing anything of the sort.'

Now, with a sense of relief this stage was over, Sasha climbed into the passenger's seat, and the removal van drove to Anna's parents' home, in Margaretting.

Mim, Luke and Paul helped unload the van and installed Sasha in Anna's largest spare bedroom. She didn't realise she had no furniture to speak of, since it had all come with the house. Boxes of clothes, some ornaments and kitchen equipment seemed to be the sum total of her life. She felt slightly down at the mouth as she surveyed the contents of her room.

Is this it, all I've got to show for forty-six, nearly forty-seven years on this planet?

Closing the door, she then walked downstairs, slowly, one step at a time. She was greeted in the kitchen with a cheer from her core group of volunteers. She smiled. They stood around the table, with a cake in the shape of a cat, with *We Did It* written across the middle.

Sasha sat at the table, exhausted to the core of her bones. It had been weeks of sleepless nights, worrying they'd receive an eviction notice from the landlord, that the team of volunteers wouldn't appear, that they'd be forced to house too many cats in too few homes, over-relying on a small number of volunteers as usual. That she'd forget something…

Sasha did as they asked and cut the cake, cheered and congratulated everyone. After a small mouthful, she left the room. It was all a bit much for her. Too emotional. Too people-ey. She longed to return to the cats, spend time in one of the pens. The celebration continued in her absence which, when she thought about it, was precisely what needed to happen.

Anna met her in the hallway. 'I said it was too soon. I told them you'd want to settle in before we did anything like this. They wouldn't listen.'

'I'm sorry. I'm just not up to this. Not quite yet anyway. I feel as if I've finished running a marathon. But I've still got to run another one. We're still in need of a new location for the sanctuary.' Sasha exhaled, the breath leaving her body as she felt deflated, bone-tired, and something of an anti-climax.

'Where would you like to go?' Anna asked.

'If I said, back to the big house at Fluffy Paws, would you be *very* disappointed?'

Anna shook her head. 'Totally understandable. What would make you feel a bit better, right here, right now?'

Lately, having gone through the long, rambling text messages stage, Anna always seemed to know the right thing to say. It was as if having the responsibility of the cats and Sasha and Luke living under her roof had given Anna cause, a purpose she'd lacked since her parents' death.

Sasha thought for a moment. 'Can we go to your cat room?'

'Which one?' Anna said with a smile.

'The one you think will cheer me up the most.' There, that left Anna in charge, as was right. She felt guilty at ever doubting Anna could do this, but after her fastidiousness and slightly unhealthy obsession with cleanliness, Sasha had worried she wouldn't adjust well to the mess fostering cats would create.

Anna stood outside a room, on the door was a sign reading:

Fluffy Paws – Anna Ward, pen 1

Although it sounded stupid, and too simple, when they explained these rooms were replacing outbuildings and cat pens at Fluffy Paws, the volunteers had understood what was required. The rest of Anna's house was kept immaculately clean, the two cat rooms were also very clean, since Anna liked to ensure their litter trays were regularly refreshed, but the cat hair and other mess, Anna was able to compartmentalise as the same as in the sanctuary, so different from normal house dirty. And therefore acceptable.

It had taken some weeks of talking therapy with a woman Anna had been put in touch with by her doctor, but soon after a diagnosis of generalised anxiety disorder she could let go somewhat of her need to keep everything excessively clean.

She told Sasha her treatment included more talking with the grief counsellor, who she'd made such great friends with, which had seemed odd, but Sasha didn't wish to pry. Anna said with enthusiasm she was having relaxation therapy to learn how to relax in situations normally causing her anxiety, how the doctor had said cats definitely helped with that, and, of course, good old medication.

She had seemed very optimistic, bright, almost slightly worryingly so, but Sasha wasn't a doctor so accepted Anna's version of events in support.

The improvements were helped, in no small part, Sasha felt, by the amount of things Anna had in her life now, the fullness of her experience. With the cats, the two lodgers, Anna soon found herself unable to focus on the things that were less important and instead give her attention to those that were more important including repaying her loan.

Along one wall was a wooden frame, covered with metal wire, divided into six spaces. Each pen had two levels, a litter tray, food and water bowls, a soft bed on the higher level and toys scattered on the ground. They had, in short, recreated part of Fluffy Paws in Anna's home.

Anna opened the nearest door, letting Sasha inside, closing it. 'Shall I leave you?'

'Stay, won't you?' Sasha asked. 'I should never have doubted you'd make a perfect cat fosterer.'

'I don't think I'll want to keep them. Which I suppose helps.'

'For now,' Sasha said with a smile. 'I'll find my own place as soon as we find a new permanent location for the sanctuary.'

'No rush.'

Sasha didn't like being in the debt of others, normally. But over the last few months, she had come to owe all the volunteers such a lot. They had rallied together to save all the cats and continue their good work, despite not having a building, and Anna had, on top of taking on two rooms of cats to foster, given Sasha a place to stay.

'I don't think I want to live alone,' Sasha said without thinking.

'Neither do I,' Anna replied. 'Like I said, no rush to move. Decorate the room yourself if you want. I'll help if you'd like.' She looked at the walls, orange and brown striped wallpaper from the Seventies. 'Fresh start. If I'm living here, I'll make it my own. It's what Mum and Dad would have wanted.'

'Definitely. No point living in a mausoleum.'

Sadness crossed Anna's face as she twirled a strand of hair around a finger.

Sasha regretted mentioning it. She knew Anna had been doing good work with her counsellor, coming to terms with her grief and loss. But there was, Sasha knew, still a long way for her to go.

Chapter 27

Paul ended a three-hour video call, with a rictus grin plastered on his face. He shut the laptop and stepped away. His phone buzzed with an email. As expected, it was the same bloody client he'd just spent all morning reassuring and trying to understand what they wanted.

Another email arrived, followed by three more in swift succession. All the same person. All marked urgent. All related to what he'd just spoken to them about.

God. FML. F M actual L.

He was going to be late, so he texted Mim to let her know.

She replied: *Get here when you get here. I'm not going anywhere.*

A while after he'd intended, Paul arrived at Chelmsford library to meet Mim. She stood by a stall with pictures of the cats needing homes, a description of the sanctuary sat on one end of the stall. People surrounded the stand and Mim was confidently talking, taking people's details.

'Here's our resident internet expert,' Mim said, holding out her hands for him to shake.

Paul blushed. 'Social media.' He turned to her. 'How's it going?'

Mim glanced at the clipboard. 'Four possible adoptions, they want to see the cats first, of course. And a few volunteers who've agreed to foster. A good morning. How's the money situation?'

Sasha had shown him last month's vet bill, it was harder to keep track with the cats being all over many different homes. It came to 20,000 pounds. He told her.

'What will we do?' Mim asked.

'Find it somehow.'

'Are you in charge of fundraising for the new premises?'

'Haven't properly discussed that with Sasha, but any spare donations once we've paid the vet bills I put into the new building fund.'

'Good-oh!' Mim smiled.

He shook his head. 'Long way to go yet. And… I've taken my eye off the ball with the socials of late. This job is kicking my arse. Talk about pound of flesh.'

Mim looked out for people overhearing. 'Sounds dreadful. But it's not forever, is it?'

Paul shook his head. 'Two months. I've done a fortnight and it feels like a year. I don't think I can stick it. They're just so bloody rude. Unreasonable. Demanding. Don't listen.'

'And the client's always right, presumably?' Mim asked.

'Even when they're not,' Paul said with resignation.

'Give me twenty minutes and I'm finished, fancy a coffee?'

'I'd rather something wet, white and cool.' He raised an eyebrow.

Mim nodded. 'I'll wrap this up pronto.' Using her impressive people skills, she answered questions, took details while packing away the stand.

Paul left the library, heading for a pub along the high road. He sat by the window with a bottle of white wine in an ice bucket. He'd finished his first small glass by the time Mim arrived.

'I've been thinking about your client conundrum,' Mim said, sitting at the table, pouring herself a large wine. She held the glass aloft. 'Are we celebrating?'

'Not particularly,' Paul said, unable to keep the glumness from his tone.

'Come on.' She tapped his elbow playfully. 'There's always something to be grateful for.'

Paul thought for a moment. 'Not telling my client to actually fuck right off?'

Mim nodded. 'Good enough for me.'

They clinked glasses then sipped wine.

Paul's shoulders relaxed, and his phone buzzed in his pocket. Removing it, he checked messages. 'Fifteen.'

Mim removed the phone from him, placing it in her handbag. 'If it's urgent they'll call.'

'What if it's the client and it's urgent?'

Mim rested her elbows on the table, her aquamarine sleeves flowing like wings. 'What does this client do?'

'Sells things.'

'What sort of things?'

'Insurance.'

'And what,' she went on, holding his hands on the table, 'precisely are you doing for them?'

'Helping them sell more insurance.'

Mim sighed. 'As suspected. No one will have died. Do you know why they're behaving so unreasonably with you?'

Paul shook his head. 'I reckon you're about to tell me.'

'Correct.' Mim sat upright, adjusting her silver neck-lace on her décolletage. 'Because you're letting them. If you're available at all hours, they'll continue to expect you to be precisely that.'

'Easier said than done.'

'Two weeks in, they're getting into bad habits. It's like pets, and children. One needs to be clear who's in charge.'

'They are. Aren't they?'

Mim shook her head. 'You're giving them a service. Solving a problem for them. And you need time to give them that.'

'How do I do that?'

'Hold a mirror up to their behaviour. Don't engage out of hours otherwise you're complicitly agreeing with their behaviour.'

'Easier said than—'

'As a holiday rep I saw all sorts of unreasonable beha-viour, ridiculous requests. People complaining the food in the restaurant, in Spain, was too Spanish. Saying the sun was too hot. The pool made their swimming costumes smell of bleach. The people didn't speak English when they went into a bar in the nearby town. Need I go on?'

Paul shook his head.

'I used to describe what they'd requested and then ask if and how they thought I could fix it. For most people, it becomes clear, very swiftly those sorts of issues are beyond anyone's control. Of course, there are others with whom there's no reasoning.'

Paul's shoulders slumped as he poured more wine. 'I'm going to tell them to get fucked,' he said with relief.

'You will not. Then they've won. This job is what's giving you the freedom to go travelling. Don't walk away from six more weeks of well-paid work and then you're done. Am I right?'

'You are.'

Mim pulled Paul's phone from her handbag. 'Unlock it and let's deal with one of their messages. Pick one that's typical and we'll write a reply together.'

Together, they drafted a reply from Paul putting him back in charge.

Paul clicked send and knew he'd receive another email, asking to talk now. Putting the phone on the table, he waited for it to buzz.

Mim poured them wine, finishing the bottle.

Paul wasn't sure if it was the half a bottle of wine, or writing the email, or simply Mim's splendidly take-charge and no-nonsense attitude, which he'd always admired since meeting her at Fluffy Paws, but whatever it was, he relaxed.

His phone did not buzz. He checked it and nothing.

'Told you,' Mim said. 'Now we're two wines deep, are you going to tell me what you *really* want to discuss?'

Paul blushed. 'How is David?'

'Very well.' Mim placed her hands on the table. She had rings on alternate fingers on both hands. 'How are your travel plans with Luke coming along?'

'I think I'm going to ask why he's coming, suggest maybe I should go alone.'

'Why on earth should you?'

'He's not particularly interested in where we go. I've done most of the organising. He sits next to me while I do the research and booking. It's a bit... I hoped he'd be more involved.'

'If he took charge, what then?'

'That's what George used to do. I left him to get away from that.'

Mim raised her eyebrows, staring at him.

Paul sighed. 'Has someone told him what George was like?'

'You, maybe?'

Paul bit his bottom lip. Had he? He couldn't remember, maybe when they first met, when Paul was oversharing and didn't think he'd develop feelings for Luke. 'So he's... so I don't...'

'Letting you take charge, so you don't feel over-whelmed and repeat old unhelpful patterns with your ex...?'

'That's it.'

'Highly likely,' Mim said. 'Very considerate of him, isn't it? Perhaps more than one would normally do for a travelling companion.'

'I didn't think he saw me like that?' *Especially after I was so clear I didn't want anything more than our casual one night together, nothing approximating a relationship.*

'He's not travelled much, so perhaps he's happy for you to take charge. Any travel is better than no travel. You are, for want of a better word, the expert here.'

'Not in relationships.'

Mim laughed. 'No one's that. Each one's different. You just have to dive in with your eyes and heart open and see where you end up.'

'Right.'

'More wine?' Mim asked.

Paul nodded. Suddenly Luke's behaviour made sense. This definitely called for more wine.

Chapter 28

Margaretting, Essex

In her large kitchen at her parents' home, Anna yawned, exhausted, after another very poor night's sleep. She'd gone to bed at 10:30 p.m., as usual, but had then been unable to fall asleep: tossing and turning, rolling in bed all night, her brain unable to switch off and let her simply rest. She'd finally fallen asleep at three or four in the morning. It was so much easier relying on those marvellous little tablets to help her sleep. But she'd been told it wasn't acceptable to rely on them so heavily, so this was her trying not to.

And sadly failing.

She put her head in her hands, resting her elbows on her parents' large wooden kitchen table. Well, it was hers now. As was the house. She'd sold her small house, cash buyer, first person who'd looked at it. Mim helped her pay off the loan to the company who, when Anna had checked the paperwork, were indeed taking the absolute piss out of her. It was only when Anna felt better and went through the details with Mim, that she saw how foolish she'd been taking out the loan in the first place. Sky high interest rates and large monthly repayments she struggled to keep up with. Sending the loan company the final payment and receiving an email to confirm it had been repaid in full were moments of such relief.

Anna felt she was returning to a more balanced, whole version of herself, rather than a strange person she'd become who made rash illogical decisions, isolated herself and worried about everything.

The sale happened very quickly. Under three months. Much faster than Anna remembered, when she had bought it all those years before. Twenty years ago, it had been, when she was twenty-two. Her parents had given her a hefty deposit and she'd secured a mortgage with the job she'd just landed at The Grove Practice. All in the wake of her divorce.

A lifetime ago, she reflected now, the local newspapers spread on the table. Unsurprisingly, job hunting had somewhat moved on since she'd last needed to properly do it. She pushed the papers into one pile, arranging it neatly to the side of the table.

There were noises coming from upstairs, a TV or radio playing in Sasha's room, and Luke's voice coming from his room, probably on the phone.

Bringing tins of cat food and a box of dried food, she walked upstairs to the cat rooms. Opening the door, she was greeted by the loud meowing of four cats and a distinctive cat smell which she had found she did, after all, quite like. She'd cleaned their litter trays and washed their bowls first thing this morning.

One pen at a time, she filled their bowls with food, stroking each cat, talking to them, asking how they were. This routine, such that it was, had become her favourite part of her mornings. Now the days seemed to stretch out indefinitely in front of her, without a job, she liked the regular cat activities that punctuated her days. She felt better than before, not completely well, but definitely *better*.

A pair of black-and-white male cats were playing in the cage where she crouched. They were brothers, had been found in a box by a busy road as kittens. No sign of mother, but fortunately they were weaned, so Anna had fed them on solids. She imagined them playing on her sitting room furniture and smiled.

Stroking one under his chin he soon purred loudly, jumped on her lap and started making bread with his paws. She wore an old towelling dressing gown of her father's and it had pieces of loose cotton from where many cats had plucked and pulled at it.

She stood as the persistent meows of cats she'd yet to feed drew her back to the job in hand. She moved to the next pen, which housed a large male ginger cat who was well over ten years old. He looked slightly raggedy, but was well-natured, letting Anna stroke him as he threaded his way between her ankles.

The next room housed four more cats. She had a viewing for two of them this afternoon. *Must ensure their pens are scrupulously clean, and that they're happy to play.* It was, Anna had soon learned, so important how well cats showed. If they remained hidden in their beds, they were unlikely to be rehomed with any speed. But the cats that played with visitors, allowed themselves to be stroked, were usually adopted very soon.

Content with a job well done, she shut the doors and returned to the kitchen. Searching for a mug, she admonished herself for having too many. She'd retained all hers *and* her parents' mugs. *Nobody needs forty-seven mugs, do they?*

'Morning,' Luke's voice came from behind her.

She turned, holding two mugs. 'Which should I choose?'

'I don't mind,' he said with a shrug.

She made them tea, knowing that was his preferred first drink of the day. 'When was the last time you got a job?'

'Before the group. When I was at uni, I suppose.' He shrugged. 'Ten years ago?'

'Do you know if there are places where I can get help with my CV and application writing?' She felt so useless, having grown hopelessly out of practice. But she knew he'd be gentle with her.

'I'll send some websites to you. Letter templates, CVs, the lot. Very helpful.' He sat at the table.

'What are you doing today?' She'd worried having both him and Sasha in her home would prove awkward, but it hadn't. They ate most evening meals together. Sasha seemed to like cooking and prepared almost all of the meals – Anna paid for the food. It was cheaper and as easy as living on ready meals as she had done before.

'I'm trying to work out how to get Sasha to meet Mum and Dad.'

'What does Sasha think?'

'Didn't say no. Didn't seem too excited about the idea.'

'Your parents?'

'They're always happy to hear from me. Now. Pleased I'm settling in here. Course, they didn't expect me to stay this long. The group members were very understanding. But I did say to Mum and Dad it would take as long as it took and I'd dip into my savings since this seemed like the definition of a rainy day and a good reason to use them.'

'That it will,' Anna said, sipping her tea. She wondered about asking him how he felt about Paul, about their travel plans. But it felt like something he'd probably want to discuss with Sasha, or his parents. Or not at all. Anna wasn't very good at the whole relationship thing. She regarded him, sipping his tea.

He sat with legs outstretched and almost hanging on the chair by his bottom perched on the seat. He had a habit of taking up more space than he ought, probably thanks to his height and build. He had an enviable confidence that Anna lacked.

'We're going travelling. So I won't be home for even longer. Mum and Dad won't like that.' Luke grimaced.

'Are you?' she asked, trying to sound clueless.

'Come on, you're telling me you don't know about me and Paul's trip?' He chuckled.

'I don't like to pry,' she said simply.

'It's probably a big mistake. We'll fall out and return separately. But I've never travelled, not properly. And he has, and well, we sort of rub along together pretty well. An interesting way to spend my savings. I thought he'd say no, I couldn't come. But he didn't, so I'm going with him.' A pause, and then: 'For good or shit reasons. I'll know which soon enough.' He shrugged and smiled.

God, Anna envied him that see-how-it-turns-out casualness. She'd never managed to even come close.

'Morning.' Sasha joined them in the kitchen. 'Heard voices. I never realised how much I missed living with others, having lived alone for so long. Mind you, I didn't have you.' She nodded at Luke.

Luke stood. 'Coffee, black, no sugar, large mug?'

Sasha smiled. 'Toast, if you're having some.'

He put some bread in the toaster, fetched marmalade and spread from the fridge, putting them on the table.

Anna took her mug, walked to the door. 'See you later.' She left them as they started talking. They seemed to have their morning routine pretty well established. She smiled as she climbed the stairs, their voices carrying through the hallway. Her phone beeped, at the top of the stairs she checked – Luke had sent her some links to help the job hunt.

Good. That's a step in the right direction. I'll get on with it now.

After the morning of CV polishing, personal statement drafting and applying for half a dozen jobs, she left for her appointment.

It was in Howe Green, at the GP surgery where she had worked. She'd tried to register with another but their lists were full, or they were much farther away, so because it felt like another piece of life admin she could do without, or had never quite got round to doing, she'd left it. Now, as she parked outside the building, she reckoned she should have changed doctors. The feeling of regret and loss and sadness at getting everything so spectacularly wrong felt heavier than her eyelids from another poor night's sleep. She still had five minutes until her appointment. Better to sit in the car, or go in and register, braving the smile of the receptionist who she'd worked with for more than eight years?

I'll stay in the car. Anna watched the clock on the car's dashboard creep forwards with painful slowness.

One of the doctors she knew left the building, probably nipping out for his lunch. He saw her, paused, didn't wave, then left.

A jolt of sadness shot through her.

Yes, definitely better sitting in here than arriving early.

At precisely her appointment time, she walked into the surgery, registered using the touchscreen, sat in the waiting room. She couldn't concentrate to read any of the aged magazines, so she flicked through one that was mainly pictures: celebrity weddings, European royal family members, actors who'd just had babies.

Nice.

Her number was called, she walked to the consulting room, recognising the name of the doctor she was seeing. Of course she did, she'd worked here most of her life. She could draw a floor plan of the whole building with her eyes closed – should she need to – not that it would be particularly useful.

'Hello, Anna,' Rebecca said, holding the door open, gesturing for Anna to sit.

Anna swallowed, the shame at what she'd done still threatening to consume her whole. Perching on the plastic chair, she said, 'Hello. Doctor Kempshott.'

She tilted her head to one side. 'You can call me Rebecca.'

Anna shook her head, stood. The shame, the sadness, it was all too much. 'I need to go.'

'I'm not here to judge. Just to listen. You'll wait another week for an appointment if you walk out. You're here now. Might as well stay.' Rebecca sounded kind. Not the same tone as the last time they'd met.

Anna was very determined not to cry. She'd done that in the phone interview the HR person had conducted as part of the investigation, trying to tell her side of the story. Explaining she'd not meant it. 'If I could do it again, I wouldn't. I just thought it was a squiggle, like when I PP signatures,' she'd said.

'You know it's very different, don't you?'

'I do now,' she'd said.

Anna had cried again when the letter had informed her of the outcome:

Dear Anna Bramley,

We have concluded our investigation into the incident of you forging the signature of Rebecca Kempshott and falsifying references to obtain a job at a supermarket.

This constituted fraud and is within the scope of gross misconduct. As this was your first incident during a twenty-year career here, we will provide you with a factual reference, omitting this, as long as you sign below to confirm this concludes this matter and you will not take it further through employment tribunal or other routes.

You will be dismissed with immediate effect. You will be paid owed annual leave and in lieu of notice, the latter is not statutory. I hope you'll agree this is more than generous.

We wish you luck with your future endeavours,
Yours, Ms Rebecca Kempshott

Anna had held the letter, hands shaking, crying, unable to believe this was where things had ended up after what she'd thought was an innocent mistake.

Sasha had read it, sat next to her at the table. 'You'll get another job.'

'With fraud on my record?'

'Not if you sign the letter,' Sasha said, pointing to the part she referred to.

'I don't understand.'

'Sign it, I'll explain later.'

She signed it, brought it in when she collected her belongings from the surgery. Twenty years of life, assembled in a small cardboard box, walking out of the surgery, no goodbye card, no leaving party, just a few nodded heads and people's hands on her shoulder as she'd left. She felt as if she stood behind glass, and the rest of the world was happening outside of the glass.

And she'd cried then, of course. Silent tears rolling down her cheeks as she packed her belongings, more as she walked out, as Rebecca had accompanied her, a hand on her shoulder, steering her out, away, to ensure Anna was gone. She placed the box in her car boot, and hunched forwards, shouted at the sky, at the air, 'Stupid stupid stupid stupid stupid!'

A howl of despair and then when she managed to catch her breath, she sat in the car, started the engine and drove home. During the journey she noticed howling noises, assuming they were something to do with the car, and it wasn't until she arrived home, she realised they were her, howling at the world, at the air, at everything. For taking her parents, for taking her job, for taking her best friend, for taking her husband, for making him seem so perfect until he'd cheated on her, for dealing her this bloody shitty hand, and making her just get on with it.

And she hadn't returned to the surgery until now, when she sat two feet away from Rebecca, the person whose signature she'd forged, who'd been her manager and confidante for twenty years, and who she now had to open herself to and share how, yet again, she needed help.

Which was why, now, sitting in that small consulting room, in the village of Howe Green, Anna was determined not to cry.

Not. One. Tear.

She bunched her hands into fists, twisting the material on her blouse.

'Might as well stay,' Rebecca said, 'I'd like to help you.' She gently put a hand on Anna's shoulder, just as she had for all those years.

'I'm not able to get rid of things,' Anna said with such shame she could hardly say it.

'Your belongings?'

Anna nodded.

'How long has this been going on for?' Rebecca asked.

Anna thought. 'Forever, it seems.'

Rebecca asked about her parents' death, their possessions, her own belongings, why she held on to them. After some reference to her computer, Rebecca said, 'I think you might have something called *hoarding disorder*.'

Sounded about right. Hoarding things, to the point that she felt paralysed about sorting them out, so never bothered, sounded like a disorder of some kind. All the time. Anna shrugged. 'Can you give me some more tablets, to help me sleep?' She'd run out of the other ones, and hadn't gone back for a repeat prescription. That was when the sleepless nights had started, that and the stuff with the letter at work. All sort of combined and she'd not been sure how she'd got up each day, and put one foot in front of the other and kept on going. Some days she hadn't. Remained in bed all day. Pretending to have a migraine. But it had been a migraine about life, about how she didn't see the point and wouldn't go on.

'I can.' Rebecca checked the computer screen. 'You were prescribed some before. I'll put you back on those, assuming they worked?' Rebecca raised her eyebrows.

'Right.' Anna nodded.

A few taps of the keyboard, clicks of the mouse. 'But I also want you to talk to someone. About how you find it difficult to let go of possessions.'

After reluctantly agreeing at first, Anna had been talking to someone for a while, first shortly after her parents' death to discuss grief, and then during the work thing, and then, without warning, the woman had said, 'This is our last session.'

And it had felt like the floor beneath Anna had opened up and she'd fallen into a deep black hole, disappearing, falling down and down until she finally landed that evening when she arrived home, with no idea what to do, how to navigate herself out of this mess. And so she'd taken to bed. At first for the afternoon, then when she couldn't face rising for dinner, that evening and that night too – although not sleeping. And there, in her bed, she'd remained for the next fortnight or so, even now she wasn't sure precisely how long it had been.

She simply *could not* cope with life back then.

She had missed the cats and people from Fluffy Paws, but she had no way of navigating her way back alone. Anna wasn't even completely sure when this had happened, there had been such a great deal of change and upheaval in her life, whisking her about like a great hurricane. Some days felt as if they lasted for a week and other times she'd rise from her bed and a few days seemed to have passed. She thought it had all fallen apart after losing her jobs. Without a structure and reason to rise, and in the knowledge of her stupidity, she had found herself floating, lost, from hour to day, to week, and she thought this was when she had entered what she called the period of falling into a deep black hole. She sent long sad messages to Sasha apologising for not coming to Fluffy Paws, saying she had flu, was in bed.

After that few weeks, when she emerged from the vortex of not being able to cope, she had pretended, very hard indeed, that everything was okay, told people she was speaking to someone about her anxiety, but instead she had been crying a great deal and taking the medication that seemed to *oh so wonderfully* numb her from the everyday worries of life.

She told Rebecca. Very slowly. One sentence at a time, the shame filling her, the sadness resurfacing as she relived the worst time of her life. The guilt at lying to her friends. The strain at pretending to be well, at overcompensating for her gutful of misery by smiling so hard her cheeks ached, making stuff up when asked, lie after lie until she couldn't remember where one ended and the truth took over.

'You could have told me,' Rebecca said. 'We'd have got you another counsellor.'

A red-hot wave of fury overcame her. Anna shouted: 'I didn't want *another* one. I wanted the one I had. I wanted to carry on talking to her. And when I asked if I could do this, she said no, I'd have to speak to the doctors. It was in the middle of the mess and I couldn't. So I didn't.' A tear threatened to leave her eye and roll onto her cheek. Angrily, Anna wiped it with a tissue from the desk.

'Have you had feelings of hurting yourself, or killing yourself?' Rebecca said it as if she were asking about what Anna had seen on TV last night.

'It's a bit late for the former. Look at the mess I've made.'

'Yes. And,' Rebecca went on with care, 'taking your life?'

Anna shook her head angrily.

'Good.'

'Do you want to know why?'

Rebecca nodded.

'Because I couldn't be bothered. I hoped I'd fade away, staying in bed, not eating, not washing, just disappear into the duvet. Be found one morning, staring white-faced at the ceiling, like Mum and Dad were in their beds at the end.' That did it, that absolutely finished her off, among this traumatic mess, remembering how her parents had looked when she'd arrived at the nursing home to visit, and wishing she herself had gone in the same gentle way. She cried, burst into floods of tears.

Rebecca handed the box of tissues to her.

After Anna had stopped crying, she wiped her eyes. 'Said I wasn't going to do that today. Promised myself.'

'We don't *always* have control of our emotions,' Rebecca said carefully. 'We don't always do the best thing. Humans aren't consistently rational, they can be messy. Although we must live with our decisions it doesn't mean we must carry them with us forever.' She wrote a prescription and typed on the computer. 'You'll resume seeing Mrs Chineham as soon as she's available. I've marked that it's urgent. She'll help you with your hoarding disorder. You can come up with a plan for sorting your belongings. Tablets should help you sleep.' She handed over the prescription.

Feeling exhausted, dejected, useless and stupid, Anna stood. 'Do you wish you could re-live your life?'

Rebecca stood, shook her head. 'You can't. No one can. That's what makes life precious. If you could redo it whenever you made a mistake, it makes all mistakes and anything good, completely pointless.'

Anna nodded, huffed to herself, closed the door, muttering under her breath, 'Easy for you to say.'

Chapter 29

South Hanningfield, Essex

Mim had printed out the invitation and handed it to David. They were sitting at the island in their airy and light-filled kitchen one morning.

'I've told you, there's no need to print out things like this,' he said before reading it.

'Read it, would you, please?'

He did. 'Trip to Spain, could be fun. See the old gang. Do you want to go?'

She couldn't tell from his response whether he wanted to. He was good at that. Mim put her reading glasses on, read the invitation again. 'I don't. If we want a trip to Spain, we'll have one.'

'Indeed we will.' David smiled, stroking her hand on the work surface. 'Shall we?'

'Not yet. What would we do about the cats? We're off to stay with Henry and co next week. And I've been so looking forward to it.' So much. When Fi had suggested it, and Henry had agreed immediately, on their last visit, after she'd spent the day alone with Tilly, hand painting, baking fairy cakes and reading, Mim had almost squealed with delight.

'Good points. Wouldn't want to let Henry and Fi down.'

'Or the cats,' Mim added.

'Or, indeed, the cats. How many do we have now?' He looked about him since there was usually at least one hanging about the kitchen waiting for scraps of food.

'Four,' Mim said.

'And they're not ours, we're under no obligation to keep them?' David asked warily.

'We've been through this. I could hardly suggest a virtual cat sanctuary and not volunteer to home any, could I?'

David shrugged. 'I think you could have, but now it's neither here nor there.'

'In short, no. They're not ours. Fluffy Paws pays for their vet bills. They would pay for their food, but I'm happy to stump up for a few tins of Whiskas each week.'

'A few,' David spluttered, 'a day, more like.'

Mim grinned, she knew he was joking. She'd packed away all her glass ornaments to avoid them being broken by cats. Once they were happy in the spare room, Mim had let them have the run of the whole house. The cats being a bonded quartet, from a house where suddenly the owners had decided they couldn't care for them any longer, had helped. They all rubbed along next to each other very happily. They were often to be found washing one another on Mim's sofa.

'I'll RSVP now, shall I?' Mim held the invitation aloft.

David grinned. 'Let's book a trip to Europe soon. Just us two. Doesn't have to be Spain, does it?'

'I feel as if we've seen rather a lot of Spain over the years.' *Just us two*, she thought, and smiled. 'Just us two.'

David nodded, smiled. 'I enjoy being near to Henry and co and Will too.'

'Not that we've seen the latter of your nephews.'

'Ours, darling,' he said with a smile.

She knew it was nit-picking, but there was still part of her that couldn't escape there was no one in this world who shared her and David's DNA. She felt like Auntie Mim, as she knew David felt like Uncle David. Great-auntie and great-uncle to Tilly, of course. 'It's different for you,' she said with a great deal of care, knowing this subject would likely frighten David off to hide in the garage or his study. Or worse, out for a long walk.

'If you mean because Hal is my brother, then I under-stand your point. But Henry and William are half Hal and half Queenie, their mother. So they're not me, me.'

'They're not at all *me*.'

'Tilly wants to be an artist. She told Fi, who told us. Don't you remember?'

She'd dismissed it as nothing. She raised an eyebrow.

'Next day she said she wanted to be a cooker, like Auntie Mim.'

'She did not.' Mim blushed slightly.

'Henry told me. We were discussing the game, over texts, and he said Tilly had just said it.'

'Right.' Mim let that thought sit with her for a moment. 'You're not making this up, are you?' She knew he was want to sugar-coat some things for her if it required, but making something up completely was defin-itely not something she'd known him to do.

David showed her the message from Henry:

> Tilly wants 2 b a cooker (cook, I spect).
> Shamed Fi bc she does no cooking
> beyond a Sunday roast. #awkward

'What's with the hashtag before the final word?' Mim asked.

'Internet speak.' David shrugged.

There was a long silence. Mim really wanted to say what she'd been thinking, but knew David would bolt.

'In my life I have many regrets,' David said, 'but being with you, is not one of them. We've had a great life. Still are. We tried, we really did.' He looked at her with love.

They really had. All the tips from the books, trips to the doctor, tests, hospital visits, and she'd started circling on their calendar the days when she was the most fertile and had taken to calling David, to chivvy him up from the office, so when he returned they could… It had soon felt rather duty bound. Less gloriously uninhibited and greedily enjoying each other's bodies, taking and giving as they had when they first met. Then, in their early twenties, married and desperately wanting children, it felt mechanical and had put so much pressure on them. David once or twice had returned from work, to be greeted by Mim, laying on their bed, in the altogether, wearing only a smile, and he'd failed to muster the enthusiasm, unable to rise to the occasion precisely on schedule, like a dental appointment, as he'd awkwardly described it.

And after a few years of *really* trying, very hard indeed, making it everything they ever discussed, in her mid-twenties, Mim had finally said, 'Fancy working in Spain?', showing him the job adverts for holiday reps.

They'd left, intending to return after one season and never doing so. Leaving behind that small terraced house, where they'd tried inordinately hard to make a baby together, had been the tonic Mim had needed. They were soon waking on mornings before work and David would disappear beneath the covers with a glint in his eyes and a waggle of his eyebrows, having no problem at all rising to the occasion. Wanting, needing great bucketfuls of each other, taking, giving, enjoying, doing it because, after all, it was such *tremendous* fun.

Secretly, Mim had wondered if that would do the trick, but soon realised, sadly, not.

'We did,' Mim said now, looking at him with as much love as she'd felt on their wedding day. He was usually not very good at this side of Mim's emotions, but now he seemed more than equal to it.

Perhaps it was discussing it this way that helped. A conversation about actual relatives such as they were now, felt more anchored and concrete than one about the imaginary children they never created. The relationship they had with Henry, Fiona, Tilly, and even Will, when Henry had said he would bring Will and his girlfriend to visit, was, she now saw, something to celebrate, to cherish, to cultivate.

'No regrets?' David said, taking her hand with a glint in his eyes.

'No point,' she said, the sadness, guilt, regret finally, joyfully, falling away. She always knew it was pointless, but hadn't been able to see what she had here and now, because they hadn't the relationship with their family they did now. Throwing herself into work, party planning, living in Spain, had been a solution at the time, but as time went on, it had prevented her developing meaningful bonds with family. *Still, no regrets.* She'd have struggled with the pain of spending much more time with Hal and Queenie and their two boys. It would have brought into sharp relief that she and David had no children for the two boys to play with.

A cat jumped onto the kitchen island, a long-haired grey, one of the proper breeds, Mim forgot which, blue something, grey something… She stroked the cat, who immediately purred, rubbing his cheek on Mim's hand, closing his eyes in pleasure.

'Where are all your glass figures?' David asked.

'Gone.'

'Gone gone, or what?'

'Packed away.'

'Are you all right?' he asked with concern.

She stood, picked up the grey cat, supporting his rear legs with one hand, and holding his body and stroking him with the other hand. 'Seemed foolish expecting these to obey my no-touching rule.'

David nodded.

'I'm selling them. Who'd have thought they'd be so popular? Paul set me up with an eBay account and I've been merrily auctioning them off.'

'Marvellous.'

'The postage is a bit of a bind, but once I worked out the best way to pack them, I was all set. Thousands of pounds.' She'd sold hundreds. She felt a slight shame at having that many, not that David would ever make her feel bad about it. 'I'm donating it to Fluffy Paws. Their need is greater than mine.' Mim put the cat down, searched in the fridge for cat food.

The rattle of the tin and fork had the other three cats arriving soon, a long-haired white one, a short-haired tabby and a short-haired white one with splodges of black, like a Friesian cow. They held their tails aloft, meowing loudly, weaving amongst one another, and around Mim's feet.

She filled their bowls, placing them in the corner, and they ate in contented silence. A slight purring noise and the odd crunch of dried cat food.

'You seem well. Perhaps we should have got cats before,' David said.

Mim resumed her seat, shaking her head. 'I don't think so. It's not just the cats, it's where they're from. The people at Fluffy Paws. It's moving back here, having the impetus to reconnect with family. It's…' She struggled for the right word – not perfect, not serendipitous, not good.

'You seem better.'

'I am. Mostly. Not always. I don't think I'll *always* be like this. It's in me, the other side of me.' The sadness, the 'off' personality. But it at least meant she had the 'on' personality, she knew now. Making peace with not having children while filling her life with people who, to all intents and purposes, were like her children and grandchildren seemed to do the trick.

'Plenty of people with children never see them. There's no guarantees.'

He often said this, but she'd not believed it, not really. Now, having seen Luke's relationship with his adoptive parents, and his developing relationship with Sasha, she understood, knew this to be true. 'Acceptance,' she said simply.

'It is what it is and we are grateful for what we have.'

'Shall I telephone Henry, ask him to bring Will here?'

'Good idea. He's very shy, is Will. Don't you remember?'

She shook her head. They'd always come as a pair when younger, and although Henry had done most of the talking, Will hadn't struck her as shy. 'Do you think he'll come?'

'If Henry tells him to, I shouldn't be surprised.'

Mim nodded, making a mental note, feeling as if she had a plan and a way to execute it. A wonderful lunch, they'd eat in the conservatory, maybe afternoon tea, sandwiches, little fairy cakes, tea and champagne for those who wanted it. A Victoria sponge, scones, clotted cream and the best strawberry jam. Best of British, would be the theme.

'You're planning it in your head, aren't you?'

Mim smiled.

David grinned, kissed her. 'I love you.'

Mim blushed, nodded. 'I love you.'

David took her hand, coaxing her to stand as he did. He led her to their bedroom, where, with the curtains open, the light shards filling the room, they made love, David enthusiastically rising to meet her and Mim joining him, softly taking him in, giving herself to him, as totally as when they'd first met. And then, great gulping dollops of sex, of love, of physical expression of their adoration for one another, for what seemed like most of the afternoon, until a while later, she sat in bed, flushed, and covering her breasts with the duvet, catching her breath.

Tigger, the male tabby cat, walked into their bedroom, jumped on the bed, meowed loudly. He smelled of cat food. He washed himself, licking his paw and wiping his face in that fastidious fascinating way Mim so loved now.

'I'm sorry,' Mim said finally, 'if sometimes I'm...' She stopped herself.

David held her face in his hands, staring into her eyes. 'Don't apologise. I've always known you had that within you. I'm sorry for not always...'

She knew it too was part of who he was. That he was so supportive, but he couldn't have the same conversation about something they could no longer change. She'd made peace with that. 'Good job we're both not perfect, isn't it?' She smiled.

'Quite.' He got out of bed, gloriously naked, his body as imperfect and aged as hers, but as splendidly unselfconscious as he'd been when they'd met. 'Tea?'

She nodded.

'In bed?' His pink and wobbly bits were delightfully pink and wobbly.

'I reckon so,' she said.

He bowed, in an attempt at humour, more wobbling. Turning his less-than-pert pink bottom was the last thing she saw before he left the room.

She smiled to herself, thinking how lucky she was.

Chapter 30

Margaretting, Essex

Luke was about to video call his parents. They were in Anna's lounge, sitting on the ancient squashy leather sofa her parents must have bought in the Seventies. Sasha sat on the sofa next to Luke, the laptop on the glass-and-metal coffee table in front of them.

Anna was in her bedroom, having excused herself, saying she'd leave them to it.

'Ready?' Luke asked Sasha.

She took a brush from her handbag and saw to her hair.

Jean and Roger appeared on Luke's laptop screen. They sat still, staring into the camera.

Sasha looked at Luke. 'Are they there?'

He nodded, showing her his parents, waving on his phone. His heart beat fast, his palms felt dry. 'Mum and Dad, meet Sasha.' Luke waited for an awkward moment of silence. 'Why don't we all say where we are at the moment?'

'Me first?' Jean asked.

Luke nodded, checking the time and noting not even a minute had passed and it felt like an hour. *God, I hope it's not going to be this awkward. Perhaps this was a bad idea...*

'I'm Jean, we live in Bournemouth. A little town on the south coast. It's full of tourists in summer. Too many.

But in winter it's nice and quiet. The sea is my favourite reason for living here. Luke used to swim in the sea as a little boy.'

Sasha blinked quickly, wiping a tear from her eye. 'You never told me that,' she said to Luke.

'Sorry. It didn't come up while we've been with the cats.'

Jean laughed nervously. 'I can't believe we're seeing you. I read about you when we... Luke, but now you're here.'

Sasha nodded vigorously, adjusting her position in the chair. 'Yes. It's me.'

'What did the form say, Mum?' Luke asked, thinking if ever there was a time to ask that, it was now.

'It's been a while.' Jean grimaced, looking to the air as she tried to remember. 'Young mother, you look much younger than me.'

'Sixteen,' Sasha said, 'I was sixteen.'

'I was twenty-five. Roger was thirty.'

'My age,' Luke said, finding it hard to imagine his dad at his age. Roger had always struck Luke as a man who had the beliefs and habits of a man much older than his real age. 'What else?'

'Unmarried. Unable to keep the baby.' Jean bit her bottom lip, looking to her husband. 'Obviously.'

Obviously.

There was a very awkward and long silence and Luke wished he hadn't gone to this conversation so soon. Maybe he should have kept it for a face-to-face meeting.

'How are the cats?' Jean asked.

Sasha coughed, looking nervously to Luke.

He nodded, indicating for her to go on.

304

Sasha said, 'We have sixty or so cats. I'm in Margaretting.' A pause, looking to Luke. 'Can they hear me?'

'Coming through loud and clear,' Roger bellowed.

Sasha went on, 'But I used to live in Wickford.'

'Why did you move?' Roger asked.

Sasha explained about the landlord selling the sanctuary, setting up the virtual one, and moving in with Anna and Luke in her large house.

Luke checked the time and they'd been chatting for short while, it felt like about that, or perhaps less, which he reckoned was a good sign.

Roger nodded. 'You must have your hands full.'

'I do,' Sasha said.

'Luke, I wanted to ask what's happening with your work. Mum said something about time off, but... well, I couldn't believe it.'

It felt very normal to have this discussion with his dad, as he was always the one Luke spoke to about his career, jobs, work, all that. 'I've been in education or work since I started school. I wanted to jump off the merry-go-round for a bit.'

'It's hardly like you're in the rat race!' Roger scoffed.

Luke knew he'd react like this. His dad's strong work ethic and the expectation of a job for life meant they often clashed about this topic. 'Even if I'm not a rat, it's my race and I want out of it. For a while anyway. I'm eking out my savings. You should be proud.'

'And they're all right about this, your colleagues, manager?'

Luke sighed. He'd been through this with his mother and Sasha, but it was typical of his father to want more details. For him to need to justify his decision, even though it was his to make and he was an adult. 'They are.'

'Don't look at me like that, you two,' he said, turning to his wife and then Sasha. 'I'm just trying to establish the facts.'

Jean grabbed his forearm. 'I have all of those. I told you. You obviously didn't listen.'

'I did. I always listen. I want to find out what makes someone throw away his dream career.' Roger became red-faced.

'That's not what I'm doing. Mum, explain it to him, will you?'

Sasha and Jean spoke at the same time. They laughed.

Luke smiled, reflecting if it meant he had two mums worrying about him, he could think of worse things in life. This thought filled him with a warm sense of love.

'Sorry,' Jean said. 'I thought you meant me.'

'And me,' Sasha added awkwardly. 'Perhaps I should always be referred to by my name.' She shrugged. 'I wanted to thank you both. For doing what I couldn't. Doing it well. He's a lovely man.'

Luke blushed.

'That's very kind of you,' Jean said. 'But you don't need to thank us. It's what we signed up for, when we adopted him.'

Sasha swallowed, looking at Luke with tear-filled eyes. 'I wish I could have... then. Except...' She shook her head.

Luke hugged her, patting her back gently.

'I'm so sorry,' Jean began. 'I wish I could hug you.'

Sasha composed herself, nodding, and said, 'I wish that too. Maybe next time...'

Obviously not knowing what to do with this display of emotion, Roger said, 'I still disagree with your decision to leave the group.'

'I don't,' Sasha said.

'Me neither,' Jean added.

'He should travel, explore. See and experience things.'

'I didn't. Couldn't. But I wouldn't change things. Luke's the thing I'm most proud of in the world.'

Luke blushed again. 'Don't, you're embarrassing me!'

'That's what mums are for, isn't it?' Jean said with a smile.

'Quite right,' Sasha added, ruffling his hair.

They moved from the sitting room, had a tour of each other's homes, then made drinks in their kitchens, all while talking. Soon they'd been on the call for nearly an hour and Luke was grinning widely.

'Shall we do this again?' Roger asked after a short silence.

'I think so,' Jean said. 'If you'd like, Sasha.'

'I would most definitely like,' Sasha said. 'And we're not too far from each other. If we wanted to, meet, you know, in the flesh.'

'Oh yes,' Jean said with enthusiasm. 'I'd like that very much.'

Anna appeared at the door, poking her head through the crack. 'Sorry, I thought you'd finished. Silence. I'll come back. Rufus has a bald patch on his back. Over-grooming, I think.'

'Who's that?' Jean asked.

'Anna, who owns this house,' Sasha said with confidence she'd not appeared to have at the start of the call.

'I can't see her. Who's she talking about?'

'One of the cats. She's gone, Mum,' Luke said. 'Next time. You can speak to her on the next call.'

'Best go, see what's up with Rufus,' Sasha said.

Luke waved, blew kisses to his parents, it felt a little over the top, in comparison with how he'd usually call them, but that call had been extraordinary.

Jean and Roger waved back, grinning widely.

Luke ended the call. 'Okay?' he asked Sasha with concern.

'Very. They're lovely. Of course they are. I expected…' Sasha looked away, blinking quickly to avoid tears falling onto her cheeks, clearly overwhelmed by it all.

Luke hugged her, holding tight as she sniffed slightly, probably crying. He couldn't have wished for the call to go better. 'Coffee?' he said finally, pulling back from the hug.

'I'm all right, actually. I think I'll retire to my room for a bit.' She stood, pulled herself together. 'Little lie down, I think.' She left the room.

Before, Luke's instinct would have been to insist she stay, talk to her, ask her if she was all right, but he knew Sasha liked her own company, had been used to living alone and that she would return in her own good time.

There was a message in the social media group he had with his parents.

Mum: well done. Went well. She's lovely.
Of course. Love Mum and Dad xxx

Luke smiled, hoping Sasha was all right, that it hadn't been too much for her, and feeling reasonably confident that, even if she was overwhelmed now, she would soon be okay, and they'd all get used to a new relationship as four adults.

Chapter 31

Sasha was with Mim and a particularly unhelpful estate agent who was showing them properties for the cat sanctuary. So far, they'd seen one with rent twice what she'd been paying, one with barely space to swing a cat never mind house sixty or so, and one next to a busy road without parking.

'Where would the visitors park?' Sasha had asked.

'No permits here,' Carl, the overconfident estate agent, had said.

'And how far should I have to walk to unload and load cats each time?' Sasha shook her head.

'Hazards on, here,' he said, pointing to the busy road, 'and then park properly round there.' He nodded away from the building. 'It's very affordable. Owner says they're happy with a change of use.'

'What was it before?' Mim asked.

'Don't know. Commercial something. Not residential is the main thing.'

Mim rolled her eyes.

Sasha said, 'We really were spoilt before.'

There followed a long journey very far into the Essex countryside until they reached a farm.

'I'd forgotten how much bullshit they speak,' Mim said quietly as they followed the estate agent walking up a long drive.

'Quite.' Sasha rolled her eyes, feeling thoroughly fed up but glad she'd asked Mim to come along. 'Is the cottage included?' she asked, as they passed a thatched building.

'No. It's just this.' Carl stopped outside a large barn on the far edge of the property's grounds.

'What's it used for now?' Mim asked.

Carl opened the door, the building was filled with hay bales. 'This stuff.' He shrugged, raising his eyes in confusion.

'Hay?' Mim said gently, with a great deal more patience than Sasha had.

'Yep. They said you can do what you like in here. All this stuff...'

'The hay?' Mim went on with incredulity.

'Yeah,' Carl said, 'it'll all be gone when you move in.'

'We'd need to build everything in here.' Sasha looked about, working out if it was big enough, and how much work it would take.

'Couldn't we use the cages we've put in some of the houses?' Mim asked.

'And put the cats where in the meantime?' Sasha shook her head. It all felt so much, and even then it wouldn't be suitable. 'Why didn't we dismantle the cages at Fluffy Paws?'

'We tried. Same problem. Nowhere to keep the cats. It was easier to build new.'

It had been, Sasha remembered. She'd left much of that to Mim to organise, it being a particularly stressful period, and her plate being, very much, full. 'Course.' Sasha nodded.

'Want a look around?' Carl asked with an optimistic grin. 'Great space, isn't it?'

'To store hay, yes. For cats, I'm less sure.' Sasha walked away from him.

'Where would you live? The cottage is out, apparently.' Mim followed.

'I've given up trying to find somewhere for me too. The cats are what's important. I'll muddle through.' She had for the rest of her life.

'You can't look after the cats if you're not secure in your own place. They tell you to put on your mask first, before helping others.' Mim raised her eyebrows as if she'd just uttered a magical phrase.

'Don't follow. What?'

'On a plane. Emergency drill.'

'Quite,' Sasha said, unable to remember the last time she'd been on holiday, never mind on a plane. As she reflected on this, she continued walking about the barn. It was a large enough space. Plenty of room. But it was miles away from their vets and she didn't want to find alternatives, they were heavily discounted and very understanding with her erratic payment timescales.

'If you don't want it, someone else will. I've another viewing after you,' Carl put in.

'I know what I think,' Mim said, shaking her head.

'It's a no from me,' Sasha said with some relief.

'Right. Your decision. It's just, I think you're going to struggle to find a place, within your tight budget, that meets *all* your criteria.' He walked towards the door, taking a deep breath. 'What is that smell, it's like grass, but different, maybe drier?'

'Hay!' Mim widened her eyes, shaking her head at Sasha.

'Want me to drop you back at the office?' he asked.

Climbing into his shiny silver BMW, Sasha said, once Mim had installed herself, 'Would be great. Since it's where I left the car.'

Mim put on her seat belt, putting her hand on Sasha's shoulder in a show of solidarity.

He dropped them off, without a thanks or goodbye, leaving them standing on the pavement.

'Well, that was a colossal waste of time,' Sasha said, shaking her head and feeling frustrated and exhausted by it all.

'We can agree on that,' Mim said. 'But what I remain unclear about is quite *why* you're reluctant to accept Anna's money.'

Sasha had considered this long and hard and felt very principled about her decision. 'I don't want to take advantage of her good nature. And she is, and I mean this in the kindest way, quite fragile and a little...' Sasha struggled for the kindest word. 'In need of TLC.'

'She's doing very well,' Mim said. 'Much better.'

'Agreed,' Sasha said.

'Which is why she wants to donate to Fluffy Paws. We've transformed her life. She's never felt better. Obviously her GP and counsellor have contributed.'

'Obviously.' Sasha thought for a moment. 'There's no going back. If she gives us the money, I can't give it back once it's spent.'

'I think Anna understands the basic principles of how money works.'

'Indeed. I just want her to understand what she's getting into.'

'She could buy a place herself, and let Fluffy Paws locate there.'

'Rent-free?'

'Possibly. Up to her. That ensures Anna retains control of her money.'

Sasha hadn't considered this before, since Anna had always insisted she wanted to donate the money for Sasha to spend as she wished. 'Does it make a difference that we're a charity?' It had taken a long time and a great deal of work, but they had become a registered charity a few years ago, and Sasha found it helped inordinately when asking for help such as this. The accountant had provided them with very sound advice at the time, before Mim took over that role alongside her normal volunteer role.

'It would. I'd need to check. We're doing surprisingly well, balance-wise, at the moment,' Mim said.

'How?'

'Reduced overheads since going virtual. Lots of income from Paul and his marvellous social media work.'

'A great success. I don't know how I'd manage without your help. And the other volunteers, of course.' She really would be lost. Despite sometimes wanting to, there was no way she could run the sanctuary alone. She was lucky to be surrounded by such generous and skilled people.

'That's why we volunteer. It's not meant to be the sole endeavour of one person. Not very sustainable.'

'Why didn't you suggest this to me before?' Sasha asked, as options began to percolate through her mind.

'I'm not sure. Anna was very fixed with her view of what she wanted. I knew she was fragile, so didn't want to throw back her help in her face. And…' Mim added with narrowed eyes, 'I knew how marvellously the virtual sanctuary was working, and saving money.'

'It's going well, but it's not a long-term solution. Me and the other senior volunteers are spending all their time driving around to chaperone visits to people's homes. Some people have given up, didn't like strangers coming into their homes, the cats they loved, but the people, not so much. And,' Sasha said, really getting to the nub of the matter, 'it's not the same. There's no community with the virtual sanctuary. People chatting in a social media group isn't the same as having a cuppa in a kitchen, is it?'

'It absolutely is not,' Mim said.

'So we need to find a new home for Fluffy Paws, one place, with space for the cats and volunteers to gather, before we find ourselves with too many cats and not enough space to house them. Or mutiny from the volunteers who don't want to feel like their homes are open to everyone like an auction.'

'It didn't feel like a pressing problem. Not until you asked me to view places. I thought you'd...'

'Forgotten about it?' Sasha asked, feeling slightly bemused.

'Not forgotten, but you had other priorities. You can't do everything all at once. I didn't know how unfruitful your searches had been.'

'Until today,' Sasha said glumly.

'Until, as you say, today.'

Sasha had kept the fruitless estate agent sojourns to herself, wanting to remain silent until she had good news. Wasn't it, after all, the role of a leader to shield one's team from bad news, keep them inspired to continue fighting the good fight? 'Don't think I'm trying to criticise you. You do a marvellous job. It's just I can't believe no one thought of this before.'

'We've hardly been replete with spare time, have we? At Sun Burn Holidays, we'd have regular team away days.' Mim shuddered. 'We could have...'

'Three-word horror story is that.'

'Thought so. Sometimes,' Mim said, walking towards a cafe on the high road, 'the most obvious solution isn't apparent, since it's so obvious.'

Sasha shrugged, following Mim. Was it that obvious? 'I've not had this sort of problem before,' she added as they entered the cafe.

Shortly after, they sat with drinks.

'Are you cancelling the viewings this afternoon?' Mim asked with optimism as she dunked her biscotti in her coffee.

'I'll call the estate agent, ask them to talk me through what they're showing us, then decide.' She left the cafe to make the call. Presently, she returned and updated Mim. 'Two were the same properties we've already seen, just listed with another estate agent. The third was Fluffy Paws and the fourth had no grounds useable for the pens.'

'When you say the third was Fluffy Paws, what do you mean?'

'Our previous location...' As she said it, Sasha's tired brain joined the dots as Mim's obviously already had.

'How much?'

'It's not for sale. It's to let. Otherwise I wouldn't have been shown it.'

'The landlord wanted us out because he was selling. What's happened between that and now?'

Sasha shrugged. 'Who knows?'

'Well, you, if you find out.'

'How much has Anna got to spend?'

She had said, but Sasha couldn't remember. 'Let me call them back.'

The estate agent explained the owner had wanted to sell the previous location of Fluffy Paws, but hadn't achieved their asking price, so was letting it in the meantime, while the market recovered, or became more buoyant, or some such estate agent's speak.

'How much does the landlord want?' Sasha asked, holding her breath.

'I can't tell you that. But he really wants to sell, and not let, and based on similar properties in the area I would suggest...' He gave a figure.

Sasha thanked him then ended the call.

Mim was overjoyed at the news. 'We must tell Anna now.'

'Does she have that much?'

'No idea.'

'It sounds like an awful lot of money.'

'She sold her place. Said it was more money than she knew what to do with. Which was why—'

'I know, but it doesn't mean I can go cap in hand to her.'

'Except, it precisely does mean that.'

'Does it?' Sasha asked, very unsure and uncomfortable about this turn of events. She'd never liked relying on others, asking for help. But she knew without help she'd have lost Fluffy Paws long ago.

'It all comes down to how we tell her about the plan. She has to feel comfortable, you have to feel comfortable. Nobody can feel as if they've been had over.'

'Absolutely don't want to have Anna over.' And yet, Sasha still felt a certain unease about this suggestion.

Chapter 32

Paul waited at the restaurant for Luke to arrive. He'd chosen from the menu, having eaten here many times before. An Italian chain restaurant, he knew what he was getting from their simple menu. This was absolutely nothing like a date, simply two friends, who happened to have slept together a few times, casually discussing their plans.

The waiter arrived, asking if Paul wanted a drink. He said he was awaiting his friend's arrival and would order then, but could he have water in the meantime? The waiter left.

Luke arrived, on time actually, not late, pale yellow shirt showing off his enviable biceps and a little bit of chest hair through the open buttons, skin tight dark blue jeans – giving an uninterrupted view of his impressive thighs and behind – apologising for his tardiness. 'I was chatting to Sasha, trying to organise when she can meet Mum and Dad in person.'

'How did the great meeting of the parents go?' Paul asked, still trying to focus less on how devastatingly handsome Luke looked and more on what they were here to discuss. He hadn't wanted to pry before, about Luke's grand meeting of the parents, and had picked up from

Sasha via others that it had been emotional, awkward but basically a good start. He wanted to hear it from Luke himself, gossip and second-hand info being what it was.

With enthusiasm, Luke talked about how it had gone; the laughs, the jokes, the difficult start.

The waiter arrived to take their orders.

Paul said, 'Spicy sausage pizza and dough balls, please. Glass of this white, please.' He pointed at the wine menu.

Luke looked at his menu. 'Sorry I've not even...' He looked at Paul for reassurance maybe. 'I'll have...' He gave the names for what Paul had chosen in perfect Italian. 'So, same. Thanks.'

The waiter wrote their order. 'Would you prefer a bottle, it's the same price as two glasses.'

'I don't mind,' Luke said.

'I'm driving,' Paul said, feeling unfairly irritated.

'I got a cab.'

Of course he had, because Luke made everything look so effortless, as he slid through life, in his designer Italian leather shoes, with his good looks, charm and ability to speak two, or was it three languages?

The waiter looked at them both. 'The wine?'

'I don't mind,' Luke said.

Paul wanted to shout, *He knew that*, since Luke had made it very clear at least twice. 'Bottle, please.'

The waiter left.

'You didn't have to do that, copy my order,' Paul said, trying very hard to keep frustration out of his tone.

'Spicy sausage pizza, dough balls, what's not to like?' Luke sat back, looking about the room, relaxing, doing that commanding-the-room-with-his-presence thing that Paul so envied.

Paul said, 'I was expecting a joke about your spicy Italian sausage.' *God, why did I say that?*

'I was about to make one, but you've beaten me to it.' Luke grinned. Full lips, straight white teeth.

Those lips had felt so nice against Paul's, and how he longed to feel them again. *No, I absolutely don't!*

'You all right?' Luke asked.

'Miles away, sorry. Tired. Work. In the last few weeks of this contract. Counting the days.' *Until I have to spend a few months travelling with you, but not with you. Oh goodness, this really is the worst idea ever.*

'You don't look tired. In charge, I'd say. Organised. Telling them what to do.'

Well, he had done that obviously. Since Mim's little pep talk. He told Luke.

Luke nodded slowly. 'I can totally see that. Nice.'

'Aren't you pickier than that? Choosing your Italian food? You didn't need to have the same as me.'

'Why not? I know you like good food. I trust your good taste, choices. The water's medicinal.' Luke sipped his water, his Adam's apple bobbing up and down on a freshly shaved throat.

I do not want to touch his skin again. I absolutely do not want to kiss his neck again. And he's just complimented me, my taste, choices. Medicinal, I'll tell him what's medicinal in a minute... Why did I say I didn't want a relationship with him?

'Keeping hydrated, as you're driving I don't want to drink all the wine and have to be poured into a taxi at the end of the night.' Luke grinned, his eyes twinkling. 'I like Italian food.'

'I know, it's just I thought you'd... It's a chain... More authentic maybe...' *Because your birth dad is Italian? Because you made a big song and dance about wanting to know who he is? Because you speak it perfectly?* Paul shrugged. 'So it went well, the virtual meeting of the parents?'

'Very. Nervous. Terrible. Didn't sleep the night before.'

Paul found that hard to believe, he narrowed his eyes. 'I can imagine.' He couldn't. Not remotely. 'I just wondered...'

The wine arrived, it was poured.

'You wondered?' Luke said.

Wish I could have a very large glass of wine, take the edge off my nerves. Driving, what was I thinking? 'Why leave when it's just starting?'

'Leave?' Luke thought for a moment. 'With you? Travelling?'

Is he deliberately being obtuse, Paul wondered. 'It seems a bit delicate at the moment.'

'I wouldn't say that. They mentioned seeing each other without me.' He laughed.

'What do you think about that?' Paul asked.

'Love it.'

Of course he does. 'I've been thinking about this trip.' Paul's throat was dry. He swallowed with a great deal of effort. Sweaty hands, rubbed them on his trousers.

'So have I. I can't wait.'

Paul had felt the same, until the dawning realisation — of spending all day, every day for a few months, sharing hotel rooms with Luke — had seized him in the middle of the night, wondering what the actual fuck he'd done. When, as was apparent now, he still very much fancied Luke. Liked him even. Maybe they could keep it to no-strings sex during their trip? Perhaps that would make this easier, Paul wondered.

No, he decided firmly, that would make it worse. The thought of *having* Luke, and Luke *having* Paul, repeatedly and not anything more than that, while ignoring what Paul *really* wanted with Luke, was much worse than having nothing.

Much. Worse.

'I think it's a bad idea,' Paul said, deciding that was the best thing to say in the presence of everything frothing through his brain.

'Not cos we… before?' Luke frowned, shaking his head in total disbelief.

'Not that,' Paul lied, gritting his teeth tightly. 'It's that you've not spent so long with one person. It's not like going on holiday with someone. It's a warts-and-all kind of thing.' For a few months.

'I've been on tour with the group. It'll be fine. I'm very laid-back.'

Of course he was. *Obvs.* That was what Paul was afraid of. Luke lying back and Paul wanting nothing more than to… 'How about someone else coming with us?' Paul said without thinking, desperately grasping at straws.

'Who? Although, three's a crowd.'

Which was precisely what Paul wanted. 'Shirley.'

'Who?'

'From the tap-dancing group.' Paul really was desperate.

'I can't remember her.' Luke frowned, obviously trying to remember her. Finally, he shrugged. 'But if she's interested, I don't see why not. The more the merrier.' Luke had more wine, drinking it with as much abandon as he seemed to live the rest of his life.

God, he's so bloody perfect and relaxed and I am jealous of him and want to be him at the same time. I think I want him, to be with him too. Shit, I've absolutely fucked this up, haven't

I? Paul did not have more wine, instead observing Luke with more than a tiny bit of envy.

Luke finished a large glug of wine, sat back in the chair, resting his large hands on his lap. 'If you want to do this alone, or with Shirley, just say.'

And Paul, after *absolutely not* imagining himself sitting on Luke's lap, *definitely not* thinking what it would be like to kiss Luke, found himself perfectly unable to. Say, that is. Because, when he later considered it, he did want to go with Luke. But he wanted to go *with* Luke, not just with him. And Paul wasn't about to put himself out there and say that, especially when Luke was the sort of cool, handsome, confident Lothario who would inevitably realise how underwhelming Paul was, as with other similar men Paul had known, and would swiftly dump Paul.

No.

Paul would *not* let himself be hurt again, not after George. He couldn't work out if he was putting up barriers around his heart *because* of George and how hurt he'd been, or *because* he thought he ought to keep things no-strings, casual, pre-empting his inevitable dumping that would follow. But whatever, put up barriers he did.

They ate, Luke talked about the European countries he'd visited, but not seen, what he wanted to visit when there with Paul, he didn't order dessert and Paul did, just because he wanted to be contrary.

Luke was, of course, perfect and non-judgemental, asked for a tiny spoonful of it, to which Paul acquiesced, then Luke insisted on paying for it all, and Paul agreed because Luke had said it in such a generous way that Paul couldn't argue with, unless he wanted to sound particularly ungrateful. And later, after hugging goodbye, lingering with that longer than he ought, Paul found himself walking back to his car, as he'd waited for Luke to get his taxi, wondering how he'd managed to entirely fail at his mission of telling Luke they couldn't go travelling together.

Because for Luke, *this* was the trip of a lifetime and he wanted to learn and experience how to do travelling properly, from Paul who he saw as an expert in this. Paul didn't have the heart to shatter that, especially as Luke had taken a break from work, partly *for* this. Paul couldn't be the person who'd bring all that shattering down around Luke's well-shaped, perfectly tanned ears.

'Shit, shit, shittedy shit.' Paul held the steering wheel tightly, his knuckles white, knowing, without a doubt, he had to go ahead with the plan. Excluding Shirley, who he'd absolutely made up out of thin air, on the spot.

Chapter 33

Margaretting, Essex

Anna woke in the large iron-framed double bed her parents had shared, in what had been their bedroom, to the gentle noises of people making their breakfast in the kitchen. Her kitchen really, but now she shared it with Luke and Sasha she felt it was *theirs*.

There was a knock on her bedroom door.

'Yes,' she said.

'I'm making coffee, do you want some?' It was Luke, his deep voice so comforting and familiar.

'Yes, please,' she replied with enthusiasm. It was so much nicer living with people than not. At first she'd found navigating her way around other people's belongings quite stressful, but she'd soon realised they had far less stuff than she.

Anna threw back the duvet – new, IKEA, keeping her parents' had felt creepy – stepped out of bed, into her wardrobe, now empty of her parents' clothes, all gone to charity shops, except half a dozen items she'd kept as keepsakes – her mother's wedding dress, the suit her father used to wear whenever he dressed up – and felt her way through her clothes. There were far fewer of them now and the labels about when and where she'd got them had gone too.

Bit of a wrench, that had been. The labels were in a drawer, meaning she didn't forget that — what to her was important — information, but it didn't dictate what she wore each morning.

She slipped into the shower in the large shared bathroom. No en suite bathroom for her parents, they'd felt it unnecessary.

Much later, after their first visit to help with Anna's kitchen, Anna was ready to let Mim and Luke return and help her sort through her clothes in her small Moulsham home. It had been the hardest and best weekend she'd ever known. The water poured on her head as she closed her eyes and recalled...

'I don't understand what these are?' Mim had said, holding the clothes labels. Peering through her glasses, she read one: 'Lakeside Shopping Centre, nineteen ninety-nine, Mum and Dad, birthday present, Miss Selfridge.' Putting it down, Mim went on, 'Is this what I think it is?'

Luke read one: 'Solo shopping trip to Oxford Street, with birthday money from work, Top Shop, August two thousand and five.' He put it down. 'Bit far to go for a Top Shop, don't you think? When there were about twenty-five in Essex?'

Anna took the low-necked T-shirt from Luke, replacing it on the hanger. 'You can both go.' She sniffed, *I'm not going to cry, not getting upset, just moving on from this particular conversation.*

They all sat on her bed.

Mim put her hand on Anna's, holding it gently. 'Is this something you've done for a long time?'

Anna nodded with a great deal of shame and embarrassment.

'How long are we talking, and is this why you don't get rid of any clothes?'

Anna nodded. She'd never got rid, as Mim put it, of any clothes since her grandparents had died, when she was a teenager. They had bought her a shell suit in the Nineties, when they were all the rage, and Anna hadn't been able to let go of it, when she'd outgrown it, and when, twenty years later, it was far from in fashion. She looked at Mim and Luke. 'I felt like I was letting them down,' she said very quietly.

'Who, dear?' Mim asked gently.

'Granny and Grandpa.' She retrieved the purple and turquoise shell suit from the wardrobe. It had a label with the key information.

Mim nodded. 'Understood.' She shot Luke a look. 'How about the items you bought yourself, or people bought you who are still… with us?'

Anna shrugged, her eyes filling with tears, feeling terribly silly and almost on the verge of telling them to get out of her house, but knowing they were helping her, that she needed this assistance. The counsellor sessions had helped Anna realise she retained belongings in lieu of the people she'd lost. She'd been advised to sort through her possessions with someone else, but Anna hadn't liked the sound of it, didn't want to ask for help. And here it was, help, being offered.

'How would it be if we sorted them into items you wear and ones you want to keep for other reasons?' Mim asked, holding Anna's hand carefully.

Anna nodded, knowing she had to take this offer of help, and they had, over that weekend, done so. She ended up with far more in the former pile of clothes to wear than the latter. But the pile of those she wanted to keep for other reasons lay in the corner of her bedroom on the Sunday morning. They were like a huge heap reminding her of all the people she'd lost in her life.

Mim and Luke found her that morning, sitting on the floor, in floods of tears, absolutely unable to part with a single item.

The following weekend, with Mim and Luke gently discussing their plan during the week when they'd seen each other at Fluffy Paws, they had resumed the sentimental pile of memory clothes. Anna agreed to keep a few very precious items, including her grandparents' shell suit, and for the others she no longer wore, she took photos and stuck them into an album with the labels. It felt as if she were still honouring the memory of those people, but she was left with more space in which to enjoy the clothes she still wore.

At the end of the second weekend, she had said goodbye to more than half of the memory clothes and stroked the pages of the album she'd created. She had far more space in which to see the clothes she wore and to wear a greater variety. Gradually, over the following weeks, talking to the counsellor woman her doctor had put her back in touch with, she'd weaned herself off the labels. She retained them, but stuck them in a scrapbook, with a picture of the clothing items. It meant she could choose what she wore each day without being weighed down by the history of each item.

She, Mim and Luke had celebrated this, when she had freed herself from the final clothing label, a month or so ago. Anna had taken photos and put them in her memory scrapbook, which was her way to manage how much ephemera she retained from her everyday life.

It meant finding space for her clothes from her small house in her parents' was a much simpler job, and she found it easier choosing what to wear every day.

Now, in her parents' home, she stepped out of the shower, dried herself on a new towel – all her parents' old ones were being used as cat beds for Fluffy Paws – and stood in front of the wardrobe, picking her clothes for the day. Acid-washed high-waisted jeans, a bright pink T-shirt and high-top trainers were what she stepped into the kitchen wearing.

'Very nice,' Luke said, handing her a mug of coffee. He wore loose faded jeans and T-shirt, the latter seemed to make him look even more dashing and muscular than usual.

She blushed at the compliment and at noticing his biceps maybe a bit too much, and sipped her drink.

'I see the Nineties are back in fashion,' Luke said, sitting at the table. 'Did you buy them recently?'

Anna shook her head.

'Where…? From the actual Nineties?' Luke's eyes widened in recognition.

Anna nodded, smoothing out the T-shirt. She didn't want to give all the clothes' details, for she worried Luke would think she'd returned to her old ways, so she simply said: 'Nineteen ninety-seven, I was sixteen, seventeen. Top Shop.'

'Amazing. Love that for you. I bought new, obvs. On account of the fact that I was born in nineteen ninety-three, I don't think I'd fit anything I wore then.'

Anna wasn't sure if he was being sarcastic, with the 'love that for you' and raised an eyebrow.

'Genuinely, do love it for you. Go you!' Luke hugged her.

They sat at the table drinking coffee. 'Where's Sasha?' Anna asked.

'Gone hours ago. Emergency vet call. The usual. Owner can't pay, so we are.'

The rescuing-cats-from-the-jaws-of-defeat aspect was something Anna didn't think she'd ever quite get used to. She knew there was so much sadness and cruelty in the world, but the way some people treated their pets broke her heart every time she heard about it. She'd asked Sasha if she could be excused from such rescues, because it left her shaking and in tears for weeks afterwards. Sasha had been very supportive, said there were plenty of other things Anna could do.

She wished Luke wouldn't leave, but didn't say. It sounded a bit pathetic. Besides, he was going travelling, with Paul, how could she and her house compete with that? 'This virtual cat sanctuary idea is much better than I expected.' She missed having the sanctuary as a space to gather with the other volunteers, a focal point for the cats, but knew all the important work Fluffy Paws did was continuing in this new form.

Luke nodded, smiling. He opened his mouth to say something, then stopped himself.

'What?' she asked.

He shook his head. 'Nothing.'

'It really isn't.' She rose, put her mug in the dishwasher, wiped the work surface, hoping if she said nothing he'd talk of his own accord.

Luke left his mug on the table, walked to the door. 'Are you ready to go soon?'

'Where?' She frowned, disappointed he hadn't said more about whatever was on his mind.

'Adoption check-up. Those two tuxedo boy cats. Remember?'

She'd fostered the two brothers in her home for a few weeks. They'd been surrendered when their owner had gone into residential care. It was, at the time, all a bit raw for her, having not long had her parents go through the same. But their new owner was so happy to find two boy cats who got on, since she believed they were more affectionate than girl cats, and loved their markings, that it had taken away the sadness somewhat.

'Is it far? Are we going to be late? Ought I to change into something more... professional?' Anna felt the worry beginning to rise, her throat went dry, her heart beat faster.

'You're spinning.'

I really am. 'I'm fine.'

'If we leave now-ish, we'll be on time. Plus, it's not like a hospital appointment, we won't lose our slot if we're a bit late. You're fabulous as you are.'

They went in Anna's car and Luke dealt with the satnav. She decided she'd ask what he didn't want to say, it felt better sitting side by side than sitting opposite one another. She'd noticed she found it easier to talk about difficult subjects if she wasn't facing the other person. Her counsellor had suggested it for some of their harder sessions.

Carefully, she asked, 'How's Sasha?'

'Busy. Stressed. Happy. Despairing of humankind and being grateful to them too.' Luke shrugged. 'Hashtag, standard.' He pointed to a mid-terrace small house. 'It's here.'

Anna parked and they were soon standing at the door having rung the bell.

A thin woman in her fifties, in a baggy vest and denim skirt, opened the door. Her blonde-grey hair was tied back in a ponytail. 'Fluffy Paws?'

'No,' Luke said, 'we have feet. Is that okay?' He smirked.

The woman, who introduced herself as Val, laughed.

Anna showed her their Fluffy Paws photo-ID badges and Val let them in, showing them to the drawing room.

They sat on low leather sofas. The house smelled of washing powder and mild bleach.

'Tea or coffee?' Val asked, standing in the sitting room.

'Is it okay if we have a look around, see the cats, please?' Luke asked.

'Course. Fill your boots. They're on my bed.'

Luke and Anna stood.

'Yes or no to drinks?' she shouted from the kitchen.

'Coffee for both of us, please,' Luke shouted from the bottom of the stairs.

Val was singing along to a song on the radio as she clattered mugs and spoons in the kitchen.

The cats were sitting on the bed washing one another. They were two large neutered males, short black hair, white bibs and paws. Tuxedos, as they'd been known at Fluffy Paws.

Anna perched on the bed and stroked them. The first rubbed his cheek on her hand, purring as she stroked underneath his chin. The second, Anna still struggled telling them apart, rolled onto his back, letting her stroke his stomach, black except a small white splodge in the middle.

Luke surveyed the room for tell-tale signs such as over-flowing litter trays, dirty food bowls, empty water bowls. Nothing.

Anna walked around the other rooms upstairs, but didn't find anything that concerned her.

'Want me to bring the drinks up?' Val shouted from the bottom of the stairs.

'We'll be down now,' Anna said. To Luke, she said, 'I'd move in if I was looking for a home.' She smiled.

'I know, right?' Luke said.

They joined Val in the sitting room. Anna took out her checklist from her bag. 'A few questions, and then we're done.'

Val grimaced. 'I hope I don't fail. I was never much cop at tests at school.'

Anna turned to her form, biro poised. She asked about the cats' vaccinations, for which Val showed the records, then their flea treatment, and Val retrieved some packets of treatment from the kitchen. Anna confirmed they were up to date. They hadn't found fleas on the cats, but you could never be too careful, Anna knew.

'Do they go outside?' Anna asked. The road was quite busy and the house not set back far.

Val shook her head. 'No. Since I lost Bobby, I only wanted house cats.'

Anna remembered, Val had called Fluffy Paws after Bobby had been hit by a car and died. She said she couldn't even think about another cat just yet, but wanted to know if they had indoor cats she could adopt. Sasha, or Anna, or maybe Mim had said they absolutely did and they'd be ready to meet her when she was able.

Anna wrote in the form. 'Can't be too careful,' she added with a smile. 'Can we have a look round downstairs please?' There were cat toys on the floor and a scratching post by the TV.

Val gestured with her hand. 'Be my guest.'

Anna found clean food bowls in the kitchen, a bowl of clean water, and on the opposite wall, two clean litter trays. A scratch mat was attached to the wall by the door. Anna returned to the sitting room.

'Can we go upstairs to see you with the cats, please?' Luke asked.

Val frowned. 'Why? Can't you see they're as happy as Larry?'

'We can. It's just sometimes the cats aren't happy with their new owners. Cats remember.'

Val nodded solemnly, leading them upstairs. She sat on the bed, holding her hand for the cats to sniff. She stroked one, then the other. The cats purred, stood and rubbed themselves around Val's body, nuzzling into her chest, and one sat on her lap, making bread with his paws.

Luke looked to Anna, raising his eyebrows. 'Thanks. We'll leave you to it.'

They said goodbye at the door.

Val said, 'Fostering, how does that work? And do you think you'll go back to what you had before, or carry on with this virtual thingummy? Not that there's anything wrong with it, I just wondered.'

Luke explained what fostering cats entailed.

Val listened. 'Sign me up, please.'

'The virtual idea, is just for now. Sasha, who runs Fluffy Paws, is looking for somewhere we can move into, but...' Anna trailed off, realising she didn't know anymore. She looked to Luke.

'It's hard finding somewhere suitable, nearby, so we keep all our existing connections – vets, suppliers, donations, etcetera.' He looked at the floor, shuffled his feet about a bit. 'Difficult.'

Val thanked them again, said goodbye and they returned to the car.

'Tell me what you don't want to tell me,' Anna said firmly, her hands on the steering wheel.

'What I just said. It's hard to find somewhere.'

'And has Sasha found somewhere?'

'The old place was up for rent, and she was going to look into that. Last I heard.'

'The old place? Where we were before? Why's that to let, I thought they wanted to sell it?'

'Same.' Luke shrugged.

'Anything else I should know?'

Luke looked up at the car roof, closing his eyes, sighing. 'I said I wouldn't say. Promised Sasha.'

'Because she wouldn't ask?'

Luke pursed his lips.

'Right. What won't she ask me? I want to donate my house money to them. I'd just like to know what they're using it for. Wasn't sure it would make sense while they're still virtual, but...'

'Talk to Sasha.' Luke shook his head. 'Very proud woman. Won't ask for help.'

'Except we're a charity. And we ask for help all the time.' Anna felt the frustration and anger building in her. She wasn't going to fall out about this, but she certainly *was* going to have the conversation with Sasha.

'And,' Luke said quietly, obviously knowing he'd already said too much and might as well be hanged for a sheep as a lamb, 'it's the giving of the money she's uncomfortable with. If you found a way around that. So you spend your money, but it still helps Fluffy Paws.'

Anna narrowed her eyes, trying to follow what he'd said. 'In English, please?'

'You buy somewhere and Fluffy Paws moves in.'

'Got it. Why didn't I?'

'You were very focused on giving the money away.'

'I was. Right, I shall have it out with Sasha.' The idea settled in Anna's mind. It seemed so obvious now Luke had said it. She supposed other things may seem perfectly obvious, once they'd been suggested. But she'd been fixated on giving the money away, making sure it went to good use. Hadn't considered anything else.

They drove in silence. Once back at the house, Anna noticed Sasha's car on her drive.

She was in the dining room, looking at paperwork on the table.

Anna marched in, hands on hips, standing in the dining room. 'What's wrong?'

Sasha tidied up the paperwork. 'Nothing. Just… people. You know.'

Anna picked up a piece of paper, it was a printout of property details. And another one. 'Why didn't you tell me you couldn't find somewhere for Fluffy Paws?'

Sasha looked like a child who had just been found with her hands in the sweet jar. 'I thought I'd find somewhere.'

'How long have you been looking?'

Sasha counted on her fingers. 'Since before we went virtual. A few months.' She shook her head. 'There's nothing out there. I've registered with all the estate agents. I've seen the same places more than once. Very hard.'

'And you're doing this all on your own?' Anna was very angry, she barely contained her rage.

'Luke and Mim have accompanied me.' After a long pause, Sasha said, 'I am lost as to what to do. Absolutely at my wit's end.'

Anna sat at the table, realising anger wasn't helpful. She put her hand on Sasha's as it rested on the table. 'I want to help. I know you don't want me giving you the money, and I understand there are tax implications of me doing that. How would it be, if I bought somewhere and Fluffy Paws moved in?'

Sasha looked up. Despair drifted from her face, replaced with hope. 'You'd do that?'

'I would. It's still my place.'

'We'd pay rent, of course.'

'Of course.' Anna would cross that bridge when she came to it. A peppercorn rent, of course.

'It's all the restrictions when you rent somewhere. If we're... you're buying it, there's none of those. It's ours... yours, to do with as we... you wish.' Sasha looked at the property printouts on the table. Nodding, she said, 'Yes. Yes.' She stared at Anna. 'Are you sure?'

'One hundred per cent sure.'

'Right.' Sasha looked a little overwhelmed, lost maybe, taking time to process things.

'So we'll contact estate agents, and ask to view places to buy?' Anna asked, wanting to move forwards with the plan, now she had Sasha's agreement.

'We will. I will. And you'll come with me. With us. And we'll find the best place the cats could ever wish for.'

'And for you too?' Anna asked gently.

'Don't worry about me.' She looked about the room. 'I've quite liked living with people, not just cats. Think it does me good. I'll find my own place.'

'No, you won't,' Anna said.

'Oh.'

'Because you've already got one.' Anna looked about the room. 'For as long as you want.' It felt like a good solution for them both. Friends helping friends.

They hugged.

Luke appeared at the door. 'Am I in trouble?'

Sasha looked at him. 'Not *very* much.'

'Very little,' Anna added. 'It's fortunate you're leaving soon, otherwise, you have no idea, the sort of punishment we'd mete on you.'

Luke put his hands in his pockets, leaning against the wall, staring at the floor. 'I'm terrible at keeping secrets.'

Sasha stood, met him, hugged him. 'Some secrets are better not kept.' She looked up at him, brushing a stray dark hair from his eye. 'You need a haircut. My gorgeous, wonderful boy. I'm glad you turned out like this, in spite of me.'

'*Because* of you,' he said, looking down at her, staring into her eyes.

'You will come back, won't you?' Sasha said with concern.

'Mum and Dad said the same. It's like... three-dimensional parenting. I'm exhausted by it all!' He threw his hands in the air dramatically.

'He used to do that,' Sasha said quietly, waving her arms about.

'Who?'

'Who do you think?'

'Well, at least now I know why I'm such a drama queen.'

Anna quietly slipped out of the kitchen, leaving them to it, a broad grin on her face, grateful to be part of their lives, of this new family Sasha and Luke had created.

It took more than a few weeks, but did not stretch into a couple of months. Anna sort of lost track of time, maybe that was the medication she was on, but after viewing about a dozen properties with Sasha, one bright morning, they found what would become the new home of Fluffy Paws.

The estate agent did his usual spiel of 'it's just come on the market' and 'if you don't want it, someone else will snap it up', which by now Anna and Sasha completely ignored. The estate agent stopped his car on the road outside the property. It was sort of nowhere, not in the countryside, not in a town or village. Anna hoped it looked better very soon. It was a short drive from a junction on the main road through Basildon all the way to Southend on the coast, tucked away off the busy road on a little cut through that led to the small town of Pitsea.

Away from the road, there was a concrete yard with a few barns, some abandoned cars, a rusty tractor and other farm equipment. *Not very good really*, Anna thought. Then a small white thatched cottage, with a large garden covered in lawn and well–developed flower beds. Across the lawn were about a dozen cages and pens, a few sheds and a newish static caravan at the far side. *This seems better*, Anna thought.

'What was it previously used for?' Sasha asked.

The estate agent, Carl, said, 'Farm and another small business.'

Anna walked up to the nearest pen. 'Boarding kennels, I should say.'

'Want to look at the house?' Carl asked. 'It has three bedrooms, a conservatory, recently built, a large airy—'

'Can we look around the garden first, please?' Anna asked.

He was about to lead them around the lawn, showing them each building in turn, but Sasha shook her head. 'We'll take it from here. Meet you in the house?'

He stepped away.

Sasha and Anna toured the large garden, which had a well-kept lawn, a good number of pens, and small buildings that had been used to house dogs, it seemed. A small shed which would work for an admissions and paperwork room. The static caravan had seen better days, but they'd worry about that later, Anna reckoned.

'Is it in budget?' Sasha asked, standing under a tree.

Anna checked the paperwork, nodded. 'Seems too good to be true. It seems too cheap?' This worried her. She didn't say, but it obviously crossed her face.

'Let's see what sort of mess the house is in and then we can decide.' Sasha strode towards the white cottage, where they met Carl.

'Ready to see inside?' he asked.

They both nodded.

'Before you enter, I've found out a little more about the circumstance of the sale.'

Anna held her breath, this was going to be where it all fell apart, she was sure.

'Go on,' Sasha said.

'Farm, elderly woman, passed away, used to run it as boarding kennels for dogs, and the children don't want the business or the property.'

'Splendid!' Sasha said with confidence Anna lacked.

'The house is in need of modernisation. She refused to refurbish it for decades, saying it was a waste of money, she'd soon be dead. Apparently, or so my colleague tells me, who spoke to the family when they put it up for sale.'

'Are you going to show us inside, or what?' Sasha asked.

Carl unlocked the door, stepped aside and Sasha and Anna entered.

There was a damp, musty smell, the décor was orange and brown, probably from the Seventies, reminding Anna of her parents' place. The kitchen had a dark blue Aga that predated both Sasha and Anna, with a green dresser, table and deep sink. A twin-tub washing machine was stowed underneath the draining board. There was no double glazing, no central heating, the bathrooms had toilets with a cistern high up, a long chain and pipe running down to the bowl. Orange and faded blue porcelain wear in the bathrooms completed the retro feel.

The conservatory was the newest addition to the house, dating back to the Nineties, Anna reckoned. Light and airy, it was larger than the well-proportioned sitting room, which had an open fireplace.

Sasha saw Anna's worried look. 'It's fine. Perfect, in fact!'

'Perfect? Some of the stuff in here is antediluvian. Most of this stuff wouldn't be out of place in the Imperial War Museum.' Anna shook her head, it all felt like such a great deal of work to do.

'We'll take it,' Sasha said.

'Will we?' Anna asked.

Sasha nodded. 'The house is secondary. We can sort that out later. The grounds and kennels mean we can get the cats in sooner rather than later. Get Fluffy Paws up and running once again, in one place, where volunteers, visitors, can all gather.'

Anna felt a slither of excitement. 'You don't think the house is too much to take on?'

'I'm not planning on living there, you certainly aren't. If we wanted, we could convert most of the rooms into cat pens. In time. That's why it's so ridiculously cheap. Most people will want the house more than the grounds. We, however, don't.'

Carl nodded. 'She's right, you know.'

'Yes,' Anna said. 'We want it.'

'How much do you want to offer? Bearing in mind you're chain-free and, from what I understand, a cash buyer?'

Sasha nodded to Anna. Suddenly it all felt very real, very scarily real. Anna suggested twenty per cent under the asking price. After a great deal of rigmarole, it was agreed at ten per cent under the asking price.

D'arcy Farm was taken off the market the day it had come on. It was Anna's.

The sale went through swiftly. Once Anna became used to the fact it was *her* property, and she was the person to make the decisions, to drive forwards the refurbishment, she worked with Sasha to fix it up as the new home of Fluffy Paws. Anna even started to enjoy herself. Under the expert supervision of Sasha, who'd already set up one cat sanctuary, Anna spoke to builders, decorators, carpenters, electricians, to make their vision of a modern Fluffy Paws, with double the capacity than the old location.

'There will always be cats needing our help,' Sasha said. 'So let's go big, now we have the space.'

Anna wanted to do everything possible to look after and save unwanted cats in their little corner of the world. 'Then that's what we'll do,' she said confidently.

They transferred the cats from the network of volunteers' homes into the cleaned and refurbished pens and outbuildings. The shed became Sasha's office, with her computer and the paperwork. Anna worked with Sasha choosing the materials for the pens and fitting out the office with a modern desk, office chair, filing cabinets and a new computer. The house would wait, it was left as they'd bought it.

Mim's charity ball aimed to raise funds to refurbish the cottage. The decision about whether to create more accommodation for the cats, or refit it as a place for someone to live, therefore generating rental income for Anna, had yet to be taken.

Anna didn't mind – in fact, she preferred not having to make all the decisions together. 'Now the cats are safe, it can wait,' she said, not needing the money, nor wanting to rush what would be a long-term plan for her involvement with Fluffy Paws.

Pitsea, Essex

Some weeks later, she walked around the garden, checking on the cats, moving from pen to pen. They were standing on the platforms, snuggled in beds, playing with their toys, using their litter trays, or sleeping. There were almost one hundred cats and kittens under the care of Fluffy Paws.

Anna was seeing her counsellor this afternoon, for the last appointment, she thought. *Yes, it is the last time.* She didn't think she'd ever not worry about things, but she'd learned to put the worries aside, with perspective, she knew the world wouldn't actually end.

Content the cats were all okay, Anna entered the cottage, the walls were clear of wallpaper that had probably been older than her, now painted white. The smell of fresh paint hit her, replacing the dampness of before. She could imagine living there maybe, or perhaps Sasha would prefer it. Although she'd said living and working in two separate places was better for her. Anna touched the freshly painted walls of the hallway, walked into the kitchen, empty but for the sink. The sitting room had low black wooden beams overhead, the walls uneven, the fire grate clean and ready for the first fire.

I did this. I made this possible. I dared to try something different.

She wished she could sit at the kitchen table with a cup of tea and appreciate how far they'd come. But alas, no table, chair, kettle or fridge. She turned, appreciated the kitchen, imagining it filled with volunteers, discussing the cats. She left the house, locking the door, and stopped by the office which was a wooden shed.

Sasha sat at the desk, frowning at the computer and shaking her head.

'Everything all right?' Anna asked.

'Some bright spark thought it would be a good idea for us to be a cattery too.'

'You are a cattery, aren't you?'

Sasha shook her head. 'Short-term stays, for when people go on holiday. Bring in some extra money. Mim thinks it's a wonderful idea.'

'But you don't?'

'I do, well, I think it could be. I'm trying to work out how we manage it with everything else that's going on.'

'Something to bear in mind when we finish doing up the cottage.'

Sasha looked away from the screen. 'Yes. With your approval, of course. I want you to be happy.'

'I am. Very. It's your cat sanctuary.'

'Technically, it's yours.'

'I may own the building and the land, but *you* are Fluffy Paws. Even when we went virtual. It was always you, at the fulcrum of it. The way we care for the cats, the way we never put one to sleep, unless it's the last resort and for health reasons, the way you get the best out of the volunteers, it's all you. Even if you don't like it, *you* are Fluffy Paws.'

Sasha shook her head, waved away the compliment.

'I'm going home. Coming?' Anna asked.

'You go, I need to finish this.'

'Luke and I are making dinner. Seven.'

Sasha nodded, returned to frowning at the computer.

Anna drove home, relieved Luke and Paul had postponed their travels, citing money, time and 'wider sensibilities' according to Paul. Whatever their reasons, it meant she had more time with them. She smiled, thinking, *Life really can be wonderful sometimes, can't it?*

Chapter 34

'Now we know where we shall be laying our hat, so to speak, I'd like to organise a charity ball,' Mim had said with enthusiasm, when Sasha showed her the new Fluffy Paws premises and explained they needed to raise money for the cottage refurbishment.

'If you're up to it.'

'Up to it,' Mim replied, 'I was *born* to organise something like this. Been itching to get started.'

'Then I'll leave it in your hands,' Sasha said.

Mim still hadn't quite grasped how Paul persuaded people to donate money for their vet bills by sharing pictures of cats on the internet, but she decided there were some things one was simply not meant to understand and instead merely accept. Although, when Paul finally left for his travels, someone would need to understand enough to take over.

Mim enjoyed a challenge and put many hours of work into the charity ball while the others moved the cats into their new home.

The invitation list included: vets, food suppliers, grooming product suppliers, all the volunteers, she'd even managed to get it partly sponsored by two well-known cat food manufacturers. It also coincided with the last week before Luke and Paul were leaving for their travels.

It was, Mim had learned, only Luke and Paul who were travelling. The mysterious third wheel, a woman from their dance classes, apparently, had never materialised. Mim suspected she'd been manufactured purely from Paul's imagination, as an elaborate ruse to convince himself he didn't feel so strongly for Luke as he did. And Luke, bless him, had asked what to do if Paul had intimated they should be more than friends.

'Grab it, him, with both hands and hold on for dear life,' Mim had said with a grin. For it was precisely what had happened when she first met David.

Luke and Paul had gone shopping for all the paraphernalia required for such a trip: backpacks, cheap clothes for various climates, travel toiletries, an eBook reader and something in which to write a travel journal, among other things. Mim knew Luke and Paul were unlikely to find time to write their travel journals; she instead imagined them making love, under a red, gold and orange sunset, in a sun-drenched island somewhere in Europe. Just as her holiday rep friends had done, and her and David too, all those years ago.

Sasha had shared Mim's hopes, but they hadn't told either of the two young men. 'Sometimes, it's often easier for others to see the love between individuals than for the people themselves,' Mim had commented to Sasha when they discussed what to do about the charity ball.

'Here's hoping,' Sasha said.

'It'll be a farewell-fond-travels event and a charity ball,' Mim replied.

Sasha agreed, adding, 'And a thank you to Anna for her generosity.'

'Very important we thank Anna,' Mim had replied.

And on that basis was how Mim had ploughed on over the weeks, organising, calling, booking, choosing. Mim had rolled up her sleeves, cracked open a new spreadsheet, opened her contacts book and been in her element. This was the pinnacle of her organisational skills, feeling similar to organising a wedding. Each decision she relished making, ensuring it was appropriate, thrifty, while not giving the impression of cost-cutting.

Until now, this evening. The date had arrived.

They were in the grounds of Fluffy Paws, under a marquee that Mim had secured free of charge, thanks to a tip from Anna who knew someone who hired them. And although not quite as grand as she'd hoped, it felt appropriate given the purpose. Banners proclaimed it as a charity ball, with a small concession to Luke and Paul's travels provided by a cake.

Mim inspected the table decorations, moving from one to the next. There was a table along one wall that would be covered in the buffet food. Silver service had felt a bit *de trop*, so she'd plumped for a self-serve buffet. The volunteers had done a potluck, bringing their signature dishes, and Mim had resisted over-controlling it, she knew they'd provide a good range of dishes, having approved them in advance as each volunteer pitched in with their food.

Sasha arrived, looking frazzled. 'What's wrong?'

'Nothing. All under control,' Mim said, greeting her with a hug and kiss on both cheeks. 'You look as if you've seen something terrible.'

'I can't believe they're leaving. Together. And that all these people want to give us money.'

'*Have* given us money,' Mim said with emphasis. Tickets were priced reasonably, and all costs had been kept to a minimum. A charity ball's main goal should be to raise money for the charity in question, surely.

'Are they definitely going, *together*?' Sasha asked. 'Or just together?'

'They're definitely going. As for the rest, I believe Mother Nature will take her course. I've had them both coming to me, wobbling slightly. Soon put them straight.' She raised an eyebrow. 'If you forgive the pun.'

Anna arrived, looking radiant in a black and red puff-ball skirt. Mim had owned one like that, back in the Eighties. 'Anything I can do?' Anna asked.

'Lovely dress. New?'

'Mum's. Original.'

Mim nodded in approval. 'Splendid.'

'Car park is filling.'

'Wonderful. Ready?'

Anna nodded nervously. 'If you are, I am. You're in charge.'

'I'm ready.'

Guests filtered in over the next half an hour, milling around for a drinks reception by the table on which the cake sat.

Henry, Fiona and Tilly arrived, looked around the marquee.

Mim walked over to greet them, hugged each in turn. 'You came. Thank you.'

'Very impressive,' Fiona said.

'How do these premises compare to the old ones?' Henry asked.

'Bigger, more indoor space and, best of all, the landlord is one of the volunteers, so it sort of staves off that little worry.' Mim smiled. Henry had said he'd ask his brother to visit her and David. 'Heard from that elusive brother of yours?'

'Sorted!' Henry said. 'We're descending en masse. We three, plus Will, Chloe and their new baby Lottie are lunching at yours in a fortnight. Since we already had the date in the diary. I asked him to come along.'

'And he said yes?'

'Chloe's heard so much about you, she can't wait to meet you. If that's okay with you.' Henry looked about. 'Where are we sitting?'

It was more than okay, it was thoroughly splendid. A house-full of family to entertain, Mim's cup absolutely overflowed with joy. She smiled, squeezing Henry's forearm affectionately. 'I'll show you, I've put you near the front.'

Fi put her hand on Mim's arm. 'We'll manage.'

Mim nodded in thanks.

Fiona waved her away. 'Go, host, organise.'

Mim left, wondering what Will and his family would be like. She had no time to dwell on that thought, as there were checks to complete for the table decorations, the music, the portable loos, and before she knew it, it was time to begin.

Mim called everyone to attention, nerves bubbling in her stomach until she caught David's eye, as he sat near the back. A calm confidence descended on her. 'I wanted to thank everyone for coming. I'm so pleased you all think Fluffy Paws is a worthy cause for your support. But before we move on to the business of the evening, I wanted to wish a fond farewell to two people who are very special to me. Luke and Paul.' She looked about her. 'Where are they? Can you come to the front, please?'

They were soon standing next to the table.

'We made a cake to wish you well on your way. Who knows how well you'll be eating on your travels? Perhaps stash a few pieces in your backpacks.'

Anna and Sasha carried the cake towards the table, letting it rest carefully, then joining the crowd.

Paul went bright red. 'I can't believe it!'

'Love. It,' Luke said, walking closer to take photos of the cake. It was in the shape of a rainbow-coloured plane, upon which two men rode like a horse. It looked slightly odd, but Mim agreed it was fun and funny and reflected Paul and Luke very well.

'This is a thanks from those who love and care about you. Travel safely, have lots of fun, but return and tell us all about it, okay?'

Luke put his hand around Paul's waist. 'We'll look after each other.'

Paul shared a look with him. 'Worked it all out, didn't we?'

Luke nodded. 'We did.'

Paul bit his bottom lip, looked to one side. 'Once I realised how stupid I was being, with my pre-emptive strike, it was really rather simple.'

Mim smiled, raised her eyebrows, hoping they'd say a little more about Paul's withdrawal from the relationship before it had started.

Luke kissed Paul's cheek. 'Can I explain?'

Paul shrugged, blushed, held Luke's hand.

Luke went on, 'I liked him and he liked me. So once he was convinced I wasn't going to find him not interesting or handsome enough, he decided not to run away. From me. Us really. Which was one reason why we delayed our travels. Gave us time…' He blushed.

Paul kissed him, fully, on the lips. 'To get to know each other.'

How splendid, Paul's realised there's no point fighting what his heart wants, finally got into his heart that Luke is not George, Mim thought, excitement and satisfaction bubbling in her stomach.

Mim grinned, they'd been getting to know one another very well, from what she saw. Taking herself back to the job in hand, Mim asked, 'Who's cutting the first slice?' Mim looked from Paul to Luke. 'From the nose or tail of the aeroplane?'

Paul cut a slice from the plane's nose, pointing to one of the men on the cake. 'Is this me?'

'This one's taller,' Luke said, pointing to the other icing-sugar man on the cake. 'So I reckon that's you.'

'I reckon you might be right,' Paul said, holding his hand out. 'You're often right.'

Luke, after a brief hesitation, took his hand, squeezed.

Paul pulled Luke closer, resting his hand on Luke's broad chest as they kissed. Eyes shut, not a peck on the cheek, but a proper passionate, desirous open-mouthed kiss.

David nodded, mouthed, 'I told you,' at her, then smiled.

There was applause, then Mim blushed at the romance of it all, gathered herself in, said, 'I'd also like to thank Anna, who has very generously bought this place for Fluffy Paws to call its own. We are very grateful.'

Anna blushed, shook her head, waved away the compliment, hid behind a table decoration.

There was applause.

Mim went on. 'Please can everyone take their seats? The seating plan is at the entrance of this marvellous marquee.'

Representatives from the companies who'd donated goods, services, or money, or provided discounts to Fluffy Paws, each spoke in turn, according to Mim's list.

The food was eaten; Mim reckoned it was better than most weddings she'd been to. Content it was all going smoothly, she placed her cutlery on the plate.

Henry waved from a table at the other side of the marquee. Tilly climbed on her mum's lap and Fiona held a thumb up, checking if Mim was okay.

Mim nodded. *I am so lucky, to have them in my life. All the fun of being a grandma, a cool auntie, the person who can spoil them, give their parents respite, before handing them back, and retreating to my own quiet solitude.*

Wonderful.

After everyone had eaten, the tables were pushed to the sides, the disco arrived, a man with two record turntables and flashing lights.

David had let her get on with leading everyone through the evening, but now the music played he asked her to dance.

She gladly agreed, and they twirled and jived and danced with wonderful youthful abandon, just like when they had danced in their twenties. When the music changed to a ballad, David held her close, whispering into her ear: 'You really are wonderful, you do know that?'

I really am not. Tears filled her eyes and she blushed, didn't dare nod, but shook her head for she felt terribly embarrassed at such praise for something she felt she could do almost without thinking. 'I could do nothing without you, you do know that?'

And then he kissed her. It was as wonderful as their first kiss, as passionate as the one Luke and Paul had shared earlier, and he held her tightly, gently swaying on the dance floor until the music changed to something more upbeat and they slid to the side of the room, drinking and talking, watching others dance.

Paul and Luke danced to the fast song, moving as if they'd rehearsed their moves. Luke's professional dancing had rubbed off on Paul. The tempo changed, slower now, something Mim had heard on the radio. Paul pulled Luke closer, encircling Luke's waist with his arms. Paul looked into Luke's eyes, said something Mim couldn't hear, but it looked like 'sorry'. She couldn't be sure.

Luke nodded, smiled, stared into Paul's eyes.

They kissed, while slowly dancing to the music, and it went on for so long that Mim felt embarrassed for staring.

She looked away, blushing.

'That,' David said with confidence, 'is two people who are very much in love.'

'Why did it take them so long to come to this realisation?'

'Because people are complex, and love is messy and difficult.' David nodded. 'Heartbroken people don't always behave logically.' She'd told David about Paul's ex and him not wanting to dive head first into a relationship with Luke.

'*People* don't always behave logically,' David said.

When the music changed to something louder, the men left the dancefloor, joining a man and woman in their fifties or sixties. Luke introduced them to Paul, who shook their hands. *It must be Luke's adoptive parents, he asked for two tickets.* Luke held Paul's hand, spoke to his adoptive parents. The small birdlike woman in a plain blue long-sleeved dress hugged Paul, kissing his cheeks. The man shook Paul's hands.

Luke's just introduced Paul as his boyfriend. How marvellous! She told David. Mim's heart beat faster with the excitement of it all, with the matchmaking success she'd had, over such a long time. She couldn't feel happier even if she tried. Satisfaction, romance and joy whizzed through her veins, and she felt a little light-headed. *Or is that the free champagne and table wine*, she wondered.

By the end of the evening, CEOs and vets were dancing with the volunteers. Anna was talking to a chief executive from a cat grooming company, shyly looking at her feet as he spoke.

At midnight, the music stopped and Mim stood on the stage at one end of the marquee. 'That's it, I'm afraid, folks. Carriages await!'

Everyone clapped and Mim told the volunteers to leave the clearing up until the next morning.

Later that evening, tallying the money against the costs, Mim worked out they'd made enough for a few months of expensive vet bills, or to give the cottage a very thorough refurbishment, which felt very satisfying.

'How do you think it went?' David asked.

'Perfect. Wonderful.' Mim stood as she felt joy and relief bubbling up in her chest. She wiped away a tear from her cheek.

David hugged her. 'Why the tears?'

'I'm really happy.' She didn't feel as if she were sliding into one of her 'off' moods, she was overjoyed at the success. At her life. At finding purpose, the people, from Fluffy Paws, who gave her such meaning and joy.

Wonderful.

'Sure?' David asked with uncertainty.

'Positive.' And Mim led them to bed, with a satisfied grin.

Chapter 35

Luke and Paul sat on an outcrop of rock overlooking the sun, watching the sunset. The sky was orange-red and people were gathering to enjoy the best place in the Balearic Islands to view a sunset.

Travelling, really seeing all the places they visited, eating food bought in markets, visiting churches, museums, shopping streets, was far better than Luke had imagined. He'd had holidays, dozens of them, fly and flop next to a pool for the week. Recharge his batteries after a busy tour, and between rehearsal schedules. He'd visited European countries, and not seen anything more than the hotel, performance venue and airport. But this experience of travelling was totally different and Paul had shown him precisely how to do it.

I must say it to him. It's getting stupid. I'm not imagining it, am I, he must feel the same? Just three little words. I know this is how I feel.

Paul was looking into the distance. He wore a yellow vest and denim shorts that had seen better days, having been washed and rewashed every few days over the last few months of travelling. But Paul somehow managed to look delightfully laid-back, as if he'd been travelling his whole life and took everything life threw at him, completely in his stride.

Luke knew this to be mostly true, while they had been travelling, and he smiled. Every time there had been a problem – missed trains, delayed flights, lost hotel bookings, swallowed credit cards – Paul had responded calmly with a practical solution. Paul looked as if he was born to travel.

Paul's arms were lightly tanned and he sat with legs outstretched. By now Luke could practically draw the shape of Paul's calves, arms, the way the bits of hair lay on his chest, falling in two U shapes around his pectoral muscles.

'All right?' Paul asked, shifting backwards on the rocks and sitting in front of Luke's legs, which formed a V. 'I can smell myself.' He smelled his armpit. 'Sorry.' Paul moved away.

Luke put his hands around Paul's torso, really wanting to pull him closer, to kiss his neck. 'You smell fine.' *Much better than fine.* Luke knew Paul's scent was citrus, woody, with just a hint of muskiness that had Luke's desire bubbling from deep within himself, until sometimes it had boiled over.

Aha, the lust and desire had been perfect. And no need to hold back now.

'Do I?' Paul shook his head, sniffing his armpit again. 'Doubtful.' He scrunched up his face in disbelief.

After sharing rooms, and beds, for a few months, they had become very comfortable in each other's company. Relaxed. Travelling as a couple had made all that easier; every time they booked accommodation they shared.

They had travelled by train around France, Spain, Portugal, Italy. Luke said what he wanted to see, Paul

came up with the itinerary. Luke arranged the accommodation, checking in with each other about what they
wanted to see in each location, how long they would
remain there. They'd developed this sort of shorthand
with each other: when Paul remained silent, Luke knew
he didn't want to do what he had suggested.

'You know you don't. You never smell of anything but
soap. It's almost superhuman,' Luke said now.

'No one's ever called me that before.' Paul shrugged.

You're much more than superhuman, to me, Luke thought.
I love you like I've never loved anyone else.

Luke nodded, his throat dry, worrying that he'd mess
this all up. 'I happen to think you're pretty perfect, as it
goes.'

Luke reached around Paul's torso, putting his hands on
top of Paul's. 'Sorrento was fun, right?'

'Bit touristy, but good. Yeah. Glad you got to see where
you were conceived.'

Maybe it was the mention of his conception, maybe
it was the half-light, maybe it was the scent of salty sea
spray on rocks below, or perhaps the gentle, happy chatter
of people around them, but there and then, Luke decided
he'd had enough of dropping hints. Whispering into Paul's
ear, he said, 'I know you were hurt. I can't imagine what
it was like being with *George*.'

'I—'

Luke gently kissed Paul's neck. 'If we can travel
together, I reckon we've got a good chance of living a
normal life together. Whatever that is. I've seen you first
thing in the morning, when we've got hangovers and
insomnia and need to get an early flight. And after all
these months we didn't kill each other. And,' Luke went
on, 'so...'

359

Paul turned around to face him, nodded, grinned, checking to the side, probably to see if anyone was watching. 'Paris wasn't bad either.' Paul shrugged. 'Or Portugal. Or Spain.'

That's good. Joy bubbled in Luke's stomach, he was right, he'd read the signals correctly, Paul felt the same way. 'I just wondered if you wanted to carry on this, us, when we get back?'

'And they say romance is dead!' Paul winked.

'I can get down on one knee, if you want.' Luke grinned.

Paul shook his head. 'A kiss'll do.'

That would do for Luke too, very nicely, thank you very much. He kissed Paul. 'Can we do another one?'

'They're not rationed, not as far as I remember.'

Nothing when I'm with you feels rationed. Luke held the camera at arm's length, checking they were both in shot.

'This is for Sasha, isn't it?' Paul asked.

'How did you know?' Luke grimaced. *Am I that obvious?*

'Same reason why we've spent all day and night together for the last few weeks, without anything approximating an argument.'

This hadn't occurred to Luke since their travels had been so much fun, effortless, hanging out with Paul gave time an elastic quality, a day seemed to pass in an hour. Easily. Luke waited. And waited. And waited. 'Which is?'

'Because,' Paul said, kissing him on the nose, 'I know you inside out and back to front.'

Luke laughed. *Perfect. Magic. Bloody wonderful.* 'Sounds rude. I'm in.' Luke kissed Paul's lips, the salt of the sea spray, the sweetness of the wine they'd shared earlier and something that Luke knew very well to be one thing and one thing only, Paul. And then he took the photo. Click! *I'm going to tell him. Right here, right now.* 'I love you, you do realise that, don't you?' Luke asked.

'Right!' Paul laughed. 'I suspected as much.' A pause, and then: 'I love you too.' Paul blinked, moistened his lips. 'Very much.'

Luke smiled and kissed him, and he closed his eyes, lost to the outside world. No one and nothing else existed, except him and Paul, as they disappeared into their own world together.

Chapter 36

Pitsea, Essex

Sasha wiped the kitchen work surface, having fed all the sanctuary's cats living in the pens in the garden. They were nearly at capacity of one hundred and ten cats and kittens. The expansion required more volunteers and they were a merry band, coming from all walks of life, gathering in the cottage's kitchen, drinking tea and talking cats, life and helping each other, as Sasha had with Anna, Paul, Luke and Mim. She couldn't have done any of this without them, and she would forever remain grateful.

She stood in the new kitchen, canary-yellow cupboards, wooden surfaces, dark-tiled floor, a deep sink, it had felt a bit much, refitting the kitchen mainly for cleaning cat bowls, but Anna had insisted – besides, the funds had been raised by Fluffy Paws to use as they saw fit. *Two dishwashers, very fancy*, she thought, one for the cats' bowls, one for the volunteers' cutlery and crockery. A microwave sat on the surface to heat volunteers' food, and a large fridge-freezer stood in the corner.

She could easily have moved into the cottage, but she wanted to keep it nice for the cats. All rooms except the lounge and kitchen had been converted to house cats for a few days, and sometimes much longer, when their owners went on holiday. She couldn't believe how much people paid for this. It made an interesting addition to the cat sanctuary; seeing spoilt cats needing care while their owners were sunning themselves on holiday reminded Sasha not all people were bad. Some pet owners were good people. It felt better to rent the cottage to cats than people.

She filled a dozen crockery bowls with cat food placed them on a tray, and walked towards the first room of holiday cats, as she liked to call the cattery customers. There were three rooms in the house used for these holiday cats. They each had their own pen, with its own webcam so owners could check on their pets from anywhere in the world. The pens had toys brought from their owners.

There was a catio built on to the back of the cottage to give access to the outside for some cats if their owners agreed. It had a wooden frame covered in chicken wire, and a transparent roof to give the most light. There were shelves, climbing trees, water features and beds scattered about.

She checked each of the holiday cats, feeding them in turn, then put the pair who'd enjoyed time in the catio into their carry cases, taking them to the back bedroom, which would be their home for the next week.

Now one final check on the pens in the garden. She walked past them, cats meowed, came to the front of the cage for attention or food. Everyone was well, the younger kittens and any cats needing more attention were housed at Anna's parents' home. All the cats at the main site were safe and happy, awaiting their perfect human parents' arrival.

She was busier than ever, but she loved it, more cats in her care meant more cats who would live a happy, safe life. The emails, pictures and messages she received from happy adoptees, or failed fosterers – people who'd agreed to foster their cats temporarily and then fell in love with them, keeping them forever – made it all worthwhile. She was busy, but felt supported and without the threat of the landlord's will changing, for Anna still volunteered, Sasha had some stability for Fluffy Paws now they were at D'arcy Farm.

Content the cats were okay for the night, Sasha checked the cat cams were working. They showed every pen and room, the feed went to a computer screen in her shed office. She also monitored them while at home, just in case.

She locked the gate, set the alarm, then returned to the home she shared with Anna. Anna insisted she shouldn't call it her place, since Sasha lived there too. Not just in one room. Sharing it all, Sasha's belongings were in the sitting room, kitchen, dining room, as well as her bedroom.

Anna was making dinner in the kitchen. 'Long day?'

Sasha sat at the kitchen table. 'Very.' She'd left at eight and it was six now, so yes, it had been a long day. At least she wasn't living where she worked, so it gave her some degree of separation.

'Good though?'

'Very good.' After a pause, Sasha said, 'I don't suppose you'd like to take on some more foster cats?'

'You don't suppose correctly.' Anna continued chopping vegetables by the sink, put noodles on to cook.

Sasha's phone beeped with a message. It was from Luke, a picture of him and Paul kissing, looking very tanned, unkempt hair going in four directions at once, stubbly chins and joyously happy, with big smiles. There was a sunset in the background. The message said:

> Loving Ibiza, luv u Second Mum xx

She smiled at that. She showed Anna. Sasha felt the lightness of romance, young love, at the optimism of their relationship, reflected back at her. She couldn't stop grinning. Nor did she want to.

'Are you all right, not missing Luke, both of them, too much?' Anna asked after they'd stared at the picture, zoomed in.

'I never expected Paul to stay long. Young man like that, he's not going to stay volunteering in a place like this. He should be travelling, tasting life, doing all the stuff his ex didn't with him.' She replied:

> So happy for you, Sasha / Second Mum
> xxx

'Think it'll last when they get back?' Anna asked.

It was sad how cynical Anna remained about love. Perhaps she hadn't met the right person. Sasha had, but it had been a decade too early. Or in the wrong country. She wished she could meet Luca now, see how his life had turned out. But life wasn't like that. And she'd had the next best thing, better in some ways, by having Luke return to her life.

Sasha smiled. 'I think if you can spend every day, all day, with someone, when you're living on fifty quid a day, you can do pretty much anything. But what do I know,

I've only been on package holidays, not as adventurous as those two.'

They sat in silence for a moment.

'Stir-fry?' Anna asked, removing some prawns from the fridge, adding them to the wok.

'Perfect.' Sasha fetched glasses, poured them wine from the fridge, laid the table. She'd underestimated how much she missed spending time with people when she'd been alone for so long. She sat at the table.

Anna cooked the vegetables, added sauce, then served up, putting noodles in the bowls and covering them with the stir-fry, before joining Sasha at the table. 'Thank you,' she said, holding the wine aloft.

'You're the one who cooked!'

'I chucked some prawns and veg into a wok, it's hardly cordon bleu.'

'Come on.' Sasha waved her glass.

Anna joined in the toast. 'What are we toasting?'

'Us, getting through the last year. You, for saving us. Luke and Paul. Take your pick.'

'All of it sounds pretty good to me.' Anna sipped the wine, in obvious thought. 'I almost forgot to tell you. I got offered my old job back.'

'At the doctor's surgery?'

Anna swallowed her wine, nodded. 'Rebecca, she rang me. Someone had left. Did I want to come back?'

'I hope you told them to stick it?'

'I didn't. I said I'd think about it. But Nicholas told me to tell them that.'

Sasha narrowed her eyes, she felt she should know who this Nicholas was. 'Nicholas?'

'Met him at the charity dinner. Works for that cat food company.'

'The chief executive?'

Trying her best to sound laid-back, Anna said, 'He didn't mention it. I thought he did something to do with marketing.' Anna ate a mouthful of food, chewing for a moment. 'He said,' she waved her fork in emphasis, 'I should tell them I'm better than that, I'm considering my options, and to stick their offer up their—'

'You didn't?'

'I thanked her, Rebecca has been good to me. I did commit fraud. They gave me a reference for the time I'd worked there. I said I was considering my options. I left out the stick it up their... bit.'

'And are you? Considering your options, I mean?'

'It's embarrassing, and I can't believe I'm going to say this. I sound like one of those trust-fund people from the Eighties, roaring around in their sports cars and sticking all sorts of stuff up their noses. But...'

'But?'

Anna blushed. 'It's strange how not having to work changes how you think about work.' Anna covered her mouth. 'Sorry. I am officially one of those rich idiots from the Eighties. Am I a yuppie four decades too late?'

'If you want to be,' Sasha said with a grin.

Sasha had insisted Fluffy Paws pay Anna rent for their new location. All cattery pens had webcams regularly attracting thousands of viewers per week and providing a healthy income from people who tipped them for providing remote cat therapy.

'You've been through a lot.' Sasha felt it was something of an understatement. And they had all been through significant change over the last year or so.

Anna looked at the floor. 'If I could have them back, I would. For all the money, I would.'

'I know.' Sasha stroked Anna's forearm on the table. 'Doesn't work like that, does it?'

'Nope.' Anna sat up straight, composed herself.

'Anyway,' Sasha went on, 'I'm not letting you get away any time soon. What would you do?'

'Nicholas reckons I could do anything.'

'Is *he* actually an Eighties yuppie?'

Anna shrugged.

'Anything?' Sasha found that hard to believe, but she wasn't going to extinguish some joy from Anna's life that had been, up until recently, pretty joyless.

'I can go back to uni, set up my own business, whatever really. Sounds stupid, but I don't know what I want to do. I keep thinking what would Mum and Dad want me to do with myself, now I've got all this free time.'

The fact she was no longer caring for her parents was left unsaid, for that was what Anna had done for most of her adult life, putting others' needs before her own and now, finally, in her early forties, she could put her needs first and she didn't know where to begin. 'It'll come to you.'

'I know who I can ask: Mim,' Anna said brightly.

'You can ask at her next dinner party. She's timed it so Luke and Paul will be back. Although I'll believe *that* when I see it.'

'You don't think they'll come back?' Anna looked worried.

'Grey and drizzly Essex, or sun-filled Ibiza, which would you choose? Besides, Paul's a travelling digital, whatever it's called. Why would he ever come back?'

'He's really a homebody. It was his ex's idea to go travelling. Paul would have stayed, with his cat.'

'Right,' Sasha said, wondering if maybe they would return, and settle down together, adopt some cats maybe. She smiled at the thought of Luke and Paul sharing a home with half a dozen cats.

'Digital nomad is what he is,' Anna said.

'That's it.'

'Can't see the appeal myself. But then again I'm not much for big change, travel.'

'Maybe you will be now? With your yuppie by your side, perhaps?' Sasha asked gently. 'Mind you, Luke's got his dance group, so he won't abandon that.'

'Or his parents, all three of them.' Anna exchanged a look with Sasha. 'I'd never have put them together, Paul and Luke, would you?'

Sasha shrugged. 'Don't know.' But, she admitted, with the benefit of hindsight, Paul had seemed broken and Luke was adrift, searching for his roots, in Sasha, but also charming, romantic and charismatic like his birth father, so Sasha had felt they would, inevitably, find their way to each other, just as she and Luke's father had. Both hurt from love and needing someone who accepted them for their whole selves, without judgement. That, Sasha reckoned, was the definition of true romantic love. She'd had it for that holiday with Luca, in the Italian sun.

The phone rang, shaking Sasha from her romantic vision that although she and Luke's father couldn't have their happily-ever-after, it was somewhat right that she'd helped Luke find his with Paul.

Sasha answered the phone. It was a man: 'I'm moving and I can't keep my two cats. Can you take them?'

She didn't bother asking why he couldn't keep them, knowing it wouldn't change his mind. She took details in her notebook. 'What are they?'

'Cats.'

Taking a deep breath, Sasha said, 'Male, female, how old?' *And on we march*, she thought, *because if not us, who will?*

A Letter from Charlie

Thanks for picking up a copy of *The Cosy Cat Society*. I hope you've enjoyed meeting the human and feline characters, and sharing their journey.

I've loved cats ever since, as a boy of six, my mum showed me a litter of black and white farm kittens in a barn, before we adopted two sisters, Sooty and Sweep. When I was a little boy, Sooty used to climb in bed with me, and I would read late into the night, as she purred and snuggled against my chest. Since then, Mum had Tilly and her kittens, Jasper, Phoebe, Chandler and Kiera (spot the Nineties names from *Friends* and *This Life*).

I've found, whenever I'm feeling below par, not quite myself, cats sense it. If I'm feeling a bit wobbly and take to bed during the day, it's never long before I'm joined by a cat.

Shortly after my dad's funeral, I rushed to pack and drive from the New Forest back to university in London. Mum said I didn't need to leave so soon, but I was on a mission to return, so left. Twenty minutes into the two-hour drive later, I remembered I'd forgotten my diary, so returned to Mum's house. I slumped on her sofa, in tears, acknowledging it was all too much, and perhaps I should stay a little longer. Mum's three cats, Tilly, Jasper and Chandler, jumped on my lap and chest and I was unable to leave. I remained for another week until rested, before returning to university in London.

Reviews help others find their next story to enjoy. It would be wonderful if you could add a review of *The Cosy Cat Society* on your favourite review platform. Even a few words and a star rating make all the difference.

If you're interested in meeting my alter ego, who writes gay romance and gay fiction, check out liamlivings.co.uk where you'll find my social media links and newsletter sign up form. I love to hear from readers who've read my stories. You can also check out charlielyndhurst.co.uk where you can find information about my other Charlie Lyndhurst books, my latest news and social media links.

Love and light,
Charlie Lyndhurst xx

Acknowledgements

Thanks to Tim who is supportive of my writing, does all the things I should do around the house when I'm 'at keyboard', and understands when I'm absent due to a deadline.

Thanks to the cat sanctuaries I follow on Twitter: Stray Cat Rescue Team West Midlands, Bradford Cat Watch Rescue and Sanctuary, The New Moon Rescue, Montreal Animal Rescue Network, Loudoun Community Cat Coalition, Ernesto's Sanctuary for Syrian Cats, Henry's Haven Cat Rescue, The Scratching Post, Yorkshire Cat Rescue, Battersea Dogs and Cats Home, Cats Protection and Celia Hammond Animal Trust. Thanks for the work you do, the information you've shared about rescuing and caring for cats, and the inspiration you've provided for some of the cats' stories in this book.

Every cat's story in this book is either true, or based on the truth. Some are cats I've adopted, others are from cat sanctuaries across the world. Fortunately, there's a worldwide army of excellent people rescuing, caring for and adopting cats.

Thanks to Tim, Paul, Nick and Lorna who were with me in sunny Gran Canaria during autumn 2022, as I forged through half the structural edit of this story. Every morning, as they relaxed, I quietly slipped away and made myself comfortable to write in the morning sun on the balcony overlooking the pool. I've found I write best in the morning, in the sun's warmth, with the promise of a cool glass of pink wine as a lunchtime reward.

Thanks to Lucy, for introducing me to the concept of 'let her be her' which seemed the best way to describe Luke's difficult relationship with Sasha. Which is why I've used your phrase.

Thanks to my school friend, Miles who—the joyful evening we reconnected after losing touch since school, while reminiscing about our teenage friendship—told me he enjoyed tap dancing and talked about 'guys I've been tapping with,' which instantly sparked an idea for Paul's character.

Thanks to Nick and Lorna for sharing pictures of their friend's painted glass ornaments. As soon as I saw them, Mim and her flowing dresses and no-nonsense attitude appeared, almost fully-formed from my mind onto the page.

Thanks to everyone in the Hera Books team including Keshini and Jennie, and cover designer Rose Cooper for helping me bring this story to the world.

Love and light,

Charlie Lyndhurst xx